BLOOD MONEY

Also by Johnny 'Two Combs' Howard

Boat Troop

BLOOD MONEY

Johnny 'Two Combs' Howard

LONDON NEW YORK SYDNEY TORONTO

This edition published 1998
by BCA
by arrangement with Orion Books Ltd

CN 3050

Typeset by Deltatype Ltd, Birkenhead, Merseyside.
Printed in Great Britain by
Clays Ltd, St Ives plc

For my children
Jamie & Yaisa
Your love and support is
my constant inspiration

GUINEA

GUINEA

FALABA
GBERIA FOTOMBU

Wara Wara
Mountains
KOINADUGU   BENDUGU

KAMAKWIE

KUKUNA   KAMALU

SIERRA

Gbenge
Hills

Loma
Mountains

KAMBIA
ROKUPR
MANGE
MAMBOLO
KASSIRI

Sula Mountains

MAKENI

KAYIMA

Tingi
Mountains

PORT LOKO

MAGBURAKA

KOIDU-SEFADU (KONO)
YENGEMA

LEONE

Malal
Hills

MASINGBI
Nimini
Hills

LUNGI
FREETOWN
ABERDEEN
GODERICH
HASTINGS
WATERLOO

YONIBANA

Kangari
Hills

NJAIMA-
SEWAFE

Kongotan Range

YORK

Makondu
Hills

BAUYA

TAIAMA

Peninsula Mountains

Moyamba
Hills

MOYAMBA

Mokanji
Hills

JAIYAHUN JUNCTION
and
SIEROMCO MOKANJE

Kambui Hills

KENEMA

GBANGBATOK

GBANGBAIA
Imperri
Hills

Gbonge
Hills

KPETEWOMA

Gola
Hills

TURTLE
ISLANDS

SHERBRO
ISLANDS

BONTHE

PUJEHUN

LIBERIA

North Atlantic Ocean

0 10 20 30 40 50km

0   10   20   30miles

PROLOGUE

or hours, apart from the occasional hooting of an owl, the only
sound had been the wind hissing through the tops of the trees. A
stiff breeze had at least kept the frost at bay, making it marginally
less cold for the hidden SAS teams. One group was in the bushes that lined
the northern side of the road, the other in the rape-seed field opposite. To
avoid detection they'd taken up their positions the night before. That
meant a long, cold and patient approach, very necessary to avoid the well-
mounted IRA surveillance operation.

Terrorists weren't mugs, nor were they just mad, gun-happy fanatics. In
a war that had lasted twenty-five years the British Army now faced men
who had been born into the Troubles. They'd taken their first lessons in
terrorist tactics with their mother's milk; grown up in houses where adult
talk was all about the best way to fight, with limited resources, a successful
guerrilla war. In the school playground they'd acted out the roles of
gunman and victim and fought imaginary battles with a more numerous
enemy. In later years, emerging from classes in physics and chemistry,
during which they'd paid a great deal of attention, they'd probably argued
about the best way to construct and plant a bomb.

Like any army, the fighting men had plenty of backup. The terrorists
who would do the forthcoming job might have looked over the target, but
that would have been so long ago that their presence would have gone
unremarked. The plan had been made, maps and diagrams drawn, and a
scale model of the area constructed. Despite tight secrecy, the IRA
commanders knew the risks of betrayal. And that brought into play the
support tail, which in South Armagh, the heart of bandit country,
amounted to almost the entire population. There were 'dickers' on foot,
placed at strategic points to warn of an unusual army or police presence.
Up to a dozen cars would be used for mobile sweeps. Other sympathisers
walked their dogs not only over the firing point, but the ground
approaches as well. Some of these watchers were men from active service
units, with radios so that they could control the overall situation. Only

when they were sure the area was clear would they radio for the attack to go ahead.

The teams designated to stop them had coped with all of that, and got themselves into the right position to react. Training had got them there, constant practice in covert tactics that bore out the regimental mantra, 'Train hard, fight easy!' Working in such a hostile environment, you never knew if an op was going to go down or be aborted. And that applied to the first few minutes as well as the last. The guys they would be up against had a mental advantage. When they went to their hide and drew a weapon or a bomb, they expected to use it. Any trooper who'd served in Northern Ireland could list more operations that went sour than those that went right; times when their weapons had never been raised, let alone fired. But you could only get a result, when the plan worked out, if you trained for success. That's what the SAS did, day in and day out.

Right at that moment, on this job, the fat lady hadn't sung. For the Northern Ireland troop commander back at the ops room, as well as the men on the ground, failure was still an unwelcome possibility. A strong moon meant that visibility was good. But that, given the amount of deep shadow, would provide only limited aid to the IRA 'dickers'. And for the men tasked to stop the attack going in, it meant that when they were called upon to move they could do so quickly, with a clear sight of the enemy.

As commander of one four-man patrol, Blue Harding had the added task of running not just his own orders through his mind, but those of the others. Thrown together for this op, the three men under his command were unknowns, part of a six-man group from G Squadron heli'd into Northern Ireland to assist B Squadron especially for this job. They'd revealed little of themselves at the briefing, cautious in the presence of the two older NCOs tasked to lead the operation. Both were seasoned operators who were serving a second year-long tour in Ulster.

There was no Chinese parliament. Everything had been worked out in advance. Blue and Paul Hill knew the terrain and the enemy. They spent most of their time in civvies, walking the deadly beat of the areas populated by the hard-liners, Republican and Loyalist. They drove unmarked cars and engaged in covert surveillance. And sometimes, not often, they had enough hard information from an A1 source to mount this kind of operation. The reinforcements had listened to their orders,

2

and when questioned had repeated their detailed tasks with commendable brevity. And the troop commander, Roddy Forwood, had passed Blue's plan without comment.

It was simple stuff on the face of it. A terrorist attack was expected on the local police station, home-made mortars fired from the back of a van. The informer had passed on the firing point and the date to his RUC Special Branch handler. Now, a ferociously effective counter-terrorist team was here to stop it happening. They'd got in without being detected, the first task to inform Zero back at base that they were in position. Blue had checked the links with all the other units on what was a very busy comms net. Everything was in place. If all went to plan, they'd stop the attack and arrest the perpetrators.

Cammed up and chilled to the marrow, they lay absolutely still, waiting for the first sign of activity. On a cold night, in open country, a car can be heard a long way off. There had been one or two false alarms, the guys stiffening at the sound of a distant engine, only to ease their trigger fingers as it faded. This one was different, coming right on towards their position at about twenty miles an hour, headlights full on, the last mobile sweep searching for any sign of an unwanted presence. Even with a blackened face there's a temptation to cringe as the light sweeps over your face. That has to be avoided. The trick is to stay absolutely still, merely closing your eyes to maintain night vision. The 'dickers' are looking for movement, which is the only thing that, in darkness, will betray an enemy presence. The second sweep was done with just sidelights, the engine noise kept to a minimum so that the sentries on the police barracks wouldn't perk up their ears. The stop was brief, and the three passengers piled out. The engine was killed for a second so that they could listen to the sounds of the night, while the driver put a radio handset to his ear, ready to blast out the abort signal the second anything untoward was spotted.

One Republican came within four feet of Blue Harding, standing right at the edge of the road, his hand gently pulling branches aside so that he could peer deeper into the gloom. A wood pigeon took off, its wings beating loudly against the leaves of the tree. That made the Republican jump back and caused Blue to smile, firstly because he hadn't reacted, but secondly the buzz of success: his patrol had remained so still that a pigeon had felt it safe to return to a nest no more than ten feet away. The voices murmured softly and indistinctly, reassuring one another just before the engine on the Sierra came back to life. Then they were gone, and the fringe of the forest settled down, the wood pigeon eventually returning to its original perch.

The troopers exercised to keep themselves from stiffening, minimal movements that merely tightened and released individual muscles. They knew that action was imminent, that the van would arrive shortly after the recce, too close in time for the Brits to put in a force to ambush them.

The engine was diesel with a much heavier note than the Sierra's. And the occupants made no attempt to contain the noise, probably working on the principle that stealth was suspicious, speed was paramount. On the slightly damp surface of the roadway the tyres, as the van braked, made a slithering, gravelly sound, followed by the metallic clunk of hard hit door handles, as the four-man firing team piled out. They'd done their dummy run and knew exactly where to park, so there was no need to guide the driver into the innocent looking marks made days before, the ones that would aim the home-made mortars they intended to fire right on to their target.

'That's Charlie One,' Blue whispered into his mike. 'Static, four up.'

There had been a constant stream of traffic on the net, very necessary in an op that involved over a hundred people. But that had diminished as attention began to concentrate on the point of action. Blue Harding's words would be picked up by everyone, but were primarily aimed at Zero manning the ops desk back at base. They told Captain Forwood what he needed to know: that the van had been positively identified; that it had stopped; that there were four terrorists in the IRA unit. His next words informed Zero that his teams were moving to initiate the hard arrest.

'Stand-by, stand-by, go!'

The move out of cover was made with the minimum of noise. The patrol knew they had at least a minute. The mortars had to be armed, since not even the most dedicated terrorist would drive over potholed roads with ready-to-explode bombs in his van. And what noise they did make was covered, first by the movement of the Transit, then by the clacking sound of the idling diesel engine.

'Bad mistake, boys,' Blue said to himself, moving into position, Heckler & Koch G3 up and ready. 'You should have switched that fucker off.'

As patrol commander Blue was close to the trees, behind one of the G Squadron guys, Tosh McKinnon, while the other pair took up station on

4

the opposite side of the road. Off to the right of the target, Paul Hill's patrol merely had to stand up to be active. The eight men were in position before any of the terrorists spotted them, Blue shouting as soon as he saw the first guy react.

The message was simple and standard. 'Army! Stop or we'll fire!'

Common sense must have told them that they'd be covered from two angles, front and rear. Common sense said, 'Don't do anything stupid, just lie face down on the road with your hands behind your head.'

That was when they made their second bad mistake. They should have surrendered. But either through bravado or stupidity they elected to fight. If there had been a real shoot-to-kill policy they would have died right there and then, but the Rules of Engagement gave them a window. Still, it was never on. When eight guys have their weapons up and aimed to cover their targets, it is foolish to try and haul out even an automatic pistol. One or two seconds to get it up and aim it, an age against ordinary squaddies with standard kit, never mind the SAS, half of whom were using the best nightsights on the market.

Blue had elected to fit a Streamlight torch, operated on a pressure switch and zeroed to his weapon. There was no guarantee they would nail their targets right away. They might have to chase these guys into the surrounding woods. The Streamlight was brilliant for close work at night, especially when searching undergrowth. It illuminated the target and gave the operator a chance either to force surrender or blow his opponent away if he turned out to be armed.

The van driver dived out of his seat, Armalite in his hand, heading for the ground and nearby cover. His mates, one right behind him and a pair by the back, pressed themselves close to the vehicle as they fired off their automatic pistols, wildly in the hope of sowing confusion. McKinnon, in forward position and down on one knee, knew the Rules of Engagement. Once the terrorists had ignored the command to surrender and committed themselves to a fight, he had precise orders regarding what to do. Blue Harding was vaguely aware of Tosh desperately slamming at the side of his G3 as he himself opened fire, his rounds skimming the top of the lead man's head. The Armalite was the danger, accurate and with a high rate of fire, so Blue deliberately followed the driver as he rolled, leaving the rest to the other pair of troopers.

The first of his shots hit the driver. He stopped rolling and somehow got halfway to his feet, rifle still in his hand, when the second controlled shot from the patrol commander took him in the chest. Tosh must have cleared the stoppage to his weapon then, since he opened up on rapid fire and cut the already dying man in half. Blue had already switched his fire to the van to take out one of the others, but that guy was already wasted. As he saw him drop, he noticed the writhing bodies of the other Republicans, both of them taken when Paul Hill's patrol opened up from the rape-seed field.

The silence as both patrols moved forward was eerie, the only sound the ticking of a hot engine under the Transit bonnet. Blue's guys checked the bodies, making sure they were dead, while Paul's troopers made sure that the mortars were still unarmed and that the van wasn't booby-trapped. At a signal from them, Blue spoke into his mike again to tell Roddy Forwood that the situation was stable. 'Zero. Three One Contact. We have four dead gunmen. No casualties. Mortars are safe.'

Forwood came on the net to pass that on. 'All callsigns, this is Zero. Contact four dead gunmen. Mortar tubes are safe.'

At a further sign from Blue both teams withdrew up the road and back into the woods, making for the clearing on the opposite side where the heli would come in to lift them out of the contact area. For the two teams, the op was over. All around the area, since the call had gone out to say that the job was going down, the mobile intercepts had been moving. SAS troopers in upgraded high-performance cars, their task was two-fold. If the job going down was successful, they would seal off the incident so that no one, innocent or involved, could get close to the vicinity. If the terrorists evaded the covert teams and made a run for it, their task was to intercept and carry out the hard arrest. Backing them up, to provide a more extended cordon, came the Quick Reaction Force, local troops provided by the Green Army, but led by one very pissed-off SAS trooper, who was so far from the action that he knew he'd never get involved.

The RUC's own guys from the Heavy Mobile Support Unit would take over after everything was secured, the work coordinated by Forwood on the ops desk. Next to arrive would be the Scenes of Crime Officers. They would take over the incident and do the necessary. The Green Army boys would, of course, be credited with the kill, the usual guff going out on the news that a passing patrol had disturbed the IRA as they were preparing to launch. The SAS didn't exist as far as Ulster was concerned. The troopers would go back to their barracks to debrief and to see if they could learn anything from the night's action. They would also repair to the base bar, have more than a few drinks, then do their very best to get a leg over one of the females working for DET 14, the intelligence-gathering section.

The first part of that was the patrol debrief. They went over everything: the approach, the level of hostile surveillance they'd encountered, and a detailed eight-way observation of the contact and the outcome. It was a situation where honesty was highly desirable. Nobody was a superman: they couldn't be everywhere and do everything. You learned from every experience in the regiment, and what you saw and did was added to the total sum of knowledge on which every trooper could draw.

Blue listened as Tosh McKinnon gave his version, only flicking his eyes to the man's face when he failed to mention the stoppage on his G3. Blue knew that there was a lot of difference between theory and practice: that applied to the SAS as much as any other organisation. In the regiment you didn't bleat, especially to Ruperts. There was no way Blue Harding was going to speak out and drop another trooper in the shit, even if the guy was a total stranger. So, called upon for his contribution, he played down the way in which Tosh's weapon had jammed. Nor did he point out what he should have done. When it happened Tosh shouldn't have fucked about trying to clear the thing, he should have gone for his secondary weapon, the 9mm pistol each patrol member carried in his op waistcoat. That was standard drill, which they'd all trained for, over and over again. Weapons jam. It happens to the best. But the very best don't compound the problem. It was a fuck-up, and one that could have cost lives if the terrorists had been more alert.

Once the briefing was over, Blue confined himself to a private bollocking, satisfied that the ex-Guardsman showed proper contrition, and quite a bit of gratitude. Tosh knew that he'd panicked and done the wrong thing. Rubbing salt into the wound to his pride wasn't necessary. But it was an action which Blue put away in the memory bank, a mental warning in case he should he ever find himself on an op with this bloke again.

He then sat down to compose his own patrol report, written in the same vein as the debrief, before going on to his obligatory interviews with the Army Legal Service and the RUC Special Branch. What followed that was, for Blue, a real surprise. He heard Forwood praising Tosh for dropping the driver, hinting that it could well warrant a Mention in Dispatches. Other ranks loyalty only extended so far and even if hogging glory was something Blue hated, when Tosh showed no sign of correcting Forwood and admitting his weapon had jammed, he was very tempted to give the guys the good news.

Years in the regiment had inured Blue to that kind of shit, however, and it would have stayed private if he hadn't slightly over-indulged in the supply of free booze in the base bar. He'd started on the beer before moving on to his favourite get-pissed juice, red wine. The combination of that, plus the presence of so many people being fed a line of bullshit, proved explosive.

'Excuse me, boss,' Blue said, interrupting the Rupert.

'Yes, Blue,' replied Forwood.

Forwood had consumed a fair amount of beer too, so the upper-class drawl seemed somewhat exaggerated. The captain was a tall slim guy with black, swept-back hair and heavy, defined eyebrows, the skin on his face and the dark patches under his brown eyes carrying a sallow hue that indicated a confused bloodline. Forwood didn't look him in the eye as he spoke, and he stiffened to hold himself erect, as if to confirm by this Guardee pose, even sitting, that he was the fellow in command. 'Typical fuckin' woodentop,' thought Blue. He didn't have much time for Ruperts or Guardsmen, and if you combined them the whole was, to his way of thinking, less than the sum of its parts.

'Did Tosh say in his statement that he downed the driver?'

Drink made Blue's voice a shade louder than normal and the buzz of conversation was suddenly muted. The place was full of support staff as well as almost the entire Ulster SAS contingent. But the people who stiffened most were those closest, the guys who had been on that night's op.

'I can't see that's there's any doubt that he did,' replied Forwood, eyeing the G Squadron trooper, whose beer glass had stopped halfway to his mouth. 'You told them it was your burst that cut the bastard near in half. That certainly accords with what I observed when I read the SOCO's reports after they'd examined the bodies.'

Blue pushed his own glass away from him, as if to clear a space in which to move. 'Are you going to tell him, Tosh, or will I do it?'

McKinnon had the good grace to drop his head when he responded. 'Tell what, mate?'

'The truth, arsehole.'

'I don't think we need that sort of talk, Blue,' said Forwood, flushing slightly.

'Don't we? You're talking about giving this guy the hero treatment when he nearly got the rest of us killed.'

'You can fuck off,' growled Tosh, stung into anger.

'You were front man, mate. It was your job to take them down with me as backup.'

'Which he did,' insisted Forwood.

Blue was angry. Drink meant his self-control was not as good as it should have been. That bastard Guardsman was telling porkies, and looked as if he intended to bluff it out. Paul Hill was sitting beside him and, sensing the coming outburst, put a hand on Blue's forearm to restrain him. It didn't work.

'Tell him, shitlegs!'

'This stops now!' barked Forwood, slamming his glass down hard. There was no conversation now. The rest of those in the bar were either staring at Blue or at their glasses, in a clear attempt to indicate a desire to remain uninvolved.

'Tell him you had a stoppage. That your weapon jammed. You didn't down the driver, I did.'

The silence wasn't long, but it was telling. Blue, looking from one to the other, suddenly realised what was going on. The regiment had enjoyed a wee bit of success. The public might guess it was an SAS op, but they'd never be told. Only those who mattered would know: the politicians and the Army brass. And, as usual, when there might be a bit of praise to follow the Guards mafia was trying to hog it. Forwood was Welsh and McKinnon was Coldstream, but that didn't matter. Both from the Woodentop Brigade, they would look after each other. The CO of the regiment was another fucking woodentop, so he would be delighted to be told that a Guardsman had done enough to earn a reward.

'Can it, Blue,' said Paul Hill, softly. 'You're wasting your breath.'

'This is formal, and to go on the record,' said Blue, in a voice he hadn't used since he joined the regiment. 'Trooper McKinnon had a stoppage.

His weapon jammed. He then failed to take the appropriate action in using his pistol, and so jeopardised everyone's security.'

'You didn't say that in your patrol report. It makes no mention of a jammed weapon, and I don't recall you saying anything at the debrief.'

'If you read it. It says what I told you at the debrief, that I put two shots into the driver.'

The Rupert flicked a casual hand at McKinnon. 'Which is a lot less than Tosh here. You were patrol commander, and that will result, within the confines of the regiment, in some degree of distinction. But you really can't come along afterwards and try to claim a credit that belongs to another man. Tosh here took out the most dangerous terrorist on that team, and to my mind that qualifies for extra recognition.'

'I've told you, he's lying,' Blue insisted.

'I believe him.'

'Maybe he told you what he did and you decided to cover it up?'

'Careful, Blue,' Forwood replied, edgily.

'There's not one of you worth a wank. As a Rupert you're a fuckin' disgrace.' Blue dragged his arm free from Paul's second attempt at restraint, and jabbed an angry finger at the other Guardsman. The red wine he was drinking was not exactly Château-bottled. It was cheap, Spanish and cheerful, and had stained both his tongue and his lips, making the threat he issued through bared teeth that much more intense. 'And you, McKinnon, if I see you in Hereford, stay clear of me or I'm going to kick seventeen different kinds of shit out of you.'

'In your dreams, pal.'

Captain Forwood was smiling slightly. And so he should, since he had all the aces. It was his report that would be read by his superiors, not Blue Harding's. And protest as he might, there wasn't a Rupert born who wouldn't back up a fellow officer. And that went in spades for the CO. They might smile at the troopers they supposedly commanded, and cosily use first-name terms. But they were, to a man, career soldiers, using the SAS as part of their path to promotion, each one a past master of the art of the double handshake. This Rupert might even write himself a personal medal citation to go with McKinnon's MiD. As an officer he had that right.

But there was another reason for that smile, because it told Blue Harding just how far he'd gone over the top; that he was, to all extents and purposes, finished. He should never have spoken out in front of so many witnesses. Forwood would recount with glee to the CO what Blue thought of G Squadron and the Guards Brigade, and the other woodentops would confirm it. He wasn't too popular in that department as it was, given the way he generally took the piss out of the Ruperts at mess dinners.

They wouldn't RTU him. But there were fates in their gift just as bad as being sent back to your regiment. They could stick him in an office, or in the stores; denying him any kind of meaningful job, bore him to the point where he would leave of his own accord. It was no good looking for justice. Blue Harding might be one of the longest-serving members of the finest élite fighting force in the world. But it was still the good old British Army, run, as far as he was concerned, by the brain-dead offspring of the rich and well connected.

When he spoke, he tried to make his voice sound contrite. 'I'd just like to say one last thing, boss.'

Forwood walked straight into it. 'What's that, Blue?'

'Fuck you!'

A shared interest in fine wine made dinner with Sir Patrick Molloy an occasion to savour. Sir George Forgeham-Lowry enjoyed the first-course Montrachet, but the 1962 Petrus left that fine white burgundy in the shade. They'd already discussed at some length what would follow and the Château d'Yquem was chilling nicely. Such wines, even to a very senior civil servant, were rare treats. The salaries of permanent secretaries ran to a fairly decent cellar. Careful, early buying of promising vintages, allied to patience, meant Sir George could hold his own in most company. But he couldn't compete at the level of the Petrus. He'd never see the bill, but if that bottle of thirty-year-old wine came in at less than a thousand pounds he'd be amazed.

Mutual friends had been discussed, the parlous state of their old Oxford college bemoaned, government economic policy coruscated (but then it always was, regardless of the prevailing Treasury nostrums) and international events commented on, those where Sir Patrick's various companies were active receiving special mention.

'And how goes the anticipation of retirement, George?'

'It gets better by the day, Paddy. I've told you before, the higher you rise

11

in the service, the more you come to see what an absolute shower these politicos are.'

'The world of commerce would suit you much better.'

The offer had never been formally made, but George Forgeham-Lowry knew there was a place for him in Sir Patrick's mining to shipping conglomerate. They were friends, and had been since Oxford. But when a major international financier treats you to a wine costing one thousand pounds, old comradeship has nothing to do with it. GFL was a senior civil servant with unrivalled contacts in the corridors of power. He might not know or esteem the men with the ministerial titles, but he knew just whom they listened to for advice, which in lobbying terms was a priceless asset.

It wouldn't last for ever, of course. Within five years the personnel would have changed and he'd be out of touch. But in that period he'd justify a fat salary to top up his substantial index-linked pension. Sir Patrick Molloy would get his pound of flesh, and Forgeham-Lowry would get the payoff for years of climbing his way up the slippery civil service ladder. That wasn't mentioned either; with people of like minds, so little actually has to be stated.

The cheese and port moved them on to company business; the bits that were doing well, those that were causing problems, and the genuine worries. How this information would be used was also not discussed. GFL would disseminate it as he saw fit, definitely using it to impress his own minister, but making sure that the necessary bits were dropped into appropriate ears. The emerging Russian market was interesting, but difficult; but it was nothing compared to Africa.

'Always troublesome, George, you know that.'

'Not just for commerce, Paddy. In the FO they give the sub-Sahara desk to the man they most want rid of. It's a pig of a job. SA sanctions, wars in Angola and Mozambique, all those tinpot dictators like Kaunda.'

'He's one of the better bets. Very steady with the old copper supply.'

'Which only goes to show how impossible it is. If he shines, what in heaven's name are the rest of them like?'

'Any hope that things will settle down in Liberia?'

'Not from what I can observe, but I'll ask Jimmy Heriot.' He paused, seeing Sir Patrick struggling to place the name, before putting him out of his misery. 'Second in charge at the FO, you remember. I introduced him to you at Henley.'

'Ah! Yes, got him. Seem to recall you saying he's one to watch.'

Sir George allowed himself a smile, knowing that if Jimmy Heriot played his cards well, he'd follow him into the embrace of his powerful host. 'Jimmy is right out of the top drawer, Paddy. Fearfully bright! I'll ask him for an appreciation if it will help.'

'I'm really only interested because of Sierra Leone. There's bugger all in Liberia worth bothering about. But they have set things alight in that part of the Dark Continent. They could spread.'

'Remind me.'

'Rutile.'

'Ah yes,' replied Sir George, frantically trying to remember what rutile was.

'Poured a fortune into extracting the stuff. Have to, or you can't get at it. And now we have two coups in two years. Unstable, that. Not good for business.'

'This stilton is perfection,' said Sir George Forgeham-Lowry.

'Bliss,' replied Sir Patrick Molloy.

CHAPTER ONE

The battered old Peugeot looked like what it was: a utility vehicle poorly suited to the terrain. Sub-Saharan wind, rain and sun had combined to strip off most of the original blue paint. It bounced and bucked over the potholes, creaking and groaning in a way that showed how useless both springs and shock absorbers had become. The only thing that was fresh was the white patch on the roof carrying the Red Cross insignia in the middle. The protection that was supposed to provide was a hope rather than a certainty. There were few hostile aircraft to worry about: a couple of Nigerian ground attack jets and, when the military council paid for the fuel, some helicopter gunships. Both had a bad habit of firing at anything that moved, even if they were on the government side.

The Peugeot was going too fast for the state of the road; red, dusty and rutted. Occasionally the back would slew round, skidding perilously close to a deep rain ditch that ran along one side. The doors didn't close properly, which meant that a lot of that red dust entered the driving compartment, to mix with the leaking exhaust fumes. Sister Francesca was at the wheel, the look on her lined and weather-beaten face denoting the deep level of concentration she put into the task. Beside her, eyes tightly shut as she prayed for deliverance, sat Sister Gabriella. Young, fresh-faced and terrified, she gripped the clasp that anchored her seat belt in case it should jump out, something it had done many times before.

'Smoke,' said Sister Francesca. The voice had a dry, rasping quality that went very well with her sharp features. Having spoken, she turned her head just enough to see the closed eyes and moving lips of her young companion. 'Open your eyes, girl!'

Gabriella obliged, obeying automatically a command from one of her superiors in the order. She saw the black plume rising into the bright blue sky, her nose twitching at the first hint of an unfamiliar smell. Acrid, yes! But there was also a sweet odour in the air. She looked at the older nun, and saw that she was now praying too, slowing the car as she approached the two smouldering lumps that partially blocked the road.

14

It took two hands to wind down the window, one on the top rim to push it down. Sister Francesca was, for a moment, steering with her bony thighs. The mechanism worked properly on the other side, and both women were presented with very similar sights. Only the way the bodies lay was different. Both were young, male and naked, with dead and empty eye sockets that stared into oblivion. The dark flesh was cratered and uneven where the petrol had scorched the skin, the edges of the deep panga scars pale where the blood, with only the white cells left, had congealed. In contrast, the earth around their cadavers was dark, because the melting body fats had run out to stain the roadway. Gabriella gagged as she reached for the door handle, but she would do her Christian duty despite the turmoil in her guts as soon as the car stopped.

'We can do nothing for them,' said Sister Francesca, gunning the engine, which coughed twice before engaging. She steered expertly between the bodies. 'They are in God's care. Better we seek the living or injured.'

There were more bodies on the road, and in the bushes to either side, with vultures screeching as they lifted slowly into the air at the vehicle's approach. The old nun, after a quick glance for signs of life, ignored them all. They had to stop where a huge earth-moving Caterpillar lorry had been slewed haphazardly across the road. It was big enough to fill half the ditch and block access to the main gate of the quarry site. Sister Francesca had seen all this before, in Liberia two years previously. Untrained bush fighters trying to steal things they couldn't drive, only to abandon them when they ran out of control.

With some difficulty, Sister Francesca turned the car round. Experience told her it was best to be prepared for the worst. It was eight months since that Dutch doctor and his family had been murdered, but that didn't make things safe. And she had no faith in the protection of the cloth. A priest had been hacked to death as well. Each side – government and Revolutionary United Front – blamed the other. A quick exit from a scene of destruction was always advisable, especially when you knew it could be the work of either side.

Finally she stopped the engine and got out, signalling for her young companion to follow her. The older nun kept a close eye on Gabriella as they entered the Salco compound. She had a good idea what to expect, the younger nun would not. And regardless of what people tell you, nothing prepares you for your first sight of mass murder and wanton destruction. There was paper everywhere, fluttering in the air as a breath of wind took hold. The fence that enclosed the property had been torn down, probably by the RUF soldiers driving that stolen Caterpillar. Part of the offices of the quarrying company had been set alight and still smouldered, though the main, stone-built structure was intact. Smashed equipment lay everywhere: a computer monitor and keyboard; desks, chairs, telephones and dented, empty filing cabinets. But there were whole objects too: TVs and fridges, an air-conditioning unit, several fans and a couple of small generators, as well as engine parts and tyres in an untidy pile. And there were bodies, all black and all dead, one or two in pieces.

The older nun sniffed the air, in a way that was almost animal in its intensity, peering back the way they'd come for several seconds before signalling to her companion to come with her and look for survivors. It was a futile search. Where the people came from was a mystery; they appeared as if by magic in a place which had looked totally deserted. That happened often in this part of the world, a seemingly empty landscape suddenly full of a mass of individuals, male and female, of varying ages, adults and children, all talking at once.

'They think it is safe because we are here,' said Sister Francesca, when she'd managed to quieten the most voluble. 'To them it means the men with guns have gone.'

'And have they?' asked Sister Gabriella.

Sister Francesca shrugged. 'They left quickly. But they will not be far away.'

Then, standing relaxed, her hands inside the pants of her baggy beige slacks, she proceeded slowly to question the crowd. It was a long-drawn-out process; each question delivered to one was answered by many, with much high-pitched argument about details that mattered little. The RUF had come from nowhere, appearing, as usual, out of the bush. They had killed what men they could find and abducted the women. Did the sisters know that when the RUF attacked, there was a government inspector present? That led to even more high-pitched wailing and informing, each gory detail of the unfortunate man's agonising death related with relish: the slashing of the skin, the gouging out of the eyes, the way the arc welding equipment had been used to scorch off his testicles, and finally

16

the cutting out of the heart from a still living body. They were shown what remained of his carcass, which lay beside that of his driver, hacked so badly after death that few limbs remained connected. Both, again, were naked. Someone would be marching through the bush wearing a smart city suit now, probably sporting polished shoes of the type you only saw in Freetown.

And the crowd confirmed the rumour, picked up from those who had fled as far as the displacement camp, that when the rebels departed the Italian quarry manager and his two Pakistani assistants had been taken away as hostages. Not that Sister Francesca understood much of what was said. Her language skills were good, but there were just too many voices speaking at once. The nun was all patience, listening with her head bent, interjecting a word or two only very occasionally. The babble subsided because of this, and the garbled information began to make more sense.

Neither of the nuns heard the truck. But the locals did, and the compound emptied as quickly as it had filled, the crowd dispersing through holes in the fencing to hide in the bush whence they'd come. The grinding of the gears eventually reached their European ears. That was followed by shouting, the discharge into the air of numerous weapons, then the sight of dozens of ragged men, each wearing a white headband, cautiously approaching the compound.

'Army,' said Sister Francesca, without any hint of relief. 'Stay still and do not move.'

They came through the fencing, rifles at the ready swinging left and right, their eyes clearly showing varying degrees of fear. Commands shouted from the rear had them fanning out to search any place that could hide an enemy. The search was noisy, since the method of exploration was simple: any place that looked like it could remotely harbour an enemy was sprayed with enough automatic gunfire to kill any human within. What glass that remained in the windows was smashed, adding to the infernal din. The nuns, standing in the middle of the compound, were ignored, treated as if they did not exist.

A full ten minutes of this mayhem passed before the officer who'd directed his men's efforts deigned to enter the danger zone. Both sisters knew him: Colonel Nyomo, who held the command in the Bo district. He'd visited their camp on many occasions, none of them pleasant to recall. The contrast between him and the men he led was striking. The officer wore crisp, new-looking fatigues with a stiff peaked cap over eyes hidden by a very expensive pair of sunglasses. His high-quality laced jungle boots were, under the slight coating of red dust from the road, as well polished as his belt and holster. The shirt he wore was open-necked and short-sleeved, exposing the gold chain around his neck, and the expensive chronometer watch on his wrist. His soldiers were in rags by comparison, and that was if they had anything approaching a complete uniform. Most did not, though some part of their dress tended to be camouflage fatigues. Few had boots of any description, and those who did were coming out of them at either heel or toe. The rest wore trainers or the kind of canvas shoes a white man reserved for the beach. They were all young, some mere children dwarfed by their weapons.

The wimples the sisters were wearing, the only part of the order's uniform that suited the climate, earned a salute. But there was little real courtesy in it, and no shortage of arrogance in Colonel Nyomo's eyes. Looking at him, Sister Francesca found it hard to be Christian and forgiving. She'd worked in Africa for two decades, watched the colonial powers leave, and seen at first hand the chaos their departure had created.

The small, educated élite in every country had come to power on a wave of happy promise. Once there, they had plundered the resources of their nations, lining their own pockets at the expense of the ordinary citizen. Seeing how much money there was to be stolen, the men in command of the army had ousted them. They'd kicked out the corrupt civilians and begun to line their own pockets, in a country a lot less wealthy than it had been before. Income from mining and extraction went to Swiss banks instead of hospitals, roads and the provision of fresh water. The generals traded their Land Rovers for the essential Mercedes-Benz with blackened windows, their ordinary homes for luxurious villas, filling them with booze, luxury goods and young nubile concubines. Rarely, if ever, did they spend any money on the army they commanded.

Embezzlement on such a scale created jealousies in the lower ranks. The junior officers, mouthing slogans about equality and democracy, had mounted the next coup, then once in office begun to emulate those they'd replaced. Sister Francesca had seen it all before, in Liberia. If matters ran to form, she knew the final phase in the destruction of the state was when the army fragmented into factions, so that civil war, continuous and unstoppable, followed as night followed day.

18

'I would be obliged to you for any information that you can give me regarding the rebels,' Nyomo said, removing his sunglasses and swinging them by their arms.

'We have no information,' Sister Francesca replied. 'Whoever did this was gone by the time we arrived.'

'Whoever did this? Can there be any doubt it was the RUF? They seem to have left in some panic. Which means they must have known of our approach.'

She didn't answer, or even shrug to show indifference: she simply held the man's gaze. Sister Gabriella saw the anger in his eyes. This was a fellow used to creating fear. That he was not doing so annoyed him immensely.

'I must ask you, what brought you here?'

'Rumours we heard.'

'Where?' he snapped.

'Where else, Colonel Nyomo? At our mission.'

He snorted, throwing his head back in mild disgust. The sisters worked in the Tiama displaced persons' camp. DP camps like Tiama, to him, were a source of nothing but trouble, full of either rebels hiding from the government, refugees from the civil war in Liberia, or European trouble-makers. Like all of his kind, he would dearly like to drive the whole lot over the southern border to a death from starvation or Liberian bullets.

'We need to know what is happening,' Sister Gabriella added, 'to stop our people leaving the safety of the mission.'

'They have nothing to fear,' Nyomo replied, without the slightest trace of conviction. 'That is what we exist for, to protect them.'

It was Sister Francesca's turn to snort. Her charges had everything to fear from anyone toting a gun. Seeing her look past his shoulder, the officer turned round. His men were poking with exaggerated caution at the various artefacts of value that had been left behind, as though worried that they might be booby-trapped. Nyomo snapped a command, obviously an order to stop messing about and start shipping the goods to the waiting lorry.

'Your fee, Colonel?' said Sister Francesca.

If she'd hoped to shame him, she failed. Nyomo grinned, hooking one arm of his sunglasses on his lower lip, which took some, if not all of the sting out of his reply. 'These things cannot just be left lying around to rot, can they, sister?'

'I don't suppose they will for long, Colonel. I expect they will turn up in Freetown market before the week is out.'

'Do not put too much faith in either your head-dress or the Red Cross sign on your roof. You are a long way from those who you would need to appeal to if the RUF decide to attack your camp.'

'What have we got that they could possibly want?'

'Recruits, sister.'

'We can be sure if they do come, Colonel, that you will be many miles away,' growled Sister Francesca. 'But they are close now, and from what we have already learned they have with them the mine manager and his two assistants. It might be better to go in pursuit of them than stealing their property.'

'Who told you this?'

'People who do not fear to talk to us.'

'Tell me what they said!'

'Signor Assitola and his two assistants were led away, hands tied and with ropes around their necks.'

'That has to be a lie. The RUF has never taken expatriates hostage.'

'Until a month ago the RUF rarely came out from the western heights. Do you see Signor Assitola here? And if he had survived, would he go off and leave all his property to be plundered?'

Nyomo became more tense, gripping his sunglasses tightly. 'He may have left for Freetown before the attack.'

'We did not pass him on the road, and neither, I suspect, did you.'

What Nyomo said next really hurt him. The tone of his voice had an odd, strangled quality and he put his sunglasses back on quickly in an attempt to disguise the fear in his eyes. There was no way of knowing how deeply he was connected to the RUF: they certainly seemed to be able to operate with impunity, always appearing when the army was absent. At best it was a mutually beneficial arrangement designed to share out plunder from the area he controlled. But it could be more than that, which would lead to a certain death if his superiors on the military council ever suspected it to be the case.

'Can it be confirmed?'

A lengthy pause followed before Sister Francesca replied. For Nyomo to find out anything would be difficult. The people didn't trust the army, and would lie to him if they thought it prudent. He would use torture, of course, but that would take time. Much as he hated to admit it, they would open up to these sisters, even to the point of telling them which way the rebels had gone. The older nun smiled. On her lined and narrow face was not something inclined to warm the likes of the man before her.

'The camp is in need of generators.'

It was now Nyomo's turn to make a pause, but his was shorter and his reply unsmiling. In reality it was a small price to pay. But he hated doing it nevertheless. 'I will have the two we just loaded transferred to your car.'

'Then if you will wait here, Colonel Nyomo, Sister Gabriella and I will go and find out what you need to know.'

'Would we become thieves too, sister?' whispered Gabriella as they walked away.

'Never fear, child. In such a cause God will forgive us many things.'

John Little might have become a victim if he'd stayed on the road, but as a dedicated twitcher he'd moved into a clearing, pausing to watch the flight of the Elenora's falcon. The bird, which had never been spotted this far south in West Africa, hovered before landing in the high branches of a cotton tree, where there was probably a nest. But all thoughts of birds and their nesting habits were banished as he heard the unmistakable crack of gunfire. Above him every bird in the forest rose, screeching and wheeling.

A knot of apprehension formed in his stomach, and he mentally cursed himself for ignoring the advice he'd been given. The security chief at Anglo-African, Frank Wintour, had cautioned him against going too far past the Sieromin compound at Mokanje, even if he had been told of a rare sighting. He'd abandoned his pickup about half a mile back by an old, dilapidated mud hut, to walk slowly, carefully and as silently as possible towards the sighting point.

The rapid fire of a heavier weapon followed. John Little's long-buried military training surfaced, and he found himself weighing up odds and alternatives. Should he run for his pickup or stay on foot? The vehicle was white and conspicuous. It was a large target even at long distance on a straight road. A heavy-calibre machine gun would rip it, and him, to shreds. But to stay on foot would mean he could move no faster than anyone else, and what he wanted most of all was to be well away from here.

He was moving back towards the pickup, parallel to the road, doing everything he could to minimise the noise of his passage, listening hard, hoping to pick up any hint of a pursuit. There was a faint buzz of sound, but with the birds still screeching it was hard to place or identify. He made it to the abandoned mud hut in about ten minutes. As he inched out from his cover and focused his binos up the road he saw it was full of armed men. They were coming down the road in no sort of order, more like a crowd leaving a football match – if you could ignore the weapons some of them carried.

They seemed to be of all shapes and sizes, about fifty in number, grey-haired elders right down to kids who could barely cope with the weight of their rifles. The clothing was real dress-optional: bright T-shirts or plain, once-white singlets; fatigue caps mixed with hats made out of palm leaves; the odd part of a uniform; some wearing trainers, others with proper boots. Unarmed men carried ammo boxes on their heads. One toted what looked like artillery shells bound into a pack with leaves.

It didn't take a genius to figure out that these guys were RUF. When it came to swearwords Little went through the card, cursing Africa, his employer Anglo-African Rutile and himself in equal measure. The pickup was like a beacon so he moved straight back into the bush, to a point where he could just see the road past the side of the abandoned mud hut.

He'd been counting without at first being aware of it, that military training again which surfaced unbidden. It had been drummed into him at God knows how many lectures, the rules of what to do if you were caught behind enemy lines. That you were still a soldier with a job to do, that you should assess the threat to the rest of your group, then get back on the right side of the forward edge of the battle area and let your commander know the score.

'FEBA, for Christ's sake,' he murmured, amazed that he still knew that kind of jargon.

He heard the engine of his pickup, quickly followed by the crunching of gears as the guy who'd decided to drive it tried to figure out how the thing worked. Whoever was at the wheel got it going eventually, after two attempts that ended in a stall. They stayed in low gear, the roar of the engine drowning out all the other sounds of the passing men. John Little moved, pushing himself closer still, kitten-crawling along the ground until he was at the rear of the hut. From there he could count the numbers accurately, nose wrinkling at the faint odour of cannabis that wafted in his direction from the passing rebels.

This was no small raiding party. That notion was dispelled by the time he got over a hundred, but he kept counting till he'd doubled and trebled that. His heart sank when he saw the prisoners. The three men were secured at the neck by a bright yellow rope, the ends held by two of the rebels who were joshing them along with what sounded like insults. Two were Asian. Their clothes were torn and grimy, especially the shirts, as though they'd been dragged along the ground. It was the expressions that made him pull back to a safer place, the look of sheer terror etched in the faces, mixed with pain as the jerked ropes dug into necks that were already raw. He'd been stupid to move forward, like some bloody boy scout. If they'd seen him, his neck would probably have been added to the rope.

For John Little the next thing he had to do was simple: he had to get to a phone or a radio, one that was out of the route of the rebel's advance, and let Freetown know what he'd observed. There was a displaced persons' camp at Mobela, about three kilometres back up the main route. They had a radio.

As he moved out he heard the first burst of what became sustained gunfire. It wasn't hard to figure out the target: the head of the column must have reached the Sieromin compound by now. Staying close to the road was paramount, so it wasn't surprising that he witnessed the killing. In fact, the use of his binos got him so close to the action it was as if he were taking part.

The remains of the makeshift checkpoint had been rearranged into an execution block. The victim had been stripped to the waist, and two men had twisted his arms to force him over the empty oil drum. The man doing the work was obviously a somebody, dressed in proper fatigues and boots. The long, hooked panga he held seemed to swish audibly as he took several practice swings. John Little was too far away for the sound to carry. It was just his overwrought imagination at work. What he could hear clearly were the pleading cries of the intended victim, and the way the man threatening him was haranguing the others present. Some were armed, watchful of the other group, which stood disconsolate or terrified, scared to look at the scene before them. The panga, accompanied by more passionate shouting, swung viciously, but stopped, coming to rest gently on the victim's neck, producing a wail from the prisoners and a laugh from their armed attendants.

The next swing was no pretend. The arm of the holder was high enough to lift his heels off the ground, his body arcing to get maximum force into the blow. It hit a point just below the joint of the neck and shoulders, cutting deeply into the flesh and bone but not severing anything. The scream of the victim rent the still hot air and the second blow was struck, missing again, this time splitting the man's lower skull. The blade swung a third time, more accurately, and it took the already dying African right on the joint, cutting through about halfway. The head fell forward in a great fount of blood, but not off, the skin of the front holding the two corporeal sections together.

The last blow was delivered into a stream of gore that splashed everyone close by, most of all the executioner. He bent down and picked up the severed head, rushing then to confront the prisoners, who cowered away from the horror that they believed to be their certain fate. The leader was jumping around, screaming imprecations, pointing towards the roadway where his fellows had advanced. One by one, the men he was shouting to started nodding, then murmuring themselves. Their hands, tentatively at first, then with more force, began to punch the air, their voices rising as each fist became more active. The guys who'd been guarding them started a sort of dance, feet pounding into the red dust, rifles raised in a form of salute. One fired off a round into the air, which seemed to galvanise both sections of the group. Then they began to move down the road, chanting what John Little could only suppose were RUF slogans.

'Some method of recruitment,' he said softly to himself.

CHAPTER TWO

After he'd delivered the punch there was claret everywhere. The arsehole with the Barry Manilow nose and the Brezhnev eyebrows was trying to stem it, both hands cupped over the smashed bone. The way he'd tackled he had it coming. Five times beaten for skill and pace, he'd chopped at Paul Hill's legs to stop him creating a scoring chance; five falls on to the hard-packed West African ground. To a man less well trained in unarmed combat that could have caused real injury. Already pissed off, the last tackle had produced an automatic reaction. And it had been the full Monty. When you're trained to kill by the very best in the world, a soft, measured blow is not an option.

The ref's whistle had gone immediately. He rushed to stand over the two men – big, sweating buckets and angry. As a crowd gathered round, Paul heard the swearing coming through the bloody fingers, a stream of very comprehensive Gallic curses. Having worked in casinos on the Côte d'Azur, Paul understood every word. This Frog didn't like the Brits in general. And he especially didn't like the *sales garçons* from the 22nd pecial Air Service Regiment.

The noise grew, a mixture of a dozen languages with even more opinions. People from the various embassies and consulates had come off the touchline to put their oar in. The bleeding figure, half crouched over, was led from the field while Paul faced the wrath of the referee. Poor bastard. This was supposed to be a friendly match between two embassies, and it would have been if that one ugly bastard had just played football.

'Nice one, Paul,' said Jimmy Forrest.

With hair the colour of carrots and a million freckles on his pallid skin, Forrest looked like something out of a *Peanuts* cartoon. Jimmy was a Royal Signals cipher clerk at the High Commission who was playing on the wing. It was his sharp passing that had put Paul through with a scoring chance. He jerked a thumb at the retreating wounded.

'That shite has had it coming for yonks. He plays like that every match.'

The ref was writing in his little book, then searching his pockets for the card he needed, just as if this was the World Cup.

'Then why the fuck do the Frogs pick him?' Paul demanded as the red card was lifted aloft.

'Have to, old son, he's the bloody ambassador.'

There are moments when you can see your whole career slipping down the tubes. Right then, Paul Hill had one of them. A full nine years in the regiment and he might well be out on his arse for decking the French ambassador. They were in Sierra Leone to give close protection training to the bodyguards who looked after Valentine Strasser, the leader of the military council, but half of that job was to be diplomatic. Being in the SAS wasn't all gung-ho. One day might see you out in the bush crawling through mud, another at some reception, suited and booted, chatting away to another African leader, helping to sell the service.

As he walked through the crowd towards the tiny pavilion, he was aware that people were patting his back sympathetically. The voices were benign, and some of the buggers were commiserating in French!

'Well, Paul?' demanded the High Commissioner, in a loud, cut-glass voice that easily drowned out the buzz of comments as the game resumed. Donald Quentin-Davies had also come off his seat to stand at the touchline. He was one of those tall, rangy bastards that litter the Diplomatic Corps. You could find them in every British embassy around the globe. They had the same dried-up skin over gaunt features, the same bony ineptitude. And they all went to the same bad tailor who dressed them in suits several sizes too big. Added to that, looking pissed off was a facial expression they had perfected to a fine art. The military attaché, Major Alan Delane, stood at a discreet distance to the rear, beside his own troop commander, Captain Roddy Forwood.

'Sorry,' said Paul.

He tried to assemble his body into something approaching respect. But that came hard after a dozen years in the SAS, where it was almost a point of honour not to stand to attention for anyone. Forwood was looking skywards, a blank expression on his swarthy face. Given his past behaviour, he wondered if this Rupert would back him if the HC turned nasty. He should do: that was the way in the regiment. But Forwood gave every indication of a man trying extremely hard to avoid getting involved.

26

'I need hardly remind you,' said Quentin-Davies, in the same penetrating tone, 'that you were not sent to West Africa to indulge in fisticuffs, at least not with diplomats. And in your position, as the senior NCO of the close protection team, I would have expected a little restraint, especially in front of such an impressionable crowd.'

He could hear them yelling! All the local kids from the Freetown schools had been fetched along, presumably invited to see a demonstration of the superiority of Western sporting culture. Valentine Strasser, surrounded by bodyguards, was in the small stand along with all the flunkeys who constituted the so-called government. Even here in Freetown, the capital of the country, these guys didn't feel safe.

'If an apology would help.'

Quentin-Davies dropped his voice and leant closer, the grin exposing badly tended, yellowing teeth. 'Apologise? Over my dead body! The man's an absolute scoundrel. I would have biffed the bugger myself if I thought I could get away with it, and so would half the staff in the French embassy. They hate his guts.'

The High Commissioner snorted, in that way which passes for a laugh in the British upper classes. 'Shouldn't be surprised if half the diplomatic corps want to buy you a drink after the match.'

'Hear, hear!' croaked Delane.

Quentin-Davies looked over Paul's shoulder as a cheer went up from two thirds of the crowd, the big bony hands coming together slowly in an excuse for a clap. 'Oh! I say, well done, well done indeed.'

Paul Hill heard the words echoed by the two attendant officers, and turned in time to see his team-mates celebrating their first goal.

'You are being stupid, very, very stupid. You will tell us who you are and what we want to know in time, so you may as well speak before you are subjected to even more discomfort.'

Colonel Eustace Tumbu delivered these words, slowly and clearly, in what he liked to think was his most polished Sandhurst accent. He then rubbed a finger across his mouth. Handsome and elegant in his crisp jungle-green uniform, he allowed a slight smile to play round his lips, the interior edges of which exactly matched the pink of his manicured fingernail. Tumbu considered himself an impressive fellow, oozing vanity from every one of the brightly coloured medal ribbons that adorned his chest. The harsh overhead light reflected not only the gold of these, but also his shoulder insignia and the smooth, even skin on his wide forehead and full cheeks. Beside him, on the desk, lay his cap and swagger stick, the red band on the hat denoting his staff rank.

The underground room was as cool as his demeanour, the only person sweating being the naked victim tied by ropes to the beams in the ceiling. He was bleeding as well, from his nose, and had some broken teeth. The eyes, staring out from the puffed-up flesh that surrounded them, were white with fear. Everyone in the country knew of this place, the underground cells of the Battery Street police barracks. Rumour had it that many entered this building, but few left. It was only a rumour because it was rare to find people alive to attest to the truth.

Tumbu looked at the three soldiers of the defence force. Thick sticks in hand, the trio leant against the wall. Square-faced and impassive, with massive hunched shoulders, they looked at the man they'd just beaten with total indifference. Their once white overalls were dark where the blood of previous interrogations had stuck and dried, the odd patch glistening with this morning's fresh layer. He knew them to be thugs and prized them for it. They would do whatever was necessary, either instructed by him or working on their own. And even if the man tied up before them was a complete innocent whose only crime was to be in the wrong place at the wrong time, they would extract a confession of guilt.

Did he have to be here at all? Perhaps not! But when he'd heard word of this new arrival, he'd felt compelled, for the sake of security, to have a look. Besides, it was a good idea to remind his subordinates that he was ruthless; that he could do to them, if the need arose, what they did to others. Tumbu stood up, picked up his swagger stick and stretched himself to his full height of six foot three inches. Moving forward, he raised the stick until it was waving fractionally in front of the victim's eyes. A sudden slight tap on the broken nose caused the man to moan.

'Yes, yes,' said Tumbu, nodding approvingly. His voice was pitched just the right side of amiability. He always spoke English, and liked to listen to it here, in this chamber, where the slightly damp walls and low ceiling bounced his intonations pleasingly back into his ears. This underlined to him that he was an educated man, a coastal Creole who had travelled, not some upcountry savage whose horizon was bounded by the limits of his commune. 'You must not cry out too loudly. Save your screams for the time when they are your only release. And you will scream, and call to your father, mother and the gods of your village to come to your aid. That will really not be of much help. The question is, how are we to persuade you that it is in your own best interests to cooperate?'

The victim's head was shaking, his eyes rolling, and he was sobbing his innocence to a man who was completely indifferent. Suddenly Tumbu's brow creased, and as he spoke he studiously ignored the shaking head of the prisoner. 'It is very galling, you know, that you are so stubborn. Why deny that you are a member of the RUF? What were you doing on the road from Moyamba to Sembehun, an area where we know you rebels are operating?'

He pointed to the heap of stained fatigues that had been slung into one corner. 'Those clothes give you away. Why not tell us where your compatriots are? Your commanders would have given you instructions: which tracks to follow, what targets to attack and where your fellow rebels are so that should you come across them you will not shoot them by mistake. All you have to do is pass that on to me and we will cut you down and let you go.'

The voice turned slightly querulous. 'Do you know, boy, that I am supposed to be enjoying a very fine football match? Instead I am stuck here, in this awful room, with you.'

The movement was slow as he looked around, his gaze followed by that of the prisoner. It took in the walls, lined above head height with manacles, the concrete streaked with dried blood, excrement and the gouging of innumerable scrabbling hands. The floor was earth, hard-packed but porous enough to show no trace of the gallons of bloody butchery with which it had been irrigated.

Tumbu finally made a great play of looking at his chunky Rolex watch, then smiled conspiratorially before continuing. 'But if you are quick to confess, I may just be in time to catch the second half.'

The swagger stick was used to lift the man's penis from below, the act itself gentle, but the reaction one of even more terror. Tumbu was looking into the victim's eyes, this the moment when he would seek the most effective torture, the one this fellow most feared.

'There are various things we can do with this piece of your anatomy. Such a delicate part of the body, is it not? Have you ever met anyone who has had a red-hot piece of wire forced up the urethra?' Tumbu smiled, like a benign schoolmaster addressing a dim but favoured pupil. 'You do not know what that is, do you? It is the hole you piss through. I have met such unfortunates, been as close to them as I am to you while they watch it being heated by the blowlamp. Some were already aware of what was coming. Very unpleasant! Nearly as bad for your prospects as what we can do to you with just a plain wood table and a heavy hammer.'

He looked to the three men by the wall, as if seeking confirmation, but they'd heard it all before and didn't react. The swagger stick jabbed gently at the scrotum. 'Then we can take pliers to these. When we squeeze it really does make you cry.' The amused tone, along with the half-smile, evaporated simultaneously, and the stick swung viciously. Tumbu's voice rose slightly to cut across the cry of pain. 'Or we can just remove the whole bloody lot, boy, with a knife or a blowtorch.'

The victim's eyes were shut now, the swollen lips moving in silent prayer. Tumbu motioned to one of his men, who moved forward with his stick. It was a well-seasoned piece of rounded timber four feet long and two inches in diameter. The soldier took up a position behind the prisoner, snorted up some phlegm and spat it on to the end. The victim felt the head of the stick against his sphincter and arched his back, trying to tighten his anal muscles. Tumbu poked him hard in the solar plexus and stamped on the bare, stiffened toes that only just touched the ground. That made him bend forward. He screamed as the stick was rammed deep into him, his body wriggling in a hopeless attempt to avoid penetration.

'Are you now prepared to talk?'

The victim shook his head. His voice, when he spoke, was strained from his pain, and distorted by the swollen lips and broken teeth in his mouth. 'I know nothing to tell.'

'You are an awful bore,' Tumbu replied wearily, looking at his watch again.

He really should be off to the football match. Everyone would be there, including Strasser and his coterie of arse-lickers, as well as all the diplomats. More importantly, it was an attraction that would be attended by all the leading foreign businessmen. He had a horrible vision then, that one of his rivals might at that very moment be extracting a promise of funds that should rightfully be his. But then there was the victim, and the example he must set his men, who could then gossip and spread the fearful reputation of which he was so proud. That, on consideration, was not really a problem. He suspected the man had little information that

30

would be of any use. His clothing meant nothing, since many people dressed in what was the most convenient thing they could find. And when it came to examples he could always have another victim picked up.

'I really cannot waste time with this nobody,' he snapped, as the soldier at the victim's rear pushed a little harder. Tumbu examined his hands before he reached for his hat to make sure that they had not attracted any blood or dirt. Satisfied, he picked it up and put it on, taking care to square it properly. 'If he does not respond in an hour give him the salt-water treatment.'

Having sentenced this man to a certain, excruciatingly painful and lingering death, Colonel Eustace Tumbu smiled at him in a friendly way, scowled at his impassive subordinates, and left the room.

'You must not worry unduly, Mr Razenbrook. The rebels may advance upon the area around your mining interests, but rest assured the army will chase them away.'

All Africans, if they are well fed like Captain Joshua Lumulo, have big smiles. The white of their teeth and the contrast of the skin colour acts to create a jolly whole. Tony Razenbrook had volunteered to act as spokesman for the businessmen who were present. He reckoned he could spot insincerity on any face, white, black or yellow, even one so determined to avoid his eye. Lumulo was gazing with singular intensity at the football being played in front of him. He was convinced that what he was getting from the Minister of State for Defence was pious hopes rather than stark truth. He was also aware of the eyes boring into his back, the concerned stares of the community he'd been elected to represent.

'The reports we are getting say that there are no Sierra Leone Defence Force soldiers within fifty miles of the place. The whole of Moyamba district is under rebel control. If they take Sembehun, they will cut the road between Freetown and our mine sites again.'

There was a touch of asperity in Lumulo's voice as he replied. 'You must not worry because we don't make the big splash. When the road was cut before, we reopened it within a day or two. Our men are there, but in a quiet way. Around Moyamba we have contained them. If they move south, east or west they will run into our forces. And then the rebels will be as surprised as you at the bloody nose they get.'

Razenbrook, like every businessman present, had a sheaf of reports on his desk saying otherwise. They told him that the army had melted away

31

before the rebel advance. The charity aid workers, since they operated in the villages and displaced persons' camps, were the most sensitive. They'd been sending in reports for weeks of the fighting taking place around Bo, just twenty miles from his own mining concession. There was a report that had arrived that very morning, rumours of damage done at a quarry operated by Salco, an Italian company. Though unconfirmed, it stated that plant, vehicles and equipment had either been trashed or stolen and dozens of people killed. Even if the army retook the area, operations would have to be suspended.

Everything he'd heard from them since the turn of the year indicated that the Revolutionary United Front were becoming more active, spreading the area of their operations to the extent that the government was losing control of whole sections of the country. Reports were coming in from the missionaries and voluntary agencies to add to those from his employee sources. Those Razenbrook was inclined to trust, but experience told him that other reports, from local tribesmen, had to be taken with a pinch of salt. The problem was, the ruling council seemed to be relying on the latter, which went some way to explaining the rosy air of confidence they maintained.

But even then there could be no way of doubting the general thrust of the reports. The RUF was moving in numbers into the area where he and several others present at the football match had a great deal to protect. The Sierra Leone Defence Force, meanwhile, seemed moribund. It wasn't just investments that left him and his colleagues with a difficult decision to make. The rebels, in the two years they'd been fighting the government, had never gone after foreigners or their commercial interests, but a recent announcement had pointed to a complete policy change. The aim of the revolt from now on, since they couldn't defeat the men in power, was to target their source of income; this accompanied by high-sounding calls for the national wealth of Sierra Leone to be given back to the people. Foreigners were invited to leave the country before they became victims of the revolution. Quite a few people had told Tony Razenbrook that it was a bluff, but part of that unconfirmed report he had received that morning suggested the rebels had taken a European hostage from the Italian quarry site.

Right in front of them now, if the rebels kept moving, lay the Sieromin bauxite mines at Mokanje. The compound that enclosed the mines was huge, overshadowing the nearby village. It was also a tempting target

32

since it contained a lot of expat accommodation, and thus a huge quantity of very valuable loot. Fenced off, with its own guards and mobile patrols, access was controlled through a set of double gates. It was like a small town, totally self-supporting to the point of having its own generated electricity, swimming pool and company shop.

The notion that they might attack such a facility was really worrying, but for Tony Razenbrook what lay beyond that was what really scared him: his own rutile deposit and production sites at Bemba, covering an area over a hundred square kilometres. You couldn't fence that in. The only way to protect such an operation was for the army to stop the rebels before they got near the place. He too had an expat compound to worry about, home to the skilled workers, European and local, who operated the extraction sites as well as the plants that processed the raw product. There were wives and children there, and if the slightest hint existed that they could be threatened he was duty-bound to pull them out. He'd tried to open a line of communication to the RUF, in order to get some guarantees, but that, as yet, hadn't borne fruit.

It was damned frustrating. He wanted to shout at the man, to tell him he was a complacent bastard, but Razenbrook was in a difficult situation. Lumulo was a member of the National Provisional Ruling Council, one of the guys who, in theory, ran the country. If you mined, dredged or built things in Sierra Leone, then upsetting someone as powerful as him was not a good idea. Against that Razenbrook had leverage with the government as a whole, since he and the other businessmen who operated here provided eighty per cent of the national revenue though their export duties. If the concessions closed, the money would dry up. These junior officers, who'd mounted the last coup and who'd now got used to a comfortable lifestyle, might find that they in turn were ousted. The army was in a bad way as it was, underpaid and poorly trained. If the NPRC couldn't fund a defence, then they wouldn't last three months.

He half suspected they were stuck firmly in cloud-cuckoo land. Half their men lacked proper boots, and things as simple as rifles were scarce. Fuel for the helicopters necessary to suppress rebel activity took a back seat to the need to keep their Mercs running. Yet all around the small stadium, covertly assessing the performance of Strasser's bodyguards, were men from the SAS team brought in to train them. They didn't come cheap. In fact, although he had no idea of the actual figure, Razenbrook suspected

33

they cost a mint. That money, put in the right place, might have gone some way to easing his concerns.

Anglo-African Rutile, the company he worked for, had a big and as yet unfulfilled investment in the place. Well over two hundred million dollars had been laid out and, though the profits were commensurate with the investment, they could not afford a stoppage. Quite apart from a break in the revenue stream there was the plant to look after. That was spread over different sites and comprised everything from conveyor belts to huge oil-fired vats, generators and computers, the massive dredgers used to extract the raw material from the virgin African soil. There were Caterpillar trucks, forklifts and riverside cranes, plus a sophisticated production control system at the Plant site. Stuff like that didn't take long to deteriorate to the point of being useless in Africa. The investors, including some of the bigger banks, would get jumpy and might pull the plug on the whole deal, prepared to cut their losses rather than pour in any more money. So it was essential to establish the accuracy of the rumours. Then, if they proved true and the army failed to materialise, he'd get through to the RUF and offer them money. Razenbrook opened his mouth to continue the argument, but the minister beat him to it.

'Ah!' cried Lumulo, 'here is Colonel Tumbu. He will be able to reassure you, if I cannot.'

'About what, minister?' Tumbu asked, sitting down. As he did so, his fingers brushed his shoulder boards, as if to emphasise that although Lumulo was a member of the ruling council, he was superior in military rank.

'Mr Razenbrook is worried about our ability to keep the area around the Bemba rutile deposits clear of rebels. He also fears that criminal elements will cut the road at Sembehun.'

Tumbu's grin, in terms of the degree of insincerity, outdid Lumulo. The voice didn't help either. Tumbu might think he was speaking cut-glass English, but Tony Razenbrook was an old Harrovian, so he knew better. The tone was too mannered and contrived to be real. The head of the Bureau of State Security sounded like a complete phoney every time he opened his mouth. 'Then I am in a happy position of being able to ease your concerns. As luck would have it, I have just had occasion to question an RUF suspect, a very superior person in their ranks. He was, I can tell you, most forthcoming about the rebel's movements. They are nowhere near either Sembehun or Mokanje, at least not in any kind of numbers. As always, their true aim is to take Freetown, and their concentrations are directed to that ultimately futile end.'

'The reports I'm getting hint otherwise,' Razenbrook insisted. Then he decided that a certain amount of exaggeration would do no harm. 'I have one on my desk stating that a hostage has been taken. A European! I need hardly tell you the effect that will have on my own expatriate workers.'

Tumbu laughed, exposing his huge white teeth. 'Rumour, Mr Razenbrook, nothing more. The RUF would not dare take hostages. That would bring down on their heads the odium of the whole world. You know what these scoundrels are like. They talk a great deal and do very little. And, Mr Razenbrook, they are masters at scare tactics. These are just scurrilous tales put out to frighten you.' Tumbu turned just enough to aim a grin at the assembled businessmen sitting to his rear. 'Trust me, gentlemen. I am certain I speak the truth. And both you and your friends will be happy to know that we value your investments as much as you do. Just in case, we have alerted the local civil defence groups to block all roads that provide access to the area around both Mokanje and Gbangatok.'

'That makes me feel really secure.'

If either man detected the deep irony in Tony Razenbrook's voice, they chose to ignore it.

Razenbrook managed to corner Quentin-Davies just after the match, at the point when he'd said goodbye to his guests and, in the company of the military attaché, was about to climb into his official car. The High Commissioner, his long bony face full of concern, listened carefully. He then oozed sympathy about the military situation, but could add nothing practical when it came to the notion of trying to force the NPRC to move.

'Understand the requirements of diplomacy, Tony. The leverage I have with these people is limited. It looks like a great deal, but it's actually very little. A bit of a myth, really, which tested to extremes could prove hollow. I am also constrained on the other side by Whitehall, who have no wish to see the situation here deteriorate.'

'That would take some doing, QD. The place is a bloody mess.'

'You are fairly new to Africa, Tony. I, in my time, have served in Uganda, Kenya and Angola. Things here in Sierra Leone are not perfect, but believe me when I say they are a great deal better than things at their worst. There is a propensity for uncontrolled violence in this part of the world. The trick, in my view, is never to let the cat out of the bag. If we once lose sight of our major aim, which is a degree of stability, we will inevitably end up with chaos. That, as I'm sure you're aware, is inimical to the success of any mining operation.'

'I have to make some pretty hard decisions, QD. And my board of directors is worried. If you have any access to information that would be of help to me, I'd appreciate your sharing it.'

Quentin-Davies patted Razenbrook on the back, like an elderly uncle encouraging a favourite nephew, an act that made the victim, who hated to be patronised, inwardly fume. 'We have little more than you. In fact, since we depend on the government for most of it, probably less.' Quentin-Davies climbed into his car, and continued as he closed the door. 'If, however, my people come across anything that might be of interest to AAR, rest assured we will immediately pass it over.'

'Well fielded, sir,' said Major Delane as the Daimler pulled away.

'Mustn't let the buggers think HMG is on the ball.'

Delane frowned. 'There is a downside to that, sir. The likes of AAR often pick up snippets we have missed. And Razenbrook is actually in contact with the rebels, though my information is that they have yet to respond.'

'Is he, by damn?' said Quentin-Davies, without much in the way of gravity. 'You think, then, we should confirm the hostage report?'

'As long as we can do so without compromising our source.'

'The quarry is an Italian-run concern?'

'Yes, sir. The manager is an Italian national.'

'Then say we got the word from their embassy, a sort of diplomatic courtesy.'

'Right.'

'But not immediately, Delane. Try to time it to the point where they'd have it confirmed anyway.'

'I think that is going to be very soon, sir. And we would lose credibility if we were too late with the news.'

'Very well. You may phone the blighter when we get back to the HC. He's an odd fish, Razenbrook. Harrow I know, but not quite out of the top drawer, if you get my drift.'

'And should we issue a proper warning regarding the threat to AAR's facilities?'

'No, Delane, we should not!'

CHAPTER THREE

They hit the Sieromin compound long before John Little got anywhere near a radio. The guards, who were there to protect against theft, didn't stand and fight. Alerted by negligent discharges and the odd fleeing native they abandoned their posts and ran in all directions, leaving a trail of various bits of uniform in their wake: hats, shirts and anything that carried the company insignia. What, an hour before, had been a badge they were proud to possess suddenly became a mark that could get you killed.

But in their flight they were well behind the expat workers and what remained of their families. Everyone had a vehicle of some type, usually a bit of an old banger, since Africa was hard on quality. But when you're in a real hurry the only thing a car has to do is start right away. Everything else, things that couldn't go into a coat or a trouser pocket, was left behind.

The sight of Europeans fleeing ruined what little control the RUF leaders had over their men. Shots were fired indiscriminately at the absconding vehicles, though the aim was so poor that only one old Fiat was hit, both its rear tyres shredding as the driver kept going. His car slewed back and forth across the road before slamming into a tree, the sound causing a jubilant chorus to rise from the men close enough to see. The driver was out of the car and running within seconds, diving into the bush at the roadside, so intent on escape that he didn't even notice the offers of help he received from other refugees.

Most of the black workers who had turned up for work were running too, clambering over the fence on the opposite side to the gateway in such numbers that they eventually brought it down. They knew that if there were going to be victims, it was their kind who'd suffer. Several were brought down in flight by sprayed gunfire. It would have been more if the rebels had concentrated on that task instead of looting. There was a race on to be the first into Sieromin offices and the expats' houses to steal televisions, radios, hi-fis, fridges, clothes and furniture. But the first thing to do was drink down the ample supplies of wine and spirits the Europeans had left behind. Men and boys already high on dope tipped whisky and brandy down their throats, followed by wine from the pits dug under the floor, bottles passed out through windows so that those still in the compound could join in.

Some of the servants had failed to run, a few who had that rabbit-in-the-headlights complex that froze them in terror when common sense told them to flee. Hiding under beds and in cupboards only inflamed the looters, who, when they found them, beat them savagely. Drink destroyed what little restraint they might have had and the servants began to die, from gunshot wounds, stabbing knives, blows to the head with heavy clubs and vicious swings of razor-sharp pangas. In the compound, those who'd been thrown out to face the larger mob fared even worse, repeatedly run over by looted pickups or crushed under the huge tyres of Caterpillar earth movers. Shots rang out continually, exuberance egging on itchy trigger fingers so that some of the rebels received wounds as well. One or two died from negligent discharges, such stray bullets making the compound a dangerous place to be, a fact underlined by the way in which all of the leaders, who in theory controlled this raging mob, stayed well out of the way.

Mario Berti, the Sieromin security chief, just had time to send off a flash message telling his bosses in Freetown that they were going down, before the rebels got to him. There was a moment when his white skin kept him safe, an ingrained fear of the consequences of touching a European, and the first blow was gentle, no more than a tap that made him stagger backwards. But that made another of his captors bolder. He hit him, though not with full force, with the butt of his rifle. The next was aimed at his skull. Berti went down then, covering his head and cowering in a ball as the blows rained in, certain that he was going to die.

But some fragment of discipline existed; one of the group remembered his orders, and knew a European was more valuable alive. It took a lot of shouting and shoving to persuade his companions to stop, but eventually Berti was hauled to his feet, blood streaming from a deeply gashed forehead, and dragged out across the compound to be thrown at the feet of the rebel leaders.

'Razenbrook, Alan Delane here. Just thought you'd like to know the

Eyeties have confirmed that their manager at that Salco quarry site has been taken hostage by the RUF. Assitola's his name. His two Asian assistants were grabbed as well. Place was thoroughly trashed apparently.'

Delane could have been discussing the results of the football match for all the passion he had in his voice. The man he'd phoned was silently cursing his indifference, the typical attitude of the feather-bedded civil servant to the harsh world of commerce.

'That's damned worrying,' Razenbrook responded, deliberately suppressing his emotions.

'I'll say!'

'Any info on where they're heading next?'

Delane traced the lines on the map which lay on his desk, using index finger and thumb to measure distance. These were the last reported positions he had of any RUF activity. It was not a line of march or a linear advance, more a series of sporadic appearances dotted around the approaches to both Sieromin and Anglo-African's sites. Coming from north, west and east, there was no doubt what they were after. 'None, I'm afraid. They're out there somewhere in the bush, but we don't have a clue as to their actual objectives.'

'Is there anything more you can tell me, Major?'

'Sorry. That Eyetie info came in on the old boys' network. It's not actually official yet.'

'So Strasser doesn't know?'

'If he does, old chap, he's not letting on.'

That didn't make sense. The Italian Embassy must be screaming at Strasser to do something, with cables flying back and forth to Rome. Delane might not know that, but he surely should have had the wit to guess. 'Military boneheads,' Razenbrook said to himself.

'Sorry?'

'Well, thanks,' Razenbrook replied quickly, unaware that he'd actually spoken out loud. 'We're obliged.'

'Don't mention it. If I get anything else I'll get back on the blower to you. Might see you for a drink tonight perhaps.'

'My shout, I think.'

'There's no need for that, old man. Part of my job really.'

Delane put the phone down, and rolled up the map. He half thought of telling Razenbrook about the dead and mutilated government minister, but he'd find that out soon enough for himself.

What he'd just heard, added to what he already knew, made Razenbrook feel seriously gloomy. He rifled through the reports on his desk. Each slip of paper accumulated by his operations manager, Mike Layman, pointed to RUF advances along the Bo–Mokanje road with no sign of the military means to check them. Where would they go next? It was all so damned vague! Part of the problem was the way the rebels moved, never using the roads unless it was essential, to avoid aerial observation and, just occasionally, the more mobile army. By operating along the tracks through the bush they could melt into the forests at the first hint of an aircraft, fixed wing or helicopter. They would then turn up in strength, without prior warning, fifty miles from their last known halt.

The other paper he had before him was a printout of the latest production figures. This showed that he had over fifteen million dollars of processed rutile, one month's production. It was sitting on barges tied to the quay at Port Nitti. There was another batch bagged up and ready to be shipped out from the Plant site, but he had nowhere to ship it to. The barges were not designed for deep water; the Sherbro Channel was the limit of their travel, but the freighter which was due to lift it out for deep-sea transportation was still north of the Azores.

'No response from the feelers we put out?' Razenbrook demanded, having told Layman the latest news.

'Jack shit.'

Mike Layman was pleased to observe the slightly pained expression on Razenbrook's face as he looked up. Boyish, pink-skinned and with floppy blond hair, when he was put out it showed. It was a bloody stupid question anyway. If there had been any feedback from the RUF it would have been the first thing he'd have been told. Layman wasn't fond of Razenbrook, though he was careful to keep it well disguised. He saw him as a stuck-up arsehole who'd only got the job because he came out of the right drawer. Harrow and Cambridge had kitted him out to run a mining and processing company, a man who could barely tell one end of a shovel from the other.

'I think we should try again.'

There were a dozen reasons why Layman disagreed. It might be fruitless, and even if they wanted to the RUF could be in no position to respond. Running a rebel army was no picnic. Communications were horrendous. You couldn't just call the forward units up on the net and tell them to fall back. Likewise, they'd had little time to process the request through what had to be a loose-knit organisation. But the main reason was that if they did want to talk, and perhaps take a bribe to leave AAR's sites alone, it was a bad idea, and potentially very expensive, for the company to be so much the supplicant.

'Shall I do it now?'

'If you don't mind,' Razenbrook replied, in a tone that really said get the fuck on with it. 'Meanwhile, get hold of Frank Wintour for me.'

'What's the picture, Frank?' Razenbrook asked as soon as he was patched through to the main admin building on the Plant site.

'Fog, guv,' Wintour replied, in a voice that would have sat well on a London cabbie. How someone like that had ever got the job of security chief in such a sensitive location foxed his superior. 'Some reports we're getting say that the bastards have taken Sieromin, others that they are still on the other side of the Mokanje hills. It's mostly loose gossip, which is why I ain't bothered to send it in.'

'Army?'

'Not a single one of those tossers in sight. My guess is the few buggers that were here have pulled out.'

'We might have to call for an evacuation of non-essential personnel from all of our sites.'

'Most of those have already gone, guv, they say to do some shoppin'. Everyone out here is ready to follow.'

'How many are left?'

'A hard core, includin' one or two of the women. You know the type, they won't even shift with their kids when their blokes tell them to.'

'That's how the men feel, is it?'

'They ain't daft, boss, and they talk to their own servants. Everyone has got a bag packed, I reckon.'

'Does that include you Frank?'

'No, boss,' Wintour lied. 'I've gotta stay here ain't I, and look after the gaff.'

'I think you should go up the Mokanje road and see what's what.'

41

There was a pause before the security chief answered. The normally chirpy Cockney was thinking if such a job was in his contract. Being AAR's head of security was all about looking after the company assets, not traipsing around Sierra Leone looking for armed insurgents, or standing around waiting to be shot at.

Razenbrook picked up the hesitation with commendable speed. 'I know it's a bit outside your brief, Frank, but I would take it as a personal favour if you'd do this for me.'

Wintour wasn't fooled, either by the soft voice or the pleading tone of the question. He'd served ten years in the forces back home and he knew the leadership type well. From a hard-nosed bastard like Razenbrook that translated into 'How would you like to hang on to your job?'

'I'm not taking no weapons.'

'No one is asking you to, Frank,' said Razenbrook smoothly. 'That might provoke entirely the wrong response if you do meet the RUF. Can't risk you getting shot at, can we?'

Frank Wintour glared at the radio as the connection went dead, then turned to look out of the window of his office. From the top floor of the only two-storey building he could see the whole of the central site. Not that it amounted to much. A dozen evenly spaced low buildings: the processing sheds, the packing plant and the warehousing. Added to that was the accommodation, tin-roofed huts lacking windows and doors for the native workers, more substantial but still tatty-looking villas for the expats, their compound stuck on the only piece of highish ground on the site. There was no fence of any kind, just a perimeter road, mainly because Razenbrook had refused to pay for one. But for Wintour, an ex-military policeman, safeguarding this place presented few major problems. Most of the stuff was too big to nick or like the rutile product, unsaleable locally. He was left with standard pilfering: petrol, engine parts and food from the canteen stores. AAR had given him a budget big enough to employ plenty of Africans, so his job was what he was fond of describing as 'cushy'.

He turned angrily to his operations assistant, Gareth Evans, who'd listened to the whole exchange lounging in a chair. 'That Razenbrook is a right wanker!'

'And no mistake, Frank,' replied Evans, in his heavy Welsh accent. 'Question is, are you going to oblige him?'

'Got to, old son. Though nuffin' says we got to go all the way.'

'We?' demanded Evans, suddenly sitting bolt upright.

'You don't fink I'm going all up that bleeding road alone do you?'

'What about taking Geoff?' Evans protested. 'He'd enjoy that sort of thing. A right bloody Rambo, if you ask me.'

'Mr Hinchcliffe has gone sniffin' after that CARE tart, ain't he.'

'Not Mary Kline?'

'Who else?'

'Disincline, I call her.' Gareth waited for his boss to laugh at the pun, but Wintour was too preoccupied. 'Geoff's got more chance of a leg-over with a Rwandan ape, I say.'

'Hope springs, old son. John Little's out there as well, looking for some bleeding bird.' He saw Gareth's eyebrows begin to rise and added quickly, 'The feathered variety.'

'So he says.'

'I believe him. Anyway, it makes no odds one way or t'other. Just get your boots on.'

'Who is going to mind the shop?'

'Fuck the shop, sheep shagger! Our boys'll look after it, just like they always do. Just get out a pickup, and you and me'll be on our way.'

'I didn't sign on for this sort of thing, Frank.'

'Neither did I, me old mate, neither did I.'

'I just want to run this past you, Mike,' said Razenbrook about an hour later. He was wearing what his deputy called his 'keen' look, the one that was supposed to imply his total commitment to the company cause.

Layman was aware he'd been on the phone continuously since talking to Frank Wintour. It was too small an office not to know, and the girls were, like all Sierra Leonians, very loud, gabby and wonderfully indiscreet. His first call had been to the High Commission. He followed that by making contact with all the other businessmen who stood to be affected by any trouble up-country, asking if they had any further reports to add to his own.

'Nothing we have done has got the army to where we need them. I got on to Quentin-Davies to ask if he could finagle us some of those bloody Gurkhas.'

'How did he respond?'

Razenbrook used a hand to push back his blond hair, his boyish face full of pleasant recall. 'Bugger was furious because I mentioned them on the High Commission line.'

'I bet he was.' That made his boss frown, and Mike Layman spoke quickly to cover what was a bit of a gaffe. 'They aren't supposed to be public, Tony. And any notion that the British High Commission helped recruit them is a real no-no. Not even the locals refer to them by name.'

It was a tribute to West African ignorance regarding the outside world that the National Provisional Ruling Council had come up with the term 'Israelis' as a cover name for a mercenary force made up exclusively of Gurkhas. Nobody, it seemed, questioned this appellation, even when faced with a small brown-skinned number in a floppy green jungle hat, with a knife of a quite distinctive shape at his hip. The fact that the man who led them was an American allowed people like Quentin-Davies to distance themselves from their presence, even though the British government had been quite happy to see them employed as mercenaries in Sierra Leone. Ostensibly on hand to help train Strasser's army, they were almost exclusively employed as combat troops.

'Rubbish!' Razenbrook spat. 'Everyone knows they're here. Go to the bar of the Cape Sierra on almost any night and you can see their officers getting pissed. I've seen that Buckhart fellow, their commander, so drunk he was barely able to walk. How his wife puts up with it I don't know.'

Layman was about to defend Buckhart, a man he was fond of for his utter lack of side. A Vietnam veteran, he was dedicated to fun and fighting, both pursued with outrageous vigour. This was an attitude that had earned him the sobriquet. 'Fizzin' Frank'. The look in the younger man's eyes stopped his protest, since it would be pointless. Razenbrook didn't like to be checked. Looking as youthful as he did, exercising authority was important. Knowing nothing about mining, especially when he was in the presence of a qualified engineer, made him doubly touchy.

'Apart from blasting me for talking about them, it seems none of them can be spared from whatever it is they're engaged in.'

'What about bombing the rebels?'

Razenbrook rolled his blue eyes. 'They have to take somewhere before they can be bombed out of it, Mike. Even I know that. The buggers are out in the bush, and no one knows for certain where.'

'Did you serve in the army, Tony?' Layman asked, knowing full well that the answer was no.

'I was a sergeant in the school cadet force.'

'Really.'

Tony Razenbrook was no fool. He knew that Layman, as careful as he was, didn't like him or rate him. That didn't matter. He was the boss, and there was no way he was going to allow an underling to wind him up. He deliberately sat back in his chair, forcing his muscles, especially those in his face, to relax. 'If you knew anything about the political situation here, Mike, you'd know how hard it is for the military council to ask the Nigerians for air cover.' Pleased that his patronising tone had made Layman clench his jaw, Razenbrook continued. 'It just underlines to them how much they suck the hind tit in the combat pecking order. Every time they go to the airport they see those two Nigerian jets just sitting there. But they don't see any of their own. And nor can they find the money to buy them, even second hand, so busy are they filching from the public coffers. Besides, if they did, who would fly the buggers? It must really hurt when they have to call them in. The lads from Lagos extract a hefty price for every intervention.'

'A price we pay.'

'Only indirectly. It does the government no good, as far as it is concerned, to see its hard-won peculations being passed south to some Nigerian general.'

'I take it you have a solution.'

'You agree we need to get the buggers to move?'

Layman hesitated deliberately. He'd been advocating a different course ever since the rebellion looked to be hotting up, one that involved some expense. Other companies had begun to move in mercenaries, disguised as all sorts of workers, to safeguard their sites. If you couldn't rely on the army or provide sufficient local protection, the only way to keep the mines working was to import your own defence force, one strong enough to make any approach by the RUF too bloody to contemplate. Every time he mentioned it Razenbrook countered with the opinion that the NPRC wouldn't wear it, but in reality, it was the effect on the bottom line and his career prospects that scared him. The cost was, to be fair, horrendous. Yet it was peanuts to the losses they would incur if the mechanics of the rutile extraction were compromised.

45

'Yes,' he agreed finally.

'And do you agree that to give them money to do so in a specific instance might set an unwelcome precedent?'

Since that had been his opinion all along, Layman readily conceded the point, even if he did object to the manner in which it was put. 'The dredge and plant sites would be under threat for ever, with us shelling out in both directions.'

'Quite!' Razenbrook snapped, picking up a handwritten note on his desk. So, I intend to apply pressure another way. This is the outline of a press release. I intend to evacuate all European women and children from our sites. We need some photographs to go with it. Once we have those I want both sent out to all the major wire services.'

Layman read it slowly, partly because of the poor handwriting. The gist of it was straightforward enough. The plan was obvious, since it was written like a horror story: to ratchet up what info was already out on the wire services and so make an international media meal of the need to pull out.

'If this gets the right response there will be camera crews flying in from everywhere,' added Razenbrook gleefully. 'I can just see the headlines: expats, children in hand, forced to flee from the fear of rape by murderous African rebels. Questions in the House, the old embassy bod in London forced to get the Merc out and go crawling to the Foreign Office.' Razenbrook grinned, which made him look even more like a sixth-form prefect. 'Sweet, don't you think? The world's press will be on our doorstep before the day's out, screaming that something has to be done. That'll liven those thieving bastards up.'

'Did you tell Quentin-Davies about this?'

'Not on your Nellie.' The use of such a quaint phrase threw Mike Layman for a second, until he recalled that his boss was public school, a group of people linguistically stuck firmly somewhere in the 1950s. 'He'd put the block on it if I did.'

'He'll make life even more difficult for us if you don't.'

'Only if he finds out, Michael. And I am certainly not going to tell him.' Razenbrook adopted a mischievous look. 'Who knows, with a crisis like this we might get Kate Adie. I've always rather fancied her.'

'Do we have a contingency plan, Tony, if we hit the worst-case scenario?' asked Layman, dragging Razenbrook back from his imagined celebrity shag. He continued as his boss blinked. 'Like if the RUF do overrun the Plant site, and a bribe fails to shift them. A bunch of journalists won't be much help if that happens.'

'That, obviously, is the next point I need to address.'

Razenbrook had responded swiftly but, to Layman's mind, unconvincingly. The look told his number two to leave, and as Layman departed he heard Razenbrook telling the girls to place a call to London that to his mind should have been made a month before.

'Charter Security, my love.'

Much as they tried, the Sisters of Mercy couldn't, at night, keep their charges inside the confines of the displacement camp. In daylight the men were worried, with fearful eyes searching the nearby bush for the first sign of trouble; when the darkness descended, all the demons that afflicted these primitive people rose to smother what thin veneer of Christian feelings they had taken on board. The apprehension was too great, the knowledge that the people these refugees feared so much could come in on them silhouetted by the light of the moon. Some, very few, a handful of Liberians who'd fled their own civil war, had actual experience of this, and were alive to tell the tale because of a freak of good fortune. The others had heard tales from too many sources to feel reassured by the nuns that their safety was more certain if they stuck close to the makeshift convent.

Death could appear from nowhere, silent men with guns, machetes and a mad look in their eyes. It was the face without mercy, not affected by screaming, praying or pleading. Babies unable to walk would be sliced in half in front of their mothers' eyes; pregnant women would be raped before having the foetus cut from their wombs, left to die looking at their own umbilical entrails; young girls and boys would be impaled on spears or the bayonets of the murderers' rifles, held up by vagina and anus until the weapons tore their guts out. Blood would flow by the gallon until the raiders tired and left, taking with them the men and teenage boys as recruits, a few of each butchered in the most abominable way so that the ones allowed to live could see the alternative to volunteering. Girls of the right age would be dragged in their wake, weeping from the degradation they'd already experienced and wailing for what was yet to come. And men covered from head to foot in the gore of their victims would sing and dance as they faded back into the bush, exulting in the power that had flowed into their bodies through the sacrifice they'd inflicted.

The nuns couldn't protect them and Sister Francesca knew it. Indeed, they were in equal danger, and the instructions from their superiors were quite explicit: to pull out if there was a threat of either death or of being taken hostage. But how do you, if you believe in God, abandon thousands of souls to save your own miserable body? Who would feed them, dose them and keep them tied to the Catholic faith if she and her fellow nuns were to depart?

So they watched them drift out at sunset, unable to look in the eye those who maintained their bodies, those to whom they lied regarding their souls. Small knots of people, some single families, others more substantial tribal groupings, all sure that their numbers made them targets, and that individually they were safer. They would spend the night hidden in clumps of bushes, chanting under their breath the mantras they'd learned as children, seeking the protection of their own local spirits and river gods, sure that they provided a security denied them by this alien religion.

At dawn they would return, to eat the free food and sleep part of the day in the tents that distant charities provided, drinking the clean, disease-free water of the well they could not themselves have sunk. When those with ailments heard the bell they would gather in a long line to be dosed and treated by the nuns. Laughter would emerge slowly as the day wore on, especially from children free to play. At some time in the heat of the afternoon the squeals of the *bambinos* would mingle with the chatter of the women, the steady thud of the generators providing a backdrop that suggested tranquillity. Then it was almost possible for the old nun to half-close her eyes and pretend that everything was normal.

But that didn't last, even in a mind that believed God would provide. The first sign soon came that some of the fear her charges displayed was justified. That was the Friday when the trucks from Freetown didn't turn up. The drivers, employed and led by the UN, had noses like ferrets. No matter how bad the roads, how numerous the checkpoints, or how outrageous the demands for bribes, they could always get through to the camps. The excuse that they were late held for a day or two, but by Sunday, when no message came and the United Nations workers at the depot in Freetown could give them no information, it was obvious that the roads must be cut.

The people of the camp were out that night as well, but this time the morning did not bring the full number back. Some had gone for good, to God alone knew where. They would just walk, asking those whom they met for news of a safe place. Many would find it and end up under the protection of some other organisation dedicated to keeping them alive. Others would not. They would starve, and die either by the roadside or in the bushes they'd crawled into for a short rest.

'There is nothing to do but pray, child,' Sister Francesca said, patting the inclined head of Sister Gabriella. 'God's will be done.'

But there was a catch in the normally firm, gravelly voice, as visions of times past filled her mind: of other camps and other wars, of years of effort blown away on the hot African wind. The first sign of real trouble was always the day the supplies dried up. Her spirit was struggling with the reality, her faith under pressure from what her eyes could see and her ears could hear. But that was as nothing to her imaginings, in which innocent people screamed, their bodies and their souls in torment.

'Please God,' she whispered, 'please grant me the strength and the faith to continue.'

CHAPTER FOUR

No bodyguard training job is destined to run like clockwork, but this one had started as a bit of a bummer and then got worse. It didn't take long for eight very bright guys to start wondering what they were doing in Sierra Leone in the first place. It wasn't so much that Strasser didn't need protecting; that was established beyond doubt as soon as the team undertook the first step on the assignment – the assessment of the risk to the client.

The leader of the National Provisional Revolutionary Council could take his pick. He had a full-scale revolt going on in the inland areas, run by people who would happily cut him into Oxo cubes. In the military council there was endless jockeying for position. Some of his so-called friends were of more danger to him than his avowed and very public enemies. He had to deal with urban terrorism as well as a countrywide revolt. The power generating station had been blown up, and RUF supporters had cut the main water supply. To walk the streets was to see how much fear was prevalent. It was in the eyes of the ordinary people, in the way they behaved at checkpoints or shied away from the endless military patrols.

Corruption was endemic and he was pulling in the biggest slice of the cake, sure grounds for jealousy. They'd just sentenced one of the most senior officers, a brigadier-general, to death for associating with the rebels. Nobody knew, since it had been held in secret, whether his trial had established the truth or if it was a farce designed to get rid of a potential rival. Whatever the truth, it could do nothing to make Strasser feel safe. He was well at risk of being bumped off; at home, in the presidential offices, or out in the bush by some pissed-off local unit commander.

It just seemed a bit daft to be shelling out for their kind of military aid when it was obvious the money would have been better spent elsewhere. If the guys in the NRPC had spent dough on their soldiers instead of nicking it themselves, they would probably have put down the revolt, secured the loyalty of the army and done away with a lot of the need for close protection.

The SAS team had read up extensively on the place, and added that to the information they'd gained at the Hereford briefing. Even if they didn't say so openly, each one was capable of a shrewd assessment of the situation in the country they were flying to. If that led to a moral judgement on the merits of the job, it was kept strictly private. 'Ours is not to reason why' was the order of the day. In the regiment, you take the task you are given and do it to the very best of your ability.

Next there was Captain George Roderick Forwood. Not noted for hyperactivity, he was on the last three months of his three-year attachment to the regiment, and gave every appearance of being content to work out his time, leaving the bulk of the work to do with the assignment to his staff sergeant. A keen tennis player, he practically lived at the High Commission courts working flat out on two things: raising his game and dropping the knickers of the female staff members of the entire diplomatic corps. Nationality was not a consideration, only age and beauty, and with the cachet of the SAS behind him he was serving and volleying brilliantly in both departments.

Paul Hill was glad, since it left him free to operate in his own way. When he made a decision or laid out the schedule for a training programme, Forwood was more inclined to rubber stamp it than interfere and get fussy. Personally, the two got on reasonably well, Forwood too idle or preoccupied to worry about his authority and Paul Hill too disinterested to bear grudges. That didn't apply to everybody. The business with Blue Harding, who'd left the regiment in disgust, still rankled. Forwood must have known that as far as G Squadron was concerned he was filed under the heading of 'no good bastard'.

When they'd arrived and carried out the original assessment, they'd quickly decided that Strasser's bodyguards were useless. Loyalty wasn't the problem since they were all related to him in some way, at the very least tribal cousins, but they were overfed, lazy and, with their boss well entrenched in power, addicted to the good life. Looking after their leader, to them, had more to do with keeping his glass and his bed full than saving his life. Half of them, when asked to run round the assault course, didn't manage more than half a lap before collapsing. They weren't left to lie and pant. Paul and his team had great fun beasting them over the course again from the beginning, adding smoke grenades and flash bangs to liven things up.

For all the laughter that such a beasting provided, it did nothing to alter their uselessness. In a place like Sierra Leone, close protection wasn't confined to walking down the High Street. Strasser, even if he didn't like it, had occasionally to go out into the countryside. That meant trips by helicopter or Land Rover in which his bodyguards would be in a potential combat situation. They had to be able to double up as effective close protection and counter attack teams if they were going to be any use. Paul Hill and his trainers spent a week working on them, only to report that they were wasting their time. The mental attitude was simply not there to turn these flabby specimens into a proficient team.

Naturally, the leader of the military council was attached to those who flattered his ego and indulged his whims, men who'd been with him since he came to power and were clearly devoted to keeping him there. That was a real hurdle, which involved the High Commissioner and his Military Attaché in an endless series of meetings. Strasser found it hard to grasp that some things, when he was paying good money for them, were impossible. It was Paul Hill's idea, one cleared by the High Commission, to mount a mock attack in order to convince the man that his cousins couldn't protect him even from a half-arsed assassination attempt.

It was easy to plan, embarrassingly simple to execute. Strasser's men had no idea, or chose to ignore, the first principle of close protection, that in order to safeguard your man from an assassin, you must learn to think like one. It never occurred to them that there was any risk within his own family compound. The SAS team got him on his way from his own front door to his car, the uniformed guards, still half hung-over from the previous night's boozing, in no sort of shape to prevent it. Disarming them was child's play, and the leader of the military council found himself surrounded by the full eight-man team, half their weapons aimed at his head, the other half pointing at the pillocks employed to protect him, spreadeagled on the ground and pleading for mercy.

The old man didn't take this too well, and with Forwood's permission the team stood down until it was sorted out. It wasn't entirely free time. They were told to stick together, which seriously pissed off the trio of golf-mad bastards that were included in the assignment. In the early part of the year the climate was dry and hot without being uncomfortable, so the best place to spend the day was at the beach. Facing north, it was protected from the great South Atlantic rollers, a beautiful sweep of bright white sands with great water for swimming, as well as any number of locals willing to serve them beer and scoff. There, sitting around in T-shirts and shorts, or working hard on the tan, they spent their time chewing the fat. Old mates were recalled fondly, especially if they'd failed to beat the clock. It was one of the risks of the job, getting killed: downed by some IRA guy; a balls up on a free-fall jump; car crashes. These were the risks of action, even down to expiry from hypothermia in some total fuck-up in the Arabian desert, where a group of dickheads had gone out without wheels.

It was natural that past ops were discussed and dissected, the qualities of troopers past and present filleted: some wise, others foolish, but when push came to shove, effective and mutually reliant. The comments, in the main, tended to the comical rather than the serious. There's not often much humour to be extracted from smooth, unruffled success, so the chewing was generally on the downside. For all their skill and ability the SAS had been no different to any other organisation. In places like Dhofar, Oman, Brunei, Ulster, Malaysia, Afghanistan and South America fuck-ups abounded. Things had gone wrong all over the world, stories to be traded with each other but guarded from outsiders with more secrecy than the regiment's successes. They were the best and they knew it, without arrogance – or at least not much.

And, in a desultory way they came back round to discussing the present assignment. Strasser, apparently, had called in a meeting of the entire military council to discuss his personal safety. Which made Paul Hill wonder out loud what it must be like being an African leader, sitting talking about personal security to a bunch of people at least half of whom must be scheming to do you in. Harry Fielding's opinion was delivered in his usual West Country drawl: 'Imagine what it's like when they're having their dinner, dipping into your soup knowing every bastard there is thinking his arse ought to be in your chair.'

A Cornishman and ex-Para, Harry Fielding was Paul Hill's backup man, a troop sergeant and commander of one of the four-man teams. Burly, red-faced and jolly-looking with tight gingerish curls, the slow speech fitted the image he projected. He looked like a farmer, the kind who chews a stalk of hay. But he was as hard as fuck, a karate black belt, and a good enough linguist to worry about his accent sounding too provincial in French and Spanish.

'Perhaps we should lend them our COs when they pack it in,' added

Tommy French. 'They did it in the old days, with the old colonels, sent 'em over 'ere to run a country or two.'

'Away yersel',' hooted Kenny 'Crazy' Collins. 'If ye did that there'd no be any cunt left to fuck up the British Army.'

'There would,' replied Harry, with mock gravity. 'If there's one thing we're not short on in the Rupert brigade, it's dickheads.'

Trevor Lipscombe, who was lying flat out on a beach mat, spoke up, his voice given added gravitas by the fact that he had his hand half covering his mouth. 'I won't hear a word said against Ruperts. How can they be bad if they get us a billet like this?'

'You've had too much sun, mate,' said Paul. 'We're out here working, while that bastard Forwood is practising for Wimbledon.'

'You call this working?'

'Slavery, Trev,' said Paul, sipping his beer, his head tipped back to take the sun. 'That's what it is.'

'You must be right, Hillbilly,' he replied, drawing his towel over his head. Trevor was the one who'd first given Paul that nickname, a monicker in direct opposition to the man's fashion conscious self-image. Trev was Mr Sarcastic, well known for debunking everything, especially the Ruperts. He had a wonderful way about him, a mixture of respect just bordering on taking the piss that left them nowhere to go. But underneath the sarcasm was a streak of reality. 'Never trust a Rupert' was a mantra in the ranks of the SAS, underlined by each trooper's personal experiences. 'But given the shit service round here dehydration is more likely than too much sun.'

Paul picked a can of beer out of the icebox and laid it on Trevor's back. This was a good job, even if he reserved the soldier's right to moan. Doing a bodyguard assignment was a breeze, a sort of payoff for all the discomfort they suffered on other operations. There was none of that Ulster boredom, or sitting in wet shell scrapes for a week, freezing your bollocks off on some Afghan hillside or in an Iraqi foxhole. And it was a damn sight better than picking leeches off your dick in Indonesia or Thailand. Sure, there was work to do, and it was valuable, even to the people giving the instructions. Nothing fixed the tenets of good practice in a soldier's mind more than teaching. As they trained a close protection team their own skills would be honed. Her Majesty's Government weren't daft; they knew that Special Forces men sent on BG training assignments came back better and sharper.

And, especially on a good climate job, they came back tanned and happy. It was nine to five most days and weekends off, with good booze, great food and crumpet galore on the menu. Freetown, like any capital city, had good bars like Paddy's and the Cape Sierra Hotel, and a decent nightclub, the Lagoona, to go on to, each place stuffed with hookers by the several dozen. True, you didn't always end up on such an assignment with an eight-man team of wits and players, but generally, unless you got a real tosser along, it was easy to relax and enjoy yourself.

That was something, along with his job, that Paul dedicated himself to. He was single, the only one of the party not either married or divorced. He was one of the trio of real players on the scene which included Trevor and Crazy Collins, when the Scotsman could be dragged away from writing software programmes on his portable PC. They would be out every night, parading the Armani and the Yves St Laurent suits, the Cartier watches and the Gucci shoes. Paddy's Bar, to these guys, was a real forward battle area. Oneupmanship was on Standing Orders, honours going to the guy who could pull the best floozie that night.

Three of the others were what Paul called occasional players; one-or-two-nights-a-week men, and to some extent they dressed like it. Harry Fielding was one of the nicest guys Paul knew, but when it came to putting on a suit he was a disaster. He'd taken his £200 clothing allowance, which every one of them got for the job, and bought pinstripes. His excuse was that he'd look good at the embassy receptions. The truth was that he was the wrong shape, and he ended up looking like a happy, smiling, charming bag of shit. The LOVE and HATE he'd had tattooed on his fingers as young Para squaddie did nothing for the overall image.

Tommy French was gadget mad, an inveterate fiddler who could fix almost anything. Give him a dozen bits of metal and he'd hand you back a ground attack jet. But he couldn't hold his drink too well, and being married to a really tough number he had a total terror of catching the clap, so when the hookers sponged a meal off him, which was their first priority, they usually got it for no service in return beyond a blow-job. Paul Hill reckoned that the number of times this had happened he was in danger of going home with a dose of plaque.

Bob Deighton liked to think of himself as Mr Responsible. He was doing an Open University course in politics and philosophy, working for his degree with the same tenacity he applied to everything, determined, when his service was over, to become a lecturer. So he was strictly a Saturday night player, his intentions on going out to have just one or two before coming home. That never happened. In fact it generally turned into a get-pissed-and-get-laid-bonanza, with much muttering on Sunday through eyes that looked like pissholes in the snow about what a stupid wanker he was.

The other two barely drank. Owen Saddler was a fauna and flora freak, who thought that being in Africa was too good a chance to waste on boozing and women. Nicknamed 'Horse', he was more interested in orchids than whores. He was also heavily and recently married to a girl expecting his first baby, so spent a lot of time on the phone home. But he was discreet, never letting on what players on the scene got up to. Which was just as well, since SAS wives tended to get very close to each other when their men folk were away. Jerry Fallon was a *Times*-crossword-in-ten-minutes guy, steady as a rock, who looked like a travelling solicitor when he put on the cream suit he bought from Gieves and Hawkes. If anybody failed to look like an SAS trooper it was Jerry, with his lanky build, fine-boned features and high forehead, all complemented by a bit of a grand manner. But he was a bloody good soldier, a weapons and demolitions expert so talented that he had been all over the world telling other people how to do the job. Jerry could take down a bridge with no more Semtex than would fit into a fag packet.

Forwood suddenly appeared at the top of the beach, racquet in hand. He'd been playing with some French embassy tarts at the Cape Sierra Hotel and was dressed in his whites, the shirt streaked with damp patches and his black hair plastered to his forehead. Judging by his face, he was not pleased.

'Paul, aide of a chap called Tumbu has just come to see me. Stopped me in the middle of a bloody tie-break as well. His boss has been given the job of selecting personnel for a new close protection team. Wants to see us in the attaché's office in twenty minutes. Double back to the HC. We'll just have time for a quick shower.'

Then he was gone, and Kenny opined, his Glaswegian accent extra strong and his ridiculously young face full of piss-taking wonder. 'Would you look at the state of him. Those French floozies must a' put the man through the mill. Ah know wit a sixty-nine is, lads, and the missionary position, an 'aw, but what in the name o' hell is a tie-break?'

'You're too young, Kenny,' joked Harry Fielding. 'Too much of that kind of knowledge and you go blind.'

'Does that mean I won't be able tae enjoy the porno on the Internet?'

Paul was on his feet, heading up the beach, wondering which suit to wear, the black Armani or the bespoke pale cream number he'd had made for the trip. The black won, since he would not then need to get changed again before heading for Paddy's Bar and the company of a very beautiful Lebanese floozie he'd connected with the night before.

Roddy Forwood, when they joined up, was just as crisply attired, in a Hackett's blazer, brigade tie and tan slacks. Brown suede brogues completed an ensemble that was Guards officer hot-climate mufti. Like the battered winter tweeds it was designed to tell whoever was looking exactly which drawer he came out of. As they crossed from the residency compound to the High Commission building, the sergeant was slightly amused at the way the change of clothes affected the man. Forwood, normally a rather louche creature, was striding out as if he was on the square at Chelsea Barracks, chin thrust to the fore, steel-tipped heels cracking on the flagstones of the path.

'Roddy, Paul,' said the attaché, beaming, 'do come in and sit down.'

Even in civvies Major Alan Delane looked like a uniformed soldier. The hair was short and carefully groomed. He had his regimental Welch Fusiliers tie on, tightly knotted over a blindingly white, starched, short-sleeved shirt. The wristband on his watch was regimental too, blue background with a red central stripe. He was a fussy sort of man, of medium height, a red face full of broken veins, with a plummy sort of voice so well past the point of caricature that the training team had immediately nicknamed him 'Carruthers'. He was, as he described himself, the liaison 'chappie', for all that his charges knew, the very bloke who'd sold the idea of an SAS training team to Strasser. That was his job; flatter the locals: flog them the arms and the services, so that a goodly part of Britain's military budget could be financed by the poor fuckers in the ex-colonies. As his two visitors obliged, entering the room and making for the chairs, he frowned slightly, forced by his own good manners to move from behind his desk and personally shut the door.

'Your glass, Colonel Tumbu, can I top it up?'

'Thank you, no, Major,' said Tumbu, grinning at the two newcomers.

'Then, if you don't mind, sir,' Delane continued, 'I leave you to brief Captain Forwood.'

Tumbu moved in his chair, pulling himself up to arrange his body into a more self-important pose. He was running a finger round the rim of his glass, staring at the contents as though he needed to collect his thoughts. Finally he spoke, in a voice so grave he could have been announcing the start of World War Three.

'Gentlemaan,' he intoned. 'You have demonstrated beyond doubt that the men assigned to be trained by you were of no value as bodyguards. The leader of the military council has entrusted to me the task of finding replacements.'

'An absolutely top-hole choice if I may say so, Colonel Tumbu,' said Delane, his voice silky and his face beaming.

Paul was wondering which came first for MAs, the sycophancy or the job? Did the powers that be think here's a right oily bastard, let's send him to the embassy in Wonga Wonga to kiss arse? Or did they take perfectly ordinary Ruperts and turn them, especially, into the type who could slip under a closed door? And who was worse, Delane or this Idi Amin lookalike who took the phoney compliment as his rightful due?

Tumbu frowned, looking worried. 'The leader has faith in me to do the job properly.'

'Hardly misplaced, sir.'

'Yet, Major Delane,' Tumbu said, sitting upright, 'I have to admit that choosing men for such a task is outside my own experience. I will therefore have to rely very heavily on you and your experts for advice.'

He'd turned to Forwood to include him, giving him the full 'I'm just a simple soldier and I trust you' smile. Delane was in like Flint, for which Paul was grateful. He was well aware that what they were being handed was a bonus, the chance to select their own team. It was a bug on any job, since even if most of the guys were malleable material, there were always one or two who were graduates of the two-left-feet academy. They also generally turned out to be personal favourites of the client, and very difficult to shift.

'Naturally, we will do anything we can to help,' Delane oozed.

Tumbu nodded, slowly, pausing again to collect his thoughts. 'My suggestion is this; that I provide the candidates from my own military police units, of necessity a numerous group, but that you select from them the men you think best.'

'Happy to, sir,' beamed Delane.

Tumbu followed that with a slight shrug, and an embarrassed air that was totally unsuited to his nature. 'It will please our leader if I can say to him that this is a service you are willing to add on to the original contract at no extra charge.'

Delane hesitated. To Paul's way of thinking, it was not because he needed time to decide but merely to imbue his assent with the gravity it deserved. That applied especially to the 'no charge' bit, since the contract was at a fixed price over an agreed time. Delane's pause allowed a quizzical look to be aimed at Forwood to get his nodded assent, even though essentially it was none of the captain's business. But no acknowledgement was made to the man who would actually have to do the job.

'I know you have said they will be numerous,' Paul remarked, 'but might I ask how many candidates we will have to select from?'

That made Delane frown. The locals were sensitive to a very exceptional degree about hierarchy, something he'd advised the whole training team about when they'd arrived. Part of the problem was their actual rank – low in terms of the army, even if they were ministers in the government. Captain Strasser ordered brigadiers and generals around; that was when he was not accusing them of treason and blowing them away with a firing squad. Delane's lecture hadn't gone down too well. These were men who'd had plenty of practice at the art of dealing with senior officers. Good manners were drummed into them by steady attendance at formal mess dinners. In the army, they didn't just give you stripes and responsibility and nothing else; they took you into a world where by example and encouragement you were taught the rules of polite behaviour. Most people, even the most touchy sod, would have seen Paul's question for what it was: a courteous enquiry. Not Tumbu. He was clearly displeased. Paul surmised that in his kind of army no mere ranker would even have been invited to such a meeting in the first place. The notion that they might speak was anathema.

'That is a very good point, Paul,' Delane said, giving Tumbu a smile as he drew the question on to himself.

'You have the entire military police to select from,' the Colonel replied, pointedly ignoring the NCO, 'as well as the men of my internal security forces.'

'We will require the fittest and brightest you have,' added Paul, just to drive home the point that, regardless of Tumbu's love of rank and privilege, it would be him doing the work.

'If you don't mind, sir,' said Forwood, abruptly standing up, 'I believe the details would be best left to be worked out by you. Paul and I will go and run up a selection programme. We'll beast them round the assault course to begin with. That's the best place to start. Basic fitness, that kind of thing! Sort out the wheat from the absolute chaff. Shall we say 0800 hours the day after tomorrow?'

Tumbu had been giving Paul the full Idi Amin glare, but he suddenly smiled as his eyes left the sergeant's face. 'That will be perfect, Captain Forwood.'

'Touchy sod, that Tumbu,' said Forwood softly as the door closed behind them. Paul growled his assent, but couldn't help wondering if the next time this master of the double handshake shared a drink with Tumbu he'd be calling Paul a bit of bolshie bastard.

They were out of the building and halfway back to the residency before Paul spoke again. 'Why doesn't he want to select the men, boss? Surely he knows their capabilities better than we do.'

'That's easy, Paul. He doesn't want the responsibility. If that bugger Strasser gets slotted, regardless of who pulls the trigger, he can shrug his shoulders and blame us.'

The walk down to Paddy's Bar was spoiled by the stoning. The poor guy the crowd had cornered literally shat himself with fear. You could see it, mixed with piss, running down his legs. His eyes were terrified, his voice cracked as he pleaded, hands held out in a gesture of innocence. The people around him didn't believe him or didn't care, and were whipping themselves up into the kind of frenzy that kills, shaking their fists, spitting, stamping their feet and shouting insults. The soldiers nearby, MPs in their bright red caps, showed no inclination to interfere. Neither did Paul, Trevor or Crazy Collins. The mob, which looked to be about a hundred strong, was growing by the minute, filling the street and blocking their route. All three stopped and moved so that their backs were near a wall, tensed by the presence of violence.

The first stone missed and hit the wall behind the guy. He must have known what was coming. The mob, mostly Creoles, thought he was a spy; more than likely he was just some up-country bumpkin who couldn't speak their lingo. The Freetowners were nervous, especially those same Creoles. Better educated and prosperous, they saw the RUF as outsiders, ignorant tribesmen who with their revolt would bring them all down. Every time they heard a gunshot or an explosion, or had their water or power supply interrupted by sabotage, they felt threatened, and what education they possessed was no more than a thin veneer over more primeval instincts. All it needed, in such an atmosphere, was a pointed finger, a shouted accusation, and they were off. If they had sticks they would use them. Here, on the site of a derelict building, they had stones.

They arrived by the dozen in the next volley, half at least pounding into the man's body. He screamed in pain, more like a wounded beast than a human being. A big lump took him on the forehead, splitting his skin and sending forth a rush of bright red blood. Tears were streaming down his face, leaving clear tracks on the dust that coated his skin, soon to be joined by that very same blood. The noise of the mob rose to drown him out, and the stoning increased in tempo.

When he went down, which didn't take more than half a minute, the mob didn't close on him. They continued stoning from a distance, as if he were contaminated and too lethal to touch. He reacted for a while, his body twitching and jerking as each projectile made contact. The sound of breaking bones was all in the imagination of the men watching, but the number finding the hands he was using to try to protect his head were doing just that, until he could no longer keep them there.

He was still howling when they knocked him unconscious using a huge flat slab which one rioter was brave enough to take in a bit closer. Emboldened by this, another followed, practically standing over the victim as he raised a lump of concrete in his hands and threw it down with all the force he could muster. They heard the skull go with a loud plop, saw the brains oozing out of the crack which now became the target of every stone that could be cast.

Eventually even the involuntary twitching ceased, the only body movement caused by a projectile forceful enough to induce it. Then they came forward in numbers, murmuring now rather than shouting, pointing and laughing in that gruesome way people do when they have

61

just let fall a civilised façade. They didn't hang around long, no more than a few seconds to poke the victim with a toe. Then they shuffled away. The normal buzz of happy people emerged, getting more and more excited as each one reprised the action of every stone that had been cast, no doubt arguing and claiming to have been the one to strike the fatal blow.

The three troopers walked past the victim slowly, which kept the vultures on the rooftops away for a few seconds more. The clothes were in tatters and covered in blood; so was the roadway, a long trickle running towards a small gully where it gathered into a darkening pool.

'Poor fucker,' said Crazy Collins.

CHAPTER FIVE

ake a hostage anywhere in the world and certain people notice. There was obviously, by this time, a great deal of activity in Rome on behalf of the Italian captive, Signor Assitola, but that was political. Sierra Leone was an ex-British colony, and if any action was to be taken on that turf the natural place to look was London. A senior official of the Foreign and Commonwealth Office, the permanent under-secretary chaired the committee which oversaw such problems. The committee comprised representatives of the Cabinet Office, the Home Office and the Ministry of Defence. But when it came to a reaction to any perceived threat, the most important member was the Director of Special Forces. A Brigadier, he is almost invariably an ex-CO of the 22nd Air Service Regiment, which means he has been, in the past, a Troop and Squadron commander. He oversees the activities of his old regiment, plus the Special Boat services and two Territorial Army groups.

As soon as a hostage crisis is identified, even before it has a chance to develop, this committee will meet. But by that time Hereford will have been alerted. There is a permanent Special Projects Team always on alert, their main task to provide an instant response to any act of terrorism. Avid readers of the newspapers, as well as watchers of the TV news, they are a very switched-on group of people. By the time the request came in from Rome to London the men in Hereford were already looking at maps of West Africa and thinking about exercises that would hone the skills necessary for action in combat and jungle warfare. These men trained constantly. The decision about what to do on a daily basis was random, and shared out between the team members. Some would be practising close reconnaissance techniques or organising lectures on tracking and bush patrol skills. Requests to use the Close Quarters Combat House, the specially constructed building where the Counter Terrorist team practised hostage rescue from confined and darkened spaces increased. Other teams spent the day firing at Hun head targets on the sniper ranges. And since West Africa was suddenly on the menu, the conversation, the constant search for knowledge and improvement, moved to spotlight the guys who'd seen action in that environment. Any information they'd gathered from previous ops or training exercises was readily passed on. Everybody learns from everybody else in the SAS.

In the headquarters buildings the green slime guys opened their lines to Freetown and the Foreign Office and started gathering intelligence, the first thing necessary to build up a profile of the RUF, its leadership, and its strengths and weaknesses. The names of the combat leaders were fished out, and where no photograph was extant an identikit was made up from what knowledge existed.

The fax machines whirred as information poured in from official archives as well as those belonging to companies that operated in the area. They might have guessed where the info was going, but discretion ensured that they never knew. Maps were pinned up and points of advance and territory held were marked, as well as the location of any forces that could be used to support an incursion. Key locations holding supplies that might prove useful were flagged, as well as sites that could be employed as forward operation bases.

The same applied to the headshed of the stand-by squadron, ready to put serious numbers into any world troublespot at short notice. They were right on the case and had already started to call back personnel from less important tasks and liaison jobs. The CO, the Squadron commander and the Squadron sergeant-major had already looked at various ways of getting in, preparing for two main eventualities: an invite from the locals, or if that wasn't forthcoming an operation mounted from the UK that would have to be deniable. One of their first tasks was to request information on what sea transport was available, an act which had the Admiralty detaching a frigate from Gibraltar with orders to commence exercises off, but out of sight of, the West African coast. All of this happened with very little reference to the political masters in Whitehall. Ever since the Iranian embassy siege at Prince's Gate it had been a maxim of the regiment to have as much in place as possible before they were asked.

Only one other department was ready to act with such speed. Scotland Yard's SO10 branch, the trained negotiators whose job it was to get the hostages out without bloodshed. It didn't matter if it was one person or a hundred, they always worked in pairs. Superintendent Eddie Welford and Inspector Ian Cannon were rostered to be on stand-by when the signal came in from Freetown. Within an hour they were booked on a flight and ready to go. They had spoken to, and had arranged their rendezvous with, the two SAS minders they would take with them.

Colonel Frank Buckhart had reports on his desk too. He also had a representative from United Nations Commission for Refugees sitting in the outer office. It wasn't often a mercenary commander got a wholly formed unit to play with. Normally they were recruited piecemeal, the first task being to weld them together into an effective fighting unit. But thanks to the British government and its policy of military retrenchment, added to the endemic poverty of Nepal, that was what he had: two complete Gurkha companies.

Disbanded, well trained and homogeneous, it was an inspired idea to have them recruited as instructors for a government struggling to suppress a revolt, especially one that had little faith in its own army. They liked a scrap, so they were pleased when Buckhart insisted that the training they were tasked to provide should be very hands-on. Not for him the rear-echelon stuff – combat drills and mock battles; he loved to be in the thick of the action. Which meant that when the Sierra Leone Defence Force got into a firefight, Buckhart's instructors would be right alongside, and in some cases well out in front of them.

Centred on his headquarters at Kabala, the one hundred and sixty men of his Gurkha Guard Force were spread out along the northern border with the Republic of Guinea. A mixture of high mountain and thick jungle, the country was ideal for guerrilla operations. This was the location from which the RUF leadership operated; hard to find, always willing to withdraw if threatened, determined to maintain their threat to the Strasser government, able to move through the jungle at will and cross the border at a point of their own choosing.

There was a map behind Buckhart showing the latest sitrep, as well as the routes covering the main crossing points into Guinea, a country whose forces either could not or would not do what was necessary to suppress the rebels. Also displayed on the map were the numerous DP camps, the responsibility of the man waiting to see him. Yet the wall map didn't show the whole truth. Some of his men were over that border, his secret assault units, there to disrupt RUF preparations. Frank Buckhart believed very strongly in pro-active defence.

He had hundreds of miles of open border to protect. To sit and wait for rebels with his limited forces would be madness. He'd learned most of his combat skills in Vietnam, and had seen the downside of taking up static defensive positions. 'Get to the enemy before he can get to you' was the Buckhart philosophy. That had to be deniable, of course, sometimes to the point of not telling his paymasters in the NPRC, who wished to stay on good terms with their northern neighbours.

The tactic had produced some success, luck playing just as much a part as skill. Intelligence was patchy in a country where power was fractured, and the rebels could move at will. Locating them and avoiding the Guinean forces was no picnic, but his comms were excellent, and so were the tracking abilities of his Nepalese troops. Yet it was still a hard, hot grind, sometimes for little reward; only occasionally his forward reconnaissance patrols found some base, and could then call in the assault groups to hit the enemy, destroying arms caches and forcing the RUF political leadership to move their location.

The strategy he favoured was simple to enunciate, more complex to execute. Buckhart and his officers had concluded that just holding the border would never produce either a military or a political solution. To survive the Freetown government had to defeat the insurgents, a job that could never be achieved by letting them retire at will to a safe haven. By attacking those bases, the Gurkhas had forced the RUF into a more offensive posture, one that meant most of their guerrilla fighters were now obliged to operate inside Sierra Leone. The downside of that was the damage they were inflicting on the economy and the country. But the gain was obvious: as a force in the field they could be attacked and defeated, if the NPRC could get the units in place to tackle them.

The strategy seemed to be working. The enemy had come out of the highlands and had occupied positions around Moyamba. They were now spreading out from there, attacking economic targets. A determined response now, employing his forces, could inflict such a defeat on them as to destroy the revolt. The whole thing had a sweet smell to Frank Buckhart, the prospect of a real battle with the chance to prove his command capabilities.

Less pleasant to contemplate, right at this moment, were the other reports. These came from the aid agencies, which told him of supplies drying up and an increase in the number of refugees coming in from the displacement camps to the south. That was an inevitable result of enticing the RUF out to fight, but what had been a trickle was rapidly turning into a flood. The problem was simple: with Freetown the only major port in Sierra Leone everything was processed through there, including his own supplies. Transport by road was essential. Part of his brief was to keep the routes open. That he could do, but only in his immediate area. The increasing number of incursions being made by the RUF in a sector that was not yet under his control was lengthening and sometimes disrupting that logistical support. Not just food, clothing, ammunition and replacements for him, but the supplies needed for the refugee camps. That, with the increasing number of dependent mouths, could only get worse, which had to be why the UN representative was here.

'Best wheel him in, Toby,' said Buckhart to his adjutant, his Texas drawl made all the more pronounced by the sigh in it.

Major Toby Flowers, an ex-Green Jacket, was the antithesis of the American. Fizzin' Frank Buckhart was big and brash, a cigar-chomping motivator who wore a big pistol and swore as much as he shouted. He was like a character in a Hollywood war movie. But inside that larger than life behaviour was a commander who cared for his troops and was personally brave enough to impress these members of a Himalayan warrior race. In fact, being so different to what they'd experienced under British command, the men adored him. Flowers was what these Gurkhas were used to. He was slim, of average height, with a quiet but efficient and very British demeanour. Always immaculately turned out, Flowers never shouted except when the noise of gunfire and battle demanded it. He spoke softly to his juniors, leaving them to pass on his orders to the troops.

The Englishman was tempted to sigh himself. The man who would come through the door in a second was not one of their favourite people. Fizzin' Frank hated to be told what to do by military superiors. The idea that a civilian would try such a thing was enough to make him explode with rage.

'Let's hear how hellish life is for the bureaucrats,' Buckhart added.

'Shall I arrange some tea for him?'

'Tea, for Christ's sake?'

Flowers opened the door and called out, in his very correct, clipped voice, 'Mr Ammera, will you please come this way.'

Lani Ammera bustled in, a busy little man of five foot six inches. He had a well-developed sense of his own importance. Buckhart loathed him, called him the 'poisoned dwarf' and being six foot four, always stood to his full height when in the UN representative's presence. This did nothing to intimidate Ammera. He was a man who'd wag a reproving finger if he was talking to God.

'I have been kept waiting twenty minutes,' he snapped.

The lips pursed in suppressed anger, that expression followed by an impatient look at his gold, wafer-thin Swiss watch. He was immaculately dressed in a pale grey suit, just a shade darker than his hair, wafting in front of him the gentle smell of an expensive eau-de-Cologne. The briefcase was Louis Vuitton, the shoes hand-made, the silk tie discreet but decidedly expensive. He dressed like that wherever he went. Even on the rare occasions during which he visited, in air-conditioned comfort, some of the camps whose budgets, on behalf of the UN Commission for Refugees, he controlled.

'It was necessary for me to look over the reports from the aid agencies, Mr Ammera.'

'Good. I hope you have drawn from them the same conclusion as I.'

Buckhart grinned, but it was more rueful than friendly. 'You haven't actually told me what that is, but I guess you're going to.'

Ammera sat down. A Ghanaian, he had the arrogance of the race who held themselves superior to all other West Africans. He'd spent his entire working life in the service of the UN, avoiding a return to his native land by continuous employment. It was generally accepted by anyone who met him that if he ever went home he would be shot within weeks, an act which would be barbaric, but justified.

'It is, if I may say so Colonel, as plain as the nose on your face. The supply routes are being severely disrupted, and the number of refugees in the border camps is increasing by the day. If this is allowed to continue, we will face a disaster. It is therefore necessary that you alter your priorities. The transport routes must be protected, and any impediments cleared.'

Flowers thought impediments a nice bureaucratic word for armed rebels, but it wasn't a wholly outrageous demand. Buckhart had sent troops on that kind of mission many times, usually when a particular bottleneck became too greedy in its demands for bribes. His men were just as effective with lathis as they were with guns. A sound beating usually sufficed to clear the road completely, but if that showed signs of failing then the sight of a few razor-sharp Gurkha kukris usually turned the natives into willing listeners.

But now something quite different would be required. To secure the supply routes they'd have to provide enough manpower to ensure that the roads to Freetown stayed open, a task that would severely deplete their ability to mount the kind of response Buckhart had envisaged. He needed to keep his forces together. And it was not a job the Gurkhas would enjoy; split up into small packets, manning hard-to-protect road junctions, at grave risk of being overwhelmed if the RUF decided to take them on. Yet the man in front of him had to be humoured. Ammera had clout and his own agenda, one that was never going to coincide with purely military objectives. The only option was to play him along a little, to try to prevaricate, to make the time Buckhart needed to impress on his paymasters the advantages of his approach.

'That is not, strictly speaking, a good use of my troops,' said Buckhart. 'They are fighters, not traffic cops.'

'It is a proper use of your men, Colonel, something that Captain Valentine Strasser confirmed to me personally only a few days ago.'

'Then I'm surprised he didn't tell me that as well!' snapped Buckhart.

Flowers cut in, his voice soothing as he headed off his superior. Ammera was well able to offer a payment to get his way. Strasser took money from everywhere, and was not always fussy about delivering on the promise that went with the gift, so it was reasonable to suppose that when it came to dealing with the UN, he adopted the same tactic.

'You must understand, Mr Ammera, the size of the task we face.'

The UN representative produced a particular look in response to that, one that indicated how much greater were the burdens he had to bear.

'The Colonel and I believe,' Flowers lied, 'that our troops are best deployed in keeping the rebels pinned down in Guinea. If we start acting as policemen all over Sierra Leone, I doubt we will be half as effective.'

'I have people at risk of starvation within a mile of this office.'

Buckhart should have been tactful, but that was something he found difficult to do. But when he spoke, it was without much passion. In fact, he stuck the knife in slowly. 'The contents of your icebox would go a long way to relieving that, sir.'

Ammera responded with a bland expression, totally unfazed by the remark. 'I'm afraid that your American witticisms quite escape me.'

'We were merely trying to point out,' said Flowers, 'that what you propose may make matters worse, rather than better. If we denude the border, there will be a greater rebel presence inside the country. That may result in even more trouble for the DP camps.'

Ammera looked at Flowers, making it very plain he thought he was talking nonsense. He addressed his next remark to Buckhart. 'I doubt there could be many more rebels inside the country than there are now. And do not treat me like an idiot. You may think your notions of how to fight the RUF are secret, but they are not. Indeed they are plain to anyone with half a brain. Glory-seeking is all very well for people like you, but it does not excite me. I represent the UN and I have a responsibility that I cannot put aside to convenience your military ambitions. I therefore must insist that you accede to my request.'

It didn't sound like a request, but then Ammera wasn't capable of asking for a favour with anything approaching supplication. Too many years of UN bureaucratic comfort had quite killed that concept.

'You can ask, mister, but you can't insist,' Buckhart replied. 'I do not take my instructions from the UN Commission for Refugees.'

'There seems to be some confusion about where you go for your orders,' the Ghanaian snapped. 'Did Strasser sanction those incursions you have just made into Guinea, or did you think of them yourself?'

Frank Buckhart produced such a look of injured innocence that Toby Flowers had trouble trying to stop himself from laughing. 'My dear Mr Ammera, what are you talking about?'

'I am talking about you exceeding your instructions and endangering the delicate relationship between Sierra Leone and the Republic of Guinea. You have spread the conflict, rather than contained it. Perhaps, in order to get you to comply with my wishes, I should report the truth of this to Captain Strasser.'

'How are you getting on with New York these days, Mr Ammera?' The voice was bland, the look wistful, not threatening, the total change of subject treated as a natural progression. 'Are they still having trouble trying to understand the difficulties people like you have to cope with on the ground?'

The UN official didn't blink, but his jaw clenched slightly. Buckhart was making plain that he too could issue threats. As an American with good newspaper contacts, he could get to people in the UN. Ammera was in charge of a great deal of cash, some of which was handed out to people who were not only in transit but could neither read nor write. The opportunities for corruption were obvious. Even if there was no actual proof, some of the money seemed to get stuck in his fingers. The man was just a shade too well groomed.

'As it happens,' Buckhart continued, 'Major Flowers and I planned to fly up to Freetown today to consult on this very problem.'

'But will you obey the instructions you are given?'

Flowers moved forward quickly as he saw Buckhart bare his teeth and begin to move. Booting the supercilious little bastard out of the office was a temptation to which he was subject himself, but it wouldn't help. 'We will contact you as soon as we return, Mr Ammera.'

'That will not do.'

'In the meantime, we will detach some mobile unit to find out what is happening at the major road junctions.' Flowers had to look at his CO then, who waited a long time before coming up with the required nod. 'But I must warn you these measures are temporary. Without specific orders to do otherwise, the units will return to Kabala.'

Ammera stood up, and without even any pretence at politeness walked out of the door.

'I have to tell you, Toby, that my toes are itching like hell.'

'Mine too, Frank. But we need to stall the sod, not boot him. A week or two from now, if we get our way, every road in the country will be clear.'

'Just in,' said Mike Layman, rushing into Razenbrook's office and throwing a couple of hastily scribbled notes on to his desk. 'Sieromin's gone.'

'Are you sure?' demanded Razenbrook, but it was more an automatic reaction than a proper question.

'Read the signals. The first is from one of our own guys, John Little. He was up past Mokanje, God knows why. He saw the RUF moving in on the place and got to a radio as soon as he could. The other one is from Mario Berti, Sieromin's security chief. One of the head office guys did a translation for us and sent it over.'

71

'Stopped in mid-transmission,' Razenbrook said, his hand pushing anxiously at his flopping blond hair. 'That means he's been taken.'

'If he's still breathing.'

'God!'

'We've got to get our people out, Tony, now!'

'What about the processed product?'

Layman lost his temper then, and actually shouted at his boss. 'Fuck the product!'

Geoff Hinchcliffe and Mary Kline knew there was trouble about without needing radio messages. The villages they'd visited seemed half empty, the men nowhere to be seen and a large number of the mothers and children Mary had come to treat missing. Those who'd stayed were frightened, but that, in itself, was commonplace in this part of Africa. The people here were blown about by the winds of fear and rumour, the decision to stay or run very much down to individual choice. There was no certainty anywhere, just an all-pervading sense of terror.

But the sound of distant gunfire was something more than a rumour, regardless of who was pulling the trigger. The first thud of a faraway shot stopped the babble of conversation around the hut in which Mary was inoculating the youngest children against smallpox and diphtheria. Only the hungry infants, or those who objected to the needle, maintained their noise. The second crump of something like an artillery shell made the whole group flee for their huts.

Geoff Hinchcliffe had a hand to his ear, trying to place the source of the sounds, while the CARE nurse packed her containers, exercising the same degree of caution with syringes and phials of vaccine as if the day were normal and no hint of panic surrounded her.

'Up Moribatown way, I reckon,' said Geoff, looking worried, 'or maybe further away on the other side of the Bemba deposits. The water on the dredge sites would carry the sound on a bit.'

'You'll want to get there quick then?'

'For what?'

Mary put her hands on her hips and gave him an arch look. 'It's where you live.'

'Soldiers rush to the sound of guns, Mary. I'm a civilian. I go the other way.'

'Is this for my sake?'

'Like hell. It's pure cowardice. Besides, what have I got in Moribatown? A few clothes and some stuff that belongs to the company. As you're always reminding me, I'm a slob and I haven't been here long enough to acquire much. Certainly not stuff worth getting shot at for.'

He grinned, bent down, and picked up one of the metal cool boxes containing vaccine. Mary Kline had been in Africa for two years, Geoff for four months; he didn't care for the place much, she loved it. She was always correcting him in the way long-serving folk do with people they consider newcomers.

'Come on, I'll take you to Mobimbi.'

'The CARE mission might have to pull out of there if trouble's that close.'

'In which case, sweetheart, a nice pickup with nowhere else to go but Freetown could come in real handy.'

'Don't call me sweetheart,' Mary snapped.

Geoff wasn't the least put out by this rebuke. His grin didn't slip even a fraction. 'You certainly know how to respond to a generous gesture.'

The village, by the time they left, seemed to be completely empty. What had been a bustling settlement only a few hours before was now a ghost town. The gunfire had stopped, making the resulting calm seem somewhat eerie.

'It couldn't have been someone from AAR using explosives, could it?'

'I doubt it. I think I would have known.' Geoff made a gesture designed to emphasise the lack of human beings. 'Anyway, you're finished here, regardless.'

'Roadblock,' said Mary, pointing her index finger through the pickup's windscreen. She could just see a hint of the barrier across the road, partially hidden by the throng of Africans milling around. Some must be from the village they'd just left, all shapes and sizes, men, children and women with bundles on their heads and babies on their backs.

'Got it,' Geoff replied, pressing the brakes.

The crowd, wild-eyed and noisy, parted to let them through, until the bull bars on the front were right up against the barrier. It wasn't much of a checkpoint, just a long, freshly chopped pole on a couple of empty oil drums. The main question was who had set it up. You never could tell who was who in the confused state of the countryside. It might be civil defence, the army or even the RUF, since possession of territory for those two forces was the ground under their feet. And to tell them apart was near impossible, given that they inclined towards the same uniform of camouflage fatigues. Often, whichever faction they supported, and it could be both at once, they faced boys acting like men. But, given they had guns with real bullets, that made them all very dangerous.

A bribe usually got you through without fuss. Everybody carried a few dollars to ease their passage, but the money didn't oblige on this occasion. The kid with the gun took it, but made no move to open the way. Geoff responded with an impatient gesture that totally backfired. Wild-eyed and voluble, waving his AK47 excitedly, he ordered the two Europeans out of the vehicle. Slightly confused, they both obliged. You don't argue with a loaded weapon, especially in the hands of someone that excited.

'Who are you?' demanded Mary.

'Civil defence,' the kid barked, puffing out his chest.

'Then you must let us pass. You are here to stop rebels, not us.'

'No car,' the kid shouted. 'No car down road.'

'Till when?' asked Mary.

'Never,' the gunman replied, with a huge gesture. Then he pointed his gun at them and told both to back away. Behind him they could see his companions searching the other travellers with a thoroughness that was rare.

'Okay Mary,' said Geoff as they stepped backwards. 'You're the expert. What do we do now?'

'We'll probably be fine if we just wait a while,' she replied, though Geoff noticed the words were delivered without much in the way of conviction.

'Is that Joe Folani over there?' asked Geoff, standing on the tips of his boots to see over the heads of the crowd.

Mary followed his look. Joe was standing by one of the oil drums, smoking and trying to look relaxed. He was also trying to act more than fourteen years old, but the size of his rifle made him look small and vulnerable. 'Yes.'

What the hell's he doing in the civil defence? He's got a job at AAR.'

'You don't always get a choice,' Mary replied.

She gave a slight wave to try to attract the kid's attention. The way he suddenly looked away was clear proof of recognition, hardly surprising since Mary had dosed him more than once with medicine. And Geoff, as the AAR training officer, had recently had him at his classes.

'The little bastard's ignoring us,' snarled Geoff, but he dropped his voice when the kids nearest to them swung their rifles round. 'I'll have his guts.'

'Maybe if he waves back his mates will do that for him.'

'What a bunch of no-hopers.'

Given the ragged nature of the uniforms, Geoff was right. Most of the boys who were refusing to let them pass looked about twelve, but there were one or two more mature guys and these youths seemingly took their duties seriously. The fellow who appeared to be the leader, having barked a string of unnecessary orders, came over to the side of the pickup. He told them in a solemn tone that he was the leader of the local civil defence, that the rebels were close by and might be heading this way.

'We need to get back to the CARE headquarters at Mobimbi,' Mary insisted.

'Not safe. Rebels coming.'

'Then you must let us pass.'

'No one to pass,' the African said. 'Road closed ahead by orders.'

'Does that mean the rebels are ahead of us?'

'They everywhere. Not safe,' he barked before turning to shout at the milling crowd of Africans, gesturing that they should get away from the roadblock and make for the nearby buildings.

'D'you think he's right?' asked Geoff quietly. 'Can they be ahead as well?'

'Who the hell knows in this place?' Mary replied

She shook loose her blond hair, adding a physical gesture of anger to add to her spoken one. Geoff reckoned she must be rattled. Mary was a lady who, when it came to temperament, made ice look liquid, and she never had a bad word to say about Africa. The tribes were noble, the country beautiful and the traditions wonderful. The whole thing had been a paradise spoiled by greedy white men.

She then went through the ritual of scrunching up her hair in both hands and putting the ponytail band back again. Geoff couldn't help looking at the way that defined her breasts through the pockets of her bush shirt. He thought her handsome rather than beautiful, the face a bit too square and the figure too full. But in a place like Sierra Leone, especially out in the bush, that was enough to ensure a lot of attention, as well as determined competition he had some trouble fending off.

'That would mean we are cut off.'

'Looks that way,' she replied, biting her lower lip, 'though I really can't believe it. Not after all the false alarms.'

Both Geoff and Mary fell silent then, alone with their own thoughts. Even with that sound of gunfire earlier it was hard to accept, because if ever a revolution could be termed low-key, this was it. The RUF claimed to occupy most of the country, but that was a particularly African form of bullshit. Their preferred tactic was to occupy an area, loudly trumpet their presence, indulge in some looting then melt back into the bush when the army finally arrived. Any violence they employed was against their own, and after a raid and a retreat, it was hard to tell who had done the more damage, the government troops or the rebels. Occasionally, if they stayed too long, they were caught out by the Nigerian jets and given a taste of some napalm. Sometimes the army even got mortars and machine guns up to make a proper fight of it. But it seemed to be more of a dance than a war. The rebels couldn't take Freetown, the one place that mattered, and the Sierra Leone Defence Force couldn't, or wouldn't, pacify a huge swathe of country that would support anyone against any government.

'Where's the bloody army?' asked Geoff.

'Boozing it up in the barracks, Geoff, where else? And don't tell me you'd be happier if they were here.'

'They all stink, the lot of them.'

'You'll get used to them, Geoff. They're really nice people when you get to know them. And you can't blame them, can you?'

'Don't go giving me that crap again, Mary.' He jabbed a finger at the boy who had stopped them. 'If that little turd at the barrier didn't have a Kalashnikov I'd boot him up the arse and out of the way.'

The boy might not have understood every word, but he saw the red face on his bull-necked detainee and he caught enough of the drift to get very agitated. He started shouted in Mende, his own tongue, that they should go. Mary translated, and Geoff was happy to oblige. He made to get back in the jeep, gesturing to Mary to follow, but that sent the kid even more haywire, and he shouted for the rest of his gang to join him. Suddenly the two Europeans found themselves surrounded by a gesticulating mob, which forced them away from their vehicle and towards a church hall, the only sizeable building at the crossroads.

CHAPTER SIX

John 'Blue' Harding cursed when the phone rang. He was on a plank in the middle of the dining room, trying to fix a length of lining paper to the ceiling, and he'd forgotten to switch on his answering machine before he started. It didn't help his temper, the notion that he shouldn't be bloody well doing the job in the first place. But things had been a bit slow in the security business lately, and with a new house to pay for he'd decided on a bit of DIY to save money.

'Yes?' he snapped as he picked up the receiver. His whole attention was taken up with the way the lining paper was slowly, but gracefully, detaching itself and falling to the floor.

'Blue, Dave Heffer here. How's it going?'

He wanted to say 'fucking awful', but when the head of an international security firm rings you up, it's best to be positive, even if the bastard knows you're lying. 'Great. Lots of work, you know. Bits and pieces, but steady. How are things at Charter?'

'Busier than ever.'

'Pleased to hear it.'

'How are you fixed for a fastball?'

'How fast?'

'Fly out at noon tomorrow. Party of four.'

'Where?'

'Sierra Leone. They've got some trouble brewing at a rutile mine out there and they need a security assessment.'

'What the hell is rutile?'

'Titanium dioxide in the raw state. Refined, it's the stuff they put in paint to make it nice and white. Worth very serious money, like in millions of dollars.'

'What's the pay?'

'Two fifty a day plus expenses, minimum two weeks, but it could be long-term.'

The last inch of lining paper, which had held for a few seconds, finally gave up, and the whole piece fell, via the plank, on to the floor. Blue was thinking that being a qualified boat troop instructor, a weapons and explosives expert, as well as a Grade A sniper was no fucking good if you couldn't hang wallpaper.

'Will you be at the airport?'

'Yep!'

'See you there.'

They came into the Tiama displaced persons' camp like welcome visitors, walking slowly, a group of men smarter in dress than those she had seen before. They all had guns, but kept them shouldered. Sister Francesca could easily guess why they showed neither fear nor caution. They'd obviously intercepted some of the ex-inmates fleeing the place, and they would have told them that the only people at the camp were unarmed nuns. And they would also know exactly where the army was – they always did!

Some of the prayers she could hear, even if her charges were trying their very best to keep them silent. They were lined up under the overhanging roof of the long low hut that comprised their sleeping accommodation, each one visible to the approaching rebels, so that there could be no hint of threatening behaviour. Only when the leader was close did Sister Francesca move forward. He was a small, compact fellow in full uniform, tight-fitting khaki instead of the ever-present fatigues. He halted, and as she greeted him in the name of God he responded with a slight bow, then gave a peremptory gesture designed to stop his men from coming on.

'I am Tarawali,' he said, pausing, as if that should have some significance. The voice was quite educated and cultured. When the nun didn't respond he continued. 'Your people have run away.'

'From fear.'

'Fear of those who are trying to help them, people who wish to liberate them from the poverty and exploitation that keeps them in places like this?'

'They do not believe that to be true.'

He sighed. 'And who can blame them for that?'

Sister Francesca was amazed, even if she fought hard not to show it. This small man in uniform had almost admitted that he might be at fault. That was something very uncommon in Sierra Leone or indeed anywhere else in Africa, a land where shifting the responsibility for everything from theft to murder was a continental custom.

Tarawali raised his voice so that his own men could hear his words as well as the nuns 'But when we are successful everything will change for the better.'

It was a litany Sister Francesca had heard before, that these men were liberators who would kick out the crooks who presently ran the country, and install honest government and true democracy! All the mines would be run by Sierra Leonians, all the wealth of the country given to the people. Men would die, but that was necessary to cleanse the rotten system. Sister Francesca couldn't help but wonder why he bothered. His men must know what they were supposed to be fighting for, and even if the nuns cared, they were in no position to help or hinder him.

His peroration ended on a high note, a shout that was answered by his soldiers, guns raised. It took several deep breaths before he calmed himself enough to talk normally. 'We must destroy this place.'

'Why?'

'For what it represents,' Tarawali replied. 'Servitude.'

'All that it represents is God's desire to stop disease and starvation.'

For the first time, in his sharp response, as well as the bright look in his small eyes, he showed a hint of fanaticism. 'There will be no disease or starvation in the new Sierra Leone. We shall abolish it.'

Sister Francesca was so tempted to tell him he was wrong, that these things would exist for a long time in Africa because of men like him. She would pray that he was different but with little faith in the truth of the proposition. He would succeed or fail, more than likely dying if it were the latter, going on to embezzle if it were the former. He must have seen it in her look, that opinion. The calmness evaporated, and he began to shout at his men to set fire to the buildings.

'You will come with us.'

'Where to?' she asked, alarmed.

'That is for me to decide. Your government supports Strasser and his criminals. They keep him in power. Perhaps, when we have you to bargain with, they will get out of our lives and give our country back to its own people.'

His men were looting before even thinking about burning. Everything

80

was being taken out of the huts: the refrigerators that kept the medicine cool, their books and the rest of their meagre possessions.

'We will not go!' she snapped.

'Then, sister, you could die here. All of you!'

Their eyes locked, but Sister Francesca knew he had the upper hand. Was he bluffing about killing them? He might be, but that was too much of a chance to take. Her mind was racing, trying to think of what was the best thing to do. One thing struck her, the need to let the outside world know that hostage-taking was happening. It might not help her, but it would alert others and give them a chance to get to safety.

'You intend to use us to bargain with?'

'I have just told you.'

'Then before you rip out the radio, I will send a message to Freetown.'

'Saying what?' Tarawali demanded suspiciously.

'I'll tell them that the RUF has taken seven Italian nuns hostage. Nothing more, nothing less! What is the point, if you wish to bargain, in those you wish to bargain with having no knowledge of what is at stake?'

The pause was long, the idea carefully considered, but Tarawali finally shouted to his men to leave the radio in place, before nodding to Sister Francesca to tell her to proceed. 'But you will say that we are rescuing you, offering you the protection of the RUF.'

'Who from?'

'You cannot travel safely. You must say that.'

She nodded, aware that whatever message she gave to Freetown they would not be fooled. By the time she got through, the first of the buildings, which had been their little hospital, was ablaze. She spoke with the smell of smoke in her nostrils and tears in her eyes.

Tarawali shouted at her. 'And tell them that we are treating you well.'

Sister Francesca held the mouthpiece towards him. 'You just have, signor.'

Joe Folani had been scared all morning, convinced everyone could see just how much his knees were shaking. Even the grass he'd smoked had done little to calm his fears. The leader of the civil defence group had initially been the same, but consumed with his own personal terror, Joe hadn't noticed that. Now he would never know. Victor Johnston's confidence had grown as the day wore on. The more chances he had to throw his weight about, the louder he became. The gun made him a real man. The high point had obviously been turning back the two whites, and impounding their Toyota pickup. He had barely stopped laughing since, almost dancing with joy as he recounted, over and over again, the way he had stood up to the boss people.

Joe had sought to avoid eye contact with Mister Geoff. Not Victor! Also an AAR employee, Victor worked as a general labourer at the dredge site. In the company hierarchy he was the lowest of the low, an illiterate fetch-and-carry man, sometimes entrusted with a shovel or a hosepipe. Not any more! His family connections had got him the commander's job. Now Victor was somebody. Geoff Hinchcliffe hadn't recognised him. He would the next time, when things returned to normal. The boss training officer would notice him all right. He wouldn't just walk by as though Victor Johnston didn't exist.

Geoff and Mary Kline were watching from the window. The room behind them was now full of Africans, many talking volubly, others silent and staring into space, as though wondering what the future held. Mary had spoken with them and had picked all there was to know about the movements of the RUF. These people were used to the bush trails, and they knew their own locality like the backs of their callused hands. They had sixth and seventh senses to add to rumour, and they knew just how to gauge the level of danger, whether to move out or stay still. The number of them in the room made the main question she asked – how close are the RUF? – a bit superfluous. Most of these people wouldn't be here if there were no imminent threat.

'They don't think they're ahead of us yet,' she said to Geoff.

'Makes sense. Why run for Mobimbi if they're already there?'

'There's a rumour that the RUF have taken some hostages.'

'What? Instead of just killing them?'

'White hostages, Geoff.'

That raised his eyebrows. 'Who said?'

'One or two of the people on the run from Tinanhun.'

'That's a new one.'

'Which doesn't mean much, does it?'

Geoff jerked a thumb at the crowded room. 'But is it true? They'd love to wind us up, I reckon.'

Standing next to her at the small, dust-encrusted window, listening to what she said, Geoff Hinchcliffe was very aware of Mary Kline, even in what was becoming an increasingly fetid atmosphere. The heat of the crowded room had made her sweat a bit more than usual, adding a very alluring smell of musk to a presence that already held a strong attraction for him. He shifted very slightly so that his bare forearm brushed hers, feeling the delicate shock as contact sent a surge of highly charged feelings through his body.

Mary didn't react at all. 'I know that one's face,' she said, pointing with her arm at Victor Johnston and breaking the contact. 'But I can't place it.'

'He's related to the last baboon you saw,' Geoff replied, without thinking. 'Closely related.'

It was the wrong thing to say to a CARE worker, and it showed in the heavy frown on Mary's face. He reckoned she saw him, as well as all the other expat miners, as parasites, living off the poverty of the Africans and exploiting their lack of skill to steal their natural resources. To him it was just a job: well paid, relatively easy and tax-free. Her job was different. The pay was a joke and the work could be back-breaking. It was a life spent trying to make up for the faults of the crooks who ran the country. It didn't matter to Geoff who they were, civilians or soldiers. They were all lining their pockets, stealing the wealth of one of the richest pieces of real estate in the world.

And the suspicion existed that Mary Kline was just using his interest to get around the country quickly and for free. Geoff was half hoping she'd have a go at him. That at least would represent conversation, a chance to explore the truth. Did she like him or not? Her self-contained way of behaving was driving him nuts, especially when the guy they were watching was doing his very best to imitate the animal Geoff had mentioned.

'If you had his life, you might be just the same,' she said quietly.

'If I had his life I'd do something to improve it.'

'We had a hundred years to do just that.' Geoff opened his mouth to reply, but an upheld hand was turned to stop him. 'I don't think it's something we'd agree about, Geoff, so it's probably better left. The main thing we've got to do is get out of here.'

'And back to civilisation,' he added, not trying to hide the sarcasm.

'Maybe if I go and talk to him again, he'll let us go on.'

'I don't think that's such a good idea.'

'Why not?'

'Because it's dangerous, woman.'

'I don't need your chivalry, Geoff.'

'Just my pickup truck!'

She smiled instead of wincing at what he'd intended as a rebuke, which didn't please him.

'You stay here.'

'You're kidding.'

Mary turned to face him. 'Geoff, you've got a bit of a temper, and you think you're superior to these people.'

'I don't just think it.'

Mary finished the sentence for him. 'You know it, fine! But you say it too, and that's the problem. It won't help. Right now your baboon is in the driving seat, not you. Go talk to these people yourself. They don't think the rebels are in front of us, but they're damn sure they're behind us and heading this way. If we're going to get anywhere, we won't do it by threats. It will have to be done by persuasion.'

'I wish I'd brought a gun along. I'd show the bastard some persuasion all right!'

'Stay here,' Mary commanded as she squeezed past him.

Watching from the church hall, Geoff and Mary had seen the leader dance around, climb in and out of the pickup waving his automatic rifle, and generally show off to his compatriots. But judging by the sudden flurry of activity, someone had spotted something up the road, and the celebrations stopped abruptly. Victor began pushing several others to the barrier, including Joe. Scared before, the youngster was petrified now. The road leading up to the checkpoint gave them plenty of time to examine those approaching: three men, one carrying a rifle slung over his shoulder, walking as if they didn't have a care in the world. Mary Kline was halfway between the building and the barrier when Victor Johnston spotted her and waved in an agitated manner to send her back. She stopped, and stood watching as the scene unfolded.

To her, everything about it was African. In a situation in which any armed man approaching the checkpoint should be cautious, these guys were relaxed. They'd be full of dope, of course, grass or cannabis. That tended to exaggerate their loose-limbed way of walking, a trait that underlined their natural arrogance. Who where they? She had as little idea as the men of the civil defence. They might be army or they could be RUF, and in Sierra Leone, such was the rate of cross-desertion, they could be both in the space of a week. The weaponry was no clue. All over the world the gun of choice was the AK47, the Russian masterpiece that stayed efficient even when it was barely maintained. The rebels had either deserted with their weapons or had stolen what they had from the army, so both were similarly armed. Likewise their appearance gave no clue: ill-fitting camouflage fatigues and T-shirts, just like those of the men they were approaching.

Victor Johnston had his gun up and aimed, his voice rising to fever pitch as the men got closer. The one with the automatic rifle, the only real threat to the guys at the checkpoint, didn't react, didn't either raise his hands or lower his weapon. He walked straight up to the point of Johnston's AK47, pressed his chest into the barrel, and laughed a greeting. Johnston freaked, screaming at his men to surround and disarm them. They obeyed in the frantic, voluble way that was also very African, too much pushing and jostling for position with very little actual attempt to carry out the task they'd been given. Joe Folani finally got hold of the rifle and prised it out of the owner's hands without much in the way of resistance. Johnston's steady stream of screamed questions was met with shrugs and grins, accompanied by much languid waving of large black hands.

The trio were uniformly tall men, slim and wiry, with tribal scars on fine-boned features Mary Kline thought belonged more to the highlands than the plains. Johnston probably thought so too, since he ran through half a dozen tribal tongues trying to find out who they were and where they were going. Whatever answers they gave, which Mary couldn't hear, didn't give the civil defence leader much confidence. He kept poking them with the barrel of his own weapon, eyes wild with a combination of fear and mastery. Finally he ran out of either ideas or patience and ordered that the men be tied up.

'What's the baboon up to now?' asked Geoff, who had joined her without her noticing.

'How much have you seen?'

'Enough. Are they rebels?'

The trio were pushed through the barrier and on down the road. Joe

Folani followed behind the two other men designated to escort them, now armed with two rifles rather than one.

'I don't know, and neither, I think, does the guy questioning them.'

'Are they going to waste them?'

'I doubt it,' Mary replied with an impatient sigh. 'You don't go shooting people in this part of the world unless you're dead sure who they are. And sometimes not even then. There must be some authority around here. Our man has done the sensible thing and passed them up the line. Let someone else make the decision.'

'We need this someone else, too.'

Mary Kline was just about to say she would ask him, but then Victor Johnston turned round and saw them watching him. The rifle jabbed forward again, and he ordered them back into the church building.

'Give us another shufti,' said Frank Wintour, holding out his hands for the binos.

Gareth Evans passed them over, sat down in the driver's seat and reached for the water flask. So far they hadn't sighted anyone, black or white. That was unusual given the amount of foot traffic you generally encountered on an African road, but the sound of distant gunfire was explanation enough. They'd stopped for a break on a high point in the road, and had pulled off into the trees to stay as much out of sight as possible. For the tenth time since starting out, Frank Wintour, looking up the empty road towards Mokanje, repeated how strangely quiet it was and expressed some fears for the occupants of the missing company pickup. 'They should have been back by now.'

'They've probably just stopped for a brew.' The Welshman snorted. 'Or maybe dived off into the bush for a bit of nookie.'

'Right now, old son,' Frank replied, 'that ain't funny.'

'I just meant that they'll be okay, Frank.'

'Maybe.'

The sound of another vehicle had Frank wheeling round in hope, but when he saw what was approaching he ordered Gareth to start the engine. The Land Rover was painted in camouflage colours, the driver an army officer. He stopped when he saw them and got out, walking over to the very obvious white pickup with a degree of swagger.

'Captain,' said Frank, half raising his hand.

'Mr Wintour,'

There was no warmth to go with this greeting, but then Captain Sam Gilbert was not a smiler. Frank had met him dozens of times down at Nitti, the port AAR had opened up to take out the processed rutile. Gilbert, a member of the military naval wing, had command of an armed fast patrol boat that he used to monitor the river and the approaches to the waters around Sherbro Island. A slim man, with prominent cheekbones and a high forehead, he was not gifted with anything approaching a sense of humour. By local standards, he was pretty efficient, keeping his boat and the crew up to the mark. When Sam Gilbert said he was going to arrive somewhere at a given time, he was always there. That, in itself, was rare in West Africa.

One of the things he turned up for regularly was the envelope Frank Wintour gave him every month. This was a payment to ensure that the river between Port Nitti and the sea was kept free of risk. As the main supply base for the various AAR sites, everything – food, medicine, clothing and booze – was shipped through to Nitti on the barges which then took the finished product out to the freighters waiting in the deep-water channel. That made them a tempting target for thievery. Since the biggest thieves in Sierra Leone tended to wear military uniforms, bribing the man responsible for that stretch of the supply line made sense. It was cheaper than having him help himself.

'We got a load of information about rebels heading this way,' Wintour said.

'I have heard the rumours.'

The Londoner's response was one of suppressed anger. 'Is that all they are?'

Gilbert shrugged. Frank Wintour was thinking that said it all. How could he talk of rumours when they'd heard gunfire in the distance? The bastard was indifferent when he should be concerned. He'd have loved to be sarcastic, to exercise some Cockney wit on this arrogant sod, but that would only cost money in the future so he kept his gob shut.

'Something on the road ahead,' said Gareth, who'd taken over the binoculars. 'Half a dozen fellows on foot.'

Gilbert spun on his heel and made for his Land Rover, climbing back in and gunning it down the road. His wheels set up a huge cloud of the ubiquitous red dust, through which the two AAR security men had to drive as they followed him. The two vehicles pulled up in front of the men walking, three of whom were armed. Gilbert was already busy questioning the person who appeared to be in charge. Joe Folani saw Frank and tried to dodge behind another, bigger African, but he was too slow. Wintour walked over and smiled at him.

'They prisoners?' The youngster nodded. 'Where are you taking 'em, Joe?'

Joe just nodded towards Sam Gilbert, who was still asking questions in an incomprehensible tongue, and grunted. Clearly the decision about what was to happen was the captain's. The three prisoners didn't seem alarmed by Gilbert's presence, but young Joe did, which earned him another Wintour smile. Deep down, Frank would dearly have liked to blast the little sod for what he was doing. Joe Folani was an AAR employee. He should be doing his job or sleeping, not running around toting a bloody rifle.

Gilbert had started on the prisoners, firing rapid questions at them, in that way people do when they are trying to trip you up. Not that either of the Europeans understood a bloody word. There was much eye-rolling from these three tall men, accompanied by groans and what were internationally recognisable wails of innocence. It was hard, with a humourless git like Gilbert, to know what he thought of all this. Eventually he turned and gave instructions to the escort leader, before heading back for his Land Rover.

'Well, Joe!' demanded Frank. 'What's he said?'

Joe replied, his voice light and fearful, as Gilbert's Land Rover roared away, heading up the road towards Mokanje. 'He thinks thay is deserters boss, army men who have raan awaay.'

'Ran to where?'

Joe gave another one of his elegant shrugs. 'He say we is to take them back down the road to Colonel Lumulo. They'm belong to him.'

'Are you sure?' asked Gareth, before turning to Frank. 'That bugger is on the NPRC.'

'I know that berk!'

'Then what's he doing here?'

'He's the Minister of Defence ain't he? So if it's true, he'll be doin' his fuckin' job, mate. But I wouldn't bet on his being anywhere near the place. He's more likely tucked up in Freetown.'

'Then you'll have a long bloody walk, old son,' Gareth hooted, as he looked at Joe.

'Where did Captain Gilbert say to go?' asked Frank.

'Lago Junction.'

'Get back in the pickup, Gareth.'

'Where we goin'?'

'Same place. Let's see if Lumulo is there, as Gilbert says. If he is, we might find out what the army intends to do.'

'We could give them a lift.'

'Don't be a divot, Gareth. Those guys 'ave got guns.'

'But they're on our side.'

'Is that right? I'm glad you're so sure who's who. 'Cause I ain't, an' am not about to risk finding out.'

Back behind the wheel, Frank signalled for Joe Folani to approach. The kid did so reluctantly. 'When you get to Lago Junction, dump that rifle and get back to the dredge site where you belong. That's where you work, for Anglo-African, not the bleeding government.'

The youngster walked away, his hunched shoulders showing how disconsolate he was.

'Second thought,' said Frank. 'Let's go by the Plant site and see if there's any news from Freetown.'

There was, and it all boiled down to one word: evacuate.

CHAPTER SEVEN

A very bleary-eyed employer was waiting for Blue Harding when he arrived at the Skyways Hotel. Dave Heffer, a man inclined to take some care in his appearance, looked like shit, and Blue's polite enquiry, 'How the devil are you?' was met with an unfriendly and out of character growl.

'How the fuck do you think I am?'

'What's up with you?' Blue replied, bristling at the unfriendly tone.

'Don't tell me you can't guess. I've been up all night on the poxy phone.'

'For why?'

'Have you heard the news?'

'No.'

Heffer grabbed Blue's arm, pulled a newspaper from the rack and thrust it into his hand, then led him towards the elevator, punching impatiently at the button. 'Then you must have been on the fuckin' moon. It was on all the late main bulletins last night. The whole thing's gone pear-shaped in Sierra Leone. The bloody rebels overran the sites we were sending you out to look over. You have to be blind, deaf and dumb to miss it.'

Blue was none of those. The night before he'd taken his girlfriend out for an Indian meal, retired early and, after some real gymnastics, got to sleep very late. He had then spent the whole morning from just after five dozing in the back of a cab from Hereford to Heathrow without the benefit of a newspaper or a radio.

It wasn't the top story; that was as usual about Tory rebels, not West African ones. But it was front page, with a photo of a forlorn-looking family, mother clutching a child's hand, suitcase in the other, fleeing their bungalow. There was also an insert in the main article about the rumour of European hostages being taken.

'So the job's off?'

'No way. The situation still has to be assessed. But a look-see team can only do so much. The client might want a unit strong enough to defend

90

the place. You'll go today as planned, but we need to get a minimum of twenty lined up so that we can secure the sites if they ask us to.'

'How many have you got?'

'Not enough. I want you on the phone trying to get the people I couldn't raise last night. I've got to sort out the briefing papers.'

'Any restrictions?' Blue asked as the elevator door opened.

Heffer looked at him hard, well aware of what he was being asked. The security business was like any other trade: there were good people, mediocre people and there were cowboys, the latter a danger to everybody, including themselves. 'In the first phase it's likely to require numbers more than quality. Charter, if asked, needs to impress Anglo-African Rutile with speed of reaction. If they come on the line and ask for what they're hinting at, I want to be able to say yes. That means bodies on the ground, mate. Right now it's a stand-by job. If it goes off too quick any bummers will have to be sorted out on site and replaced.'

'How long do you want them standing by?'

'A month, minimum.'

'Costly.'

'The client will pay, Blue.'

'Even if we don't use them?'

Heffer grinned, which made him look even more weary. 'There are ways.'

'What time am I out?'

'Twelve noon check-in. And don't be late or we'll never get you out today. Every spare seat has been nabbed by journos. They've done everything they can short of hijacking to bump us off. Cheeky bastards!'

When they got to Heffer's room he made straight for the loo. An ex-super boozer, he was now teetotal, with a pancreas problem that made him piss endlessly, his insides constantly processing the gallons of mineral water he consumed. Blue took the chance in his absence to put through a call to his home. The voice that answered was full of sleep. 'You still in bed?'

'Mmmm.'

'Quick one.'

'Yes please.'

'You'll hear about where I'm going on the news when you surface. Don't worry about it. This ain't front-line stuff we're doing. I'll call you when I get there.'

He hung up before she could reply, and started dialling the first of the unscored numbers on the list by the bed. Heffer came out of the bathroom and went to the desk to sort through a heap of photocopied papers.

'Answering machine,' he said, before leaving a message to call the Skyways Hotel.

'Leave my mobile number,' said Heffer, pulling his phone from his pocket. 'Or they can contact the Charter Security office after two. I'll be going back there as soon as your flight lifts off.'

'I could use some breakfast,' said Blue.

'Help yourself. I'll just have coffee and a bottle of Highland Spring. A big one.'

Blue was on the phone for an hour, in between bites from bacon sandwiches, with Heffer dodging in and out of the room. It was hard graft finding people, though Blue hadn't anticipated it given the sheaf of lists he had. There were a lot of guys in line for work, ex-Paras, marines, as well as retired Special Forces. He went to the latter first. If you're going to be stuck out in the bush with a spear aimed at your arse, you want the best guys around you. But if he wanted the cream, so did most other people. And it was frustrating, especially when you contacted someone you'd really be happy to work with only to find they had a two-day job in a fortnight that made them unavailable.

By the end of the list he had six possibles and four definites, a lot of pending messages left on machines plus the information that he wasn't the only one on the phone. Insurance assessors were on the ball, ready to fly out to Sierra Leone to adjudicate on any claims that might arise from RUF activity. They never went to any troublespot without protection, and each had been on to their favourite bodyguards to line them up for a trip. A couple of the guys he'd contacted had already been on the receiving end of a call from Sierra Leone, trying to recruit them for another team being put together by Willy Rakiba. He was man Blue knew well, a great bear of a Fijian, ex-SAS, who drank like a fish and fucked like a rabbit. He also had the loudest laugh Blue had ever heard and a bear hug for his friends so tight that it bordered on GBH.

Heffer came back from making his own calls, his reaction to Blue's news mild surprise. 'Willy was out there on a job for Group Four, looking after some geologists, I think.'

, 'I wonder if they had a look at the bastard's head then?'

Heffer grinned. That was another of Willy's traits, a little drink-induced head butt that, with his rock-hard skull, could lay you out. He handed Blue a printout of info from Grolier Electronic Publishing. This told him all about the place he was going to: size, population, annual GDP, literacy levels and the latest political appreciation. What it didn't tell him was the most important thing: how dangerous was it going to be?

'Do you mind if we wait,' Heffer said, when Blue posed that question. 'I'd rather brief all four of you than do it piecemeal.'

'Who else have you got?'

'I've had to change the guys going out today, since it's a much bigger op now. First thing is to get some kind of command set-up in place.'

'So?'

'Sandy McPherson and Wally Aitken.'

There are times when it's hard to keep a straight face, and this was one of them. Heffer was looking at Blue quite intently, for the very reaction the subject of his scrutiny was determined to conceal. Being in charge of the arm of a security company that looked after close protection and international intervention meant that Dave Heffer knew everybody in the business. And he knew, from gossip and sometimes from furious rows, just who got on with whom.

Sandy McPherson was an ex-Royal Marine RSM. He was known to be a prickly bastard, a six-foot-four giant who could never get over the fact that he'd once been a WO1, the kind of guy to whom young RM lieutenants showed respect. He liked to be obeyed. That didn't sit well with most of the others he now worked with, especially ex-SAS troopers, who valued their independence of mind even more in Civvy Street. He would hate Blue, a staff sergeant, telling him what to do, just as much as Wally Aitken. Wally was an ex-quartermaster sergeant-major in the regiment who, since retiring, had become very attached to McPherson. They'd done so many jobs together that they'd earned the moniker Mork and Mindy.

'The other guy's a Rhodesian, Jamie Padden.'

'Don't know him.'

'Ex-Selous Scouts and South African SAS. Signals buff, as well.'

Again Blue kept a straight face. He didn't like McPherson or Aitken.

People who cared about their old service rank in the field could be a menace. Aitken was doubly a pest because he was 'army barmy' and loved it, never questioning ex-RSM McPherson regardless of how stupid the instruction. But then, to Blue's mind, Aitken had never been anything other than a glorified storeman, better at issuing weapons than using them. It was all 'bullshit baffles brains' anyway. The client needed to be reassured, and the best way Charter could do that was to send out a team that looked imposing as quickly as possible. A white African could be a shrewd move too, since he'd be happy with both the ground and the job, very quick to adapt. That is, if he wasn't one of those Kaffir-loathing lunatics who liked booting black folks around.

'I've got some calls to make,' Heffer said.

'Don't mind me, I'll just bone up.'

Blue learned a whole load of stuff he really didn't need to know, like the information that the place had been named by a Portuguese guy, Pedro de Cinta. He was told what the annual GDP amounted to as well as the average wage, all about independence and who'd shafted whom in the political past. Eighty per cent of the country's income came from exports: diamonds, bauxite and this rutile stuff he'd never heard of. It was always the same on these jobs. They gave you a background briefing that was just that, but Blue read and absorbed on the grounds that no information was totally useless.

Sierra Leone was coastal swamp and inland mountains with a bush-covered plain in the middle. The capital, Freetown, was on a handy, easily defensible peninsula, home to most of the Creoles who really ran the place. It was the usual story of Africa. Independence brings out a leader who looks the part until he starts ripping off the national income. He's deposed and replaced by another set of greedy bastards from the army. Then the junior officers take a leaf out of their superiors' book and toss them out. In Sierra Leone, these guys were now busy lining their fatigues, while a set of rebels fucked about in the bush trying to overthrow them.

'It's so bloody depressing this,' said Blue, waving the papers. 'It's the same story every time.'

'Keeps me in a job, mate,' Heffer replied, taking a swig from his water bottle. 'The more coups the merrier.'

Sandy McPherson certainly looked the part. Huge of frame, with well-defined features, he was dressed in ancient, shapeless tweeds, right down to the leather patches on the elbows. When he came in, checked cap on, stick in hand, framed in the doorway, he reminded Blue of an old golfing print. He had a carefully orchestrated way about him: stiff jaw, a thin and rarely used smile in a face that lacked flesh, and a penetrating look from his bright blue eyes, the whole designed to display his command of the situation. When he sat down, he crossed his cavalry-twilled legs so emphatically that the swinging leg seemed to go round twice, the right foot hooked behind the left ankle. That one act reminded Blue of why he didn't like him. It was an irrational thing, but he'd never trusted anyone who could do that.

The other half of the Mork and Mindy partnership followed him in. Wally Aitken was old-style SAS, almost like a hangover from World War Two, a burly man, sandy hair going white, imposing in every sense until he opened his mouth. He was inclined to stumble over words, often using the wrong one, the subsequent attempts at correction tying him in knots. As a result, in his years as a soldier he'd learned to speak little and nod a lot, trying to arrange a well-battered face into a semblance of intelligent appreciation. In the mess at Stirling Lines, the windup had been to get Wally to tell a joke. He always screwed it up, either giving away the punch-line too soon, or giving the wrong one entirely. But they looked the part, the pair of them. Bloody hardcases!

The Rhodesian, Jamie Padden, arrived last. He was a good-looking blond-haired guy with a deep, ingrained tan. The demeanour was quiet but watchful, a bit like a cat, and Blue's first impression on being introduced was favourable. The kind of security operator he hated most was the loud mouth. Padden wasn't like that at all, and he also took care where he sat, taking trouble to face the door and avoid having his back to the window, even here in a hotel room full of people with whom he should feel safe. This ex-Selous Scout was, like him, a quiet, grey man, never likely to make the mistake of being a goldfish in a bowl. That was the best way to be. Trouble was something best avoided, but if it came, when you did explode into action it was best to take everyone by surprise.

'You can read all this guff on the plane,' Heffer said, handing them the same bumf he'd given Blue. 'The bottom line is this. Our client, Anglo-African Rutile, is caught between a rock and a hard place. They provide revenues for the guys currently in power and a tasty target for the men who want to kick the bastards out.'

He paused to let everyone nod before continuing. 'Taking sides is not an option, 'cause in these kind of scenarios you never know which sod's going to come out on top. But with the kind of dosh they've slung into the rutile deposits, in the region of two hundred million dollars, they can't afford to suspend operations till the dust settles.'

'So they need to secure their property?' said McPherson, in his crisp, military tone.

'That's right, Sandy. But they need to do it without upsetting either side. Which makes what we're about defensive, not offensive. The prime objective is to get the extraction back on line. If that's impossible, they will want to cut their losses, take out what they've got already processed, and run.'

'Some losses,' said Blue.

'I want to know two things,' Heffer continued. 'Can the security of their sites be re-established and at what cost? Second, the future. Is a viable defence possible? That needs to be followed by what it would take in terms of men and equipment. Then we can give them a figure.'

McPherson spoke, the harsh Scottish cadence of his voice very clear and crisp. 'Are there not bloody Gurkhas out there, sitting on their arses doing nothing?'

'They're not our Gurkhas any more, Sandy. They've gone private,' explained Heffer.

'I don't rate the little sods, as you know, but they've got to be better than the rebels. From what I've read in the *Telegraph* this morning they're a bloody rabble. A quick attack might drive them back into the jungle.'

'For how long?' asked Blue.

'Come on, John-boy,' the old RSM replied, his tone patronising enough to make Blue clench his teeth. 'These things in the heart of darkness are always temporary. Six months from now we could be contemplating working for the very folk we're proposing to give a bloody nose to, and no hard feelings thank you very much.'

'There's a bit of a hostage problem, Sandy,' said Heffer.

McPherson's reply was quick. 'Never pays to let that sort of thing cloud your thinking, Davy.'

'I make you right, Sandy,' Aitken added, eagerly.

'We just do what the client wants, Sandy.'

McPherson gave Heffer one of those smiles that made him look like a grinning skull. 'Of course, Davy. We are now in it for the money.'

'Anyway, first thing is to get you out there and working on the problem. AAR needs to know we're on the case. I need hardly tell you that with the plane full of journos we have to zip the lip.'

'That might not be enough,' said Jamie Padden, speaking for the first time. 'It will depend on where they've been. Some of these guys have seen more action than us.'

'They'll be too busy figuring out how to shaft each other for the big story to worry about you guys. Just don't walk down the aisle and introduce yourselves.'

The military police personnel Tumbu sent them were in a different class to the layabouts Paul had originally been assigned to train. They weren't perfect – many had a limited attention span and talked too much, behaving more like children than adults. That was only lack of education allied to a natural and amusing ebullience. But they were, if not totally fit, youthful enough to be close to it.

They responded to the beasting they were given on the assault course with enthusiasm, happy to go round again and again. And unlike the originals they took a real delight in the smoke and flashes that were added to simulate a real battle scenario. Taking a break, they laughed and joked as each one recalled a particular incident, especially one in which a friend had screwed up. Paraded, they had a smartness, a care in their appearance that was also a good sign. Each one wore his red MP beret with pride. They polished their boots and kept the camouflaged fatigues clean. They looked like soldiers.

Given the numbers they required for a full head of state bodyguard team that still entailed compromises. Finding dozens of top-notch troopers was never going to be on. They graded them carefully, turning away as many as they chose, this accompanied by much wailing and vocal disappointment. That was hardly surprising, since the job carried a higher wage scale plus a good chance of actually getting paid. The best thirty-six were designated as the close escort teams; another twenty-four were sorted out as office or residence guards. The biggest problem, out of the choice they had, was finding twelve competent drivers. That was a major headache, since whoever drove the client was one of the most important guys on the team. The best they could do was take the basic ability to drive and work on it.

From this point on all seventy-two personnel would be training, but when fully up and running they would break down into groups. These comprised a dozen close escort men on daily duty in teams of four, backed up by eight office and residence guards. Out of the twelve drivers, four would always be available, one to drive the VIP, the other three to look after the escort.

The hardest thing for these ex-MPs to understand was that the training they were about to undertake would never end. With one complete group on duty and one off, the third twenty-four-man section didn't get a holiday. When they weren't acting as close protection and counter-attack teams (CAT) to cover Strasser when he left Freetown, they would go back to school. There they would re-learn the original skills they'd been taught under the eyes of those finally tasked as instructors, who would be the very best men Paul could find.

At the very first lecture, when Paul outlined the very bare bones of the duties they would undertake, he used the expression they would hear most in the coming weeks, the mantra of all top-level Special Forces: 'Train hard, fight easy.' It was always a complicated notion to get across. Paul doubted if outsiders thought of the SAS as supermen. He hoped not, simply because it was untrue. Yet even well-educated people who accepted that what they did was special couldn't quite grasp how the successes they achieved came about. They accepted that the guys were bright and motivated, but they could never quite comprehend that their accomplishments were based on simple, straightforward and constant practice.

You do the same things over and over again, using the distilled wisdom of years of hard fighting, rough living and comfortable contemplation, that added to the fitness and adaptability of the subjects. Taking hostages off a plane or out of a building while neutralising the terrorists was no blackboard exercise, and protection was not some game. All were carried out for real, time and again, just like everything they might have to do. The difference in the regiment was simple. In the green army soldiers moaned about having to work and dodged when they could. In the SAS they never even considered prolonged inactivity. If the regiment didn't have their men on a course, most of them would busy themselves honing their own skills. What he needed from these MPs, if the training they were about to give was to be successful in the long term, was the same attitude.

Having selected their trainees, the next step was to parade them as a unit, to impress on them that they were now separate from the men they'd served with before. They would have to take a special pride in themselves and their abilities. At the parade, Paul and his team met the designated unit commander and his two deputies. They were not MPs, nor were they sponsored by Tumbu, a fact he made plain at the point of introduction. Sandhurst-trained, they had been provided by Strasser, and since they were young, and looked slim as well as fit, Paul didn't enquire as to what relationship they had with the leader of the military council. And having been at the British military academy, they had no problem in being instructed by NCOs. Besides, Forwood was in the background to soothe any ruffled commissioned feathers.

The training sked started with a lot of talking and blackboard work covering three basic scenarios, everything else a variation on those themes: who stood where in what situation to protect against what potential threat. There was no way to do that without prior knowledge, so the lectures included a lot on the subject of reconnaissance and route planning techniques. Although it wasn't stated explicitly, they had to be prepared to protect someone other than Valentine Strasser. The need to adapt to changes in government personnel applied in every country. The only difference in Africa was that turnover tended to be violent rather than democratic. These men had to be taught to assess everything, and that included the personality of the VIP they were tasked to protect. If he changed, so did the job. What were his habits, at home or carrying out his duties? Did his public image invite danger or not? Was he the kind to obey security suggestions or too arrogant to listen? What kind of vehicles did he use and were they the right ones? It even mattered if he was right or left-handed.

To avoid boredom Paul didn't keep them in the classroom all day. Each morning and afternoon session started with a lecture, before the groups broke up to practise particular skills outdoors, or in other rooms. Trevor and Jerry would do foot drills with one group, instructing them on the difference between three-, four-, and five-man procedures. They had to be capable of adjusting their techniques for private social occasions, public but enclosed gatherings, as well as open political meetings, the latter requiring security in depth. Ensuring bodycover was paramount, at the same time maintaining their arcs of vision, their personal area of observation in which it was their responsibility to spot any threat.

What were the threats? They ranged from verbal abuse, through missiles thrown from a crowd, to personal attacks with knife or pistol. Each had to be dealt with differently, and everyone had to be aware of the real bummer: a rifle attack, especially one by a trained sniper. In reality, Paul explained, there is no defence against that.

'But there is a reaction, and that depends on the success of the gunman. An amateur may miss, and give you a chance to get your man away. What if the threat is from a car? Don't shoot at a moving target. Your job is protection, not revenge. Get your man to a safe place.'

Two more instructors would teach another section the procedures regarding cars. Never leave them unattended, the MPs were told, unless the environment is known to be secure, and then check the security of the surroundings by restricting non-authorised access with irregular patrols, intruder alarms and permanent guards. All vehicles should be parked in a locked garage with a single, easily observed, well-illuminated entry point. If that was impossible, then the security of the building became a factor to be assessed: look for weak points, which would need to be continually checked.

Even an ideal location didn't obviate the need for a search for explosives before use, and at other times when the team felt like it. The long list of equipment was handed out, before they were broken down into teams of two. Familiarity with the vehicle was stressed, since that made spotting an anomaly easier. They were taught always to start with the surrounding area, then once that was secure to carry out their inspection logically. Outside first, then underneath, including wheels and arches. Always disconnect the battery as soon as the bonnet or boot is opened, as that may well be the power source to trigger the device. Check both luggage and engine compartments thoroughly before moving on to the interior. Don't fuck about, because if you do and you find it, it will be you that's creamed and not your boss.

The residency and office guys had their own problems to contend with. Are the buildings overlooked? How many entrances and exits are there? What cover is available to an assassin, and what depth of security cordon is required to negate that? What are the avenues open to a car bomber?

Could the grounds be landscaped to provide better security? What is the condition of the perimeter wall? There was lighting to discuss, intruder alarms, all of which had to be able to be worked off an alternative supply system. The African bodyguards had to know the access points: doors, windows, even down to the rainwater pipes that ran from the ground to the roof. What if that fails and the threat is inside? Methods of sealing the building were shown, as well as the need to place the comms in a secure position, one that would be hard to take down so that assistance, both medical and military, could be called in. Every man had to be familiar with internal layouts and the whereabouts of those inside, everyone from the boss-man to the Joe who cleaned the loo.

Offices had their own problems, since they were more open. The VIP has visitors. Can they all be checked, or is that in some cases unacceptable? Never put your man on the ground floor and don't put up signs that tell a stranger where his office is. Put him in the middle of the building and make sure he has his own washroom facilities that are personal to him alone. Stringent parking regulations should be enforced around the complex to avoid bomb use, the preference being a security cordon with facilities to check vehicles well away from the building. Heli pads should be on the roof or in an area that has secure passage from the VIP's office. The reception should be a clear area, with minimum obstructions and a high-profile search facility. These, like the main public waiting room, should be observable through a two-way mirror or CCTV. Important visitors who cannot be searched should have their own entrance and waiting facilities, down to washrooms and toilets, but all visitors to the main office should follow a prescribed guarded route. The outer office to the main VIP accommodation should have scope to allow normal secretarial activity to operate in line with the presence of a close protection team. Check on appointments, and the person making them on the VIP's behalf. They might be bribable.

Then they would rotate to car security. The trainees were taught where to sit, and the standard operating procedures for two-, three-, four-, and five-car convoy drills; where to put the VIP and how to get him safely from building to car. They had to learn how to assess the nature of a threat and the best techniques for reacting to it, as well as how to spot vulnerable locations. It went on like this day in, day out, lecture followed by course followed by lecture.

A lot of time was spent on the range, first with Browning pistols, then moving on to rifles and RPGs. Few of their recruits could achieve the standard set by the instructors, but they all showed improvements. Paul took over an old square building that had good thick walls, and once he'd blocked up the windows he started training them in room combat using live ammunition. Diving into a darkened room and having to spot and take out a perceived target in a split second really sorted the men out from the boys.

Crazy Collins took another party away, those who showed some aptitude for communications, to teach them about the equipment they'd be using: frequencies and emergency procedures. Harry Fielding had a bunch of guys working on counter-sniper drills, and occasionally they all combined, split into close protection and CAT teams, to work on various scenarios where the man would come under attack from units of his enemy.

It was relentless, but the kind of hard work that could be fun. The headings were on the wall for all the guys to see, the things they had to work on like physical fitness, room combat and close protection drills, medical skills, search techniques, navigation, field craft and last but not least, protocol and the proper way to dress. These guys would be meeting other heads of state. It was necessary to act properly and look good so that you did not let down your man. Safeguarding the VIP's reputation went hand in hand with protecting his person.

Forwood set up and dealt with the oversight committee. You couldn't just have seventy-two guys running around like headless, dangerous chickens. They needed orders and notification of advanced planning. Strasser ran this committee, personally. His presence removed the need for a protocol man, as well as any reference to a Treasury member to oversee costs. Tumbu was on it too, in his role as security chief, as well as a couple of generals who claimed to command the armed forces. Delane was co-opted when necessary. There were no other members of the military council, which only went to underline the personal nature of the task.

Paul Hill submitted a daily report on progress and a schedule for the following day's training, which was discussed in a desultory way. Everything went very smoothly until Forwood made the suggestion that the leader of the military council should make himself available for live firing exercises. This was not met with anything approaching enthusiasm,

102

even when Strasser was informed that in the UK it was standard procedure for the head of state, her family, and all leading politicians.

The SAS trainers all took turns to have days away from the lecture hall and the range. These were not breaks but serious recces, working in pairs, searching out locations for up-and-coming exercises. There was nothing worse than complacency, or training again and again in exactly the same geography. Building and street work they had to confine to Freetown, for security reasons, but occasionally they went out into the bush to work out anti-ambush and counter attack drills.

Slowly, but surely, the trainers began to discern some progress. Valentine Strasser's close protection team was taking shape.

CHAPTER EIGHT

Blue Harding clocked the SO10 guys in the departure lounge, as well as the two B Squadron minders, both of them men he knew well. John 'Casey' Jones was a good mate, a drinking and floozy-pursuing pal. The other guy, Gus Pollard, was the opposite, one of those people who rubbed Blue up the wrong way. Gus, to Blue's mind, was too full of himself, the kind of guy who found it hard to admit he might be wrong. They had squared up to each other on more than one occasion, which had done nothing to cool the mutual antipathy. The one victory Blue could chalk up was the guy's nickname, which, once used, had stuck. Much to his annoyance, Gus was known throughout the regiment as Pol Pot.

And they spotted him too, their eyes full of curiosity, wandering to take in the trio with him. Wally Aitken they knew from Hereford Old Boy reunions: Sandy was a possible, just because of his appearance. But neither of them knew Jamie Padden, and he got a lot of covert examination. But they were pros. There were journos in the lounge, gabbing away loudly, who'd managed to get club class seats, so they only exchanged a quiet nod, so as not to draw attention either to themselves or the mercenary team.

It was Mary Kline who guessed that the civil defence men on the checkpoint were preparing to leave, though it took them longer actually to depart than she had at first assumed. There was no ceremony to it, just a final departure after a period in which their ebullience had slowly died away, to be replaced by a morose air and much anxious glancing up and down the road they were guarding. If the army came they would want to be there, to prove they hadn't deserted their post; if it was the rebels, they needed to be long gone.

The same applied to her and Geoff, as well as all the other people jammed into the small church hall. The numbers of Sierra Leonians had increased as the day wore on – few men, mostly elderly, lots of women and lots of hungry children – so that by the time they were free to walk out of the place it was jam-packed with hot and noisy humanity. It had also begun to smell really bad, as the confined locals turned one corner into a latrine. The smell of piss and shit, given the heat and numbers, was overpowering, which made it a relief for the whole crowd finally to get into the open air.

But that presented another dilemma for Geoff and Mary. Should they stay or go? And if they took the second option, go where? Given wheels, they could have tried to run for Gbangatok, a regional centre that would offer them a choice of ways to leave the area. The town stood to the east at the head of a deep-water creek. It also had a grass-strip airfield that made it strategically important. The army was bound to mount a defence and there was every chance, given the present situation, that they could cadge a lift out by plane. But that was five miles away as the crow flies, a lot more by the circuitous route they would need to follow, especially since the civil defence guards had taken their pickup leaving them without the means to outrun a threat that must be close.

'What we need is food and somewhere to sleep,' said Geoff, looking up at the fading sunlight, thinking there was no long twilight to play with. Darkness in a part of the world close to the equator fell swiftly. 'And night can't be too far away.'

'If we get on to the Gbangatok road, the darkness won't matter.'

Geoff made no attempt to keep the sarcasm out of his voice. 'If you want to try walking along a pitch-black road full of guys with rifles, be my guest. I'm not sure I'd be too happy to try in daylight.'

'It was just a suggestion.'

'Try another.'

'There are some expat houses at Kpanguma belonging to friends of mine. That's less than two miles away, but we'd have to go through the bush.'

'They might still be there.'

'Not if they've got any sense. Anyway, that's got to be better than the roads right now.'

There was no way they could leave without being observed, just as there was no way they could stop the others following them, a long stream of locals unsure of where to go themselves but convinced these white folk had a way of getting them to safety. The party formed a long string of refugees weaving through the bush, heading due south, using the sinking sun and the hills to the east to keep them on track. It was like, as Geoff observed acidly, a bloody biblical exodus.

The sound of occasional gunfire added a bit of zest to the pace that Geoff set, heading for what was no more than a dozen houses grouped round a well, home to the expats who worked one of the AAR dredge sites. It was Mary's local knowledge that saved them from wandering past the place. It wasn't on a proper road, but at the end of a dust track, one they would have just crossed over had she not recognised the way the trees were arranged around a particular bend.

Geoff went ahead, to find the place deserted. And once more there was no way to stop the locals from following on, then filling up the available accommodation. By the time they had squeezed into the bedrooms and the living quarters, they'd crowded them until the last arrivals could only find space on the verandas. Forced to share with nearly fifty people, Geoff was thinking that he and Mary Kline had merely swapped one prison for another.

They did manage to find some of the food that had been left behind. Geoff was all for hoarding it, but Mary stopped him. She insisted that the whole amount, from storerooms, fridges and larders, be pooled so that everyone got something. Her first concern was the children, now so hungry and weary from the long walk that they'd fallen silent. He, meanwhile, got the lights going so that they could see what they were about. Then, through a combination of bullying and cajoling, he tried to get some order into the chaotic sleeping arrangements, commandeering the kitchen for himself and Mary.

In the war room at Hereford the pictures were going up on the walls. The news of the nuns being taken had jacked up expectations quite a bit; people don't take hostage folk dedicated to good works and saving life unless they mean business. Passport photos had come in from the relevant offices, to be blown up so that men who might have to go in and get them out could familiarise themselves with their faces.

Lists of RUF weaponry were also on the wall, what they'd bought and what they'd stolen. It wasn't complete, it never could be. But when it comes to hostage situations everybody cooperates, including national governments who are not too fussy who they sell to, so that the only variables were what had been supplied to the rebels by fringe arms dealers.

Every reported sighting was there too, a trace made to try to establish the locations where they might be held. The CO had already talked to the director of Special Forces and discussed the possibility of moving the stand-by squadron to Gibraltar. Lists of kit had been drawn up to cover for every type of entry method. Weapons and comms systems to be used collectively were itemised and pinned to the wall. It didn't have to be got ready, since it was always ready.

The whole of the loading quay at Port Nitti was ablaze with arc lights, the thud of the generators a constant as Frank Wintour oversaw the loading of the empty barges. Long and deep-hulled, they were designed to carry processed rutile not human beings, so comfort was at a premium. But few were willing to complain. Anything was better than staying still with the RUF approaching.

The briefings the security chief had attended stressed that the RUF had a certain amount of discipline, many said much more than the army. But Frank was disinclined to put that notion to the test. It wasn't prejudice that had him loading expats first either, it was the knowledge that the rebels had started to take hostages. There was no way they were going to take any of the people he was responsible for.

Gareth Evans was at the entrance to the loading site, surrounded by a cordon of AAR security guards, ordering, sometimes at the very top of his voice, the drivers of vehicles to abandon their cars and pickups. And he was being strict about the number of possessions they could take with them: one suitcase per person was the limit, which for most of those fleeing was a lot less than they'd hoped. That led to a lot of arguments, mostly from people to whom Gareth would normally have been obliged to defer. Not now! The situation was too dangerous, and he and Frank had their local workforce to think of. They wanted to get as many of the rutile workers to a place of safety as well.

Victor Johnston should have made for Port Nitti. Instead he abandoned his weapon and went back to his village, intending to melt into the background. All the bravado he'd demonstrated that morning had gone, and he was now once more the humble plant site fetch-and-carry man. When the rebels arrived he smiled over hunched and submissive shoulders, claiming his own adherence to the aims of the RUF. That might have worked if the people who knew him had kept quiet. But it only took one loose tongue, trying to curry favour or to protect his own family, to put the whole group at risk. And the one in most danger was the leader.

They shot two of his men and threw them into the marsh grasses before they ever got round to Victor. He was not allowed to die so quickly. While they taunted him politically and personally, a dozen rebels used their bayonets to torture him, never coming close, jabbing forward with their rifles into his soft flesh and turning them slowly, their laughter mixing with his agonised wails. Not one of the stab wounds was deep enough to kill, or even to stop him staggering around in a vain attempt to escape his fate. His upper arms were slashed, as well as his chest. The blood from the wounds in his thighs ran down to mix with that coming from the cuts to his shins that exposed his bones. The heaviest blows were delivered into the yielding skin of his buttocks. The people he'd lived with all his life, some of them family, those to whom he cried now for help, stood around silently and watched him bleed, till blood loss made it impossible to stand any more.

Flat on his back, with no more tears left to cry, Victor Johnston looked up as the rebels gathered round him. They began to chant their slogans, drowning out the cries of his pain and pleading, working themselves up into a killing frenzy, their eyes like great white orbs in the sweating black skin of their young grinning faces. One word, which he didn't hear, triggered the final thrust, and a dozen blades were rammed into his chest at once. As he died, he felt the taste of the blood that had begun to fill his mouth, open in a silent scream.

You get a smell every time you enter a country. Not at the big First World airports, where the only thing which will affect the sinuses is the odour of burnt aviation fuel, but at smaller places where the special aroma of the country assaults you: the fetid corrupt stench of jungle in South America; the dry blast of burnt heat in the Gulf. Here, just outside Freetown, it was a prickly, slightly spicy fragrance that matched what they'd seen of the landscape as the jet came in to land – the deep green of the vegetation mixed with the bright red scars of the exposed earth.

The SO10 party was shown off first, whisked away from the bottom of the steps in a big embassy limo, which occasioned much curious commentary from the rest of the passengers who were told to wait. And there were a lot of them. A full plane was a rare enough occurrence in Sierra Leone, likely to swamp the easy-going immigration controls, but one full of journalists was ten times worse. They were a noisy bunch at the best of times, but never more so than when they wanted to be first out of the airport with their kit. The stars, the front-of-camera guys working for the major TV networks, rushed off so they could get the best room at the Cape Sierra. The backup mob, with a couple of dozen metal flight cases each, practically came to blows around the single carousel.

Blue took the chance to give them a good look over, especially the females. They were usually easy meat on assignments, eager to get pissed and laid on expenses. It was amusing to see that Jamie Padden was doing the same, while McPherson stood back like a country squire, leaving Wally Aitken to fight through and get both their sets of luggage.

Mike Layman was waiting for them, his driver holding a sign saying ANGLO-AFRICAN RUTILE. The handshakes were perfunctory and silent, neither side speaking until they were safe in the company minibus.

'I'll take you by the office first. The boss wants a word. We've got you a villa to use as accommodation, and possibly as an HQ.'

'Good,' Blue replied. 'What's the latest sitrep?'

'The RUF have overrun all our sites. We got most of the expats out, but our workers are scattered, and the RUF have taken more hostages. We're not exactly sure of the numbers because the up-country situation is confused, but a radio message confirmed that it now includes seven Italian nuns.'

McPherson sighed. 'The lengths some people will go to get hold of a virgin.'

'SO10 is here,' said Blue, as Wally Aitken let forth a great guffaw.

'We heard they were due,' Layman replied. 'I wish them joy. We've been trying to talk to the rebels for a week, ever since we sensed they might attack the mine sites, with no joy whatsoever.' He saw, out of the corner of his eye, the slight smile on Blue's face, and confirmed what he was obviously thinking. 'Paying them off is much better than letting them stop production, believe me.'

'Shoot a few of the bastards,' said Wally Aitken, for once expounding a personal thought. He was rewarded by a grunt of assent from McPherson.

'The High Commissioner has asked us to exercise great caution until

SO10 have made contact. There's still money on the table from us if they want it, though we've kept that to ourselves.'

'Then how, pray,' asked Sandy in a magisterial voice, 'does he expect to get them out?'

'He thinks they might bow to international pressure.'

'You'd be best to ignore that sort of shit,' growled Sandy. 'Once let those diplomatic bastards tie your hands and you'll be forever buggered.'

'You don't ignore someone like Donald Quentin-Davies.'

Blue was looking out of the open window, watching Sierra Leone roll by. The road from the airport had the usual string of huts and houses, the kind that always cling to any major route. But soon it gave way to more substantial dwellings, some of them big villas cut off from humanity by large walls, then to a shantytown, before they entered the central district of Freetown. Architecturally, it was a mix of colonial alternating with single-storey breeze-block factories and two-storey flat-roofed housing, with the occasional new glass-fronted construction that hinted at the twentieth century.

Blue's main interest was in the nature of the locals, hard to discern at speed, a task made much easier when they entered the busy downtown area with its crowds and traffic jams. There were a lot of uniforms about, checkpoints on side streets and occasional patrols. And the guys were alert, a sure sign of trouble, especially in a capital city. There was fear in the people's faces, an easily identified look of tension, as though trouble could arrive at any second and claim a victim at random. He'd seen that look before, and it wasn't confined to countries where the skin colour was shaded. It was the look, too, of the streets of Derry or Belfast.

AAR's offices were in a new block, taking up the first two floors, with a manned barrier gate and a big open courtyard in front. Habit had him examining that too, sizing it up for a security risk, mentally seeing the ways he could strengthen the access with decorative concrete bollards to prevent a car bomb. There was too much glass for his liking as well, though it was hard to see what was threatened by it if it shattered because of the copper tint. Blue couldn't help himself. Once a man has been trained for that sort of appraisal, it's very hard to stop doing it.

'Right,' said Layman, as he climbed out of the bus. 'Leave your kit here, and let's go and see the boss.'

The director of Special Forces made his report to the committee in a dry, matter-of-fact way, but the import was clear enough. At this stage there was no plan, nor was there a definite intention to intervene. There was merely a developing crisis that might go out like a damp squib. But it was quite clear that any contemplated reaction from the UK risked adding to what would be an already tough assignment, so the decision to move the stand-by squadron to Gibraltar went through on the nod. Likewise, they passed the need for the frigate as a method of exfiltration.

The orders went out from Duke of York's barracks to Hereford. Because of its nature the job was handed over to B Squadron, the current stand-by squadron, much to the dismay of G Squadron, who were on counter terrorist duties. The SAS always prepared for two simultaneous major incidents without in any way jeopardising existing ops. This job had come in at a very busy time. The need to back this up with extra resources meant that R Squadron, made up of Territorial Army personnel, was tasked to remain in Hereford. B Squadron was well aware of the potential, and had already packed their personal kit. Few of them had to be paged to come into Stirling Lines. The Chinooks lifted them out to Brize Norton within three hours of the order being received, two hours behind their HQ group who had left by Learjet from Cheltenham.

Jimmy Heriot, who chaired the committee, had a desultory chat with the DSF before he left, then went to the phone when the committee room was finally cleared.

'George, Jimmy here.'

'Dear boy,' replied George Forgeham-Lowry.

'Are you at the club tonight?'

'Can be. Why?'

'Few things I'd like to bring you up to date on.'

'Seven do?'

'Splendid.'

'By the way,' Forgeham-Lowry added, just to put a little sealing wax on their unspoken bargain. 'Paddy Molloy was asking after you the other day, suggested he might like to have you out to dinner one evening.'

'I'd be delighted, of course.'

'I'll let him know then.'

Superintendent Eddie Welford and Inspector Ian Cannon sat opposite

Donald Quentin-Davies, as the High Commissioner went through his briefing. It was standard stuff, the kind of thing both men had heard before: the difficulty of dealing with the RUF and the fragmented nature of their leadership, plus the need to get the people on the ground to obey. He nodded towards the closed file in Welford's hand.

'Chief bod is a chap called Foday Sankoh, but the man who deals with the world press is Alimany Bakaar Sankoh. No relation apart from tribal, as far as we can see. But the whole thing is run by committee, so we can never be quite sure who decides what.'

'We're like salesmen, sir,' said Welford, interrupting at the first convenient pause.

He was a large man, quite as imposing as his host, with a big head, fleshy jowls, wide shoulders and a stomach that strained at his shirt buttons as well as the belt on his trousers. His brown eyes had a benign quality that matched his avuncular voice, but that was all surface. A closer inspection would have revealed the number of scars he carried on that kindly face, and time would show just how threatening those eyes and that voice could be. Cannon was the opposite: slim and very neat, a dark-suited City type to offset the rumpled state of his superior. He had dark, sharp eyes that made the object of their attention feel he was being closely examined, and elegant hands that he stroked from time to time in what appeared to be an attempt to control some inner tension.

'Salesmen?' queried Quentin-Davies.

'Our first job, sir, is to find out who makes the decisions. No good waffling away to someone who can't buy your goods.' The hands that opened the folder were huge, knobbled around the knuckles where they had been used aggressively. 'So that's where we need some help. The leadership must be in contact with other people-friendly governments, sympathetic supporters and the like.'

Cannon carried on where Welford left off. 'We need a list of those to talk to so we can establish an operating procedure. First, find our man, then get some indication of his personality.'

Welford spoke again. 'Everyone is different, and telling what they are actually like on a phone is not easy. But if you have some prior info, a way of identifying with them, it makes it easier to get inside their guard.'

'They will be guarded,' snorted Quentin-Davies, 'that I can assure you.'

The superintendent carried on as if he hadn't been interrupted. 'It could be something as simple as kids, a place they have been, or someone they admire like JFK or Nelson Mandela.'

'Anything really,' added Cannon. 'What we have to do is dominate the conversation, but let them think they are in charge. It's not easy to do that without ruffling feathers. A place to hide is essential to calm things, so the more we have before we pick up the phone, the better.'

'The sources for that are unlikely to be here in Sierra Leone,' said Quentin-Davies, 'though the local security chief, a chap called Tumbu, is bound to have a file as thick as your arm.'

'You have to be careful with that kind of source, sir. As employees of the present government they're inclined, sometimes, to put in wishful thinking just to please their bosses. If we use that we run right into trouble. We'd rather have it from their friends than their enemies.'

'I'll get on to Charlie Rochester in Conakry. They have some support in Guinea, and he probably knows just who they are.'

'If you could do that right away, sir?' said Welford, in a voice that was warm and friendly, but with a look that left no room for prevarication, even in someone as elevated as the High Commissioner.

'Bugger nearly went white when I suggested it,' said Forwood. He was sitting in the bar of the Cape Sierra Hotel, gleefully relating the incident at the oversight committee to Toby Flowers. 'The idea of him being close to armed men who would actually be asked to shoot at him and miss scared the leader rigid. We offered to do it with our guys first, on the grounds that we it do for our own VIPs, but he wouldn't buy it.'

'Then how does he expect to manage when they take up their duties?'

'God only knows. Thank Christ we won't be here to witness it.'

'Frank!' Flowers yelled when he spotted Buckhart in the doorway.

Every head turned at the call, and the object stood in the doorway for a second soaking up the attention. Buckhart had worked covering combat situations for *Soldier of Fortune* magazine when he first left Delta Force. With an ego the size of Texas, he always made sure that whatever 'hot spot' he was in, his face got maximum exposure. But he also had a lot of charm, enough to make such outrageous behaviour acceptable. Only when he was sure everyone had clocked him did he move.

'Hi, guys,' he finally replied, in a voice that definitely lacked his normal enthusiasm.

'You look glum,' said Toby, signalling for a drink.

'The best laid plans, as Rabbie Burns said.'

'Strasser wouldn't play.'

'The guy is scared shitless by the hostage thing. He thinks if the RUF bumps them off, especially the nuns, the world is going to blame him, not them.'

'He's not mister bravery in any department,' added Forwood as the drink arrived.

'It will be the companies' PR people who'll be nervous, Frank. Raping Africa is always good for a headline in Europe and the US.'

'Dammit, Toby, I'm good for a headline too!'

'Does he understand that we have a real chance to bury the bastards?'

'He can't do. All he thinks is that if we go after the rebels, they'll shoot the expats.'

'Hello, hello,' said Forwood. 'What's he doing here?'

If Frank Buckhart had put a check on the babble in the bar for a few seconds, Eustace Tumbu managed a full half-minute. The place was full of expat businessmen, the Lebanese traders who really ran the local economy and a few of the better-off locals, well leavened with a drove of hookers. They all knew Tumbu both by sight and reputation. When it came to stopping conversations in Sierra Leone, the man was in a class all of his own. The whole room got a bit of his grin, but it was clear as soon as he started moving that he was heading for the trio of white officers.

'Gentlemen,' he said, as they half stood to greet him. His hand, pink palm contrasting so sharply with his coal-black skin, was up to forestall them. 'Are your glasses ready to be refreshed?'

'Allow me,' said Forwood.

'Never,' the Colonel replied, easing himself into a chair. 'You are a guest in my country.' The grin that accompanied those words seemed to split his face in two, and he leant towards the trio, wafting before him that odour of expensive aftershave. 'Besides, the owner of the Cape Sierra likes me. Even when I entertain here many, many guests, he never gives me the bill.'

The owner was a Lebanese guy called Manoulian who clearly had a healthy fear of the Battery Street police barracks. Tumbu would hesitate to take him in personally, since his contacts were of the best, but Manoulian also employed a lot of Africans, some of whom must be RUF sympathisers.

Looking after Tumbu was a cheap way of making sure the security chief didn't take up the workers whose loss could disrupt his business.

The smile remained in place as he continued. 'I believe you had a meeting with our esteemed leader, Colonel Buckhart.'

'I did.'

'Not very satisfactory, I would guess.'

'Just the opposite, Colonel Tumbu. I've set things up nicely to give the RUF a bit of the kind of trauma they're sticking to everyone else.'

'But he is concerned for the hostages.' Tumbu broadened his grin as they nodded agreement, dropping his voice in a conspiratorial way. 'Aren't we all?'

'Hell!' snapped Buckhart, like a man whose honour had been impugned. 'Of course we are.'

'I must say it does our leader credit, the care he shows.' The insincere murmuring that comment produced seemed to delight Tumbu, but not as much as the next twist to his wind up. 'Though of course one wonders if it is wise to let it stop a more aggressive policy. The rebels cannot be allowed to dictate the pace of the conflict.'

'I think my feelings on that subject are well known,' said Buckhart. If Tumbu was trying to trap him in criticism, then he wouldn't oblige. But neither would he lie.

'They are,' the African officer replied. 'And they are to be admired.'

'You don't win a war by backing off,' Buckhart insisted. 'And if I may say so, if the NPRC don't do something they risk another coup against them.'

Tumbu nodded sagely. After all, what Buckhart had said was no more than common gossip. 'The real coup, gentlemen, the one that needs to be thought about, would be how to get them out.'

'Out of where?' said Toby Flowers.

'The location, of course, in which they are being held.'

Forwood sat back suddenly, like a man left wondering if he should be there. As an SAS officer he knew all about hostage recovery scenarios, and as an intelligent man he was wondering what Tumbu was up to. That he was up to something seemed obvious, and all Forwood knew was that he didn't want to be part of it. Drinking with the Gurkha Guard Force officers was one thing; they could even discuss, up to a point, each other's business. But there was a line beyond which he was constrained by the job he was doing, and this conversation looked as though it was drifting that way.

'Thanks for the offer of the drink, Colonel Tumbu, but I think I'd best be off.'

'More tennis, Captain?'

'It's a bit late for that, sir,' he replied, indicating the darkness outside.

'Then give my regards to the lovely lady who is about to receive your very best serve.'

Tumbu threw his head back and laughed so loud that everyone stopped talking again. He then repeated his witticism to three men who could only manage a thin smile. As Forwood left the table, he heard Tumbu repeat his question.

'What would be your reaction, Colonel Buckhart, if I could tell you exactly where the hostages are at present being held?'

CHAPTER NINE

here was little in the way of gunfire when the RUF arrived at Kpanguma, none of the sounds of battle Geoff Hinchcliffe had anticipated. War was outside his experience, something he'd only seen in the movies, so the lack of planes and exploding bombs, of screaming men and flying bullets, gave the whole thing an unreal air.

They walked into the settlement in two long lines, a leaderless straggle of men and young boys, seemingly weary from the march they'd already made, or perhaps jaded by what they'd already done in the way of murder and destruction. The lack of passion somehow made them more fearsome: the way they came through the door of the house Geoff and Mary had taken for themselves to stare at the silent mass of people who'd taken refuge. There were fifty-eight souls in a two-bedroomed villa, occupying less space now that they were standing. The older rebels just leant against the walls, rifles beside them, rolling joints and leaving it to the kids to poke and prod, with rifles and fingers, at the now cowering inhabitants.

The two Europeans were on the receiving end of a lot of unnecessary jostling, barged into at every opportunity and treated to a hard stare that dared them to react. Mary Kline kept whispering to Geoff to stay calm. He didn't bother to respond. He'd looked into the eyes of those kids before they ever laid a paw on him, and he'd seen just how out of it they were. The lack of passion wasn't down to weariness, just cannabis.

The food went first, not that there was much of that to steal. Then they started on the bundles, jabbing at them with bayonets and slicing them open. Anything of value was taken, along with a lot of stuff that was, to Geoff's mind, worthless. Both his and Mary's watch went, but there was no immediate attempt at a search of their pockets. More alarming was the noise from the other dwelling, screams and shouting that hinted at a more aggressive policy.

Finally the older men stirred themselves, first to sort out the men from the women. They were taken outside, some walking like zombies, others pleading quietly, one or two sobbing earnestly to their captors, telling

117

them of their faith in the RUF, begging them to believe their innocence. One pair had to be dragged out from the crowd, the fear so great that they left a trail of piss behind. Watching them and the way their tormentors looked at them, he reckoned they would be the first to die.

'Stop!' Mary's shout startled Geoff just as much as everyone else. They were like naughty school kids the way they froze, years of ingrained servitude working for a few seconds.

'Leave those people alone,' she continued, taking several paces forward, finger jabbing as she glared at the pair dragging one of the sobbing victims. 'You are supposed to be trying to free these people, not terrorise them. How can you listen to the way your leaders talk and behave like this?'

They didn't all have good enough English to understand what she was saying, but then they didn't need to. Her body language said it all. Her chin, her hips and breasts were thrust forward aggressively, leaving Geoff Hinchcliffe to wonder at how he could think of sex at a time like this. Mary moved even closer and got her hands on the wrists of one of the rebels, a tall guy with a mass of tribal scars, trying to break his grip so that she could free the victim. For a moment it looked as though she was going to succeed.

Then Geoff saw the change in the man's eyes, and now it was his turn to yell. 'Mary, for Christ's sake get away from there!'

There was another split second of stillness. Then they heard a gunshot, and that broke the spell. The Scarface she was grappling with swung his other arm. The barrel of the rifle would have hit her face if Geoff had moved a second later, but he'd got just close enough to grab her shirt collar and begin to haul her back, so that the blue-grey steel missed her nose by a fraction. Several kids dashed forward to push her back, easy since Geoff was also pulling.

Scarface had let his victim drop into a heap on the floor. He walked over to where Mary stood quivering, though it was hard to tell if that was caused by her anger or her fear. He towered over her, the scars made more prominent by the red dust that caked his skin, the big dark-brown eyes ranging over her face. She held his gaze until he leant forward, stopping less than an inch away. That made her shut her eyes, but she opened them a moment later as she heard the loud sound of sniffing. He ran his nose over her neck, her forehead and both cheeks, as if he was involved in the ritual of a tribal smelling out.

Then he stood back and the barrel of his weapon began to rise up slowly. Geoff tensed himself to move, knowing that if it came level the guy would probably pull the trigger. That what he was contemplating – the need to deflect the gun – was sheer madness only occurred to him afterwards. Luckily for him, it didn't come all the way up, and Scarface took another half a step forwards. The barrel was thrust between Mary's legs, which had remained slightly open to give her balance. The front sight, a half-inch sliver of protruding gun metal, was placed carefully on the spot where it would cause maximum humiliation, then jerked slowly back and forth as a low carnal laugh rose up from the man's throat.

Then he spoke softly, in what Geoff thought was Mende, to the kids behind him. Mary must have understood what he said because she tensed even more. A pair of what looked like twelve-year-olds stepped forward and began to search her, making a meal of the job. Their hands lingered in shirt front pockets, and they got a long free feel, both front and back, when they came to rifle her trousers. They got dollar bills, her CARE ID card, some sachets of water purifier and a clean white handkerchief. And all the while Scarface rubbed away with the front sight on his AK47, looking intently to see what effect this was having on the white woman. It was certainly having an effect on him, something his loose fatigue pants did nothing to disguise.

More gunshots erupted outside, accompanied by screams and pleas, which in turn set up a wailing inside the house as the women and children began to let their imaginations run riot. It was that noise which stopped Scarface and made him spin around to demand silence, an order that was quickly obeyed. While the last of the men were taken away, he walked over and began to examine the local women, poking and touching those that took his fancy. The comments started softly but increased rapidly, as his companions added verbal insults to the tactile ones he was administering.

Another rebel came to join him, a rangy guy with a hollow bony chest. They began to wind each other up, their banter, added to the laughter and salacious comments, making them more and more bold. Every female eye was aimed at the floor, trying to avoid drawing attention. One or two of the younger, more nubile girls, who had been roughly touched up, were sobbing, their shoulders quietly heaving. Scarface and Rangy were egging each other on, occasionally jabbing at their erect pricks, trying to work up the courage to take their pick.

It happened eventually. It was Rangy who grabbed first, taking a young girl of about fourteen and pulling her clear. What must have been her mother tried to intervene, but all that got her was a back-handed punch on the jaw that floored her. Suddenly every one of the rebels who had a gun raised it and swung it in front of the mass of refugees. Those with pangas and bayonets did likewise, choking off the wail of protests. Scarface grabbed his girl and both men dragged them outside, oblivious in heat to the screams and pleas.

There was silence in the hut: even the rebels were quiet, as though they were not sure of the rights or wrongs of what was happening. The whole atmosphere seemed deflated. That was broken by one of the kids who, left out of the searching of Mary Kline, was determined to make up for it on Geoff Hinchcliffe. As soon as he moved the others did too, all scrabbling for a pocket, gasping with delight when their rough search produced a trophy. Money went, his knife, his wallet, the house keys and credit cards, along with the gold chain he wore round his neck. Mary was pawed over again, the kids continuing their search long after there was anything left to find.

Finally they retired to lean against the wall, one or two rolling more joints which, once lit, were passed around. Rangy and Scarface came back after about ten minutes looking mighty pleased with themselves. Then, taking a look around at the cringing, abashed victims, they began to harangue the terrified refugees. That started everyone off, especially those revived by a fresh inhalation of dope. The words were jumbled and delivered in several tongues, but with enough English to tell Mary and Geoff that everyone was being lectured on the benefits of an RUF victory. That was accompanied by a demand to move, with a great deal of jabbing using rifles and bayonets, as Scarface, clearly some kind of leader, ordered them out of the buildings. As the refugees exited they saw the two girls crouched against the outside of the house, sobbing and wailing to themselves, arms wrapped tightly round their bodies in an attempt to protect what they'd already lost.

The roadway was soon a mass of people, all those they had brought from the church and more. The rebels who were not occupied in guarding them were busy looting the houses, taking everything that could be moved. By the edge of the trees they could see several bodies, the menfolk who'd been led away earlier, now sprawled awkwardly in death.

Blue didn't like Razenbrook much. He was too like a natural born Rupert, with a voice and manner that all but shouted the impression he had of his innate superiority. The AAR boss could almost have said 'Now listen up peasants', and it would have come as no surprise. Glancing aside occasionally, he could see that Mike Layman had no love for the guy either. That helped. It wasn't necessary to like the client, but it was good to have a rapport with the man telling you what to do. And Razenbrook had made it quite clear at the outset that Layman was the linkman.

The briefing was more or less a rehash of what they'd had in London, with all the variables that could emerge from a confused situation. But there were one or two new developments, like some evidence that the Sierra Leone forces were beginning to move in to confront the RUF, though no actual contact had yet been made.

'If we're sure they're going in, it might be an idea to get in with them,' said Blue. 'Because what they can and cannot do has to be part of any assessment we make. If we could actually see them in action it would be a plus.'

'Don't hold your breath,' said Layman, a remark that earned him a hard look from Razenbrook.

'One thing we have to establish here is that there should be no bullshit,' Blue barked.

'I beg your pardon?' replied Razenbrook, shifting that look from his number two to Blue Harding.

'I mean that everybody has to speak up, with the negatives as well as the positives. People not being up-front about their impressions can only compromise any rundown on the situation you face.'

'I assure you, John, that you will find me extremely candid.'

'I know you will be, Tony.' There was a delicious moment then as the boss-man reacted to Blue using his first name, a fleeting look that crossed his face as if to question whether such a liberty was allowed. 'But don't call me John. My nickname is Blue.'

'What means do we have of getting in there, sir?' asked Sandy McPherson. The ex-RSM was no slouch when it came to picking up and exploiting nuance. The 'sir' earned him a wide boyish grin, and a flick of the blond mop that came very close to looking like a salute.

'Mike here has convinced me of the need to provide dedicated transport for the duration of your presence here, Sandy. Don't want you stuck for the means to move about. So we have taken over the use of a Russian Hip helicopter we normally hire on a day-to-day basis. The aircrew and maintenance bods are Russians too, I'm afraid, with all the usual disregard for life and limb of their race.'

'They are all Afghanistan veterans, including the ground crew,' said Layman. 'After that little experience I daresay they hold life rather cheap.'

'Boris doesn't need a war,' Sandy responded. 'They're born with a death wish.'

Razenbrook clearly felt he'd gone too far, so he cut in hastily. 'Sergei, the pilot, does the job well. It's just that some of his tricks are a trifle hairy.'

'The whole arrangement sounds splendid, sir,' replied McPherson, an over-the-top, arse-licking response that was accompanied by an equally noisy 'Great' from Wally Aitken.

'Access by road is not on,' added Mike Layman. 'The danger of ambush is too great. But you'll be okay once we're close to the sites, we've got pickups or Land Rovers aplenty. Just take your pick.'

'Weapons?' asked Jamie Padden.

Layman frowned. 'None at this stage, and basically a bad idea in any case. We don't want to fight the bastards, we just want them to go away.'

'But you do want a defence,' Jamie insisted.

'When they're gone,' said Razenbrook. 'And just so they can't come back again. And, I must stress this: it all depends on cost. If the bottom line won't wear it, there's no point in me putting up to the board. So bear that in mind as you do your appreciations.'

'Is that Hip helo ours now?' asked Sandy.

'He should be standing by on the end of the phone.'

'Then we should go and have a shufti right away.'

'Have the RUF got any triple A?' demanded Blue, needled at the way Sandy McPherson was trying to assume control.

'Sorry?' said Razenbrook.

'Anti-aircraft weaponry.'

It was Mike Layman who replied. 'There's a chance they do. They took some stuff off the army when they captured Moyamba.'

'Do you know what it was?'

Layman shuffled a load of paper he had in his lap, found the item he was looking for, and read it out. 'A pair of twelve point seven five millimetre, fifty calibre machine guns, plus two thousand rounds of ammo.'

That, at least temporarily, shut Sandy McPherson up. The 12.75mm was a real heavy piece of kit that could rip a helicopter to shreds. But the ex-RSM was determined to be positive, so he had to say something else. He did it by posing a question to himself.

'One or two guns, in what is a very a big country?'

Blue raised his voice, though he didn't shout. 'Do we have any precise information about where the army is located?'

'Not precise, no.'

'Then I don't think we should go charging off,' said Blue.

Razenbrook looked very miffed. 'But you gave us the impression you wanted to go in quickly.'

'I do. But we need to know who is where. Let's get a bit more information first. The last thing we want to do is fly into the middle of a battle if the RUF have that kind of weapon available.'

The glance that Razenbrook and McPherson exchanged then was almost infinitesimally small, but it was there, and both faces seemed to radiate disappointment.

'We need to get ourselves housed, then set up proper comms links,' Blue continued, talking deliberately to Layman.

'I forgot. There's a message on my desk from Charter Security. Dave Heffer says he's got Ray Kavanagh coming out today.'

All three Brits nodded at that. Kavanagh was one of the best signallers in the game.

'Equipment?'

'That's coming with him. Satcoms, the lot.'

'Good. We'll need maps and equipment and personnel lists, copies of all the intelligence you've already gathered, plus a list of possibilities about where we might acquire more. I also, in the light of what's been said, need a budget to work with on a day-to-day basis.'

'Right now there is no budget,' said Razenbrook. 'Spend what you need.'

'Thanks.'

'So when do you plan to go out to our mine sites and have a proper look.'

'I don't know yet, Tony,' Blue replied. 'I don't have enough information to work out a plan. But I do know that charging in and risking getting slotted is not in any of our contracts. And it won't do Anglo-African Rutile much good either.'

Quentin-Davies and his opposite number in Guinea had moved with commendable speed. Eddie Welford and Ian Cannon had a lot of contacts with whom to talk. These consisted of politicians in neighbouring countries, several UN officials and a couple of bankers. They did look at what the Sierra Leone government had, but only as background. The feedback was generally the same: that even if Foday Sayebanah Sankoh was the RUF leader, the man who would do the talking was the other Sankoh, the foreign relations officer, Alimany Bakaar. The next job they had to work on was the need to open some kind of communication with the man so that they could start to negotiate a release, and that needed an intermediary.

They found one in Conakry, a Lebanese businessman who had been at Cambridge with the guy. The first thing he told them was the most vital: Alimany Bakaar had a visceral hatred of the white business community. For either Welford or Cannon to assume the negotiating role was to risk antagonising him. So the next search was for an acceptable well-educated African with no links to the government who, with the two SO10 men providing backup, could front the job. Quentin-Davies came up trumps on that one, digging up a qualified, British-educated engineer who worked for Anglo-African Rutile.

'It will take a day or two, sir,' said Welford. 'Our man in Conakry has a means of making contact, but it's not a pick-up-the-phone-and-call job.'

'You've done very well, both of you.'

'What we need now is to set up a comms link on an agreed frequency so that they can talk to us. The best place for that would be the High Commission cipher room.'

'Ah!' Quentin-Davies responded, negatively. He'd been prepared for this, but still felt uncomfortable saying it. With what was happening on UK traffic, the cipher room had to be kept out of bounds to all but regular diplomatic staff. Delane, caught on the hop like Quentin-Davies, undertook to sort matters out, but needed grace for a day or two.

'It's where we normally work, sir,' said Cannon, 'and we do have the requisite security clearance.'

The High Commissioner sighed, then adopted what could only be classed as his diplomatic look. It didn't impress Eddie Welford, who thought he looked like a pox doctor confirming a bad case of clap. 'The problem there, Superintendent, is that our cipher room is very cramped. And naturally right now we have a mass of traffic, certainly enough to keep our own signal staff working flat out. Things will ease off, of course, but as of this moment we are, I am informed, under tremendous pressure.'

Eddie Welford was too long in the tooth to start protesting. There was a reason behind what was being done, and that was probably none of his business. And he also reckoned that Donald Quentin-Davies, having decided to deny them ready access to the cipher room and being well aware of the need for haste, would have an alternative. So that was the question he posed.

'Well, it's really up to you. I have had an offer of assistance in the initial contact phase from Anglo-African Rutile. They have to create a net of their own for some chaps they've brought in from the UK to look over a way to defend their sites.'

'It's a bit late for that from what I heard,' said Cannon.

'They expect them to be cleared by the army. Also there is, apparently, an absolute fortune in processed product waiting to be brought out.' Quentin-Davies must have observed the jaundiced way Welford was looking at him, because he dropped both that subject and his normal measured FO speed of speech, instead speaking hurriedly. 'They've rented a villa for these chaps, and Tony Razenbrook, who runs AAR, says that you are welcome to pick their brains for whatever you need to make contact.'

'We need a signals man on hand.'

'We will provide that, of course, as soon as things settle down. But they have a top-notch chap, apparently, coming in on tomorrow's flight, and they're quite prepared to put him at your disposal.'

'You surely don't want us to operate from a private address?'

'Never. Naturally we will find somewhere in the High Commission compound for you to use as a dedicated facility as soon as contact has been established.'

'All done and dusted,' said Welford, making no attempt to hide the sarcasm. 'It's almost as if it were preordained.'

'Most fortuitous,' Quentin-Davies replied, smoothly. 'If you want to have a chat with AAR straight away I will get my driver to run you and your minder chappies over there.'

'What's this, Roddy,' said Toby Flowers, 'a sudden zealous rush to the head?'

He'd walked on to the firing range to find Forwood practising with a Heckler & Koch G3. Further along in the butts, Paul Hill was supervising a practice session with Browning pistols.

Forwood smiled. 'Going back to the brigade soon, Toby. In fact the minute I get home. I won't get the chance to blast away regardless. That is a perk reserved for the regiment.'

Toby Flowers nodded in agreement. It had been a bane of his service life, the low allocation of ammunition that regular units were given for range practice. The SAS, in a team of four, tended to shoot off in a day what a whole company of Green Jackets were allowed in a year.

'I hope and pray that Strasser and his lot are paying for what you're blasting away with now.'

'If Alan Delane is sending them the bill, they'll be paying through the nose. Park Lane prices.'

Forwood raised the weapon, slammed in a new magazine, and let fly at the target a hundred yards away.

'That was a bit of a hurried departure you made yesterday evening,' said Flowers, when he'd finished demolishing a Hun-head.

'And a diplomatic one, Toby.'

'You should have stayed. Old Tumbu doesn't shell out for his whores either. We had quite a party.'

'You know me, Toby. I don't like paying for it. And I might add, I'd be very unwilling to follow Tumbu into the nether regions of some local tart.'

'I take it you don't trust Tumbu in any respect?'

'I hope you're not going to tell me you do?'

'No, I'm not. And neither, you'll be pleased to hear, does Frank Buckhart.'

'So he didn't fall for that bull about the hostages?'

'It wasn't bull, Roddy.'

Forwood frowned in spite of himself. 'I wish I could believe you.'

'Honestly, it's true. Tumbu claims to have good info about where they are being held. He also says he knows how few people are guarding them.'

Roddy Forwood checked that the breech was clear and put on the safety before he turned to face Flowers. 'Is Frank going after them?'

'He agreed to a recce. If that confirms Tumbu's claims, then he'll take the whole of our Gurkha force in and get them out.'

'If he buys anything the locals tell him then he is even more crazy than I thought.'

'He's not.'

'I have no desire to malign your boss, Toby, and I personally like the man. But even you have to admit he's a glory-hungry sod who'll do anything for a headline in *Soldier of Fortune*.'

'Don't be so modest. Frank has moved on from that rag. He wants the cover of *Time* magazine, Roddy. Nothing less will suffice.'

'He'll run for president one day, that is if he lives to try it. I'm surprised you didn't try to stop him.'

'I did initially, but he persuaded me otherwise.'

'Were you drunk?'

'No.'

'Then how?'

'He told Tumbu, just as the sod was on the vinegar stroke, that he would only go and recce the area if the bugger went with him.'

'And Tumbu agreed?'

'He did. And just to make sure he turned up, I saw them off not an hour ago.'

'As some of my troopers would no doubt say, "Fucking Ada".'

'Those two chaps who flew in from Scotland Yard are going to be a bit irked. If Fizzin' Frank gets his way the crisis they've come to solve will be over before they get going.'

'I doubt they'll be angry. Buggers'll probably insist on a good fortnight to clear matters up.'

B Squadron arrived in Gibraltar under strength, but there was nothing unusual about that. It happened to every group in the SAS. In theory, a squadron consisted of sixty-four men plus headshed, but they rarely had their full complement available. Troopers were always on detached duties, sometimes up to no good in places they shouldn't be, at other times working as instructors in any number of locations around the world.

Northern Ireland was a special arena, where only those considered suitable would be sent. No matter how good he might be, there was no use in employing a guy who was six foot four with flaming red hair in undercover work on the Falls Road. And there was the temperament factor as well. Some guys just couldn't hack that kind of intensity, the cauldron of a year-long tour, always working, forever under the threat of a bullet that could come from anywhere. Quite a few people went through their SAS career without ever being put up by their squadrons for NI duties. Others, who were put up, doing what was essentially a selection within a selection, failed the twice-yearly course.

If any unit tasked was short for a particular op, men would be drafted in from other squadrons. Only when the shit really hit the fan, like in the Gulf War, did TA units like R Squadron finally make it to the coal face. And that was the way the regular guys liked it. A few, but not many, of the TA troopers were as good as the guys in the 22nd SAS, not that the fact would ever be admitted. The nightmare was the odd nutter. There were guys so fixated about their own totally individual skills that they could endanger a whole patrol. The Gulf War had shown that such self-aggrandisement could get people killed.

The Squadron headshed and the green slime had got there before them, so all the stuff that had been put up in Hereford was replicated in Gibraltar. It was still a possible op rather than a definite one, but everyone worked as though it was for real, taking the opportunity particularly to do air drops both on land and into water, using the fast Avon boats to mount a mock assault on a land target.

The portable computer came with them. It had in its programme an almost endless list of scenarios for target buildings. Given the outside dimensions, the positions of the windows and door, along with the height of the roof, it could produce a three-dimensional layout of the probable interior. Using a hall, plasterboard and bits of timber, it was possible to mock up various African structures, then look at their peculiarities. Some were wood, others stone, and then there were mud huts. Many had decorative stone, open brickwork rather than glass in what would have been windows. They tended not to have many doors, so the need might arise to blow open a secondary point of entry. A mud hut wasn't going to need anything approaching a large charge, if it was going to require one at all. Another consideration was the roof. If it was thatched and there were people inside you had to get out, using anything that could start a conflagration was out of the question.

They mocked them up and they trained in them, sometimes in shorts, at other times in full kit with the lights out and wearing night vision goggles. They blew up and pinned the pictures of the known hostages to strips of board, using any shots they could find of black faces to stand in for the guards. At night they sat around and chewed the fat, and either rubbished or agreed with the rumour that another one of their number, now retired and writing under an alias, had got a whole load of wonga for a book idea.

Meanwhile the wires hummed as the powers that would make the decisions communicated. That had been Quentin-Davies's real reason for denying the SO10 detectives the use of his cipher room, though he'd gone out of his way to be generous with other accommodation. To the High Commissioner there could be no question about whether the operation, if it took place, was to be deniable. In all his signals to London he stressed how unreliable the locals were; that not even the top members of the government could be trusted not to reveal an impending attempt to get the hostages out. At the same time, he concurred in the necessity for caution, the need to let the Scotland Yard negotiators have a crack at persuasion.

'One problem does arise, of course, Alan.'

Delane smiled. 'There are several I would say, sir.'

'Would I be right in thinking that the men coming in, always assuming they do, will require some knowledge of the terrain?'

'Ground, sir. In the army we always call it ground.'

'Am I right or wrong, man?' the High Commissioner said tetchily.

'You're right, sir. The SAS will go in without prior knowledge of the ground or enemy strength, but like all soldiers they have a strong preference for knowing what they are about to face.'

'That's what I thought.' Quentin-Davies paused for a moment, then continued on another tack entirely. 'What do you make of this Forwood fellow?'

'He's a Guardsman, sir,' Delane said, crisply. He was trying hard to keep out of his voice the disdain all line regiments have for the Brigade of

Guards. 'Right out of the top drawer, of course. His mother is a Tyrwhitt and the old man made a pile as a bankruptcy receiver. But you had him to dinner when he arrived in Freetown, you know that.'

'Hardly got a chance to talk to the fellow. He tended to confine himself somewhat to the ladies. Doesn't seem very active on the work front, if you exclude playing tennis and fucking everything that moves in a skirt.'

Quentin-Davies enjoyed the shock the uncharacteristic vulgarity produced, which was why he'd put so much emphasis on the expletive.

'That's standard in the SAS, sir. It's always the NCOs who do the donkey work.'

'Not like that in the FO, I can tell you, Delane. In my outfit it's the top dog that gets the most toil.'

Delane was wondering where this conversation was leading. He was also anxious to get away. As the man with the best set of intelligence contacts in Sierra Leone he had a great deal to do in terms of collating the mass of incoming information. Quentin-Davies would want an up-to-date analysis on his desk every morning.

'We'd best have him round again, Alan. Get him to dinner. Tell him he can bring a woman with him, as long as she's respectable and not French. Can't stand the bloody Frogs. They all think they're as clever as Talleyrand, when they're really as stupid as Napoleon.'

CHAPTER TEN

Joe Folani became a soldier by default. Having helped deliver his prisoners he was immediately told to join up. The officer who gave him this command had a pistol in his hand when he said it, and a heavy boot which he used to kick to the ground one of Joe's companions who dared to question his right to order them about. The bullet that he then fired missed the victim by less than an inch. Those watching had no desire to test out the idea that it had been deliberate.

In the confused situation around Lago Junction there were any number of armed men milling about. Some of them, the ones in proper if incomplete sets of fatigues, were real soldiers, but they had no more discipline or desire to fight than the others who'd been hastily conscripted. Joe was told that they were to be commanded by the Minister of Defence himself, but had no way of knowing if that was true. He also learned very quickly that not one of the men he was serving with really wanted to be there.

They were poorly fed, badly equipped, and led by officers who despised them, a hate that their men returned in full measure. Cohesion was maintained through brutality: beatings, occasional maimings, and even the odd shooting. Armed with the standard AK47, each soldier kept the safety catch off. That was caused by two things: the fear that the RUF would appear at any moment and start killing; or that they would be faced with a power-crazed officer who would shoot just to underline his authority. They also hadn't been paid for months, so most of the talk was of what they could steal, the only reason they even thought of moving forward when ordered was the knowledge that a chance of loot lay ahead. And just in case that wasn't enough to tempt them the rumour was flying about that the RUF had run out of ammunition, so beating them into a hasty retreat would be easy.

Joe found himself marching back up the way he had come. He'd been issued with a white headband to distinguish him from the rebels they planned to attack, men who often dressed the same and certainly looked

131

the same as the soldiers he was with. His rifle, which he had now been carrying for hours, felt as though it were made of lead. The youngster was scared stiff. First of all he was in one of two long files marching along either side of the road, exposed to anyone up ahead who cared to open fire. He had no idea what to do if they did, and was sure that with only the bullets in his one magazine, no training and no one around to tell him what to do, he was near useless as a soldier.

Never having been in a battle, the crack of the first bullets, so like the sound of splitting wood, had him looking up at the trees for branches breaking. He froze, adding to his own personal danger, when he saw everyone else running into the bush that lined the road. The first mortar shell, screaming over his head, broke the spell. He threw himself to the ground just as it landed, the crump and blast seeming lethal to him, though it was over a hundred yards away. Then, as he lay there with his hands covering his head, the world went mad. The mortars had found their range and the shells began to rain down on the men hiding in the trees. Explosions followed so closely one after the other that they seemed to merge into one, yet the screams of men wounded and dying could still be heard through the great booming sounds that pressed so hard on his ears. Above his head the trees were being stripped of both leaves and branches as the RUF, supposedly short of ammunition, fired off heavy machine gun rounds by the thousand.

There was a slight lull in the barrage that had Joe on his feet, without his rifle, and scurrying for the road. When he emerged he saw that it was full of running men, all heading away from the battle with not an officer in sight to tell them to stop. Then the first of a new salvo of shells screamed over his head, targeted on that same road and the retreating mob of soldiers and conscripts. Joe saw them land, black dots that dropped among the crowd, the centre of which seemed to rise up as the impact fuse detonated. Bodies flew into the air, not all of them intact, as another salvo followed the first. The great cloud of red dust kicked up by the explosions obscured the carnage for a while. The mortars were moving up the route, keeping pace with the fleeing defence forces, inflicting the same kind of death and destruction as the first salvo. But behind them the dust was settling, some of it blown clear by blast waves, to reveal the numerous writhing and still bodies who'd fallen into the well-set RUF trap.

Joe knew he could never go down that road – his legs wouldn't take him. But he also knew he couldn't stay still. The bush seemed to offer some safety and he dived back the way he had come, tripping over and recovering his weapon, searching desperately for a place to hide. A clump of bushes offered some protection, though habit made him delay for a second to search for snakes before he entered and crouched down. He was shaking from head to foot, sweating all over, and he was having trouble holding on to the contents of his bowels. Every god he knew, Christian, Muslim and tribal passed his lips as he prayed to be spared.

The rustling and the first chanting voices stopped him cold, head spinning this way and that to locate the direction. It couldn't be the army. They had fled, and no one not involved in the battle would have strayed within a mile of the place. It had to be the rebels, following up on their retreating enemy. With a start, Joe realised that he was still wearing his white headband, which he tore off immediately, stuffing it under a thick bit of bush. He heard the voices coming closer and waited for the shout that would alert them to his presence. Fear sharpened what had become frozen wits, and as the voices grew so that the men seemed to be almost on top of him, Joe stood up and walked straight out of the bush, heading back towards the place where he'd come from, Lago Junction.

All around him were the sounds of chanting voices. Every nerve in his body screamed in terror, and he dared not look left or right to see if anyone had reacted to his sudden appearance. He just kept walking forward slowly, rifle aimed ahead, until those moving in the same way caught up with and passed him. He listened carefully to their chants, the slogans they fought by, and quickly joined in, fearful of making some basic mistake. No one paid him any attention, and he felt a sudden sense of deep relief, only tempered with the idea that having been a civil defence youth at dawn he'd joined the army that afternoon. Now, as the light began to fade and the day came to a close, he was a member of the RUF.

Every room in the Cape Sierra Hotel overlooked the beach and the sea, but to Blue and his team it could have overlooked the moon. They were all in his room, sitting on either side of the bed, as an endless stream of paper was passed around. These were all the intelligence reports going back for months, detailing everything that AAR knew about the rebels: their aims, their movements, as well as strengths and weaknesses. The latter was obvious: they could take ground, but faced by the army, always assuming it stirred itself, they could rarely hold it.

They'd read all the aid agency stuff, signals from the government district commanders, as well as the internal AAR reports. John Little, who'd got out and was now in Freetown, had been debriefed, though reading his information made it clear that it was out of date. Mike Layman sat to one side, close to the phone, watching TV with the sound down, ready to respond to any request he might be given. So far he had ordered two dozen beers. Occasionally one of the four would make a comment or add a note to his personal folder, pointing up something he considered important. But the most vital aspect of the job was to immerse themselves in as much information as possible; to know the background so that they could make immediate sense of subsequent events.

'This guy Frank Wintour got out okay as well?' asked Blue.

'Yep. He's shacked up with some friends in a beach house at Hamilton.'

'That far?'

'Half an hour.'

'Can we get him over?'

'Now?'

'If you don't mind.'

Layman picked up the phone right away. Blue had a quick glance at his watch and nodded to Wally Aitken, who leant forward and switched on the bedside radio. They just caught the end of a BBC World Service play before the English language news came on. No one stopped working as the voice detailed the latest list of international troubles, until they got to Sierra Leone.

'Government forces,' the clipped voice began, 'launched a counter offensive in the area around Gbangatok and Mokanje, driving back the rebel forces and clearing the mineral and mining deposit sites of several European companies. A spokesman for the Sierra Leone government said that thanks to their swift action only a minimal amount of damage to facilities had been sustained, and that he expected the various enterprises to be back to full production shortly. And now South Africa ...'

Wally switched it off as Blue asked, 'Mike, how reliable is that?'

'You'd have to source it, Blue. If it's come from a journalist who's gone up to the front it could be true. If it's government-inspired it's not worth bugger all.'

Jamie Padden held up a typewritten piece of paper, one of the numerous aid agency reports. 'These guys are shit in every area, man. Reading this stuff they could have had these RUF guys over at any time. Like, I mean, these so-called rebels are arseholes.'

'The government ain't much better,' said Mike.

'Tell me about it,' Jamie concurred, throwing his eyes upwards.

'Frank Wintour is on his way. He's picking up his assistant Gareth Evans and bringing him as well.'

'Good,' said Blue, with another look at his watch. 'Let's can it for now. I don't know about you guys but I need a shower.'

'You've only just noticed, John?' said Sandy McPherson, adding a grin that made him look even more like a corpse.

'I'll have a talk to this Wintour guy up here, and meet you in the bar downstairs at about eight thirty.'

'Now you're talking, John. This beer is all well and good, but I need a wee dram to line my stomach.'

All three filed out as Blue began to unbutton his shirt. Mike Layman turned the sound up on the TV.

'So what's the night-life like out here, Mike?'

'Pretty good,' he replied, before listing the bars and clubs where there was some action. 'Hookers by the cart load.'

'Clean?' demanded Blue through the open bathroom door.

'The Lebanese guys that run everything are the best there are. Every girl that works their bars is given regular check-ups. Anyway, you can ask some of your old SAS mates. There's a training team here, eight of them.'

'I know. I was talking to a couple of them before they came out.'

'I thought you guys were secretive.'

'If you live in Hereford and you're ex-regiment, you know everything. You just don't tell the other Johns in the town, or anywhere else for that matter.'

The sound of the shower killed further conversation, and by the time Blue emerged shaved and shampooed, Frank Wintour had arrived with Gareth Evans. Blue, wrapped in a towel, questioned them for ten minutes about what they knew and what they'd seen, with the Londoner doing all the talking and the Welshman surreptitiously trying to watch TV.

'Just occurred to me, Frank, that I could have done this on the phone. I'm sorry I dragged you out.'

'Don't matter, mate. I wanted out anyway. Me mate I'm dossing with is a family man: cooked dinner, a bit of the box and off to bed. You got me out, and I intend to get down to Paddy's Bar and make the best of it.'

'If you don't mind,' Gareth said, 'I'll just get a cab back.'

The look on Frank Wintour's face spoke volumes as he replied. 'I don't mind, Gareth, you do what you like, old son.'

'Anyway,' Blue said, 'if you could give me a list of names in the morning of guys we can trust to bring in some good intelligence, I'd be grateful. I need to know as well how to get hold of them.'

'That's the hard part.'

Paddy's Bar was full by the time Blue and Jamie Padden got there, noisy from a lot of people who were well past their first drink. They'd left Sandy and Wally in the more refined Cape Sierra, indulging in their favourite pastime: kissing Rupert arse. Paddy's was half indoors, half open air, sitting on a hillside well above the smells of Freetown. Near the entrance was a long, four-sided oblong bar full of people of every colour, just like the seating area to the right. The music here was muted, but given the flashing lights that swept over the dance floor at the far end, it was pretty noisy down there.

It was a warm night, with a slight breeze, so even if nearly everyone was puffing away there was no smoke in the air, just the smell of the flowers that trailed around the trellis. Spotting the SAS contingent wasn't hard. They occupied what was probably the rowdiest table in the seating area, not too far from the bar, five guys with the same number of women. Paul Hill was there, big glass in hand, which Blue knew would hold his favourite concoction, a White Russian cocktail. It was only when he got closer that Blue spotted Willy Rakiba at a nearby table. He was as pissed as a fart, draped half over a very good-looking floozie, the only guy at a table with half a dozen women.

'What the fuck are you doing here?' shouted Paul Hill as he spotted Blue.

'I could ask you the same thing, mate,' replied Blue, smiling and holding out his hand. But there was a look in his eye too, one that said the answer to the question was not one for public consumption. Paul was off his seat and hugging him in an instant. Over his shoulder, Blue nodded his hellos to Trevor Lipscombe, Kenny Collins and Casey Jones. The nod to Gus

Pollard – Pol Pot – was the only one that didn't have an accompanying smile. 'This is Jamie,' added Blue. 'He's with me.'

That was all the explanation anyone needed. In any Special Forces gathering a sponsored newcomer was treated as one of the gang, until he proved otherwise. It was a very friendly bar.

'Get these men a chair,' Paul shouted, calling over Blue's shoulder for more drinks. 'Just tell the waiter what you want, Jamie, and put it on my tab.'

'Now why did I know I'd run into you here?' said Blue.

'It was here or the local church,' Paul replied, 'and I bet you looked there first.'

Blue just laughed at that. He knew Paul was, like him, a player, the kind of guy who was out every night on the pull when the chance permitted. They'd had a lot of good times together. 'I was drinking in Blairs before I left Hereford. The number of people who couldn't wait to tell me you were out here on a BG job.'

'I bet the bastards were jealous.'

'Green with it. Have you ever done anything like that, Jamie?' The Rhodesian shook his head. 'It's like being on holiday. A run in the morning, beach till noon, then lunch in here, another hour on the sand, then back to base to get togged up for a night out.'

'In other words, Jamie, these jobs are a piece of piss.'

'Blue Harding, you big fuck cunt!'

Blue knew it was Willy before he turned round and stood up. The Fijian had a huge face, pockmarked and grinning. He also had a neck to go with the face, and shoulders four foot wide. Knowing that Willy would want to hug him, Blue tensed himself for a heavy-duty squeeze.

'How are you, you old black bastard?' was all he managed before he ran out of air.

'Willy,' the Fijian yelled in his ear, 'is like he is always. A lot of drinking, a lot of fucking and a helluva lot of fighting, man. Who's the cat with you?'

'Jamie Padden,' said Blue, extricating himself, 'this is Willy Rakiba.'

Willy held out a huge paw, which Jamie took guardedly. 'Pleased to meet you, Willy.'

'That is a strange accent you've got there, man. Where you from?'

The movements were subtle but positive. Every guy there knew what

Willy was like. They knew that tone of voice, as well as the way the brow dropped over his eyes. The most amiable man alive sober, he was a bloody pest and very hard to stop when drunk. And it was well known that he was not fond of South Africans, so they were preparing to grab him if he went for Blue's friend.

'Zimbabwe,' replied Jamie, in a tactful departure from his normal response.

'You ever shoot a black man?'

'Dozens,' Jamie replied, his blue eyes steady. 'How about you?'

The millisecond before Willy laughed was as tense as it could get. But the Fijian threw his head back and let out a great bellow. 'You okay, you white asshole.'

'Nice of you to say so.'

Willy began to shout, and every head in the bar room was listening. 'Trouble is, in this fucking land, man, they don't shoot enough black bastards. I can say that, man, 'cause I'm a black bastard myself.'

'Brown, Willy,' said Blue, loudly.

'Black, brown, what difference it make to you white cunts? But these guys in this town are crap. If they was to leave it to Willy here they would have no war. Me, I'd go out into that fucking bush and shoot every black ass that moved.'

'Take my word for it, Willy,' said Jamie. 'It doesn't work.'

'Willy,' said Paul. 'Keep your voice down. There's a lot of high-powered people in here.'

Even if it had to be voiced, it was the wrong thing to say. Willy became even louder. 'These cunts! You say Willy Rakiba should play it down for these cunts? They're fucking robbers, man, else they couldn't afford the drink in here. Maybe I should get my gun in here and weed out a few of the cunts.'

'Let me know when you're going to do it, Willy,' said Blue. 'Because I don't want to be here.'

'You scared man?'

'Like fuck. But I've seen you on a range. You don't know jack shit about marksmanship principles. Come to think of it, Willy, you can't even spell it. And I mean range!'

That earned him another bear hug. 'You always did like taking the piss, Blue.'

'As much as I like breathing, Willy.'

The Fijian turned his attention back to Jamie Padden. 'You like cunt, asshole?'

'Better than I like arsehole.'

Willy jabbed a thick finger into his own chest. 'Me, I like it there best of all. Get the bitches to scream 'cause Willy he got some big meat. But if you want some cunt man, you come and sit with me. Willy Rakiba always has the best pussy on offer, no contest.' He turned and staggered away, leaving the party at the table a little more subdued than they'd been when Blue had arrived.

Blue downed his first drink in one go, then called to Paul. 'The service round here is shit.'

Paul shouted, but Blue's attention had wandered. A really hot number was approaching the table: not local, her skin olive instead of black. 'Everything okay?' she asked.

Her dark eyes were following Willy, now in the act of sitting down again, still bellowing noisily about how he'd sort out the RUF. Blue's eyes were elsewhere. He liked her voice and the oval-shaped face was stunning, especially the bow shape of the full lips. Now he was trying to pick out the shape of the body underneath what looked like a very expensive dress. The first impression was very, very good, and she was now standing so close he could smell her, a faint perfume mixed with the spicy odour of her skin, and that was an added bonus.

'Leila,' said Paul, 'it's just Willy shouting his mouth off. He's harmless.'

'No he is not, Paul. He put one of my father's doormen in hospital last week.'

Blue didn't miss any of it. This guy was the owner's daughter. The juice was flowing, the first hint of the thrill of a chase. He didn't even have to look round to know how easy it was to get laid here. The place was wall to wall with hookers, but to get hold of this floozie would be a real hit, one above and beyond the call of duty.

'He is paying for it,' Paul replied.

'That doesn't help,' Leila replied.

She tensed suddenly as Blue, still sitting, took hold of her hand. There was no aggression in it; the act was gentle, hard to react to. Her fingertips were cool, the skin smooth. He stood up until he was looking into her eyes, his body close enough to be almost touching. 'Has anybody ever told you how beautiful you are?'

She smiled. 'That is not a question I should answer.'

'You don't have to.'

'Leila,' said Paul, 'this is my good friend Blue Harding.'

'I know you're probably busy now,' Blue said, 'but if I could dance with you later, I'd really like that.'

The pause before she replied seemed endless, but she responded eventually. 'As long as Willy keeps quiet, I'm free to dance now.'

'Good. And if he starts up again, I'll deal with him.'

'Maybe he'll put you in hospital too.'

His arm went round her waist, gently forcing her towards the dance floor. 'He's not good enough.'

'That was the worst fucking chat-up line I've ever heard,' said Trevor Lipscombe, his voice taking on a mocking tone as he copied Blue. 'Has anyone ever told you how beautiful you are?'

'I agree, Trev,' said Paul, with just a hint of disappointment. 'The only trouble is, it works.'

It was getting light by the time Blue got back to the Cape Sierra, the first hint of dawn. For him there were all the smells of an African city. But for Frank Buckhart and Eustace Tumbu out in the bush country, the air was clear and fresh, with enough dew left over from the night to keep the red dust on the road from rising in the usual choking cloud. Buckhart was armed to the teeth, festooned with weapons, ammo and grenades, an M16 rifle across his lap, near-black Raybans reflecting the rising eastern sun. This might just be a reconnaissance, but Fizzin' Frank always came prepared for combat, and so did his men. Beside him Tumbu was in his normal uniform: peaked cap, khaki and all the trimmings, as though they were still in Freetown.

The two Land Rovers raced along, six men crowded into the rear vehicle, with two more Gurkhas up front sharing Buckhart's. Fizzin' Frank had his finger on the map, tracing the route and constantly checking the landmarks. The high ground, from which they would commence their recce, overlooked the potential rebel camp. That had already been identified from maps, and while they were on the wrong side of the hill there was little need for subterfuge. From that point on great care would need to be exercised. Buckhart didn't have enough force to go courting trouble; all he wanted was the kind of confirmed information that might justify bringing in his whole force to effect a rescue. There were a lot of factors to that scenario as well, such as the numbers they might face and the state of the ground approaches, matters about which Tumbu had become, overnight, a bit vague. Reluctantly, but under persistent questioning, Tumbu had revealed that what information he had came from a prisoner he'd personally and privately interrogated. The man asking didn't enquire too much as to the methods Tumbu had used. Frank Buckhart didn't care as long as it was accurate.

Right now, back at his headquarters, Toby Flowers was putting out the orders that would get the Gurkha Guard Force ready to move in on his command. It would involve pulling them off other duties so that they could form a single, powerful attacking force. If what he was getting turned out to be crap, then it wouldn't look too clever for a man who cared a great deal for his reputation. His first act, after making the decision to undertake the recce, was to alert Jack Parkin, an Associated Press journalist, to the potential of the story. The guy was told to stay in his office with a photographer. If Buckhart did get accurate information and made the decision to call in his men, he would radio and arrange a rendezvous. That would give the guy time to get on the scene to witness the rescue. He could then file a words-and-pictures exclusive to his head office in New York. The American knew that in his country celebrity was everything, that a helluva lot of money could be made from book deals, lecture tours and syndicated newspaper articles. But first you had to get your face in the papers and on TV. With this action behind him he could go home to strut his stuff with David Letterman and Jay Leno. That was just what Fizzin' Frank needed to hang up his medals and get out of the war game altogether. He'd been in it too long, from West Point through Vietnam, Central and South America, to here. Frank Buckhart was getting old and his wife wanted to settle down. It was time to quit.

They still had two miles to go to their destination, and Buckhart was mentally composing the first chapter of his autobiography when the road exploded in front of them. It could only be a prepared ambush, because the road behind went up as well, cutting the lead vehicle off from support. He opened up immediately and so did the Gurkha beside the driver. They had been covering opposite sides of the road, which was standard drill.

The job, for them as well as the men behind, was to lay down rapid fire on the most likely enemy positions. The driver was good, one of Buckhart's most accomplished Gurkhas. He slewed the Land Rover to the right before bringing it back round on to a straight path, heading into a huge dust cloud for what he hoped was a gap between the trees and the hole that had opened up before them. The right-hand wheel dropped sickeningly within seconds, but the driver gunned the engine hard. The front bumper and the steel grill above it slammed into solid earth, catapulting the occupants forward. It seemed, for a second, as though the Land Rover was going to turn over, but it stuck halfway.

'Ambush left, debus right,' Buckhart shouted, as the first bullets struck the Land Rover's metal skin.

Buckhart and his men had trained for this. Added to that they were soldiers in action on a daily basis, at the peak of their alertness. They went out the downside of the Land Rover at speed, dropping into the crater that the explosion had created, using the hollow as cover. Tumbu was slower and had to be dragged clear as bullets continued to ping off the metal of the vehicle's body. Buckhart pushed men into place left and right to cover the arcs of fire that would be required.

The first task was to get back inside the vehicle to see if the radio was functioning. He had set the frequency to Jack Parkin's office, and there was no time to go through a re-tuning process to get on to a military net. He also had to avoid the jargon that every one of his own men would understand. He gave the agreed callsign and was relieved to hear the journalist respond.

'Jack. We're in the shit. Get on to Toby Flowers at my HQ and tell him we are under heavy fire on the Matiri road about a mile out from Magbenta village. I want him on the net to my support Land Rover to tell them we are still operational. He has to get the chopper and what firepower he has out here, now! Have you got that?'

'I'm on the phone now, Frank. Any chance of an interview under fire?'

'Christ Jack, give me a break.'

Buckhart dropped back out of the vehicle. He could hear plenty of gunfire. It wasn't coming their way, but being aimed at the group from the vehicle who had been cut off behind them. They, at this point, would have to fend for themselves. Buckhart's job was to get his men out of this hole and into cover to a point where he could see, so as to make a quick appreciation of just how much trouble they were in. Then and only then could he contemplate supporting the other group. But while he was thinking about that, he was also thinking that Tumbu had been well turned over by the guy he'd tortured. Right now, there was no point in saying so.

'Going north,' he called, tapping his men on the shoulder and aiming in that direction with his hand. 'Keep spaced out. And soon as you hit good cover go to ground. Go!'

The side of the crater wasn't too steep, and the Land Rover provided good cover for the bug-out until they were on an even surface. Still the fire stayed concentrated on the men from the second vehicle, so Frank's group made the trees without encountering opposition. Buckhart checked them into position, pushing Tumbu behind them, at the same time pressing a pistol into his hand. He then rattled off a quick ammunition and casualty check, gratified to find that no one was injured and that they still had plenty of firepower at their disposal.

Mentally he tried to envisage what was happening behind that lingering dust cloud. Judging by the fire, his Gurkhas were obviously still a unit, returning fire sparingly in the face of a furious fusillade from their less disciplined opponents. They would stay still and hold their defensive position if they could, pulling back only under pressure, expecting any survivors from the front Land Rover to move in and support them, possibly even putting in a flanking counter attack. The problem was, so would their enemy. They might well have men placed just to counter such a move.

Buckhart waited for a lull in the firing before issuing a fire control order to his group, who then returned fire. This would tell the rest of his men that they were still a unit. He then looked at the Fabalon-coated map that showed their destination. That was the one place, the one direction that would surprise their enemies. There might be opposition, but it could be a lot less than they might face trying to join up, and once clear they could work round in a wide arc to get out of trouble. For a moment he contemplated getting back to the Land Rover, and sending a message through Parkin for his support party to withdraw. But that idea was killed by the notion that he needed them to stay as long as possible to occupy the available enemy forces, thus allowing him to get clear. As to putting them in danger, they were soldiers, facing an equal risk to him and his men. He also needed to get Tumbu out and back to safety. They were Gurkhas, trained by the British Army and good at their job! They would do all that they could. Then, when their situation began to look untenable, they would withdraw in good order.

CHAPTER ELEVEN

Toby Flowers moved fast, but he had a serious problem. His signals to the men spread out on their various tasks had put them on alert for a possible move to concentrate for a special operation, but that was all. There was no way he could justify doing any more until Frank Buckhart radioed in that he had a positive fix on the hostages. Flowers did have a helicopter full of fuel and a location that he should be able to spot from the air about twenty minutes' flight time away, but no more than the men of his HQ section with which to mount an attack. These tended to be the least able soldiers in any unit, what in his old regiment had been labelled the REMFs: rear echelon motherfuckers. There was no way that would be enough, so he put out a flash radio message to get a wheel-bound rescue party on the road at once, with a rendezvous map reference where he could pick them up. Then it was a scramble for kit, weapons and the kind of ammo they would need before they could take off. That meant a time on target of at least thirty-five minutes.

Buckhart had figured that out for himself. He knew the situation didn't look rosy, but he'd been there before, caught in the old Vietnamese City of Hue during the Tet offensive. It had been buildings there, it was bush here, but the job was the same. Apart from dragging him about to keep him from getting shot he'd paid little attention to Tumbu, but in the brief interlude before they would move he decided to check him out. He was pleased by the pistol in his hand, but amazed to see the colonel still wearing his peaked hat. He was tempted to ask how the fuck he'd managed to keep it on when a burst of machine gunfire ripped through the trees to his left.

'Move!'

The corporal knew to go first, a darting run that took him no more than three to five yards before he crouched down to give covering fire to the man coming after him. Buckhart and Tumbu were next, going together, with the mercenary on the security chief's left, the direction from which the fire was most likely to come. The other pair of Gurkhas brought up the

145

rear. The manoeuvre was repeated twice before they ran into trouble, fire so heavy that Buckhart knew his decision on direction hadn't worked out. If anything, they were up against more rebels heading west than they would have faced falling back east.

They immediately returned fire, moving into position to form a fire base, but they lacked the weaponry to make any impression. The only option was to use fire and manoeuvre to break contact. All they had in their favour was the primary growth bush that gave them cover from view, though not cover from fire. But they were harried, under almost continuous gunfire, and that was coming from more than one direction. Breaking contact under fire was, as always, difficult to control, and after a few bounds there were gaps. After a few minutes Buckhart knew that he and Tumbu were totally separated from his men.

Buckhart saw a dip in the ground that would give him cover from both view and fire. He shouted to Tumbu to break left, virtually dragging the African with him when he didn't react with sufficient speed. The sun, high enough in the trees now to penetrate through the top cover to the ground, threw long shadows, but they told Frank Buckhart where he was going in a general sense. What was worrying was the lack of fire from what had been his support group. He hoped it was just that they were no longer under any immediate threat and had decided that it was paramount to conserve ammo. Hopefully they'd managed to conduct a fighting withdrawal, but if it was to be a 'bad day at Black Rock', then they'd probably been overrun.

If it came to moving in the jungle he had a lot of faith in the Gurkhas. Small, dark-skinned and natural trackers, they were well suited to the ground. He, on the other hand, was big, and compared to them very clumsy in such an environment. For him, moving silently had to be set against moving quickly enough to stay ahead of his pursuit, and it was that combination that was his undoing. It was only a brief flash of light combined with some movement that told him the rebels were ahead of him as well as behind, but that was enough. A quick check showed that he had two grenades and just two magazines for his M16 – fifty-eight rounds.

He turned to the sweating African to tell him the news, amazed yet again that the bastard had still managed to keep on his hat. Panting heavily from his exertions, his words came out in short, sharp bursts. 'Go left fifty metres. Then turn east again. I'm moving straight on and opening fire. Take cover until you hear the grenades. Then run like fuck. Don't worry about cover, just keep fucking running! I'll take on the threat. If I'm lucky I'll blast my way through. All their firepower should be concentrated on me. That should give you a chance.'

Tumbu didn't shake his hand or thank him, for which Buckhart was grateful. That kind of shit only happens in the movies. When you're actually under fire, excessive speech is a luxury, brevity is the only language. He watched as the vegetation consumed the khaki-clad colonel. As soon as he saw him disappear he threw the first of his grenades. When the second one exploded he was on his feet and running, spraying short bursts to right and left. He snapped off the empty magazine and replaced it without slowing, as he entered a clearing. Experience told him to stay close to the trees, in the shadow thrown by the sun, but to keep moving as fast as his feet would allow. He had registered the lack of return fire, seeing that as a result of his own efforts with the M16. That boosted his confidence, as well as the fact that he still had a whole magazine full of ammo.

Frank Buckhart was convinced he was going to get clear just as the burst of machine gunfire cut through his lower legs. He started to try and crawl as soon as he hit the grass, making for the back of a tree, aware only of a numbing sensation below his waist. His right hand spun round pulling the trigger, laying down the last of what he had at the direction of fire. As the rifle clicked on empty he threw it clear and dragged out his pistol, rolling towards a chance of cover. The ground around him erupted in a second sustained burst of fire. He took a wound in the right shoulder that paralysed his upper arm and another in the leg. The third, in the lower stomach, made crawling impossible. The last thing he could do was to blow his own brains out, but that was thwarted by a boot that kicked his good hand as it reached out for the pistol he had dropped. Spun on to his back, he found himself looking up into a sea of black faces.

He was lifted, bodily, by powerful hands and carried at a run, as if in triumph, on the shoulders of his captors. The pain from his wounds shot through his body with every jarring movement. He fought hard against the desire to close his eyes, to let unconsciousness claim him, concentrating on the flashes of sunlight mixed with shade that marked his route through the deepening bush. The increase in noise registered, the sound of excited humanity in great numbers. He was half-lowered to face the mob, held upright so that his useless legs didn't have to support his body weight. His eyes again registered a sea of black faces, all animated, all moving. But there was an area of white too. The effort to focus was difficult, what he saw was an impression rather than absolute identification: a row of white faces in drab beige shirts and trousers, stationary, heads bent as if in prayer, not looking at the scene before them. The knowledge that he'd been close to the captured nuns registered just as he was flung on to his back, what sunlight there was blanked out by the crowd that surged to surround him.

Buckhart saw the point of the big knife and knew he was a dead man. He felt the hands that ripped at his shirt to expose his chest to the hovering knife. The blade went in just under his rib cage, slicing up and round his heart, cutting, as it went, into the great veins around the organ. He still had sight in his eyes when they lifted it out, a trail of uncut viscera following, to be sliced at by a dozen bayonets. But he had no vision to see them begin to eat it, because by that time he was dead.

The hacking at the cadaver took on the nature of a blood orgy. The legs and arms, once severed, were waved about like triumphal symbols. The severed head was raised on a spear. The fighters cheered to the news that it would be embalmed and sent round the country so that all should know that white men died easily, and that their spirits could be denied the chance to haunt their killers. What villagers they'd rounded up from nearby Magbenta showed less enthusiasm, until they were threatened into compliance. Only the nuns stayed silent, never once ceasing their prayers.

Minutes later they were dragged away into the deeper bush. The thud of distant rotor blades sent everyone in the small clearing scurrying away, the rebels to their secret trails, the villagers they'd tried to recruit back to their mud huts. By the time the noise of the helicopter was loud enough to drown out any other sound, the area was, apart from the dismembered remains of Frank Buckhart, empty.

Flowers flew well to the south of the wrecked Land Rover, coming in on the second vehicle in a wide arc. He had his binos out, searching the bush for any sign of rebels, sure they would be gone as soon as the sound of the helicopter became apparent. They never stood to fight against an air attack. A heavy machine gun mounted in the doorway always turned such a bird into a truly lethal weapon. A tap on his shoulder made him switch to the second Land Rover, to the knot of eight Gurkhas standing up and waving, a sure sign that whatever attack they had been under had been suspended.

The first job was to get his support element on to ground, with enough ammo to re-equip the men already there. When they had reported he checked the comms between ground and air, then issued the orders for a sweep. Flowers was back up in the air in ten minutes to provide cover and advance warning of any threat, hovering forward slowly to keep just ahead of his ground troops. It was twenty minutes before he saw them signal that they had found something, and he felt his heart sink as they confirmed by radio that, judging by the tattered remains of the insignia on the ripped uniform, it was Buckhart's body.

Flowers put down right away, doing what, in any other combat scenario would have counted as bad tactics. Normally the first priority was to secure the area. Then and only then could he put the chopper down in an arc that had an all round defensive perimeter deep enough for security. But the RUF were shoot-and-scoot merchants, never hanging around to hold ground, more concerned to take captives and loot, then leg it. By the time his wheels touched the grass, one of his men had found Tumbu's hat.

'Some of the locals from Magbenta managed to avoid becoming RUF recruits. When they heard the heli they went home instead of running into the bush, so we were able to interrogate them and find out what the bastards did to him. They cut out his heart when he was still alive and ate it.'

'Juju,' said Jack Parkin, who knew Africa well enough to know why it had happened. 'They think it gives them the juice of the man they've killed.'

'And they cut off the head, arms and legs so the ghost of the dead can't threaten them. The limbs they left behind, but they took his head with them.' Flowers's voice faltered slightly then. Even recounting a tale he'd already told several times, he was not immune to the horror of what had occurred. When the news got out to the expat community it was going to make quite a few people wonder if they wanted to stay in such a country. 'The plan is to embalm it and parade it round the country.'

'Holy shit!'

Flowers held up a finger and thumb, a millimetre gap between them. 'And he was that close, Jack. The nuns were in that clearing too, that was confirmed. If he'd succeeded in getting them out you would have got a huge story.'

Flowers had searched, looking for the route the rebels had taken, in the slight hope that he might accomplish what his boss had set out to do. But the RUF were adept at melting into their background. Even in a helicopter he could only see so much, and he lacked the troop strength for the kind of sweep that might have flushed them out from cover.

'I'm sorry, Toby,' Parkin replied, sadly, 'I really am. And let me tell you, Frank was more than just good copy. He was also a friend of mine.'

'I know. But he'll get his wish, won't he? He'll make all the papers in the US. He'll be a big story for a day or two. The man from *Soldier of Fortune* who finally ran out of luck. But that's it. There'll be no book, no lecture tour, and no Schwarzenegger movie of Fizzin' Frank the hero.'

'No.' Jack Parkin leant forward and patted him on the shoulder. 'What now?'

'Now,' said Toby Flowers, standing up, 'I'm going to go out and get totally pissed. Then tomorrow I'm going to see Strasser and tell him if he doesn't give our guys the go-ahead to clobber the RUF and get Frank's head back, they will probably mutiny.'

'Why did those little brown bastards love him so much?'

'Because he liked them and cared for them, Jack. And Frank was so much larger than life, with his pistols and his cigars and his give-em-hell attitude. They like us Brits, and everything to do with the way they served us in the past.'

'Even the way your nice government shat on them?'

'No. But they know we soldiers still respect them and that counts for a lot. But Frank was very different to us. And the bottom line, Jack, for them and for me, is that he was just great fun to soldier with.'

With so many ad hoc recruits, no one bothered to question Joe Folani. Having slept under the stars, he'd managed to cadge a bit of mealie for breakfast from a group of men round a campfire. It seemed they just accepted him as a rebel, leaving him to wander freely around the area, trying to find a face he recognised. His feet, without any mental guidance, took him back towards his own area, which he reached late in the afternoon.

Joe was only made aware of his folly when someone who looked and behaved like an officer apprehended him. He had staring eyes and an angry face, carried a pistol in his hand, not a rifle, and wore a proper uniform with rank badges. His elevated status was soon confirmed when the mad-eyed man identified himself as Captain Dennis. Joe, having given his name, was immediately questioned at length, in a way that taxed all his ingenuity. The tale he produced, of being a volunteer who'd joined as soon as the RUF had overrun the area, sounded totally false in his own ears, and was clearly disbelieved by this captain.

'This?' he demanded, grabbing the AK47 out of the youngster's hands.

'A soldier dropped it as he ran away. I picked it up.'

'Use it!' Dennis ordered, his finger pointing to a termite mound. 'Aim at that.'

Too scared to realise the trap he was walking into, Joe took the rifle back, raised it, slipped the safety catch, then put a single round into the base of the mound. When he looked back at Captain Dennis, he saw in his scary eyes the deep suspicion he'd aroused. The rifle was taken out of his hands again.

'Where you learn to do that, boy?'

'My father taught me,' said Joe quickly.

'And where is this father?'

'The soldiers murdered him, because he swore at them about being bootlickers to Strasser.'

The tears were spontaneous, and caused by fear, not anguished emotion. Thankfully for Joe, Captain Dennis couldn't tell the difference. He went from angry interrogation to complete sympathy in a second, and put a reassuring hand on the youngster's shoulder.

'Lots have died, and still more must. But you will be revenged, boy. You're true RUF now, a suffering son of Sierra Leone. When we take Freetown all the murderers will be brought to justice. Maybe you will be able to cut out the heart of the men who killed your father. But now you with Captain Dennis, the best commando in the true army of the nation.'

Joe kept his head bowed as Dennis lectured him, not wishing to meet the man's eyes lest his own betray him, a hard task since what he had to listen to was a long lecture. Finally the captain patted him again, finishing with words that did little to reassure Joe. 'You come with me now. The fiends in the government are telling lies to the people, aided by the imperialists. They say we are beaten and all round the world they are heard.'

The arm that gently pushed Joe ahead left little room for protest. His mind was too taken up with fear to hear fully the words that soon became a tirade against everyone who told lies. This included the English and their stupid radio station, the criminals in Freetown, the businessmen who raped the nation of its treasure and the peasants too stupid to rise up and drive them out. Dennis was working himself up into a complete lather, which reached its peak just as they came to the very crossroads where, the previous morning, he had been a civil defence guard.

The shock of that froze him, but he nearly shat himself when he saw three of the men he'd escorted to Lago the day before standing, rifles raised, holding back a new batch of refugees who had come to mill around the crossroads church. Dennis, still shouting, though now at the assembled refugees, cut off his view of them, which allowed Joe to take several paces backwards and stay out of their line of sight. The gathering gloom helped, the rays of the dying sun cut off by the treetops, creating pools of near-darkness.

Dennis went forward and embarked on a long harangue about the revolution and how cowardly these people were. He seemed oblivious to the fact that they were, in the main, women and children. The spit flew from his mouth with such venom that it covered the terrified people in the front of the crowd. Behind him, at each screaming crescendo, his men would chant in his support, throwing up their rifles in a wave of emotion. Occasionally one of the weapons would go off, adding to the air of increasing tension. Joe, who'd got behind a tree, had never heard one man speak so much. Dennis showed no sign of breathlessness or fatigue. He was still ranting, even more passionately than he had at the beginning, when the sun finally went down, leaving the whole area bathed in the light from the torches his men had lit.

They had started to dance as well as chant, stopping only to take a quick draw on the endless supply of joints that were being passed around. The air was thick with the odour of the burning leaf, that slightly sweet smell, intoxicating enough without the added thrill given to the scene by the cloud of dust thrown up by shuffling feet. When Dennis turned, Joe saw his eyes illuminated by torchlight. He looked totally crazy, his face muscles distorted as he screamed an order to his men.

They stopped dancing and moved forward, those with guns jabbing at the crowd, ordering them back into the church building. Men around Joe started to move, forcing him to do likewise, his main concern the locality of those three prisoners he'd handed over to Captain Gilbert. There was little room inside, and it was already crowded with those who kept out the people forced to listen to Dennis's lecture. But a sharp bayonet is a powerful incentive, and with shouts and the occasional thrust of a rifle butt they were forced, wailing and screeching, inside.

The windows were made up of decorative, open concrete blocks, the kind that in Europe were used to build fancy garden walls. Joe could see the faces pressed against them, the pressure of the crowd behind them obvious by the way their cheeks were distorted. Dennis was ranting again, rushing up and down before the windows telling those inside how they had betrayed Sierra Leone. They were traitors to their country and the good people who had fought for their liberation. Safe behind the walls, he was met with pleading protests of innocence. This seemed to inflame him even more, and he began to lash out with the butt of his pistol at those by the window, poor victims made scapegoats for his anger. Sparks flew where he hit the concrete, blood where he made contact with flesh. He screamed for a torch, and when it was handed to him he jabbed that at the unprotected faces. Then he stepped back, and pulling back with his shoulder, he threw his torch on to the thatched roof. His next order had the rest of the torches following, a dozen flaming blobs that lodged in the reeds.

There was only smoke at first, white wisps that drifted up from the point of contact. But that didn't last long. The first red glow appeared, spreading quickly from the epicentre to ignite a whole area of thatch, until it reached out to combine with another fire. In ten minutes the whole roof was ablaze. Dennis's men had barred the door, but once the smoke started to spread that didn't hold. It burst open and a crowd spilt out, to be greeted by a hail of bullets. Against the concrete vents people were dying as those too far from the door, cut off by the masses trying to escape, sought air. Joe could see them, the breath squeezed from their lungs, eyes open and pleading, tongues protruding and being bitten in extremis. He half imagined, over the sounds of the screams, the roar of the fire and the crack of the rifle shots, that he could hear their bones breaking.

The roof was now an inferno, great red and orange flames leaping up into the night sky. The beams that held it up were partly exposed, well alight, the reeds they'd held dropping down on to the poor victims below, burning their exposed flesh. The billowing smoke was choking people at the same time as the darting flames were scorching them, the single means of relief that one doorway now crowded with writhing, wounded bodies. But they climbed over even them, people whose sparse clothing was flaming next to melting skin, the air full of the smell of burning flesh. There were bodies inside totally consumed, those who had died from asphyxiation, lying in piles of burning rushes which had reached the temperature necessary to destroy flesh. And still Dennis rushed up and down screaming abuse and firing off his pistol. His men had stopped shooting, and were now stabbing with bayonets, cutting with pangas, almost overwhelmed by the terrified crowd. Nothing could hold them back, their sheer numbers creating escape routes where they came face to face with those less enamoured of the idea of mass murder. Joe was one of them, and faced with the spectacle of a woman whose hair was on fire, with a baby in her arms that looked dead, he could only step aside to let her pass.

The carnage continued in front of the church hall. Dennis now had a lump of wood in his hand and was rushing around swinging it wildly, trying to dash out the brains of those who had fallen to the ground, wounded or just exhausted. The roof caved in with a mighty crack, a great roar, and a sudden spurt of red flames and orange sparks. There were still people alive in there, screaming, a cacophony of sound that filled Joe's ears. And still the bayonets jabbed and the pangas swung. Dennis executed a great sweep with his makeshift club and sent human brains spurting out to cover the blood-soaked ground.

How did these people get through that cordon of murder? Joe didn't know, but somehow they did. Not one made it without a wound or a mass of burns, leaving a sickly smell of torched skin in their wake. In the clearing, some of Dennis's men had started to chop up the bodies, throwing the parts back into the still raging fire, whooping with joy as they drank some of the spurting blood. He could see his trio of ex-prisoners, each one taking a savage delight in the task of destruction.

Joe had a vision of himself joining the victims. Those men would be bound to recognise him in daylight. They would point the finger, leaving him at the mercy of the madman, Captain Dennis. He turned and ran, yelling as though he was pursuing some of the escapees, but really looking desperately for somewhere he could hide.

Ray Kavanagh was in his element, setting up communications not just for the Charter Security team but for Eddie Welford and SO10 as well. The Scotland Yard guys had been allocated two spacious rooms for their own use in the British High Commission compound. The engineer from Anglo-African Rutile, Chendor Deen, was to stay at the AAR team's villa and travel up every morning. Blue made a point of asking if he could tag along, and so keep himself abreast of developments. The two detectives were pleased with the arrangement since it gave them somebody to communicate with other than the boring fart from the RUF.

They'd got through to him on the agreed frequency, knowing that the first thing Chendor Deen would have to listen to was a long tirade against colonial injustice, present-day corruption and the purity as well as the aims of the RUF. Alimany Bakaar was an expert. He could have bored for West Africa as an Olympic sport, never mind just the rebels. Having introduced himself, Deen, with Welford and Cannon behind him, had a two-hour lecture without interruption. If they didn't know the history of Sierra Leone before they started they could have done a degree in it towards the end. To follow that they had to listen to the programme of an organisation which, they were informed in grandiose terms, had been created by the collective will of the pure-hearted sons and daughters of the country. All foreign forces must be removed from the sacred soil of Sierra Leone. The present rulers must be tried and condemned for their crimes. Every diamond mine, rutile deposit, oil well and bauxite quarry would be handed over to the people, to be worked by them so that the profits could go to Sierra Leonians. Elections, fair and free should be held, and a government of national unity formed. It all sounded great, until you examined it and realised it was the same platitudes every group in Africa had used to gain power. They never implemented it once they were in.

Deen finally got to speak, his voice deep and clear with a strong element of reassurance that had Welford, who'd coached him, nodding in approval. 'As you know, sir, I too am a native of our troubled land. I am here to talk to you, as the leading spokesman for the RUF, about the people you have in your care. Both those who were born here and those who have come from abroad.'

Blue Harding sat listening and smiling, hearing Welford's instructions to Deen. The training these SO10 guys received was great. They knew just how to play their contacts. Flattery was essential, while the word 'hostage' was a real no-no. Using that would only put the RUF's backs up. Welford's voice was like oil, even with Deen, without being in any way slippery, as he sought to impart tone as well as content. He knew this trio would talk as long as Bakaar if they had to, chipping away at his resolve. They would take each demand and examine it, looking for chinks in the RUF armour. Deen would constantly remind them that world opinion, stupid as it might be, could not tell the difference between innocent civilians under restraint and people held by the RUF for their own protection.

Blue made a sign to Cannon, requesting to use the phone, then shut the door between the two rooms. He needed to arrange for the helicopter to be ready to fly them out to Gbangatok, a town with a grass strip where they knew the army was in control. Sergei, when he got hold of him, sounded like something out of a Bond film, so heavy was his Russian accent.

'We'll lift off at thirteen hundred hours, a party of five,' Blue said.

'You have heard the news?'

'What's that?'

'The RUF ambushed and killed that Amerikanski who commands the Gurkhas.'

'Hold on while I write that down,' said Blue, telling Sergei to continue when he had. The news of the dismemberment sent a chill through his whole body, and he knew that would be the same for every expat in Sierra Leone when they heard it.

'The security chief was with him. Tumbu. A big cheese. He is missing.'

'Another hostage?'

'No, I don't think so. Him they will not give back. He's going to get some of what he hands out, I think. A very slow death.'

Blue listened to the rest of the story, then confirmed the arrangements and put down the phone. He then slipped quietly into the comms room and signalled to Cannon. The inspector, who was listening to both sides of the conversation and making notes, turned down the volume as Blue passed him the note. While he read it, Blue listened to the voice on the radio. Even at a low pitch it was bitter in complaint, denying the report on

156

the BBC World Service that rebel forces had been pushed back from the Mokanje mine sites. Having read the note, Cannon, his face pale, shoved it in front of Welford, still busy coaching Deen. The older man just read it and nodded, not missing a single beat as he continued to give soft instructions to the African engineer, stopping as Bakaar gave him a chance to respond.

'I am sure that you are right when you say that they will not be dislodged so easily,' Deen intoned. 'You have caused us to be admired around the world, sir, for the discipline and bravery of your fighting men. People who have seen many bad things in Africa commend the RUF. But that still creates a problem of credibility. You can tell them that the people you are helping are safer with you, that the army are the ones who kill and maim, but the government denies this. And those who have sympathy with your aims will find it hard to know what to believe. A quick passage to safety of the people you rescued will reassure them, and prove that their good opinion of our country and our people is justified.'

'Who do you believe, him or the BBC?' whispered Blue.

'I thought you lot were going out there to find out,' Cannon replied.

'We are.'

'Then you can tell me the truth when you get back.'

'Have a nice day,' said Blue.

Cannon pulled a face as Blue shut the door behind him.

Sergei liked to scare people, that was obvious. Even though the passenger-carrying twin-jet Hip helicopter was not designed for aerobatics, he took off as though Freetown airport were under mortar attack. Then, throughout the hour-long trip, he swooped low at every opportunity, buzzing vehicles on the road as well as innocent farmers going about their business. That was at the start, flying over a zone of relative security close to the capital, but further inland there were few cars and not much active agriculture. In fact those fields with any hint of cultivation looked deserted and untended. The only things on the roads were military checkpoints. He eased off when he realised his antics were having no effect on his passengers. The four strangers, all ex-military, were used to it, and so was Frank Wintour, judging by the way he immediately went to sleep. Blue thought it a good idea to find out if the Russian was actually mad or just winding them up, so he began a long, loud conversation over the sound of the rotor blades.

Tall, black-haired and with a dense chin growth, Sergei was from Tula, south of Moscow, and was proud of being an Afghan veteran. Blue was treated to a lecture on what a tough war that had been. He kept to himself the information that, having been there himself, in daily contact with the Mujahedin, he probably knew more than Sergei about the dirty nature of that particular war. The Russian pilot had, by his own estimation, been shrewd, this underlined by much tapping of his own forehead. He'd got out as soon as he could after the wall came down in Berlin. Russia was bad, and that meant everything: the government, the army command, the mafias, the pay, the food and the weather. As to his sanity, that was easily established. Blue invited him to go straight on to the Plant site, a request met by a wide grin and another bit of head tapping.

'Sergei not crazy, English!' Then the Russian grinned, and Blue had the distinct impression that he was playing a part, the character he'd adopted which owed a lot to James Bond movies he'd seen. The crazy-man image was just a front, which Sergei then proved by flying the twin-engined Hip in a manner that would have done credit to Rolls Royce chauffeur.

Gbangatok airport was just a grass strip to the north of the town, a utility field for the various mining interests, and a collection point for all the aid agencies. Called the seat of the regional government, the town wasn't much better. Standing at the head of a long, stagnant creek, it comprised a collection of raddled buildings every one of which needed at least a repaint. But it had a school, an empty police barracks, a church and a mosque, the minaret of which was the highest point of observation. The AAR agent's office, right next door to what was laughingly called the hotel, had been appraised of their coming, and had a Land Rover ready for their use. There were a few army people about, including a couple of junior officers, but none of them knew anything, except that Blue's notion of driving towards AAR's Plant site was likely to be dangerous. No one had any idea of the rebels' location, which made Blue certain that whatever the government said, it was unlikely they had been defeated.

Frank Wintour took a trip round the town, trying to find his ex-workers, while Sandy and Wally visited the aid agency offices, questioning without much joy some refugees just in from up-country. All they found out

158

collectively added little to what they already knew, which left Blue with the difficult choice of what to do next.

He had his map on the bonnet of the Land Rover and was pointing to a village halfway to their destination when the jets came over. Alpha ground attack planes, they were already low but still descending. Blue jumped up on to the bonnet in time to see the jets continue their descent to the point where they released rockets at a target that would be a couple of miles further on. The calculation he made was not very scientific but he passed it on to the others anyway, in his own personal impression, very close to Rupert-speak, of Michael Caine in *Zulu*.

'I say, old boy, I think I know where the bloody rebels are.'

CHAPTER TWELVE

It had been a long and very uncomfortable night for Geoff Hinchcliffe and Mary Kline. Forced out of the houses in Kpanguma, they'd had to watch as the properties were systematically looted. The rebels took everything: curtains, blinds, even the copper piping and electrical wiring. Everything loose that they didn't want had been piled high to make a fire, which blazed away giving an ethereal tinge to the scene. But that didn't last, and a great deal of time was spent in darkness, the first hint of dawn bringing the welcome relief of being able to see what dangers might threaten them. The only useful thing they could do, now that it was light, was comfort the bereaved and at least arrange the bodies so that they had a bit of dignity in death.

Their captors were initially too busy looting to observe this, but as that eased off they were threatened once more and herded back to sit in a disorganised group on the ground. That lasted till Jalloh arrived, the respect he commanded obvious from the moment of his appearance. Thin, with brown skin rather than black, he was a north country Muslim, dressed like a member of the Arab Legion in khaki drill uniform topped by one of those Yasser Arafat red and white headpieces that looked set to fall off. Jalloh paced up and down in front of the assembled refugees, trying to make eye contact with each one, determined to exert a personal dominance. He failed with the two Europeans, who returned his baleful stare with one of bland indifference, a fact that clearly annoyed him. Finally he stopped his pacing and introduced himself, adding the title 'CO' to his name. That was followed with a benediction to Allah.

'Those of you who have fear need not worry. You are now safe in the hands of the Revolutionary United Front. We have no wish to harm civilians.' If he was worried that his audience was unconvinced, it didn't show. 'It is not your fault that you cannot believe that. The people we are fighting, the criminals in the government, have fed you many lies. But that will end soon. We await orders to attack Freetown and liberate our country. The first thing we will do is kill Strasser and his cronies, so setting an example to all those greedy officers of all ranks that stealing the treasures of the nation is punishable by a certain and painful death.'

He took up a position in front of Mary and Geoff, throwing out his arm and raising his voice. 'These people have robbed you too, and they tell as many lies as Strasser does. They will say to you that you are ignorant and stupid, that the only people who can take out of the ground the things that would make us rich have white skin.' The arms went out and the head went back, very much like a Southern Baptist preacher. There was a hint of that in the voice as well, a wheedling quality intended to prove that the speaker had at one time been as foolish and ignorant as his audience. 'How can you know any different, without schooling or ever having been more than a few miles from your own tribal village? But I, Jalloh, I have been to places you can only dream of. I have been to a country that was once like ours, under the heels of white men and their lackeys, a country that has now thrown off that heavy yoke so that the people rule themselves. I, Jalloh, have been to Libya!'

'Lucky you,' said Geoff softly.

Jalloh knew he had spoken, but had not heard what he'd said. There was a slight pause while he weighed up the need to respond, but obviously he decided his message was more important because he continued to harangue them. It was the same stuff everyone had heard for years: the crime of exploitation and expropriation, the thieves black-skinned as well as white. The picture he painted of Libya was close to paradise, a Utopia where all the dreams of the downtrodden could be realised. He talked of the power of the RUF and how the government could not prevail against them, quoting as evidence a comprehensive knowledge of what had been happening well ahead of the rebel advance.

The refugees showed more interest in this than in his politics. It was something close to their experience. Mary and Geoff watched them react to Jalloh's words, the nods and shakes that first confirmed what he said, quickly followed with stunned disbelief that it could be true. The 'CO' outlined the whole defence set-up in the area, naming those who were in the civil defence units as well as where they had been deployed. He knew the strengths and weaknesses of the army too. 'That is why we will win, brothers. The good people of Sierra Leone know that they are safe with us.'

'Are they safe?' argued Mary Kline firmly, her hand pointing towards the line of dead bodies. Her remark immediately set off a degree of sobbing and murmuring in the crowd.

Jalloh blinked, then shrugged. 'Those who oppose us make themselves our enemies.'

'Those men did not oppose you.'

His smile was infuriating in its superiority. 'They must have done so or they would not have been killed. The RUF does not harm the ordinary people, only the agents of the Freetown criminals.'

'So your men don't commit rape on innocent girls?'

'Never!'

'Bollocks!' said Geoff. Jalloh didn't understand the word, but he did the sentiment. 'Two of your men raped a couple of girls right here.'

'No!'

'It was witnessed,' said Mary. 'The victims are right in front of you. I will not shame them by pointing them out, but you can ask your own people, and they will tell you that it is true.'

He didn't have to ask. What Mary had been saying was repeated throughout the crowd, both in English and the local dialects, and everyone was nodding, all eager to insist that they had been a witness, even those who'd been in the other houses. Behind Jalloh there was just as much shuffling going on as those who had not participated tried to put some air between themselves and the two culprits.

Jalloh looked round, then turned back to Mary, speaking up to make contact over the buzz of the crowd. 'You tell the truth?'

'I do.'

'Can you identify the two victims?'

'I told you—'

Jalloh interrupted sharply. 'They will need medical treatment.'

In the event, Mary didn't have to reply. Everyone present was looking at the two girls, who sat with their eyes fixed firmly on the ground. Jalloh walked over and crouched down, his presence clearing a space. He spoke to them in a soft voice, the only indication of his whispered interrogation the slow, shy nods of the girls. They were crying again, and with some gentility Jalloh helped them stand and led them out to the front. Then he asked them to identify their abusers.

Scarface was shaking, his whole body trembling, a state that got worse as the finger was pointed in his direction. Rangy was looking around in a bemused way, as though he could never be guilty of such a crime, that it was all some bad joke, but he too was pointed out. Jalloh then called a couple of men forward and in a loud voice ordered them to take the girls to Mobgwemo, where there was a medical centre. As they shuffled out of the settlement, Jalloh walked over and took away, without any protest, the men's weapons.

'Now you will see, white lady, what we do to such men.'

A volley of commands followed. Scarface and Rangy were seized and thrown to the ground. Jalloh took a long stick off one of the men, then beckoned forward those who were similarly armed. He delivered the first blow to each one, a thudding strike across the back that made them scream and arch their bodies, then ordered the rest to carry on, leaving both men to suffer under a rain of blows. Pleasing Jalloh was obviously more important than any loyalty they felt, because there was no holding back.

Blood came quickly, soaking the T-shirts that both men wore. They tried to curl up into a ball, but that was of little use since each time they managed it the points of the sticks were used to jab them into a more open position. Jalloh kept turning to look at Mary Kline, before turning back to look at the punishment. It was as if he was trying to say, 'You are responsible for this, how do you feel?' All she could do was pretend to look, trying not to be sick.

The cries had quietened down through moans to whimpers. The beating didn't stop even when the pair, now nothing but a bloody mass, ceased to twitch. They stopped only when they heard the jets, the distant roar that became, within thirty seconds, a high-pitched scream. Jalloh was already running as they flew in, shouting to his men, his yelled orders followed by the crump of exploding rockets.

Blue Harding had the sense to stay behind the forward military units using the road from Gbangatok to Mokanje. He caught up with the rear units at Lago Junction, and would have been halted there if it hadn't been for the presence of both Frank Wintour and Captain Sam Gilbert. The officer's clout and the security chief's dollars got them though the ill-disciplined throng of confused soldiers, and up close the actual guys doing the fighting.

'He's a cheerful guy,' said Jamie, when they pulled away from the unsmiling captain. 'He didn't even smile when you slipped him the dough.'

'You should see him in a bad mood,' replied Frank.

Above their heads the two jets streaked back and forth through the sky, occasionally swooping to hit a target of opportunity. The bush on either side made it hard to see anything, so assessing how the action was unfolding could only be judged by forward progress. Blue knew that as long as he was moving up the road the army was making progress and the rebels were falling back. They could hear the mortars firing ahead, as well as the sharp crack of rocket propelled grenade fire, both incoming and outgoing. It was Jamie Padden who spotted the first hint of anti-aircraft fire, white puffs of exploding shells in the bright blue sky that had the Nigerian jets throwing a tight, descending curve, before they screamed away out of danger.

'Brave boys,' said Jamie.

'They're not being paid to get killed,' said Sandy McPherson.

'Are we?' asked Frank Wintour, who clearly didn't relish either the sight or sound of battle.

'Och, you're safe enough here,' Sandy replied. 'We're well out of range of anything these fuzzy-wuzzies have got.'

'We're just doubling up here, Frank,' added Blue, 'getting our RUF appreciation in at the same time as we recce the site.'

'Well just let me tell you I don't feel safe, and it's not the fuckin' RUF that's got me rattled. I've seen these bloody SL army blokes before, and they're more of a danger to themselves than they are to whoever they're fighting.'

'Only the ones with guns,' said Wally Aitken. 'And there ain't too many of them.'

Occasionally Blue would stop and each would take turns on the roof of the vehicle, binos ranging across the landscape to assess the progress of the battle. The appreciation of the army was already made, and the general consensus was that they were bloody useless. They might have better elements ahead doing the actual fighting, but back here they were moving forward surrounded by a right bunch of wankers. The officers, a few of whom were about, tried to get them to move in a disciplined way, one line on each side of the road, close to the cover of the trees, alert to

164

any sign of danger, but the soldiers either ignored them or told them to get stuffed.

Then the AA guns, depressed as far as possible, started to fire over the treetops. There was no danger since the shells they were firing could not be lobbed into ground level. Timed, they exploded harmlessly in the air, only the odd piece of falling shrapnel any kind of threat. But that was enough for the SL army. They were, to a man, off, back down the road, moving a damn sight quicker than they had going forward, leaving the AAR Land Rover in sole command of the stretch of highway. Sandy McPherson snorted with derision. 'If they do that to the guys up front, we'll have to bug-out at the double.'

'Man, now I know why black men always win the sprints,' said Jamie.

They moved closer to the action, until they could actually observe the impact of the mortars and rocket propelled grenades. Listening to the rate of fire coming from the government troops compared to what was incoming it was obvious they were winning the firefight. All the time the country was opening up, giving a clearer view, the man-made lakes that held the rutile deposits the only thing channelling the advance.

'How far to the Plant site, Frank?'

'Three or four kilometres, no more.'

'Then I would say our boys have got the rebels beat.'

'How the fuck can you tell that?'

'Just listen,' said Sandy.

Frank looked bemused, and it was Wally Aitken who continued, speaking slowly so as not to make a mistake. 'You can tell the difference between outgoing fire and incoming. The first is steady, the second diminishing. That means they are either short of ammo or disengaging some of their mortars to pull them back to a safe defensive position.'

'Which roughly translated,' Jamie concluded, 'means that they are retreating.'

But Frank wasn't really listening. He threw himself forward to shout out of the driver's window. 'Oi, you little bastard, come 'ere.'

The kid at the edge of the road didn't move. He just stood there holding his AK47 looking totally bemused. Frank shouted at him again, then demanded that Wally stop the Land Rover. He was out before it was stationary, striding over to the dust-covered boy.

'I thought I told you to get rid of that poxy rifle.'

Joe Folani just stared at him, as though he didn't comprehend. Normally, in Frank's recollection, a lively kid, he now seemed catatonic. The AAR security chief put out a hand and took the rifle away, then stepped forward and put his arm round Joe's shoulder. 'Come on, son, get in the car. You're safe with me now.'

Jalloh had the refugees moving within seconds of the arrival of the jets. They were hurried up the road, back the way they'd come. Behind them the sounds of battle grew louder and louder, the spread of the fighting more the cause than the fact that it was getting nearer. Confusion reigned supreme in this rear area with men, some armed but many not, milling about, most of them looking for a means of escape rather than a route to the front.

Geoff and Mary, coping better than most, passed the burnt-out church hall that had stood at the crossroads, not far from where they'd lost their pickup. The smell of burnt flesh still lingered in the air and a lot of the bodies, few of them whole, lay about unburied, decomposing rapidly in the heat of the African sun. Behind them they heard a single, very loud gunshot and turned to see one of the few remaining men in their party, an old wizened fellow who'd clearly had trouble keeping up, crumple and fall, the smoke from the gun that had killed him wafting about above his shattered skull.

'Let's get to the back and chivvy the stragglers,' said Mary. 'They won't shoot us.'

'I love your certainty,' Geoff replied.

But he did as he was asked, and both of them spent the next two hours either helping those who fell or organising others to support them. Behind them the noise of the battle stayed as loud as ever, but with no real military experience they couldn't know that the RUF was in full retreat. They found that out when Jalloh came alongside in a stolen pickup. He stopped the refugee convoy, told all the Africans to go home, then ordered Geoff and Mary into the back of the vehicle.

'Where are we going?' Geoff demanded.

'To a place where you will be safe.'

'I feel safe right here.'

The pistol in Jalloh's hand stopped any further argument.

Frank Wintour's face got longer the closer they got to the main group of Plant site buildings. They'd been trashed, but most of the stuff that had been thrown out was just lying about, which actually made things look worse than they really were. The whole area was filling up with soldiers, a sudden rush forward in trucks and pickups by a lot of the guys who'd been running back down the road just a couple of hours before.

They looked through the buildings, the offices and the processing plants, where a lot of the equipment seemed to be in good order – hardly surprising as it was hard to move, and had little actual value to people outside the rutile production industry. A quick search of the expat accommodation showed them where the rebels had vented any anger they felt. The houses, including Frank's own, had been ripped apart. To stop the security chief getting too depressed, Blue led him back to the company Land Rover, now surrounded by a crowd of noisy soldiers, all busy telling each other how brave they were.

'Let's get that satcom linked up and we can tell Razenbrook his site is safe,' said Blue.

The crack of a rifle shot had them all ducking, the scream of the wounded man as the bullet took him in the leg giving the whole crowd a good excuse to run without actually knowing which way safety lay. Only the trained soldiers stayed still. There's no good running away from an unknown danger, you might just be running towards it.

'ND,' said Blue.

He rose and pointed towards the solitary guy by the main office, who was looking at his gun as if it had been magicked into his hands. It was always like that with a negligent discharge: it surprised the guy responsible as much as it did everyone else. Suddenly the air was full of shouted accusations, some of them screams of rage, the yells of the guy who'd been on the receiving end of the bullet drowned out. The four mercenaries were already moving, a situation they had trained for put into practice without thinking. Sandy and Blue moved towards the victim. Jamie went after the guy with the rifle, a man not even his own officer seemed keen to approach, and took the weapon away lest he repeat the offence. It had been known to happen, as if the culprit by firing off another shot could blame the weapon, and that would somehow save him. The other excuse was worse, when they tried to pretend they were crazy, and emptied the whole magazine indiscriminately.

Wally Aitken hauled out the medical kit and followed Sandy McPherson. They turned the guy over on to his back. Sandy got the restricting band round his arm while Blue looked for a suitable vein. He then inserted the needle and catheter until he saw the first flashback of blood. Then, with a gentle twisting motion, he advanced the catheter into the vein. Placing a finger firmly on the vein just above the catheter he withdrew the needle. While this was going on Wally had attached the giving set to the Haemaccel plasma contained in the 500ml plastic bottle. He opened the valve, running the fluid through the tube to ensure there were no air bubbles. Satisfied, he closed the valve and passed the tube to Blue so that he could attach it to the catheter hub. The valve was reopened so that the fluid could run into the casualty. The first few inches of tubing were then looped and taped to the guy's arm. Sandy, seeing Blue beginning to insert the needle, turned his attention to the gaping exit wound on the guy's thigh. Moving quickly but deftly, he applied a shell dressing to that, as well as to the smaller entry wound. He then finished off by securing a crêpe bandage around both of them. Blue, finished, glanced up to see Jamie Padden examining his watch.

'How did we do?'

'Not bad, man. Four minutes start to finish.'

'What the hell did you time it for?' demanded Wally Aitken.

'Just to see how long I'd have to wait if I went down.'

'I think it took the bone,' said Blue.

'Hospital,' said Sandy, the look in his eye making it quite clear that he doubted the ability of the SL army to provide something like that in the field.

'You take care of him. I'll call in Sergei.'

'Would you look at this!' said Frank Wintour as Blue got back to the Land Rover. All around them, the soldiers were loading stuff on to their trucks, with not an officer in sight to tell them to can it. 'I'm going to try and find Gilbert.'

Blue had the box out and was opening it to align the dish, aiming it at the Atlantic Ocean West satellite on a bearing of 260 degrees correlated to an angle of elevation of forty-two degrees. 'You'd be better staying out of it, Frank. Mike Layman told me these guys haven't seen any dough for months. This will be their payoff, with a slice going to the officers.'

'I can't just stand here and watch them nick all our stuff, can I?'

'Yes. And if you do interfere, we might just be sticking one of those medical trauma kits into you. That stuff's replaceable, you're not.'

In his ear, as he spoke to Sergei's office at Freetown airport, Blue could hear the faint swearing of the security chief. He was cursing the country and the people, especially his own trained guards, not one of whom had stayed around to protect AAR's property. Blue didn't have the heart to interfere, to tell Frank Wintour that they would only have found the body of anyone who'd been that stupid.

The trucks, loaded to overflowing, were pulling out as Sergei flew in, landing the twin jet-engined helicopter in a huge cloud of dust. They got the wounded guy on to a stretcher and loaded him aboard, Wally still holding the Haemaccel plasma bottle until he could tape it to the luggage shelf above his head. Blue was busy talking to Frank Wintour, sorting out how the chief would use his local knowledge and his contacts to get them some proper information. They could look around the immediate area, and study maps to work out a defensive strategy, but they needed local intelligence as well before they could propose anything.

'What's the plan?' asked Jamie Padden when he came back to the Hip.

'Back to Freetown for now. There's too many trigger-happy jundies around right now.'

'Is that a good idea?' asked McPherson, brow furrowed.

'It's the only idea, Sandy. What are we going to achieve here sitting in the dark? 'Cause that's what we'll have to do! If there were any genies around when the RUF pulled out there are none now. The army has nicked them.'

'Have you ever seen such a bunch of useless cunts?' said Wally.

'Only in the Parachute Regiment,' replied the ex-Royal Marine.

Jamie Padden had a twinkle in his eye when he piped up next. 'Would this return to Freetown have anything to do with a certain Lebanese lady, what you SAS types like to call a floozie?'

'It might,' Blue grinned.

'And I thought you were happy with me, man.'

'What are you like at blow jobs, Jamie?'

'Never tried.'

'Then I rest my case. We'll come back in the morning, which will give us a whole day to recce the site.'

Jamie peered out through the small round window at the mass looting still taking place. 'Man, there will be nothing left.'

'I hope you're not going to suggest we try to stop them?'

'Not even an Afrikaner is that stupid. But that Land Rover will go too.'

'Frank is sticking around. He's going to try to round up some of his guys and see what's what. He'll spend the night in Gbangatok and meet us back here at first light.' Blue looked round the trio of faces. 'All agreed?'

He had to ask that. He might have the responsibility, but you couldn't run these kinds of jobs on three-bags-full bullshit. It had to be a team approach. Jamie Padden's response was positive, Sandy's and Wally's less so.

Jalloh took Geoff and Mary only so far. In the time they spent in the back of the pickup the pair had got a chance to examine each other. Both were now filthy, Mary's blond hair in disarray, full of dust and some dried mud. Their clothes were in the same condition, but they were, apart from the odd bruise caused by overzealous shoving, unmarked, and that had to be a blessing considering what they had witnessed.

They stopped in the village of Tinanhun, a few kilometres north on the road to Moyamba. There they were handed over to a man called Tarawali, who, judging by the deference shown to him by their captor, was Jalloh's superior. The introduction, formal and polite, was in stark contrast to what came next. They were shown into the hut which had, judging by its size, been the property of a village elder. In the gloom they could just make out the white wimples of the seven nuns, all on their knees, all praying. The others in the hut – two white men, a black and two Asians – were slumped against the mud walls, their necks roped together.

'Well, at least we are not alone,' said Geoff.

Sister Francesca looked up as he spoke, crossed herself and stood up. She provided the names of their fellow hostages while they tried, as best they could, to let those who had preceded them know what had been happening. The opinion that the RUF had been pushed back was greeted with a groan.

'All out, all out.'

The cry came from the twelve-year-old who suddenly half filled the doorway. When the hostages were slow to respond, he unslung his rifle and made threatening gestures, then shouted for assistance. The hut was soon full of men, pushing and shoving, pulling the recumbent prisoners to their feet. Geoff watched the distribution of the blows with some interest. They harmed none of the whites, male or female, but the black guy, a doctor from the Sieromin compound, got the butt of a rifle in the ribs and the two Asians from the Salco bauxite quarry were pushed and kicked even when they tried to comply.

Out in the daylight Geoff could see how weak these people were. Mario Berti was in the worst condition – the Italian had taken a real beating when he'd been captured. He had to be helped along, which wasn't easy given that the whole party was roped together by the neck.

'Where are we going?' Geoff asked.

The raised rifle butt made him shy away and produced a humourless laugh from their guards.

Quentin-Davies knew by the following morning that the RUF had taken more hostages, information that was passed back to Gibraltar as soon as it came in, this time with photographs. The same signal carried his impression that the situation was deteriorating, that the SO10 negotiators were getting nowhere, and that definite plans should be made to mount a rescue. In consultation with the Foreign Office in London he considered it highly unlikely that such an operation would be carried out by invitation of the Sierra Leone government.

Major Peter Goring, B Squadron commander, looked at the signal and turned with a wry smile to his troop commanders and senior NCOs. He then read it out.

'We'll oblige if the bugger will just tell us where they are,' said Captain Gordon Ayers, one of the troop commanders.

'Deniable, Gordie,' replied Goring.

The maps on the wall told their own story. The intelligence that the RUF had been pushed back from Mokanje had already been assessed and entered. The present dispositions of the Gurkha Guard Force were there, as well as those of the Nigerian and Republic of Guinea peacekeepers. But that left a great black hole in the middle, and the hostages could be anywhere in there. No rescue could be mounted without more knowledge and they also required, once that was established, a ground recce to assess what forces they faced. Ideally, they also needed a layout of any buildings, especially those containing the hostages and those guarding them.

Given all that, there were still problems. Getting in was easy. Every man was a trained parachutist who with the modern square 'chutes could land on a sixpence. They had the weaponry and the skill to take on any kind of local force, but how to get the hostages out over miles of territory was a real problem, compounded by the need to get themselves out as well without being seen. Forward base areas that were quiet enough to be secret were not thick on the ground.

The comms hummed all day between London and Freetown, London and Gibraltar, and Freetown and Gibraltar. Options were discussed, time-scales to get Chinooks in and out proposed, sites for fixed-wing planes to land and for the stand-by team to debus. These had to be identified and rated in terms of suitability. And sitting at the centre of all this was Donald Quentin-Davies, convinced that he had a lock on the present location of the hostages, sending a message to the SAS of patience. They were on the move, but very soon they would stop.

CHAPTER THIRTEEN

Blue and his team had spent two days on the sites, looking at likely enemy approach routes and sighting possible defensive positions. They had questioned everyone Frank Wintour could find, seeking information about the RUF, even engaging some of the ex-security staff to go out and gather intelligence in the surrounding areas. The whole mine site was now overrun by government troops and an excess of officers, all very keen to exercise some authority, behaviour that stood in sharp contrast to the situation when the bullets were flying. But it was fairly obvious that having beaten the rebels back, they were not pursuing them.

Back in Freetown, every conversation in both bar and night-club was dominated by two things: the horror of Frank Buckhart's death and a lot of talk regarding the taking of the hostages – numbers, names and their potential fate. It was quite clear to the AAR team that their capture would have an effect on what they proposed, though Blue and Sandy McPherson disagreed as to how serious that should be.

The first report to Razenbrook, delivered the morning after the initial visit, had been unequivocal: any proposed reoccupation of the site was, at this time, out of the question. Local forces were not in control, were poorly coordinated, and due to careless weapon handling were a threat to the AAR team. Also there were strong indications that although they had been driven back the rebels had not been completely cleared from the area and were still active. Last, but not least, the AAR team was not equipped to provide for their own security. While it might be possible, in time, to train a local defence force that could guarantee mine security, it would not be feasible to do so quickly. The army, who had the responsibility of providing that cordon of safety, was an unreliable force that was more interested in looting than fighting; badly led, poorly motivated and with a shortage of training only matched by their lack of weapons. The primary recommendation was that the men on stand-by in the UK should be shipped out, since they were costing money anyway, and they would be needed if any actions were initiated.

In the end, it had come down to giving the AAR boss two alternatives: get the Strasser government to move a disciplined force like the Gurkhas into the area, or employ one himself. Razenbrook hadn't even reacted to the first, knowing only too well that by asking he'd be wasting his breath. It was the second one that engaged his attention, his queries centring on cost and duration. Blue had ducked that one, not prepared to answer until he had engaged in a thorough examination of the ground. Back from his recce, and having talked the whole thing over with his team, he now felt he was in a position to respond. Notes were made and conclusions drawn, all listed in a typewritten report, but it had to be presented, and as team leader that fell to Blue. Like all briefings, he began with the obvious, repeating almost verbatim the words that opened the written submission that lay in front of everyone at the table.

'The aim is to give AAR an uninterrupted dredging and processing facility, free from both the Sierra Leone army and from any future incursions by the RUF. In essence, to secure the dredge site and Plant site so that the investors get a reasonable return, with all due consideration to the hostage situation.'

'Which also means,' Razenbrook added, 'that I, as chief executive, must retain board of director and shareholder confidence, as well as that of the financing banks.'

'Understood,' Blue responded. 'What AAR requires on the ground is a strength potent enough to produce deterrence. You could never have enough men to contain the RUF if they are determined to take the sites. Only the army can do that. What we need to put in place is a force big enough to put a very high price on the operation. Providing the political situation permits it that is possible. The men would be local, but officered by expats who would run a programme of continuous training to keep them up to the mark.'

Blue paused, and looked into the row of eyes that were watching him. Those of his team were bland, Mike Layman's were non-committal, but Tony Razenbrook was looking at him intently, the kind of unblinking stare a falcon might use to watch a field mouse. It was as if the guy were determined never to let Blue forget he was the boss. It was, to the ex-trooper's mind, a total waste of energy. 'I refer you to page five, where you will see a rough sketch map of the rutile deposit sites.'

He waited while the pages rustled, thinking of the one great plus he'd observed on his reconnaissance: the company had inadvertently built the means of its own defence. Rutile was mined by scooping out huge amounts of topsoil, the resultant holes turned into artificial lakes. Dredgers were then employed to scrape the rutile from the subsoil, the mixture processed and dried to create the final transportable product. Naturally, when siting their main operations and processing centre, they'd placed it at the geographical heart of the area, and that meant the approaches to the Plant site had been canalised, making them easy to control.

Blue talked on, taking Razenbrook and Layman through the facts, forcing them to look at the ground from a military rather than a mining standpoint. The country to the south-east and east, where the main threat lay, was bush with very little primary growth, leaving the rebels routes that the locals called bypasses. These were the RUF's operational conduits, ones that avoided roads and confrontation. To the south there were rivers and mangrove swamps to provide obstacles to free movement. These protected the twin jetties at Port Nitti, one for AAR, the other belonging to Sieromin. This was the easiest location to defend, and thus it was identified as the best base area and evacuation point. But it was still under threat, and the HQ had to be elsewhere, preferably in a secure area. Blue had chosen Bonthe on Sherbro Island, which dominated the mouths of the southern river systems. That in turn led to a need for some form of reliable water transport to get men and material in and out, so part of the submission was for the provision of a seagoing boat as well as the inflatables they'd need to navigate the rivers.

He went through the rebels' strengths. This was put, in the immediate area, at a maximum of five hundred, though that was uncorroborated, underlining the fact that whatever their numbers they had to be taken seriously. The intentions were clear: to take white hostages, to prevent any mine working and to bring down the government by starving them of revenue. White faces filtering back on to the Plant site would certainly attract attention, as would any attempt to reopen the mine or move the barges from Port Nitti. Given their aims, that was something they'd be bound to try to stop and it would appear they had the means. Intelligence reports showed they were active along both banks of the Jong River, and their confidence, having already closed the mines down once, must be high.

Against that the army could muster some three hundred men, although that was uncertain because it was doubtful if even the commanders knew the true strength of their forces. But there was a big question mark over what they could achieve. Certainly they'd pushed the RUF back, but Blue had since learned that the outgoing 81mm mortar fire they'd heard when they went in had been provided, like the Alpha jets, by the Nigerians. These had now been withdrawn, leaving the army with their AK47s, RPD, RPG and grenades. The RUF had similar equipment. Mike Layman's report that they were equipped with 12.75mm machine guns remained unconfirmed.

It soon emerged that even the Nigerian jets could provide only a partial backup. The Sierra Leone Army lacked maps, so had little or no forward air control, which severely hampered the aircraft's ground support capacity. Likewise the troops on the ground had poor communication. High frequency comms were confined to company level and above, with no tactical communications at platoon level, a problem even for motivated troops.

'Our information,' said Blue, 'is that the rebels are, despite the presence of government troops, preparing another assault. Against such a soft target they might succeed. But they lack mobility or proper logistical support, and have yet to come up against a hard target. What is required is defence in depth, the first ring of that being an outlying means of gathering intelligence, so that wherever the rebels reappear, we can get patrols out to meet them before they get close.'

'It is my opinion,' said Sandy McPherson, 'that it would be better to mount a static defence. We could lay mines, with clear safety corridors for the locals to see. The markers could be withdrawn if the site was threatened, which would leave any approaching force vulnerable.'

They'd had an argument about that, but not a very serious one, and it had been agreed that any report they presented should be unanimous. McPherson had deliberately broken that, his aim obviously to ingratiate himself with Razenbrook. And he wasn't finished. 'It might also, in the long run, save money. By laying a proper, deep minefield we will cut down on the manpower needed to defend the area.'

Blue wanted to tell him to shut up, but he didn't. He hoped he wouldn't have to, hoped that Razenbrook would see the folly of what the ex-RSM was suggesting. In that he was disappointed.

'That is a major consideration,' Razenbrook replied, the look he gave McPherson and the nodding Aitken one of deep approval.

Mike Layman cut in. 'You obviously don't agree, Blue, since it's not in your proposal.'

'Two reasons. You'll never keep the safety corridors a secret. Everyone we spoke to has told us just how much the RUF know about deployments in the area, civil defence and the army. The rebels will know where the mines are before they get anywhere near the deposits.'

'Which will still canalise their attack,' McPherson insisted.

'What are the chances of the locals sticking to the safety corridors, even if they are well marked?'

'Zero,' said Mike Layman. 'You could tell them till you're blue in the face.'

He paused, realising the pun on John Harding's nickname. But Blue just smiled and continued. 'My other aim, and the reason for the secrecy, is to inflict casualties before they even get close. The RUF are better than the army, but not by much. The best way to defeat them is to go out and meet them well away from the mine site. I remind you that the dredge site is at the very edge of the area we need to secure, and is thus the most vulnerable. The only way to protect that is by aggressive patrolling.'

'Let's leave the mine idea aside for later consideration,' said Razenbrook.

'Okay,' Blue replied. 'The next thing we have to do is prepare defence positions. Trenches pre-dug and revetted, mortar firing positions, some razor wire in place, more ready to be deployed with ploughed strips denoting mortar fire ranges, and very obvious routes of communication to emphasise that we would be operating on interior lines.'

'Forgive me for saying so,' Razenbrook enquired, 'but isn't that just as obvious as minefields?'

'It is, except it's not likely to kill anyone who works for you. We're sending a card saying if you're going to attack this place, you'd better do it properly, because it's going to be expensive. Remember we will already have hit them out in the bush, which will make them cautious. To do that we need to up the intelligence on movements of large bodies, as well as spotting strange faces. That kind of info has generally proved accurate in the past. Every local and every employee should be aware of the need to pass on anything suspicious or out of the ordinary, and you will require a good intelligence coordinator to manage the inflow.' He paused again, since until now everything had been fairly upbeat. The next item was not. 'We're in a highly delicate political situation here, one that means practically anything you do will upset someone. That applies in spades to the hostage situation. I talked to the BHC and the diplomats are adamant. Their welfare has to be a continuous factor in any decision making. We need some way of getting a fast reading of how our actions are playing with the various bodies who might react. Now if you turn to the following pages, you will see the list of what we need in terms of men and material.'

'Just one point before you continue, Blue,' said Razenbrook. 'I have looked at this, and I can tell you now that to finance what you propose I need to get that processed rutile out from Port Nitti. My board will insist! Another factor is maintenance on the dredgers. That has to be carried out soon, or certain pieces of equipment, which I might remind you cost several million pounds, will become useless.'

'In spite of the hostages?' asked Blue. 'Either of those, touched, is just the kind of act that will wind up the RUF to slot them.'

'I'm afraid so,' Razenbrook replied, his lack of sympathy for the plight of those captured ill-disguised.

'I think you can rely on us, sir,' said Sandy McPherson, smoothly. 'There has to be a way, and once we're up to strength, we are just the people to find it.'

Blue had to bite his tongue again. He would give McPherson a bollocking for certain, but not in front of the client. Instead, he stuck to the job. 'It's chicken and egg, Tony. No weapons and we can't do a thing, either way. And we will have to go abroad to get it. This level of equipment is just not available locally.'

'Even if it was,' said Mike Layman, 'any attempt to buy would be like a signal of our intentions. The RUF would know what AAR was up to before it was delivered.'

'I take it you have some idea of where to procure what you need?' added Razenbrook.

'That's the least of our problems,' Blue replied, grinning.

The AAR chief executive nodded. 'Then let's move on to this personnel establishment. I find the idea of one hundred and twenty-four men rather luxurious.'

'But, Tony, they'll be mainly Africans, and they, compared to us, are cheap.'

178

Ray Kavanagh was not a happy man, and nothing, not even the drinks Blue was pouring down his throat, was making that mood any better. A slight, balding man, he had the paunch and jowls of the truly unfit.

'You've got blokes arriving every day. Use one of them, or are you going to tell me they've all got things to do?'

Blue went through the reasons why that wasn't possible, ordering another round of drinks as he did so. He was in the middle of setting up a base and training facility at Bonthe. The guys that had been recruited were a mixed bunch, and as yet they were not all here. A trio of SBS guys who would take control of the target observation and boat work, another signaller to back up Ray Kavanagh, and two more SAS men, who would arrive in a few weeks to make up a full Special Forces patrol. The rest, here now and due to arrive soon, were ex-Paras, a fact which pleased both Blue and the man who interviewed them in Aldershot, Dave Heffer.

Mercenary teams could be a bugger to put together. Blue, particularly, didn't want a whole complement of SAS guys. That situation, if they were not carefully selected, generally ended up with them behaving like Sandy McPherson, all vying for top slot. Ex-Paras were ideal: cheaper, good soldiers and happy to be employed in the infantry role for which they'd been trained. Some of them, possibly most of them, in terms of ability, would be a bit rusty. He had to get them up to scratch for a task that as yet hadn't been finalised, everything from section battle drills to anti-ambush drills, then patrol skills and finally the SAS speciality, contact drills.

'Look, Ray, you're a signaller, and right now the comms we have are well up to requirements. A week from now they won't be.'

'You're right, Blue,' Ray replied. 'I am a signaller. Look at me for Christ's sake. I ain't fired a gun in ten years. Christ, I even managed to skip my annual when I was still in the corps.'

'Good. Because the one thing this job doesn't need is a man with a gun. It just needs one that can be spared. And not looking like a hardcase is actually a real bonus.'

'Does the fucker need a brain?'

'It's dead simple,' Blue insisted, wishing he used another word other than dead. 'You fly to Bucharest, right.'

'Wrong.'

'You take a list with you, one that I have already faxed, and you meet some guys at the Intercontinental Hotel.'

'Some guys. A bunch of murderous fucking Romanians.'

'The contact will take you to an aircraft, with all the kit loaded on it. You check the manifest, and if it's correct, you call me on the mobile. I then call Zurich and release AAR's money into their Swiss account. It's a doddle.'

'What if it goes pear-shaped, Blue? It will be my arse in a sling, not yours.'

'I've told you, nothing can go wrong. These guys are pros. They do this sort of trade all the time. How much business do you think they'd transact if every time they did a deal they threatened the messenger?'

'What if it's not right?'

'Then I don't pay.'

'Exactly. So maybe they'll get the needle and take it out on me.'

'What good will that do them?'

Ray's eyebrows went up so far they nearly replaced his missing hair. 'Are you kidding?'

Blue wore him down eventually, though it took a long time, and he was distracted by the way Pol Pot was taking advantage of the fact that he was occupied. Gus Pollard was giving it big licks, chatting up Leila, his Lebanese girlfriend, knowing it was the best way to stick one to Blue. And then there was Willy Rakiba, drunk again, surrounded by hookers, making just as much noise and threatening anyone who told him to pipe down.

'You'll have a great time, Ray. First class all the way.'

'On a Romanian plane? In your dreams! First class on that kind of shit plane just means you don't see the kettle on the Primus stove in the galley.'

'Something tells me you need a woman.'

Ray laughed for the first time since Blue had asked him to go to Bucharest to pick up the arms shipment. 'Don't give me that, you smooth-talking ratbag. It's you that needs a woman, not me. And if you don't shift your arse old Gus is going to give you the sidestep.'

Willy Rakiba went off then, with a great bull of a roar and a stream of curses aimed at the blacks and Arab scum that were robbing him blind. Everybody was off their seat – Paul Hill, Trevor, Crazy Collins, Blue, Gus Pollard and Casey Jones, all converging at a run on the Fijian to take him down before he killed someone. It took all six of them, but Blue had the bonus of Leila to bathe the half-dozen bruises he received in the attempt. All Pol Pot got was a stonker of a black eye.

Geoff Hinchcliffe had very little idea of their location after the first day's march, and absolutely none by the end of the week. They headed in every direction, boxing the compass in a zigzag route that seemed to owe more to personal whims than logic. Sometimes they got shelter for the night, at other times they slept under the stars, but they stayed roped together when they moved and tied up when they stopped, the only time the bonds were removed were when they ate or were escorted to a stinking latrine.

He knew he was in a bad way himself, losing weight from the poor diet, his feet blistered from marching in stinking footwear, his wrists and neck chafed by the rubbing of their restraints. But he was doing better than most. Mary Kline, as far as he could see, was holding up well, though he couldn't be sure because she was not the type to complain. The nuns had their prayers to sustain them, though the younger ones continued to deteriorate faster than their elders.

Mario Berti was now on a stretcher, though he had received some very basic medical treatment from an RUF medic. But the guy had no drugs, and little medicine other than aspirin. His fellow hostage, Mondeh, the black doctor, was of no use, being wholly concerned with his own survival, no easy matter since every change of guards seemed to presage for him another beating. To the rebels he was a traitor who had served the whites rather than his own kind. The fact, which he imparted to Geoff in a whisper, that he'd stolen drugs and medicine from his Italian employers, and had treated his own people for nothing in his own time seemed to count for nothing. Spooning some gruel into Mario Berti's mouth one evening, Geoff learned that Mondeh's medical thefts were no secret. The Sieromin security boss had known all along that he was taking stuff, but had decided not to interfere since the doctor was not charging the locals for his services. And when the company queried the excessive bills for drugs, he invented illnesses for half his security team to cover the loss.

Assitola, the bauxite quarry boss, was close to needing a stretcher as well, the way he staggered and occasionally fell a constant source of worry. He and his two Asian assistants could never be sure that one of the doped-up guards escorting them wouldn't put a bullet in his head. Their leaders, Tarawali, Dennis and Jalloh, were not always around to impose discipline, coming and going as their other duties dictated.

They'd reached their present location, a stone building, in darkness, so were not aware of its size and complexity until the morning, when they were taken out for their ablutions. Judging by the layout this was some kind of expat set-up, a mission or a mining facility. Another stone building, which looked like offices, stood beside the one he'd just come out of. Looking around at the wooden barracks, which seemed to contain hundreds of fighters and their families, Geoff had a hope that they might stay here. The camp was under a thick canopy of high trees, possibly invisible from the air. Either that or it was too far away from the various fronts to be in danger of attack by ground or air. All of them, him included, needed rest. They might just achieve it in a place like this.

He didn't ask where they were. That would only get him a rifle butt in the ribs.

The accommodation in Bonthe, in what had once been a holiday village, was comfortable without being luxurious. The guy who owned it, an Australian, had sunk every penny he had into West African tourism only to find that coups and revolutions, faithfully reported in the Western press, were threatening to bankrupt him. Blue's request to use the place as a barracks and training area came as a godsend.

The place was on the beach, well away from the town, with its own private strand they could use for practising their infiltration and exfiltration techniques. It also had a jetty, with water deep enough to moor the boat Razenbrook had bought. The *Adelaide* was a hundred-footer, ideal for the work Blue envisaged, and had been given a thorough overhaul before being handed over. The guys were coming in now, in large enough numbers to make the training mean something.

There was a high earthen wall at the back that they could use as a butt-stop for range work. There was an open field to the west for more serious stuff, though firing there was confined by the proximity of one of the dozens of new displacement camps that had sprung up on Sherbro Island. Erecting netting and a certain amount of wood was all that was necessary to construct a makeshift assault course. Paul Hill and Owen Saddler, who were searching out training locations for their close protection teams, cadged a lift in Sergei's heli on the first weekend, and pronounced themselves impressed. The only thing that was missing was the weapons.

Ray Kavanagh had already been to the toilet three times, and he wanted desperately to go again, even if it was a stinking, shit-streaked bog hole. It might have been the grub he'd eaten on the Romanian Airways Tupolev, but then again it might just be fear. Whatever the reason it seemed to amuse the guy who'd met him at the Intercontinental and led him to the car that had brought them here, to this garishly lit airport bar. His explanation, that the cargo was not yet ready, did nothing for Ray's nerves or bowels. He was sweating too; the place was like an oven, in stark contrast to the freezing cold outside.

In Freetown, warm and humid, Blue sat by Mike Layman's phone, waiting. The AAR engineer guessed he was nervous, even if the ex-SAS trooper showed no sign of it. He was wrong. Blue had learned a long time ago the futility of worrying about things you can do nothing about.

Ray had never learned it, and had continually to stop himself from shoving his fingernails into his mouth. His minder was a genial red-faced individual in a heavy overcoat, with a guttural way of speaking English. He'd introduced himself as Behlen. At least that was what Ray thought, because he hadn't heard properly. Having checked that he had a mobile phone that was working, Behlen tried to ply him with strong drink, a white spirit that might have been vodka but could just as easily have been wood alcohol. Turned down on that, he'd indicated one of the hookers at the bar and asked Ray, one finger poking through the ring he made with his other hand, if he wanted anything in that line. The signaller was thinking, when that was proposed, that if Behlen could see the shrivelled state of his cock he wouldn't have asked.

Eventually two of Behlen's companions appeared, a couple of thickset stage hoods who kept their sunglasses on even though it was dark outside. When Ray walked out of the lounge, with Behlen ahead and one of these guys on each side, he had a vision of a mafia hit. Striding across the tarmac, under the glaring arc lights, passing various people in uniform who paid them no attention, only heightened that impression. The transport they approached had its engines running, making that soft whine that jets do when they are not properly fired up.

They filed up the steps, and Ray pulled the list Blue had given him from his pocket, trying to stop his hand from shaking as he held it up. Behlen had one too, and they went through the items together, ticking off the three 12.75mm heavy machine guns. Then they moved on to the boxes of AK47s, the RPG anti-tank weapons that could be used as hand-held artillery, the pistols, 60mm mortars, Claymore anti-personnel mines and crates of grenades, both smoke and HE. And finally, after checking the dozens of crates of ammo, they came to the two old-fashioned Soviet Army inflatables, and the state-of-the-art Mariner engines to drive them. On Blue's instructions Ray lifted no lids. These guys, he insisted, wouldn't cheat him. If they did, everybody in the arms game would hear about it and they'd go out of business.

'Satisfied?' asked Behlen.

Ray nodded and pulled out his Ericsson phone, punching in the numbers for Mike Layman's office, checking it against the one he'd written at the top of the sheet before pressing the send button.

'Blue.'

'Yep!'

'Everything's kosher this end.'

'Good. Put me on to the main man.' Ray passed the phone over. 'The money will be transferred in ten minutes. If there is any hold up I will call you back.'

'That is good,' said Behlen. 'Ten minutes.' Then the guy pulled a bottle from his pocket, and his two hoods suddenly produced glasses. 'Now, friend, we must drink.'

There was no way out now and Ray took one of the small filled tumblers, waiting until the others were ready. Then, in unison, they lifted them. Ray said 'Cheers' and the other three said something he didn't understand, but they were grinning, so it obviously meant the same thing. As the fiery liquid hit the back of Ray Kavanagh's throat he was reviewing the events of the night. Eat your heart out Len Deighton!

Behlen's phone rang and he answered, nodding three or four times. Then he asked Ray to redial Freetown, took the phone, and spoke to Blue again, in that guttural Sidney Greenstreet voice. 'Thank you, Mr Harding. The money has been transferred. It has been a pleasure to do business with you. We have a take-off slot booked at ten minutes past every hour, so the flight will be departing in fifteen minutes. Weather reports give an estimated local time of arrival in Freetown of five a.m., which the pilot will confirm once he has passed over North Africa.'

'What has the flight plan been registered as?'

'Humanitarian aid for the hungry people of Liberia. The route has been cleared at ministerial level, and will be faxed to you as soon as the aircraft departs.'

'Good,' Blue said.

Behlen killed the connection, led Ray forward to the cockpit, introduced him to the men who would fly them south and, after a strong handshake, left. The co-pilot showed Ray to a truckle bed against the rear bulkhead and advised him that once they were airborne he might as well sleep.

In Freetown, Blue Harding made for the compound that contained the trucks he had hired. In his pocket was an envelope containing the signed authorisation from Strasser himself for the importation of the weapons. The flight details of the charter aircraft were so secret that the NPRC leader had shut down the airport for its arrival. The *Adelaide* was moored off the far end of the runway, and they had a truck standing by to trans-ship the cargo from plane to boat.

Blue didn't ask how it had been done, whether Strasser had been bribed or had given permission for free. That was none of his business. He and his AAR team would have their weapons and could begin to plan properly for the reoccupation of the mine sites.

CHAPTER FOURTEEN

BSquadron HQ in Gibraltar was still concerned by the lack of hard intelligence, especially regarding the hostage location, though they had to accept the assurances of Quentin-Davies and Delane that they would be able to provide it in due course. But even if that was true, they were still left with a black hole in terms of a ground appreciation, and that led to much discussion within the constraints imposed by a deniable op about the best way such a thing could be achieved. Using the Gurkhas didn't appeal at all. They worked for and were paid by Strasser. Even if Toby Flowers was an ex-Green Jacket who might well be trustworthy, the men of the regiment had limited faith in their patrol skills. Gurkhas, in their experience, were fine for going in and executing an already identified kill, but experience in Borneo had shown that time after time they needed to be led by the hand to a target.

Forwood and Paul Hill, called into the High Commission cipher room for an opinion, initially assumed that they would be asked to participate in the job, but Quentin-Davies poured cold water on that as soon as he said the word 'deniable'. You couldn't plan, recce and execute a hostage rescue in secret and at the same time continue the training sked as though nothing was happening. The bodyguard training team was occupied in Freetown. Their only excursions out of that area consisted of an occasional sortie to locate places to test out anti-ambush drills. That was done in the company of the men they were training. The best they could offer was a pair ostensibly out hunting the sites to use for training purposes; any more absences would arouse suspicion. Even a recce was difficult, because that was an open-ended commitment. To get the information required could take one day, or it could take a dozen. There was no way of knowing until the task was in hand.

Paul couldn't confirm that they were being watched, but he had to acknowledge that any prolonged unexplained absences would blow any notion of non-SAS involvement when the job went critical. Strasser was suspicious of everyone and everything, and that included the British government. He probably had an eye on their off-duty activities. Added to that the RUF had hundreds of spies in Freetown and would trumpet British involvement to the world should the hostages be released while the BG team was unaccounted for. That applied as well to the two minders brought in for the SO10 negotiators.

Quentin-Davies, when talking to his political masters, took up that argument with surprising force. Despite the difficulties the present situation was creating for the High Commission, matters could only deteriorate if his hand in any operation were exposed. The BG team had come in on the recommendation of his own underlings. Secrecy could not be guaranteed, and who would not believe that there had been a long-term conspiracy, should the whole thing unravel? As the man on the spot he had to be deferred to, and that left the B Squadron CO and the DSF in London with two alternatives: to mount a recce themselves, a long-distance air drop without any real support, or do something that was on the very edge of the regiment's creed.

All members of 22nd SAS, Ruperts and troopers alike, were keenly aware of how much myth played a part in their success. To the public and those whom they might oppose they had a superhuman quality. Though aware of the flaws in such thinking it was a notion they were keen to maintain. They liked to repeat the mantra that they were the custodians of illusion. One of those illusions was that they never, ever worked with an outside mercenary force.

Successful Special Forces operations might have fundamental tenets, but they have no hard and fast rules. Rules are what wise men ignore and fools die for. The whole notion of the regiment and its imitators was based on a basic breach of the current military thinking and nothing had changed since David Stirling came up with the concept during the 1942 desert campaign in North Africa. You take what you have and make the best use of it, and to hell with the kind of red-tape thinking that stifles creativity. So when Major Peter Goring asked about the ex-SAS men working for Anglo-African Rutile, Paul wasn't shocked. Forwood was, which surprised his staff sergeant. That was until he remembered who led the AAR team.

'The fact that it's Blue Harding doesn't come into it, boss. If they can help the regiment do what is required, and not cause any suspicion to fall on us, then that is the obvious solution.'

'Not for you perhaps, Paul. But it certainly does have something of a bearing for me.'

That too was a touch surprising. Paul knew his Rupert was a slippery bastard. He would have expected Forwood to avoid the personal, to hide behind the argument that to use people from outside the regiment for such an important task was to court failure. But the officer didn't. He was totally up-front about his reasons. Even if he received a direct order to do so, there was no way he was going cap in hand to his ex-staff sergeant, Blue Harding, to ask for a favour.

'What is it to him if we don't get the hostages out?' Forwood continued. 'He will still be paid his whack by Tony Razenbrook. He is bound to refuse, because he has no reason whatever to oblige.'

Forwood, not for the first or last time in his life, was wrong.

Tarawali and his lieutenants treated it like a game, and the crowd responded. Now that it was night, the whole camp had become more lively; even the hostages were brought out to witness the kind of punishment that the RUF visited on people they thought had betrayed them. The three prisoners, all black and in tattered uniforms, had been brought in the previous day and stuck at one end of the room. Sister Francesca's enquiries, in defiance of their guards, revealed that they were Nigerian soldiers who'd been cut off during a rebel raid.

The glow from the fires and the fact that everybody seemed to be preparing a meal alerted Geoff to the fact that no fires had been lit during the day. It didn't take a genius to work out the reason, the need to avoid sending up tell-tale smoke that, even in this thick bush, could be seen for miles in daylight. The government didn't fly at night, which made it safe to cook a hot meal. They were fed before the spectacle, a tiny bowl of tasteless mealie which was barely enough to remind them of their hunger, never mind satisfy it. There was a savage irony to the way they fed the Nigerians too. As they ate some of the younger rebel soldiers dug four deep but narrow holes in front of them. Nothing could happen until they'd been given their nightly lecture, an hour-long harangue that rehearsed the same grievances they'd heard every time the rebel leaders opened their mouths. A cheer from the crowd greeted every point.

But this time a new subject was broached, namely that of outside interference. The nuns were the first to be targeted, the first to be told that

188

their presence in Sierra Leone was not wanted. All the ills of the nation were laid at their interfering door, Christian charity was mocked, their humility scorned, the accusation that they enslaved their charges rather than saved them levelled repeatedly. And all the time, in front of them, by flaming torchlight, the young men dug and the assembly acclaimed their leaders.

Then it was the turn of the coloured hostages, the ill treatment they underwent having a physical as well as a political message. They were cuffed around the head as each RUF leader took his turn to abuse them, shouting obscenities in their ears, berating them for selling out their own people for white dollar bills. The crowd was in a frenzy, jabbing the air with rifles and chanting RUF slogans. Mondeh, the doctor, was finally dragged out, forced along the ground by his tormentors, who finally lifted his tied hands and threw him towards the pits.

'They'll get to us soon,' said Mary Kline. 'You just look at the ground, Geoff. Whatever they say, don't look into their eyes.'

Geoff looked into hers, bright, reflective whites that threw back the flaring torches, making her look as defiant as she had when she tried to stop the rebels dragging out the male refugees.

'Don't you worry about me,' he replied. 'You just think about you.'

'This is leading up to something, Geoff.'

'You don't know that.'

'I do. If you don't believe me, ask Sister Francesca. That is, if you can stop her praying.' Geoff looked at the old woman. Her head was bent, her hands were clasped and her lips were moving. 'She knows, just like I do.'

Geoff followed Mary's eyes to the pits, now completed. If he'd thought about them at all it was in terms of cooking food, but the kids who dug them out made no move to fill them with wood. They just stood by the piles of earth they'd excavated with expectant looks on their faces.

They started on the whites before Geoff could form a coherent thought, the voices loud and penetrating, the lips of the speaker close to his ear. It was Captain Dennis, an orator he'd seen in action before. The thought of what he'd witnessed chilled his blood and he could feel the man's spit on his cheeks for a full two minutes before the RUF commander moved on. Even Berti, in his stretcher, was given a verbal going over. The final gruesome addition was the sudden appearance of an embalmed head on a stick. There was no doubt it was that of a white victim, a soldier by the look of the blue beret they'd stuck on top. The eyes were open and like glass, the skin shiny and polished. It was lowered to each one of them for a close inspection, bobbing up and down, making them feel sick.

But what they experienced was nothing to what the Nigerians got. Hatred for them knew no bounds. These were fellow West Africans, yet they had taken up arms against their brothers, bombing and mortaring them in support of the criminals in Freetown. There were no cuffs round the ear for these four; they were punched and kicked, then beaten around the head with knotted ropes. Yet they were not harmed in any vicious way; there was no blood, no stabbing with bayonets, or clubbing with rifle butts. Nevertheless the noise was deafening, and Geoff was sure he could see in the eyes of those nearest him a hint of anticipation.

They grabbed the three soldiers eventually, dragging them forward off the stoop to where Mondeh lay, by the pits that had been shovelled out. The whole camp was gathered now in their hundreds, everything else that might occupy them forgotten while this event was about to take place. The three soldiers struggled, but to little avail. They were thrown to the ground, two of the bigger men grabbing their feet while others took hold of their arms tied behind their backs. Others did the same to Mondeh. With cruel deliberation all four men were lowered head-first into the pits, until only the men holding their feet were left with a task to perform.

The prisoners' voices, screaming in fear, carried a strange echoing quality, this caused by the confined space of the pits. But that didn't last long, as the shovels went to work, tossing the loose earth back into the ground, careful aim being taken to balance it as much as possible around the victims' heads. The shovels worked faster once the voices became muffled. In the crowd, hands were pointing and slapping, as if deals were being made. As the pits filled up the men holding the legs let go, to leave them kicking in a grotesque dance.

'They're betting,' said Mary, sobbing. 'They're actually betting.'

It was true. What they were using as wager currency didn't matter, but they were running a book on how long these victims would survive. The earth wasn't packed tightly around them so there was some air to be sucked in from around their mouths. But every breath would bring with it some soil, filling up the victims' mouths. Saliva would turn it to mud, and they might swallow that. Soon they would inhale enough earth to block up all their passages. The upturned legs had gone into a fury of kicking, the feet waving about as though the effort would levitate the men out of their fate. It was a double irony to realise that the opposite was true, that the more they struggled the quicker they would die, their shifting bodies settling the soil into a more compact mass. Perhaps that was a good thing.

There was no doubting who was the first to die. His bare, black legs went into an uncontrollable frenzy, from knee to heel, stretching up to their full extent before suddenly ceasing to move. This was greeted by moans from his backers and cheers from the rest, accompanied by demands for immediate payment. The other two Nigerians were gone within two minutes, but Mondeh was the last to die, his trousers now down below his knees, a final great heave producing the biggest cheer of all. The hostages on the stoop were left with a vision of eight still legs pointing towards the star-filled sky, the air full of the kind of noisy arguments that might occur at a dog fight. Bets were settled and jokes exchanged. It was almost uncanny when silence fell over the crowd, hard to believe after what had gone before.

'Do you see the way they are looking at us, Geoff?' sobbed Mary. He wanted to put his arms round her when he replied, but his bound hands prevented that. Instead he just nodded, looking into that sea of eyes before him. Then he glanced along the row of his fellow hostages, to see if they were receiving the same message from those stares.

'That's what they intend to do to us,' Mary continued. 'It will be blacks and Asians first, but they'll get to us eventually. They're going to bury us alive.'

He wanted to scream at her, to tell her she was wrong, but there were grins on those faces as well, the grins of ghouls looking forward to their next entertainment.

'This place is very quiet and dignified without Willy,' said Blue.

Paul Hill greeted that remark with a broad grin. The Fijian, after the last bust-up, had been barred from Paddy's Bar, a ban that extended to the Lagoona night-club and the Cape Sierra Hotel. Willy had taken to drinking in the shebeens frequented by the locals, quite happy with the loss of quality in all departments: whores, drinks and decor.

'Perhaps I should get you pissed and you could take over his stable of women?'

'You know me with hookers, Paul. It's strictly two at a time.'

'With something left for the local girlfriend when you take a trip to town.'

'Leila's all right, mate,' Blue winked. 'She is one of those women who understands a man's needs.'

'Bollocks!' Paul snorted. 'If she knew what you were up to in that compound in Bonthe she'd cut your balls off, and your cock with it.'

'That's the trouble with holiday romances,' Blue sighed. 'They always get too serious.'

'How goes the holiday?'

'Well enough,' Blue replied, without conviction.

'It must be fun working with Sandy McPherson.'

'Tell me about it! How he ever got RSM in the flipper brigade I'll never know. He's as thick as pig shit.'

'He's not, Blue.'

Blue reluctantly nodded in agreement. 'You're right. I've sent a fax to Dave Heffer at Charter Security asking for him to be pulled out. Maybe he'll oblige, maybe not. Hard to know what's going on when the old bastard is talking to Razenbrook behind my back.'

'Is Razenbrook still driving you mad?'

'Thanks to Sandy, he is. McPherson makes out to him that there's nothing stopping us going in and getting his stuff out but me and my scruples.'

'Since when did you have any fucking scruples?'

'That just shows how dozy he is. But he winds up Razenbrook no end. The man wants his money and he wants his maintenance. If I hear the words "processed rutile" one more time, I swear I'll slot him.'

'I guess he says the same about the word "hostages". Rumour from the High Commission bar has it he wanted you to go in anyway.'

'He did, the bastard. But the main man put the block on it, though how the fuck Quentin-Davies found out what was proposed is a bit of a mystery.'

'Wasn't you, then?'

'I don't talk to High Commissioners, Paul. I'm just a peasant. But whoever did it, and my guess is Layman, I was glad.' Blue responded to Paul's raised eyebrows. 'Layman hates Razenbrook, and I can see why. The bastard doesn't know his arse from his elbow, mine-wise. And Mike, a fully qualified engineer, has to take orders from him.'

'Sounds like the British Army.'

'Too right!'

'He'll be out on his arse if Razenbrook finds out.'

'Nah! Bastard needs him too much. And he's like me. Layman doesn't quite see what getting the hostages killed will do for dredge mining in Sierra Leone.'

'So what's the plan now?' asked Paul.

'We gather intelligence on rebel movements, we wait and we train for an assault on Port Nitti.'

'And occasionally relax?' said Paul, hooking a thumb towards the approaching Leila.

Blue grinned. 'Got to do that, mate. I'm like JFK. If I don't get a piece every night I get headaches.'

'Now I remember why I never liked sharing an observation post with you.'

Joined by his girlfriend, the conversation had to take a different turn. Blue never discussed either his training or the AAR team's objectives with Leila. It was habit anyway, but it made sense. She was beautiful, as far as he knew faithful, and a great fuck, but she was part of the local Lebanese business circle and they might have a different agenda from him. They would have a line to the RUF, that was certain, just as a precaution. Middle Eastern businessmen had a lot of experience of war and didn't like to be caught out.

Paul Hill was coming on to her big time. Blue was used to behaviour like that from his old friend and he didn't mind too much. They'd always competed for floozies and never yet fallen out over one. It was may-the-best-man-win stuff that you had to have if you wanted to be a serious social player. You couldn't be the jealous type and have a good time. So he listened to Paul, sometimes grinning, at other times wincing at his patter, the lines he had heard so often. It brought back memories of south-east Asia, central America, Hereford and even that pisshole Special Forces bar in Belfast. Recollecting that made him a bit melancholy. He would never admit even to Paul how much he missed the regiment, but he did. The easy camaraderie, the constant work required to build on skills, the chance to test yourself against the best, the buzz that came from death and danger – it was something that couldn't be replaced in the civilian world, regardless how many mercenary teams you joined.

That led him to thinking about the men he had. There were twenty-four of them now, including the two signallers. They were good in the main. Even Sandy McPherson, when he wasn't busily engaged in double-crossing Blue. They were the kind of guys who had loved the service life and couldn't stand the idea of a normal civvy job. They had trained hard, and most had shown a willingness to learn anything that was outside their past experience. They could move as a team, shoot straight and think for themselves in a combat situation, something they'd proved as the training had progressed.

They'd been working on a reoccupation plan that involved one eight-man team armed with 12.75mm heavy machine guns occupying a defensive position covering the road and approach routes to Port Nitti, another, complete with mortars, providing defence in depth and the remainder tasked with preparing the laden barges for the move out. So far it had worked well. Their other scenario, which they were now tuned up to perform, was a fast inflatable incursion carrying a maintenance crew to the dredgers. The AAR team weren't a patch on the guys from the regiment, but they'd take on and beat the RUF, even outnumbered ten to one, and since that was the job they'd been brought here to do, Blue was satisfied.

He wanted to get on with it as much as Razenbrook, but the hostages made that impossible. The RUF message came through Welford via Deen: touch that rutile and the hostages are history; try to occupy the Plant site and start production and you'll get the same result. They never cottoned on to the need for maintenance, but the reply would be the same if asked.

Not that the AAR boss accepted it. He'd had to argue hard for a wait before the High Commission intervened. Razenbrook was livid, and made no secret of it. He was short-term all the way, only interested in his own future. The hostages meant fuck all to him and his precious career, in which he envisaged himself elevated to the main board in London and out of all this African mayhem. He rarely let a day go by when he didn't come on the satcom to ask Blue when he intended to go in and do the necessary: get out his rutile and take back the mine sites.

The long-term effect was of no interest to him; the fact that with a whole raft of dead hostages, the mines would almost certainly struggle in the future to recruit the right kind of people to operate them. Those already here would probably carry on working for AAR, but they'd go home eventually and they'd need to be replaced. There were few expats who would fly themselves and their families out to what was essentially a war zone, and the locals would never feel safe with the RUF a constant threat. Nor could AAR afford to keep Blue and his kind on indefinitely. The job needed time: time to train a proper local security force led by a cadre of expat mercenaries good enough to check the RUF without the need to call in the army.

'Are you going to let this man steal me away, Blue?' asked Leila, with a manufactured pout.

'Sorry,' said Blue, sitting forward. 'I was miles away.'

'Stay there if you like, mate,' said Paul. 'I was enjoying myself.'

'Did he tell you he was impotent?' asked Blue. 'He can't get it up.'

Leila laughed and jabbed him hard. 'No he did not, you horrible swine. And if he did it would only make him more interesting. Paul would become a challenge.'

'See, Blue,' whooped Paul. 'All I need is another hour and she'll be desperate to prove you wrong.'

'Is that so?' said Blue, his eyes fixed on Leila's huge olive orbs in mock surprise. 'Another hour and it will be brewer's droop. It won't be me that's proved wrong.'

'I've got backup,' said Paul, waggling his tongue.

'I should think that's knackered too, the amount of work it's already done. You'd better stick with me.'

'Two's up?' asked Paul, hopefully.

'Not my decision, mate,' Blue replied.

Leila understood that all right, and it nearly got Paul a slap round the ear. Not that he was worried. He'd never really had a chance anyway, and there were too many hookers available, most of whom would do anything for a decent meal, to feel that the night would be wasted.

As it was they both drank too much. Paul got stuck into the White Russians, insisting that Blue join him, thus getting both him and his mate totally shit-faced, and that was before they left Paddy's and went clubbing. Strutting their stuff on the Lagoona dance floor sobered them up a bit, but neither pulled and they ended up back at the Cape Sierra Hotel, drinking in the lounge and keeping the poor bastard who served the night-time drinks away from his bed. The talk was all old-times-chewing-the-fat by two mates getting progressively more pissed. There were a few maudlin tears shed for mates who'd failed to 'beat the clock'. The stone regimental obelisk containing the clock was full of plaques recalling men who hadn't made it on some training exercise or operation.

Blue and Paul were still at it when some of the residents came down for breakfast. Jamie Padden found them and passed on the information that there was a South African team in town, security consultants, some of whom he had recognised. 'I checked with the desk. They're from a company called Executive Outcomes.'

'Did they clock you?'

'Must have, man,' he replied, pulling up a chair and sitting down. 'Some of them worked with me in Angola. But they didn't want to say hello, which is odd.'

'It's like flies and shit, Jamie. When there's trouble about, everybody is sniffing for work.'

Paul and Blue called for another round, with Jamie insisting he was sticking to coffee. Delane arrived with the order, standing in the doorway and looking at the occupants of the room in an imperious way, as if they had no right to be there. Sighting Paul Hill, he made a sharp signal with his hand, implying that that he wanted to speak to him in private. The SAS man, needled at the peremptory way in which the message was conveyed, took his time to respond, but he eventually joined the major in a quiet corner where they immediately became involved in an animated discussion.

Blue had his back to the pair, so it was Jamie Padden who noticed the repeated looks that Delane aimed in his direction. Paul glanced at Blue once or twice himself and, appraised of the fact by the Rhodesian, Blue felt the hairs rising on the back of his neck. No one likes the idea of being talked about when they can't hear what's being said, and Blue was no exception, but he made a good job of hiding it, sipping his drink without attempting to turn round. He began discussing, with Jamie, the various possibilities as to what the South Africans might be up to, now that they'd arrived in Freetown.

'The major is leaving,' said Jamie eventually, leaning forward to stir the remains of his coffee.

Blue turned then to exchange a look with Delane that had no warmth in it, from either party. He saw Paul gesture to him, a gentle request that he join him in the corner. Clearly what he wanted to say was for Blue's ears only. Jamie Padden stood at the same time as he did, adding only a quiet 'See you later' as he made himself scarce.

'They've topped one of the hostages,' said Paul softly as Blue joined him. 'The black doctor, Mondeh.'

'Is that what he came to tell you?'

'That and one or two other things.'

Both men understood what the death of Mondeh amounted to. The whole scenario had taken a very serious turn for the worse. But suspecting his name had been included in a lot of the conversation, Blue was more interested in knowing why.

'Delane wanted to know if the High Commission could look to you for help.'

'What kind of help?'

Paul's reply was just a little bit testy. 'I don't think after what I've just told you I have to spell it out.'

That made Blue bridle in response. He jerked a thumb at the door through which Delane had so recently exited. 'That stuffed prat wants me to do something for the British government?'

'That's right.'

'Then why the fuck didn't he ask me himself?'

'Come on, Blue. You know it's not done like that.'

'I don't know what "it" is, that's for sure. Anyway, I work for Anglo-African.'

'I mentioned that. Delane thought that they wouldn't object. Just the opposite.'

Blue nodded slowly. 'I suppose that bastard and Razenbrook are bosom pals.'

Eight parts pissed, Blue still had enough sense to figure out some angles. If Delane wanted anything from him, it couldn't be to do with negotiations: that was Welford's patch, a job suddenly made a thousand times more difficult by the way the RUF had wasted Mondeh. The only thing they could ask him for, as far as he could see, was some kind of action job, not a diplomatic one. He suddenly had a vision of being set up to take the fall for something that was really the responsibility of someone else.

'Has Forwood got anything to do with this? Because if he has you can file whatever it is you're cooking up under haemorrhoids. I wouldn't spit on that cunt in the desert.'

'The major was here because of Forwood's reluctance to be the messenger, Blue. There's no way our Roddy is going to ask you for anything. But it's all kosher. According to Delane, the request comes from London, through the High Commissioner. They're having a meeting at three o'clock and he'd like to know your answer.'

'You might get it when I know the question.'

Paul was suddenly serious, in the way only a drunk can be. 'I told him you wouldn't do anything for Forwood, but you might do it for me.'

Blue looked at his old mate suspiciously. His night should have ended in bed with Leila; instead, he was thinking, he'd spent an awful lot of it with Paul talking about old times: patrols, selection, continuation training, mates and guys they'd mutually disliked. He'd had a lot to drink, but that had a limited effect on his thought processes. 'Did you set this up, you bastard?'

Paul responded with a lop-sided grin. ''Course I did, you arse. What makes you think I'd waste a whole night getting shitfaced with you?'

The ten-mile run got rid of most of the effects. Blue was aware as he stripped off that his sweat smelled like pure distilled alcohol. Paul was the same, in dire need of water and a dip in the hotel pool. Food came next, the axiom, 'if you don't eat you can't work' well to the fore. Then Blue insisted that they repair to his room and sit on the veranda to talk, radio on in the background as a security measure in case they were being bugged.

'Now, mate. Since I don't want to go on some magic mystery tour for the High Commission with my arse hanging out, you'd better fill me in. Come to think of it, what am I talking about, for fuck's sake? I don't want to go anywhere at all.'

'I only know so much.'

'Well, let's start with that. Like what the fuck are you guys doing here in the first place?'

'I don't bloody well know! And don't think I haven't had the same thought, Blue. We all have. But from what I can tell we are on a straight BG training job. Sure there was a heap of stuff going down before we got in, but all this hostage shit has blown up since we arrived. And I saw

Forwood's face when the headshed asked him if we could offer backup. He was totally gobsmacked, so I don't think he was hiding anything. And he was all for it until the High Commissioner sat on the idea.'

'Remember what a devious bastard Forwood is.'

'I never let it out of my mind, Blue. But the guy is working out his time. He's back to the woodentops when we get home. This has been my job from the start. If it makes you feel any better, Forwood was asked about you and he flatly refused to put the request for any assistance to you himself.'

'Why didn't you?'

Paul spread his hands. 'I had no reason to. It was all speculation. That black doctor getting wasted changes things.'

There was no anger in Blue's voice when he responded. 'But you set out to soften me up. All that fucking nostalgia trip we went through.'

'That was an accident, mate. I won't deny I knew a request was possible, but it wasn't firmed up. And that had nothing to do with us getting pissed last night.'

'So, what's the picture?'

'Confidential.'

'Right,' Blue replied, well aware that all Paul was saying was not to tell anyone he spilled the deal before his three o'clock appointment.

'London is talking about a hostage rescue.'

Blue wasn't surprised. He'd already figured out that was the way things were heading, but the eyebrows were still raised enough to pose the question. So Paul had to go through all the problems related to the BG team and the SO10 minders being involved. 'Quentin-Davies won't have it. He's a career diplomat, and cares more for his own arse than anything else.'

'You know where they are?'

'Not yet, but when we do the aim is, like I said, to bring in the stand-by squadron on a deniable.'

'Method of entry?'

'To be decided, mate. That depends on the location.'

'This smells.'

'I don't disagree, Blue, but I don't know who's farted. All I know is that the High Commissioner thinks we're close to finding them. It doesn't take a genius to work out that the guys coming in would like some info on the ground and the buildings of wherever that is. It also does not take a genius to figure out that in a deniable op, and with a full-time job to do, we are limited in what we can provide, especially since we don't even have the kit we need to do the job. Any more than two of our faces out of town at the wrong time, and for a long time, and deniable goes out the window.'

Blue leant forward, his face creased as he posed the question. 'That has to be bollocks! How come, for openers, when this shit hits the fan, there are already ten SAS guys in the country?'

Paul just spread his hands in a gesture of ignorance. 'There's so much going on here, Blue, that you could come up with a dozen theories for that. Strasser doesn't trust anybody and nobody trusts him, which is why we are here, to make sure that he isn't slotted. The place is crawling with guys playing both sides of the fence, and that includes the guy who is paying your wages.'

'And suddenly Jamie tells us there is a South African team here too. The town is getting crowded.'

'Don't look to me to explain that one, mate.'

'I suppose,' said Blue slowly, 'the only thing to do is for you to go along to this meeting and listen to what the main man has to say. What the fuck, I can always turn him, and you, down!'

CHAPTER FIFTEEN

Quentin-Davies chaired the three o'clock meeting, with Delane at his right and Eddie Welford on his left. The Scotland Yard man's pasty face was as impassive as ever. Further down the table, Paul and Forwood sat opposite each other, with Harry Fielding at the bottom.

'This meeting will be unminuted, gentlemen. There will be no record of it ever having taken place. If that bothers you at all, I suggest you leave now.'

This statement was followed by a belligerent look at everyone, a very theatrical one designed to let them know just how ferocious his eyebrows could be, that he was the controller. 'Right then. If I may summarise.' He coughed slightly, then took a sip of water before continuing. 'By dint of our being the ex-colonial power, and with English being the local common language, we find ourselves at the forefront of a situation which is not of our choosing. We have taken on responsibility for the lives of over a dozen people, some of them our nationals, most not, and it is our duty to do everything in our power to secure their release.'

Quentin-Davies paused, not in the least fazed by the serried ranks of blank expressions, the faces of people who were wondering why he was taking so long to tell them things they already knew.

'The powers that be in Sierra Leone,' he continued, 'either cannot, or will not undertake the task. And in any event, recent occurrences have led us to conclude that finding someone to trust who would use local forces to effect a rescue would be somewhat difficult.'

'I'll say,' said Delane, jabbing with his pencil. 'And nothing has outlined that more, of course, than the unfortunate deaths of Colonel Buckhart and now Doctor Mondeh.'

The chairman paused again, and tapped the table impatiently, like a musician trying to recall the beat of a song. Delane had interrupted his train of thought. 'And what of the hostages?' he said, picking up the thread. 'Some of them must be in pretty poor condition by now, their spirits crushed by what has happened to one of their number. All efforts to secure their release through negotiation have so far come to nought. What is your present opinion, Mr Welford?'

'My job, or that of Mr Deen, is to keep talking as long as there is any hope of getting them out unharmed. That means we cannot overreact to the doctor's demise. That would merely jeopardise the lives of the remainder.'

'But do you anticipate a positive result overall?'

The man from SO10 looked pained. Being definite was not a situation he was happy with, which made his next response sound doleful rather than considered. 'You can never tell when a negotiating situation will suddenly improve.'

'But you can sense when it deteriorates, surely?'

'Of course. We are dealing here with a tough representative, distance and a lack of communications. Alimany Bakaar is talking to us. He is adamant that the leadership did not sanction Mondeh's death. We are dealing with a group of people who are far away from their front-line commanders. Those same commanders must have some latitude in the making of decisions. I have no idea of how much power they wield, nor how often they exchange information.' Welford sighed, like a man with the entire weight of the world on his shoulders. 'They obviously don't want us to initiate direct contact with the captors. That might give us too much leverage, or even a chance to cause a split in their approach. Bakaar wants to keep control in his own hands, so we must continue to try to persuade him that holding the hostages does the RUF cause more harm than good.'

'The problem I have,' said Quentin-Davies, 'is the need to be seen to remain impartial. And let me tell you, gentlemen, given the recent successes the rebels have enjoyed, it's damned uncomfortable. Right now I must keep good relations with the people in power. In no way can I, personally, be seen even to be in conversation with the RUF. That would render my position untenable. Yet I must also take cognisance of the fact that revolts of this nature sometimes succeed.'

He paused yet again, rather longer this time to elicit sympathy for his plight. Only Delane, with a slow nod, was prepared to oblige.

'The government is running out of money, gentlemen. The mining interests only pay duties when they export product. That has been severely curtailed. The situation in the army is getting worse by the day. Drying up the stream of revenue suits the RUF. It has given them a long-term and positive strategy, something they have managed to achieve with a minimal threat.'

'I should think the hostages feel differently,' said Welford.

'I didn't mean it that way,' Quentin-Davies snapped.

Paul was bored by this. The hostages were the key to the whole thing. As long as the RUF held them and the government was determined to try to keep them alive, the rebels had all the cards. Strasser and his gang had used their time in power to line their pockets, and would retire to spend the money rather than risk anything that might threaten their future. The underpaid, underfed army was in no fit state to get them out, and lacked the will even to try, which was just as well since they'd very likely get them all killed if they did. To Paul's mind it was like any such situation, be it Entebbe or Prince's Gate. The hostages either had to be rescued, in this case by an outside force, or the RUF had to be shown that holding them made no difference to what the government and the business community would do. Yet Quentin-Davies rambled on, using ten words where one would do, underlining over and over again the risks to his position and that of Her Majesty's Government.

'So the question arises,' he concluded, 'what is the best way to effect a resolution to this crisis?'

'We still don't know where they are,' said Forwood.

'Thank you, Mr Welford,' said the High Commissioner. 'We won't detain you any longer.' The detective hadn't been expecting that. For once he was thrown. Looking around the table with a perplexed expression, he stood up and walked out of the room.

'Alan?' said Quentin-Davies, coolly, as soon as the door shut behind him.

Delane pulled a piece of paper from under his blotter and pushed it towards the troop commander. 'I think you'll find that the situation in that respect has improved.' Forwood scanned it, then angrily passed it down the table to his men, with a hard look at his superior officer. Paul Hill was just as curious. He'd had a word with Delane about Blue Harding just before they'd entered this room and the major hadn't said a peep to him about new information.

'Just in,' Delane responded, apologetically. 'I do assure you, and the source is A1.'

'Have they got this in Gib?' Paul asked.

'Jimmy Forrest was sending a signal as this meeting convened.'

'You're sure the source is good?'

'I am,' Delane replied emphatically. 'We have been working very hard to detach our man from his primary allegiance, which is to the RUF. That we have not managed, but we do know his views regarding hostage taking are at variance with the rest of the leadership. The most difficult point was the notion he had that anything we secured might be leaked to the present government.' Delane gave Paul a hard look. 'I have managed to convince him that will not happen, so I cannot stress enough that the information cannot be passed on to anyone not actually involved in this meeting without prior clearance.'

There was silence for a bit while everyone indulged in a guessing game as to the identity of the informant. The trouble they all had, amply underlined by the number of heavy frowns, was that there were too many candidates. Betrayal and counter-betrayal were in the air like disease spores, and that included the present members of the NPRC. The only one you could probably exclude was Strasser himself, and even that didn't stand up to too much scrutiny.

'How do you see this new information affecting the thinking of your colleagues, Forwood?' asked the High Commissioner.

'It will allow them to draw certain conclusions, sir. But that is all.'

The grid reference was being marked up on the map by the green slime. They'd also begun to work out distances from all the points of entry already discussed. Peter Goring had called a meeting of the troop seniors. When it convened he put his finger on the precise point, high ground close to the banks of the Yambe River, a place at which the river divided to create several islands.

'Right, fellas, that is where they are. It's the site of an abandoned DP camp set around various mission buildings, and our information is that they will remain there long enough for us to mount a rescue mission. Early indications are that we are mostly dealing with mud huts, a couple of wooden buildings and at least one dilapidated stone structure. The position is close to a river. That, thank Christ, is in range of our Avons, and so favours an approach by boat.'

Ever since the rescue mission was first mooted, the men making plans had been seeking a way to avoid moving cross-country. Given the potential start points the distance was too great for a surprise approach by vehicle, and going on foot was an even worse option. Time and distance severely limited what they could take in the way of equipment. A helicopter approach, although the very antithesis of surprise, was the option which had occupied most of the preliminary planning, with certain sites in neighbouring countries identified which could be used as forward operational bases.

The rescue teams would drop in by air, only calling in the helis to take them and the hostages out once the operation was a success. But everyone knew the possibilities, and that the plan was fraught with risk. Aircraft flying in confined spaces at night were involved in the kind of very high-risk game that had sunk the Iranian hostage rescue back in 1982.

'Is it possible to get a layout of the camp?' asked one of the troop seniors, Barry Goldup.

'We need better than that,' said Goring, 'but the info we have is that the people at the other end are taking care of that. Our task is to gear up for a fast move once we have the necessary information. The drop zone will also be selected and sponsored by them.'

Goring looked around the faces. 'Right, we will have flight times posted. As of now, operational rehearsal will concentrate on a parachute insertion into the sea, complete with MIBs.'

Within minutes the signal had gone out, alerting the Hercules transports to stand by for intensive exercises. Within an hour, the first of the medium inflatable boats was being loaded.

Paul Hill could see what conclusion the stand-by squadron would draw. So could Forwood, but then the captain could also see what would flow from that and so was keeping his mouth shut.

'That's not very encouraging,' Quentin-Davies growled.

'They need a CTR,' Forwood replied, taking a map off Delane and examining it.

'And what, pray, is that?' the High Commissioner asked, directing his question to Delane.

'Close target reconnaissance, sir.'

'Ah!'

'Someone,' said Harry Fielding, 'has to go in and look at what is there, establish the size and strength of the opposition, the precise location of the hostages, their routines as well as their condition, and the ground, routes in and out. You must understand that the regiment does not want a battle. It's not what we were designed for. We don't have the means to take on any main enemy force. Our method is surprise, speed and overwhelming short-term firepower. The longer the rescue takes, the more trouble we're in. Ideally, from inception to conclusion, it should not take more than ten minutes. For that to happen good intelligence is essential.'

Quentin-Davies held up a hand. 'I think I have the picture, Harry. In fact, I believe the need was mooted several days ago.'

'And,' Paul Hill continued, 'that has to be done quickly.'

'How?'

Paul had passed the map to Harry, so he indicated that he wanted it back, tracing the route of the river with his finger as he talked. 'With these river systems and the coastal marshes the CTR looks like a boat op to me. Whoever goes in will have the added task of keeping the nature and the aim of any subsequent operation secure.'

Paul looked at Forwood, but the Rupert declined to take up the explanation. 'The rescue mission could start from the same location. An air drop into the estuary would be straightforward enough. By boat they could move inland real quick, under cover of darkness if there is a minimum level of ambient light. They'll be on the target by the time the sun is up.'

'How far is it?' said Delane, more to keep the conversation going than as a true request for enlightenment. He probably already knew to the inch how far it was.

'About fifteen kilometres from deep, open water, in all,' Paul replied, after another glance at the map.

'Noise?'

'An idling Mariner engine is pretty quiet.'

'Would it not be better to move in daylight?'

'No. And there's no need to. The rivers are wide and navigable by small boats. We're in the dry season so we have a very high probability of moonlight.'

'Which is almost as strong,' Delane added encouragingly. 'You can see for miles in a full moon.'

'True, but you can never be sure your eyes aren't deceiving you. Maybe the rescue team would be spotted, but they'd be moving faster than the news of their approach so they could go for it up to a point where caution becomes essential. That will allow them to deploy in numbers quickly, with whatever equipment they need, at an angle of approach of their own choosing. It's the people who do the CTR who have to be careful.'

'And the enemy?' asked Forwood.

'All the assessments we have seen show the RUF to be poor fighters. True, their discipline is greater than that of the army, but that really isn't saying much. They have, it seems to me, indifferent leadership, are low on ammunition and weapons, and possess no great ability to stand and fight if it should come to a battle.'

'They don't have to, Paul,' Forwood sneered. 'They just have to cut a dozen throats to make the whole thing a fiasco.'

Paul was quick to respond. 'Not if they're up against the best-trained counter-terrorist team in the world.'

That left Forwood high and dry. As a serving SAS officer he could hardly disagree. Besides, this was all so much waffle. The decisions wouldn't be taken in this room, they'd be made by the men doing the job, not by Forwood.

'Well, Paul,' said Delane, with the self-satisfied air of a man who felt he had achieved his aim, 'you seem to have thought of everything.'

'Except who is going to assist the CTR team to get in. Remember we are limited both in time and numbers and know little about this area, as well as being short of the means of remedying this. To do it properly could take time. We, on the BG team, cannot be absent from Freetown for long without raising questions. Then there is the small matter of some river transport to get in and out in the first place.'

There was a silence then. Quentin-Davies and Delane were waiting for Forwood to speak, but he was determined to stay silent.

'So we're rather short on options,' said Paul finally, glaring at Forwood. 'The only person I know who has some local knowledge, the boat we need and the requisite skills is John Harding, who is at present working for AAR. I know, because he has told me, that the hostage situation is causing Anglo-African just as much grief as it's causing us.'

'Will he help to undertake the CTR?' demanded Forwood in a strangled voice.

'He might if I ask him, boss.'

That produced sighs of relief from the head of the table. Forwood didn't react at all, staying stony-faced, his gaze avoiding every eye in the room.

'He'll need permission from Tony Razenbrook.'

'No!' said Quentin-Davies emphatically. 'He must know nothing about this. It has to be totally deniable, otherwise you wouldn't be asking in the first place.'

'They employ him and it's their kit we'll be using.'

'Believe me, Razenbrook would sell his grandmother to be able to get safely back into production. I doubt he'll ask too many questions once success is achieved.'

Delane then spoke rapidly and comprehensively, underlining the fact that all his previous questions had been pure waffle. He was well on top of the job and the requirements. 'The task will be to give the stand-by squadron enough information to work out a plan. Obviously, it is then up to them either to go or to abort. Also, speed is of the essence. Once the CTR has confirmed the location, the rescue should follow within hours.'

He addressed his next words directly to Forwood, who was still looking po-faced. Paul doubted that right now Delane was top of his Christmas card list. As a fellow serving officer he should have backed him up, and that rabbit-out-of-the-hat trick with the hostage location was well out of order. He'd made Forwood look like a right prat.

'You can spare two men for the CTR. Being off for the weekend gives you a clear forty-eight hours, Roddy, when your men are theoretically stood down. That should give the BG team more freedom to get involved in an actual operation.'

'I need to be told when the balloon goes up,' said Quentin-Davies. 'I must inform the members of NPRC before it happens, Strasser personally if possible. Too late for them to be able to interfere, of course.'

'If we're looking to the coming weekend,' said Paul, 'the CTR would have to be gone by tomorrow at the latest.'

'We don't have an agreement with Harding yet,' Forwood snapped, 'and I for one am not convinced either that he's the man for the job or that you'll get him to do it!'

'I'd trust him, boss,' said Paul Hill.

Forwood was being an arsehole. This wasn't decision time, and he was being asked to take no risk. So apart from the personal there was no need to be so negative.

'Me too,' chipped in Harry Fielding. 'Especially if it's an entry by boat job. That's Blue's speciality. He did it twice in the Falklands.'

Forwood still seemed set to demur, but Quentin-Davies cut across him, making it clear to all present that he had the authority to issue orders if he wished. 'We conclude this meeting with a theoretical possibility and no more. Mr Welford and his colleague will continue with the efforts to effect a release. You, Paul, will provide enough information from a reconnaissance so that we may be able to push matters forward. Agreed?'

'Agreed.'

'One more thing,' said Delane, collaring Paul as the others left the room. 'We are talking about involving Harding in this. That is caused by necessity, but it will be him and him alone. No one else.'

'What if he wants to take another AAR man along?' asked Paul.

'He can't. And since he's ex-regiment, and understands the need for secrecy, he will, I'm sure, understand that.'

Blue, when Paul put the proposition to him, tried to make it sound like he was reluctant, but he couldn't hold the line, especially when Paul confirmed that he and Kenny Collins would be coming in with him. The fact that they wouldn't be a four-man patrol was a hiccup, not a problem, especially since the task was to avoid all contact. To John Harding, when they started planning, it felt just like old times. The buzz was there. The security business had its moments, but nothing to compare with this. This was, as near as damn it, a proper Special Forces operation.

Paul went back to the High Commission building; Blue went in search of Jamie Padden. He found him in Paddy's Bar and winkled him away from the company of a couple of hookers who were eating at his expense. There was no way Blue was going to let him know what was happening, but he did have a responsibility to his team and to Anglo-African. If the operation went pear-shaped they would find themselves in a whole new ball game, quite possibly one more dangerous than anything they'd planned for. That would require leadership, and not the kind that would come from the likes of Mork and Mindy.

Jamie'd had a few drinks, and Blue was pretty vague, getting Jamie talking rather than telling him much, but the Rhodesian was ex-Special Forces and even if he couldn't get to the definitive four, he could put two and two together. Something was going down and he was out of the information loop, but he didn't ask, which was another point in his favour. He was professional enough to accept the principle of 'need to know'.

Then it was back to the Cape Sierra to rejoin Paul Hill and Crazy Collins. The three men spent a long time poring over maps and some pretty poor photographs, discussing the task. It was simple: to get them up-river unobserved, map out the rebels' camp, locate the hostages, get the information back to base, then get out, again, unseen. If the op went badly wrong, as long as they were clear of pursuit, they had the option of calling in Sergei as backup to do a quick bug-out.

The simple option of starting straight from Bonthe had to be discarded. There were too many sharp eyes and loose mouths there. Blue suggested a boat recce of Nitti, something undertaken regularly, as an excuse to throw his guys off the scent.

'On your own?' asked Kenny.

'Yeah! We do it regularly so we can tell Tony Razenbrook his rutile barges are still floating. The bastard worries.'

Going back to the map he explained his thinking. The route from there was between the twin jetties, so a change of course could be achieved unobserved. Anyone watching up-river would assume the boat had gone back down to the estuary; those keeping an eye on the down-river jetty might wonder why it stayed up-river so long, but they'd have no idea he'd pulled off the Jong River completely.

'It's just a guy in a boat, stooging around having a look-see. No big deal! Sergei can drop you down from the Hip at the other end of Gbangbia Creek and I can pick you up when he's gone. Then we're on our way.'

'What are you going to tell Sergei?'

'That we are doing some old mates of mine a favour!' said Blue emphatically. 'He don't care as long as he gets paid.'

That decided, they discussed the load they'd take, which had to be curtailed. With the rivers low there were bound to be several sandbars, obstacles they'd have to get the inflatable across. Eight guys could cope with whatever they had; three men could only handle so much and still move swiftly.

There was another familiar feeling: asking questions to which you yourself had already figured out an answer, pitting that against another man's thoughts to check that nothing was being missed. Blue could recall endless Chinese parliaments that to an outsider would have sounded like an extended knitting bee. They wouldn't comprehend that repeated and sometimes apparently senseless questions were a vital part of the process of exposing everyone's thinking on a particular point. There was a great danger, in covert operations, of making assumptions, thinking that someone understood a point when they didn't. It only worked if the team knew the plan backwards. That was the reason for all the talking, as well as the constant repetition of group orders and individual tasks. Taking chances was for mugs. You stayed alive in this game by being one hundred per cent mind-on, and secure in the knowledge that everyone with you was in the same mental state.

Blue was designated as the guide, responsible for getting them in. It was up to Paul to decide finally on method and execution, using the combined brainpower and experience of all three men. They talked and planned for over two hours. One of the most obvious constraints was the lack of accurate information regarding the river route. In normal circumstances they could have asked around, pumped the locals for information, even talked to the army. Not here! No one could be trusted. Nor could they do a casual trip to suss out any early problems. Time was too short.

There were no assumptions about anything, from clothing – two sets – through rations, to weaponry, comms, surveillance equipment and navigational aids. They had one of Blue's satellite telephones, while Paul would provide a hand-held Garmin ground positioning system. The maps were studied at length, but only a visual would give them a confirmed infiltration point. It was a bonus that the rebel camp was on high ground, since a rising slope next to the river should be covered by thick forest something akin to jungle. In this part of the world flat ground, though fertile by the watercourse, gave way fairly quickly to open bush. They gave the operation a completion time of thirty-six hours.

Once they'd picked out an infiltration point, down-river from the main camp on the same bank, it should be possible to set up a small laying-up point from which to operate. There they could set up the link that would keep the CTR team in touch with Gibraltar, passing back real-time information that could be used to begin the build-up of a proper ground appreciation. The Garmin would be backed up by pacing to establish distances. Buildings, if there were any, would have to be identified as to their use, measured and put on a sketch map. They tried to cover everything, but there is only so much you can do in advance. Reconnaissance, by its very name, means that you're going into the unknown, but time spent on it is never wasted. All they really had was a grid reference, a few reports from various sources of the strength and disposition of the numbers they might face, and no idea of the precise layout of a camp that could hold anything from three hundred to a thousand people.

To maintain security Paul and Kenny would heli straight from Freetown, while Blue cruised past Port Nitti at sunset to their rendezvous. They ran through the plan for the last time, then destroyed all the bits of paper they'd used to make notes and comments.

Blue went through a packing drill he'd done a thousand times, ticking off items from his personal kit list, sometimes having to abandon a non-essential item to create space for something very necessary. He had no choice regarding the use of an AK47, loading six mags with ammo and packing another 300 rounds into his day sack, along with spare ammo for his Browning pistol. His poncho and hammock were near the top.

Number one item was his golok, which would be attached to his wrist by a piece of paracord. You didn't even have a shit without that by your side. In deep vegetation that was a man's best friend, provider of food and the means to make shelter. It wouldn't be quite as bad as Brunei or Belize, but there would be bugs and snakes aplenty, as well as bigger wildlife so close to the river. He also had two syrettes of morphine provided by Paul Hill round his neck, plus a full trauma kit in his day sack. Belt kit was water and Steritabs, first aid, spare mags, emergency rations and map, plus a fifteen-metre loopline and a caribiner for deep-river crossing.

The lack of time was, in many ways, a good thing, leaving no time to gnaw at potential loose ends. He had to get the *Adelaide* across the Sherbro so he could be dropped off into his inflatable. None of the crew asked him any questions and he offered no explanations, parting company with a silent wave.

Port Nitti was eerily silent, but they had a real feeling of being watched. The trio of loaded barges still lay untouched, though they were bound to be under RUF observation. But they wouldn't react. The presence of a man in camouflage fatigues in an inflatable had become a common sight these past few days, and there was no way a single individual could recover the rutile. The Mariner outboard, which had been held at idling speed, fired into life, sending up a scared flock of river birds as Blue spun it away to head back down-river. Blue then closed the throttle until it was again idling in near silence. The surface of the water had that sheen on it that comes late in the day, so the ripples of the passing boat formed an ever-increasing V behind him. John Harding sat with his hand on the tiller, his skin stinging from the heavy-duty mozzie cream he was wearing.

'This is the life,' he said to himself.

CHAPTER SIXTEEN

Sergei was right on cue. From a position out of sight Blue watched as Paul and Kenny abseiled out of the heli on to a small patch of sand. The Russian was gone in less than a minute, the same time it took to get them into the inflatable. Paul and Kenny started camming up, covering their faces, necks and hands with streaks of dark cream.

Habit made Blue check that the AK47s they were using had compasses already taped on and were ready to fire. Standard operating procedure said that you had to be ready for a contact at any time. He had no need to worry. Just before they exited the heli both Paul and Kenny had checked the mechanisms on the weapons, attaching a magazine, twenty-nine rounds instead of a maximum thirty to avoid jamming, solid shot mixed with tracer to make adjustments to range and direction easy. The Sig Saur pistols had been checked too and were now in their waistcoat holsters.

Blue was in charge from this point. He went through the task again, repeating orders and objectives, before re-engaging the engine. Paul switched on the Garmin GPS, recording their start position. They turned into Gbangbia Creek, which took them due east from the twin jetties of Port Nitti, running through dense, overhanging vegetation. The main creek was slow, wide and shallow, the last of the light reflected in the flat calm waters, and after two kilometres they made their final turn into the river that would take them all the way to the rebel camp in the hills near Mongeri.

The forests were alive with the noise of screeching monkeys, trilling birds, and occasionally the odd grunt of some larger creature. That and the density of what was near to being jungle helped to muffle the engine noise, allowing Blue to employ a bit of speed. The weather was good, the air dry and warm, with plenty of moonlight. The first obstacle was the town at the head of the creek that gave the place its name, Gbangbia. There was a bridge that ran over to Tinanhun, a crossing that was almost certain to have a checkpoint; but any sentries would be watching out for traffic on the road, not the river. Besides, the rebels had never been, from

213

the little he'd observed, the most active bastards on the payroll, and if one of them was actually on the bridge and was looking down into the water, then it would be bad luck for him.

Blue slowed the boat and killed the engine when they got near to the bridge, a simple Bailey job left over from colonial times, letting it drift into the riverbank until it ran out of forward motion. This ranked as a major crossing point in local terms, and needed to be recce'd. The last thing they wanted was to be going under the bridge when a piece of road traffic was going across it. Anyone in a vehicle would be certain to look down – people always did – and spot the boat in the water.

Paul got himself into a good place to observe the bridge, its open structure making it easy to see that the checkpoint was unmanned, well back from the junction at which the jungle ended and the bridge began. He had no need to go on to the bridge unless someone else did, and then what happened next was down to him. If the guy had to be silenced, so be it, but that was to be avoided if possible. The whole squadron would be coming the same way at the weekend if all went well so the last thing they needed was a guard detail on the bridge, nervous and alert.

They got past without incident. Blue kept the engine turned way down so that the noise wouldn't carry, content to make slow headway. With ten hours of darkness in which to travel, time was not their problem. Sandbars were, and Kenny Collins was in the bows, peering forward to spot the eddies that tell them the water was shelving. It was only in certain areas they appeared, usually where the landscape was flat and the river could spread out over a wider basin, the long strands of white sand on the bank a good indication of the depth of water in the centre of the channel. It wasn't too much of a problem at this speed, but every section had to be marked on the map and recorded on the Garmin. This piece of kit would provide an exact read-out for the rescue teams to work by, so that a boat travelling at a higher speed would have a good fix on where any obstacle lay and could avoid running its outboard into deep sand.

Each time they slowly ground on to a bank, they had to get out into the shallow water, and search for another route well aware that there were crocodiles about. If that failed they had to unload the boat and drag the inflatable over into the next stretch of deep water. The soft breeze that sprang up was welcome to men who were toiling hard and sweating, with every insect in Africa buzzing round their ears. Few words were exchanged, most signals made by hand. Thankfully the river narrowed again, which increased the depth and meant that the halts and humping were fewer. Blue was able to increase speed, heading for the next obstacle, the point near Sigimi where the river bent round, almost doubling back on itself.

Another watercourse from the east joined the Gbangbia at this point, just north of the site of the Sigimi ferry. This place, a second river crossing point, would have to be checked for any sign of soldiers, be they RUF or army. The way the river came round created a salient, a narrow neck of land where distance between the two parts was shortened. There was an island in the middle of the Gbangbia on the northern arm which indicated the presence of more sandbars. Soldiers, if alerted and moving quickly, could cross from the ferry to the upper reaches and present a threat to the boats, especially if they were trying to haul an MIB and all their equipment across such an obstacle.

Blue ground the boat on a narrow strand of beach where the foliage came close to the water's edge. They turned the inflatable round so that the prow was pointing out. The bowline was buried in the soft sand, just deep enough to hold the boat but shallow enough that a good kick would dislodge it. This position, too, was recorded on the Garmin receiver.

The SAS troopers put on their day sacks. In an unknown scenario you take with you everything you need to fight and survive. You don't leave it behind, because if you're compromised it's no good being in one place with all the gear you need in another. They then knelt down and went through the task, checked the time they would spend ashore, and established the inflatable as the ERV. Leaving Blue with the boat, Paul took point, as he always did, regardless of the size of the patrol. He hated the idea of threat being evaluated by anyone else. He was much happier at the front himself so that he could make up his own mind, as well as save the time it took to pass back information.

They walked forward slowly, weapons up and covering the arcs, eyes sharp and accustomed to the dark, ears tuned for the slightest unusual sound, both measuring their pacing as they went. The chirruping of the crickets made that hard, almost as hard as the insects that seemed determined to get right inside their clothes. The hut, beside the ramp that made up the ferry, was dark and silent. Paul signalled that they would go round it to a point at the rear that gave better observation of the opposite shore. If there was a guard, this was where they should be. The men off duty would be asleep. But there should be one man outside at least if they wanted to stay alive. No assumptions! Use your eyes, ears and nose. It was that which stopped Paul from stepping straight on to the sentry.

He picked up the faint smell of stale cannabis mixed with a strong body odour just before the gentle snore, followed by the outline of a leg. Paul put up his hand to stop Ken Collins, half crouched, his weapon covering the soldier, peering into the gloom. The trooper immediately took up a firing position, his AK47 aimed at the wall of the mud building. The guy in front of Paul was stretched out with his head against a pile of thatch. He had dropped his weapon when he nodded off and it lay just a few inches away from the open hand that had held it.

The ferry had a guard detail. Who they were mattered less than the fact that they were there, since they covered the route up-river. The chances of government troops this far into the interior was slim. They were more likely to be RUF, placed at this crossing to control the traffic, and no doubt to extort the odd bribe. It would be nice to know the size of the detachment, but that was secondary to their presence. There was no way of finding out without going into the hut, and that was too risky.

Paul backed up slowly, Kenny staying clear of him so that both their weapons stayed fixed on the doorway, picking up various odours as he did so. He tried to register each one on the grounds that no information was useless. There was a food smell certainly: his brain said meat, probably pork judging by the sweetness of the aroma. There was petrol too, both fresh and used, probably their means of cooking. He passed a pile of rotting rubbish, quite deep. It all pointed to a fair-sized detail, men who had been here for some time, yet the hut, judging by its dimensions, couldn't hold over a dozen sleeping bodies.

Compasses and pacing took them back to the inflatable, with only one stop to check their bearings. They used oars to get off the sand and continued with them as they paddled past the still silent hut. There was a strong eddy halfway round the bend due to the other, more potent watercourse joining the Gbangbia, and that was noted. Paul entered the new waypoint on the Garmin, pleased that the middle of the river still had water deep enough to navigate. Once they were clear Blue fired up the Mariner.

For some three kilometres the river wound this way and that, the general direction being south-west before another sharp bend just below the settlement of Pelima. This was a substantial village of around a hundred dwellings with dogs that barked unconvincingly at something in the water. There were no lights and no reaction to the yelping and growling as the inflatable slipped by.

'The war can't have touched them much down here,' said Kenny quietly.

Blue grunted his agreement. Those dogs would be dead by now, eaten, if they'd had any trouble. His mind was on the next phase of the op, the need to establish an emergency helicopter landing zone close enough to the rebel encampment but far enough away to provide some security. The spot he'd chosen, which he would have to reconnoitre, was a point at which the river did another dogleg. While he admired Sergei as a heli pilot, Blue had no great faith in his ability to read a map, so he wanted a heli landing site which was impossible to miss from the air. In the very arc of that bend it looked like flat ground, perhaps half-beach. The shape should be easily spotted from the air, so that the Russian could come in on a visual either during the day, or, if there was even the smallest glimmer of moonlight, at night.

They ground the boat again, going through the same rigid procedures designed to keep them alive. Repeat the orders and the individual tasks. The first thing to do was to check the security of the position, for now as well as the future, to a distance of a hundred metres all round. Together they moved up-river and down, before heading inland. The map showed a dwelling five hundred metres away, but that was rated as being no more than a collection of a dozen mud huts with a few subsistence farmers, their wives, kids and chickens.

The soil was sand turning to red dust. There were few trees, but Blue paced them out anyway. The landing site for the Hip had to be fifty metres in diameter, since Sergei might be coming in for a quick landing and a very fast bug-out. The one thing that was missing was an area of dead ground to provide cover fire and cover from view, which when occupied would give good defensive fire positions should they or the teams be pursued during the withdrawal phase. Before re-embarking Ken Collins waded out into the river, checking on the depth. If you couldn't mount a defence it would be better to bug out, and over the river was the best route.

'Top of my chest,' he informed them when he returned.

'Good,' said Blue. 'With no rain it should stay that way or fall.'

That, he knew, would apply to the rest of the Gbangbia. Five days would make a difference, but that was not something anyone could calculate, and since he was working to the odd centimetre he just had to hope it wouldn't matter.

They used the engine for only a few minutes, until they were within five hundred metres of what they hoped would be the infiltration point. That was too close to the rebel camp, and any sentries they might have, to risk the noise. Besides, the map showed a couple of tiny settlements, one on each bank, further potential risks. Reading off distances from his compass, Blue was heading for the first of three islands that, according to his map, occupied the middle of the stream. As a landing site and LUP it could be perfect. The island should be uninhabited, being at risk of flash flooding in the rainy season. Yet covered every so often with a rich layer of alluvial silt, whatever vegetation existed would regenerate quickly, providing decent cover. The narrow part of the river, where it split to go round them, provide a natural defence line and a good arc of fire that could be made lethal by just a pair of Minimis. The main riverbank should also have thick vegetation to cover any crossing the assault and rescue teams wanted to make. And if the Ordnance Survey map had it right, the rising ground on the western bank that led up to the site of the rebel camp was too far away to overlook the proposed LUP. If threatened, falling back to the opposite, eastern ground should give them another arc of fire. Behind that lay densely forested low hills into which the teams could withdraw.

Paul tapped his arm and then his own watch. Blue nodded. There was a limit on the amount of dark time. It was one of those situations where a decision would have to be made quickly, but both men had trained for years at this and were fully aware that when such a situation occurred the trick was not to fuck about. The mantra, 'Make a decision – a bad one is better than no decision at all' had been drummed into them.

They got ashore on the central island to find that, just past the sand at the very edge of the vegetation, it was covered in low scrub bushes that came no higher than their knees. At a signal Blue moved forward twenty paces, covered by Paul, then the trooper leapfrogged him. The third time Blue went to point he was relieved to enter a group of trees, not tall but well above the height of his head, thick without being so dense that they couldn't move through them. It took another hour to check the security of the proposed LUP. Twenty minutes was static, checking for any movement or to see if there was any pursuit or covert observation of their presence. That was followed by a small perimeter patrol, careful movement through scrub and forest, the location stored in the Garmin, the layout recorded mentally by each member of the team. The place was deserted; not even a strip of cultivated soil had been furrowed to grow mealie. The land around here, with the river hemmed in by hills, had to be fertile, so good that the locals could afford to ignore the rich soil of this island.

They brought the boat ashore, concealing it in the bushes as close to the shore as possible. That had to be the heaviest thing they'd have to move; no point, if there was to be an emergency bug-out, in having to lug it for any distance. Carrying it over the soft, dry sand left no trace, and they carefully cut enough greenery to cover it over so that it, too, was ready to go straight back into the water. The few feet of beach then had to be brushed to obliterate their footprints.

Only then did they look to their own needs. They required a spot that gave them good observation of the western shore, with security from any risk of being overlooked. Given the thick vegetation they had ample cover. With luck they would be gone from here the following night. Nature would provide them with what they needed; a place to set up an equipment cache and, when they had something to transmit, their comms. If the recce took longer than anticipated and they had to stay extra time, they could easily spend the day there.

The team just had time to eat and drink. Then still in darkness, leaving Blue behind, Paul and Kenny crossed to the west bank. There was no need to swim here either. It was the same chest-high water Ken Collins had experienced earlier, though the current flowed a bit more quickly through the narrow gap, tugging at their legs. Once ashore, they stood to and waited, back to back behind tree cover and in a position to cover all the approaches, never speaking, even their breathing regulated to stay quiet. Around them the forest was alive, birds and beasts adjusting to their presence. Then, at a signal from Paul, they faced each other and re-established orders and tasks before setting off.

The first thing to check was the riverbank and their own security. Anywhere in Africa where you had water, you also had people: women washing clothes or filling pots for cooking and drinking, kids bathing and men fishing. If there was a camp they might have to set up a daytime observation point. That required careful siting since there would also be various tracks from it to the riverside, not straight routes, but narrow lanes that twisted and turned to make ascent and descent easy. There would be rocks which the women used to flay their washing. They could then keep an eye on their offspring splashing about. The fishermen liked the kind of deep pools where their bottom-feeding catch tended to live, so would be unlikely to operate in the faster streams near these island. The trees came right to the riverbank and overhung it on both sides, creating a shaded avenue. There were no rocks that Paul could see, nor any evidence that a shaped clearing had been created by constant visitations. The river, between the bank and the island about a hundred metres wide, was deserted, and even after the most thorough examination no one would see any trace of their own movements.

Paul tapped Kenny and turned inland. Moving through the thick forest reminded him of his time in Brunei, where he'd done his continuation training after passing selection. That had been a bastard, especially to start with. Nothing was better designed to bring a newly badged trooper down to earth than a spell in the jungle. The directing staff were as hard as fuck, totally without sympathy and seemingly impervious to all the things that bothered the new arrivals. Compared to Brunei, this was a piece of piss. This wasn't real jungle; it was thinner and you could see to a distance of about five metres. The ground was more predictable, rising steadily from the riverside rather than swooping and falling in sudden gullies and bluffs, so thick with roots and the branches of dead trees that they could hide an army. But most of all it was nothing like as humid. It was hot, certainly, but it was a fairly dry heat, unlike the sapping steam bath he'd experienced in south-east Asia.

The rules, though, were the same. He could almost hear the voices of the DS minders as they issued their mantras: move slowly and use your senses; see a threat before it sees you; sniff, listen, watch where you put your feet using trees and anything else that's available to shield you from being compromised; take even paces and remember to note the distances; keep an eye on your compass and constantly check your heading, because you can get disorientated in a few minutes in deep foliage. They knew the drill and operated it with great skill.

They heard they were close before they were gifted with any sight of the rebel camp. They compared their pacings, took a reading from the Garmin, then marked the position on their maps. Then it was down on their bellies, crawling forward a few inches at a time to the spot where the forest became woods, then thinned to show the shaded clearings where the RUF had made camp. There wasn't much to see in the darkness, just a few makeshift thatched huts, with cooking pots outside.

'No sentries,' thought Paul, 'Not a single fucking one. Boy do these cunts think they're secure.'

The pair pulled back to deeper cover. They had a quick whispered conversation to confirm that the point where they exited the river was still the ERV, each checking that the other could identify it by the layout of trees and bushes. Paul had the Garmin, which was sensitive enough to tell them how much ground they had covered, though it had an overall positioning accuracy that could be fifty metres out.

They were back on their bellies, crawling carefully forwards, backwards, then sideways, searching for a point that would give them decent observation of the main part of the camp. Each incursion was followed by close observation of the movement of people. In theory they should be moving in both directions in equal numbers, but somehow the centre always attracted more.

Then it was straight back to the last ERV. Paul did a written appreciation and a sketch of what they'd observed to back up the technology, then it was a measured crawl to the east followed by another kitten-crawl approach on elbows and knees, moving six inches at a time until they could see the clearings. This they repeated four times, crossing two downhill tracks with great caution, building up a picture as they progressed.

The first substantial hut, a long and low affair with wooden walls shaded by high trees, confirmed that they were moving in the right direction. They watched that for twenty minutes, noting who went in and who came out, individuals who entered empty-handed and emerged carrying sacks. The dimensions were also transferred to the sketch they were building up. There was no talking, just a written word, 'storehouse', and a nod to confirm they'd come to the same conclusion.

They knew they'd need a daylight observation point. The site was chosen with care, since there could be limited movement during the day.

They had to get to a place as central to the activity of the camp as possible and just lie and watch. Paul and Kenny searched for a spot, where they could lie up and wait for daylight to arrive.

The buildings, as well as the babble of noise, had increased as they came closer and closer to the hub of the camp. From somewhere they could just pick up the thud of a petrol-driven generator, and as they got closer still they could feel it through the contact between ground and body. The cluster of five large huts around a central compound and two dilapidated stone structures had to be the command area. There were others, also shaded by trees, smaller huts standing alone and off to the edges, but they would have to wait. Guys with guns were milling around the entrances or sitting smoking on the raised verandas. Paul had his nightsight out, concentrating on the palm-covered roofs, looking for the one thing that was as important as the location of the hostages.

The changing angle of the still potent moon revealed it. He spotted the wire running up into the trees from the second building to the north and nudged Kenny Collins, directing his gaze towards it. Neither said a word, but both automatically recorded it. That had to be the RUF's headquarters, perhaps even the boss-man's hut as well. No commander was ever very far away from his comms. There was no moving now. This was a spot from which to observe a great deal, perhaps the only better position the one on the opposite, up-slope side of the encampment.

In daylight, when it came, the scene reminded Paul of a fucked-up, el cheapo holiday camp. On both sides of the compound there were increasing amounts of laughing and shouting, kids and women preparing food without fires. The bigger huts themselves were visited by a constant stream of human traffic, some supplicants clearly seeking favours, others men who inspired enough fear to clear a path in front of them. Some of their individual features were committed to memory.

Lying there became increasingly uncomfortable as the number of biting insects multiplied, but movement had to be kept to a minimum. They were right at the edge of the clearings and things registered in the corner of people's eyes more readily than the centre. There were plenty of chickens and goats, the latter, to Paul's relief, tethered, since they were inclined to be curious, and to aid them with the humans was the jungle dweller's habit of never going into deep vegetation if it could be avoided.

They tended to stay in their clearings where their witch doctors assured them they were safe from the evil spirits that lived in the bushes and trees.

Everybody has to piss and shit, though, and they rarely want to do it in the same place as they sleep. That located the hostage building for them. They were led out in pairs from the long, low, roofless stone building next to the comms hut. A rope had been tied round their necks, and each group was taken off to a spot well to the observer's left. Both men were on maximum alert to establish their state of health as well as their identity. Kenny had binos while Paul used a Mark 1 eyeball, but even from here, with the naked eye, they could see that a lot of them were not too kosher.

The photographs they'd studied allowed them to identify most of them. The oldest nun, Sister Francesca, was unmistakable, as thin as a rake and as brown as a walnut. She looked to be in the least trouble, but the one she was roped to was in a bad way. Her hair was hanging in thick, tangled strands and her clothing was torn, especially below the waist. The rest of the nuns followed. Most of the older ones had fared reasonably well; it was the youngsters who were struggling.

The Italian quarry manager, Signor Assitola, practically had to be carried and Mario Berti was laid out flat on a stretcher. His face was like parchment left in the sun, his cheeks sunken and his eyes hollow. Hinchcliffe tried to look like he had the situation under control, but they could see from the stiff way he walked what an effort it was. Then Paul zoomed in and saw how many swellings and cuts he had on his face. It was pride that was keeping him upright. The woman Hinchcliffe had been lifted with, Mary Kline, was easily spotted because of her blond hair. She was dirty but still in control, helping the last hostage taken, a black nurse called Amy Sekola, to stagger across the compound. The two worst-looking cases were the Asian guys who'd been taken with Assitola. They looked as though they'd been used as punch bags. Their eyes were barely visible through the swellings and their clothes were streaked with blood. One of them opened his mouth to moan in pain, only to reveal that most of his teeth were broken or missing.

But the good news was that the count meant they were all still alive, and their location established. The next task was to find if any of the heavy equipment that the RUF had stolen from the army was sited round the camp, the 12.75mm machine guns and mortars Blue had seen them firing in the fighting around the Plant site. It was a long day spent crawling round that ill-defined perimeter at constant risk of being spotted. Kenny Collins came closest when a naked kid decided to piss into the bush he was hiding under. The stream hit him, but at least, coming from a five- or six-year-old, it was as clean as piss could be.

By the middle of the afternoon they had, apart from the location of the heavy machine guns, what they wanted, and if they couldn't get a fix on those they could only assume they were not there. They knew the exact dimensions of the camp, that it had one route in and out for wheels and feet alike, well guarded and heading south-east. There were various vehicles available to the rebels, most in poor condition. When it came to the buildings, the rescue team would be infiltrating in the dark and they would use the measurements they'd made to plan the assault. They couldn't be dead accurate, but they were close.

All the heavy kit was in another of those command huts and had been brought out for a bit of weapons training to follow the drill which had taken place mid-morning. They lay there and watched the fighters jog through their paces, over three hundred guys, every one chanting the same RUF slogans, their feet sending up clouds of dust into the hot air, their faces sweating and their eyes full of courage. The commanders came out to instruct and inspect. They thought they could identify Tarawali, small but smart in his crisp uniform leaving no one in any doubt that he was the leader. Jalloh, the Libyan-trained commander, was the only other guy they could put a name to, since they'd seen a photograph taken by the CIA. He put the men through their drills, first without, then with their weapons. Jalloh was much taller than Tarawali, a man with full cheeks, a big flat nose and an arrogant look in his eye.

The exfil was executed with even more care than the entry. This was no time to be compromised, now that they had all the info needed to make a plan. The light was fading by the time they got back to the river, their progress made slower by the need to try to remove any trace of their entry, though there was no evidence of a pursuit. Being a good soldier is about having good habits.

As soon as they stood down Paul set up the satcom phone and patched through to Gibraltar. He confirmed the success of the reconnaissance and read off a verbal report on numbers, dimensions, locations of hostages and command and control before informing them that he and the team would be pulling out within the hour, after they had repeated the message to the High Commission at Freetown. Blue then called Ray Kavanagh at Bonthe, and without informing him of his present location established a rendezvous for Gbangbia creek, where the *Adelaide* would pick them up.

They then went through the drills necessary to ensure the LUP was not likely to be compromised in their absence. Paul ran through the orders before launching the inflatable. The moon was showing as they got the outboard on, a near full job in a cloudless sky that illuminated the landscape and had Blue hesitating. But time was short. The evidence they had seen showed that some of the hostages could be close to croaking. If they could get back quickly, the op could go this weekend. That might just save a life.

'Fuck it,' he whispered. 'Just pretend we're a hippo.'

CHAPTER SEVENTEEN

With the information the team provided, Blue's ground recce and Paul and Ken Collins's camp recce, the stand-by squadron could finalise a new plan. The sketch map was faxed from Bonthe to Gibraltar with copies of the maps plus a sitrep from Paul Hill. And there was a very positive payoff for Blue. He could become pro-active too, knowing that the situation was about to be resolved. He spent a long two hours with Paul Hill, listening as hard as he talked, fitting the bits and pieces Paul fed him into the plan that was forming in his mind.

'You're sponsoring the drop?' asked Blue.

'Yep.'

'And going in?'

'Me, Crazy, Trevor and Jerry Fallon.'

'You'd be better off with Harry Fielding.'

'Jerry's a good man, and he does love a Claymore. And Harry has to play boss-man, stay behind and get drunk with the rest of the guys.'

'He'll enjoy that.'

'He'd rather come to your party.'

'I'm sure he would. Just tell him to make sure Pol Pot doesn't go anywhere near my woman. He has my permission to break the bastard's legs.'

'Suddenly I'm thinking maybe Harry and I should swap places.'

'That's okay by me,' Blue said, 'just as long as Gus doesn't sneak in.'

Paul looked at his watch, then stood up. 'I've got to go.'

'I've been dying to ask. What's the shirt and tie for, a parade?'

'Memorial service,' Paul replied, fingering his regimental tie. 'That Buckhart guy, the Yank. Fizzin' Frank. The Gurkha officers are having a service at the Methodist church. The whole BG team is going. It's fitting really, since he was Delta Force.' Blue nodded. There was a strong bond between the two units. The American unit had been created after a Green Beret officer did some training with the SAS in Hereford. The regiment was like a mother to them. 'Leila's going, and her old man, as well as Strasser,

226

Bio, Lumulo and half the government. We're using it as an exercise for our guys. The widow will be there too, poor cow, and won't even know it. She'll think it's all for her.'

'No funeral?'

Paul shook his head. 'She's taking the bits back to the US for that. I just hope no prat opens his mouth about the head.'

'Oh yeah,' Blue replied, with a slight shudder. 'They've embalmed it and are carrying it round on a pole to wind up the troops.'

'Apparently,' said Paul bitterly, 'those RUF cunts have even left his beret on.'

'That'll please the Gurkhas.'

'They're busy planning an attack. Strasser's given the green light to go in around Moyamba and drive them out. No bollocks about training either. It's a wholly Gurkha op.'

'When?' asked Blue suddenly.

'They don't know it, Blue, but it will be timed to coincide with the rescue.'

'You can't be sure of that. They don't work for Whitehall.'

'Quentin-Davies has a finger in it. You've got to admire that old bastard, even if he does seem full of piss and wind. He seems to know just which button to press to get anyone he wants to do his bidding. He got Toby Flowers to allow him the decision as to the timing of their attack.'

'Without telling him anything else?'

'Not a word, mate.'

'Flowers is no mug,' Blue insisted. 'He might not know the details, but he'll figure the reason out for himself. When will we get feedback from Gib?'

'It won't be long. They'll be working flat out up there.'

'You will let me know, won't you?'

Paul grinned. 'I'll get Forwood to give you a bell.'

Blue gave him two fingers before climbing into the pickup and heading off for the AAR head office.

As soon as Gibraltar had the info the operation had to go in. No time could be allowed for the situation to change. A whole wall was covered in photographs, sketches, weapon lists, personnel lists and orders. In a full squadron operation the headshed decides the nature of the job, formulates an outline with the troop seniors, and then allocates the tasks, designating various smaller units for the detailed responsibilities. Each group works out its detailed plan then submits that back to the headshed who collate everything before commencing a final briefing. There's less freedom of choice on these occasions with the headshed deciding on almost everything, including weaponry, to be employed.

The briefing took place at the far end of the hangar, surrounded by the debris of what had been a target layout. Every member of B Squadron had been issued a copy of the sketch map and a personal set of shots to study of both the hostages and their known captors. They'd gone through the mocked-up building interiors, with the windows blacked out and using passive night goggles. Outside, there was a taped area to represent the rebel encampment. They'd already trained on that, working out times and distances, movements, attack scenarios and all the problems of identification and exfil. This had taken place not once, but a dozen times, half in the dark, and there had been plenty of activity including the use of stun grenades.

'Right then,' said Goring. 'It's light order. We will deploy in two C-130s, dropping in four MIBs per airframe. That gives us eight boats and a capacity to carry sixty-four persons on the exfil. I need hardly say that there's little chance of a counter-attack. Anyone who has dealt with people like this will know just which direction they will be going in once we're finished with them.'

Everybody could count. With forty troopers going in that left plenty of room for the hostages, who now totalled thirteen. Goring talked on, identifying and detailing the responsibilities for the four men tasked as snipers. They would take out any sentries following the actions of the four-man distraction team. They would trigger the primary explosions that would signal the initiation. Eight men were tasked to storm the building where the hostages were being held, and they were the ones who had to study layout and hostage recognition the most.

Eight men would engage in fire support with the Minimi light machine guns fitted with nightsights. The task? As well as taking out opportunity targets, they would need to create and maintain a wall of fire on both sides of the exfil corridor. The remaining sixteen troopers, armed with M203s and 66mm rocket launchers, had the job of hitting everything that moved, then assisting in the evacuation of the hostages once they had reached the perimeter. They would escort them to the MIBs, with a four-man patrol also carrying trauma packs and designated as medics.

The BG team was sponsoring the drop and acting as the rear protection unit to minimise the chance of their becoming engaged in a firefight and sustaining casualties. They would change the fuel bags on the boats and maintain the security of the drop-off point. Their secondary role was laying Claymores outside the designated exfil route. The troopers with-drawing from the rebel camp would put down a wall of fire, thus creating havoc, firing off their 40mm grenades. The final act once the last man was through the rear defence position, would be to fire off the electrically detonated Claymores with short delay fuses.

'The exfil will be as follows,' Goring continued. 'Three MIBs carrying three hostages plus three SAS. One MIB carrying four hostages and three. Four MIBs bringing up the rear each carrying seven SAS plus one member of the sponsoring Freetown team. Each MIB to have a Minimi up front plus one man wearing passive night goggles. One SAS in each hostage boat will be a medic. At present exfil for the hostages is to Bonthe, but that may change as the security of the area is uncertain. Alternatives will be notified before departure and as a last resort given over the Cougar net. Take-off is at thirteen hundred hours. ETA over the drop zone will be nineteen hundred hours. Any questions?'

They fired them in, double- and treble-checking the tasks, routes and things that could go pear-shaped. Goring and his green slime officer dealt with them patiently. When you've got the best there is, in terms of military punch, asking you questions, you'd better damn well listen just in case you've missed something. When the meeting broke up, the guys broke down into their individual teams and went back to get prepared for the off.

Blue dropped in on Mike Layman to check on the latest intelligence. As well as all the other jobs he had, he'd been landed with that one. Blue's tactic was paying off though; the picture they were building up of RUF deployment had gone from vague to firm. The AAR team now knew where they were based and in what numbers, and had an indication of their morale and weapons strength, the first high, the second low. Their informants, seemingly just people wandering about the war-ravaged countryside, had been tasked to get info on the army as well. That was less satisfying. They seemed to have stopped dead, making no attempt to gather a superior force to take the rebels on. It was easy to say that they too were stymied by the hostage situation, but that didn't extend to preparations and it was clear they just weren't making any.

'Oh Christ, no!' said Blue, picking up the last report which had details of the enemy strength and dispositions around the Sieromin compound.

'The head?' asked Mike Layman.

'How did it get there?'

'Well, it didn't walk, Blue.'

'My SAS mates have just gone to the service they're holding for the poor bastard.'

'You'll never guess what my esteemed boss said when he read it.'

'Go on.'

Layman took off Razenbrook's voice well, that combination of pukka lightness and boyish enthusiasm. 'What about if we could get a picture? It would be bound to make the front page in London. Might let them know at head office what we're up against.'

'How is the boy wonder?'

'You might want to see for yourself. Two of your best friends are in there now.'

'Is that a fact,' Blue replied, scooping up the copies of the intelligence reports. 'Then maybe I should drop in.'

Sandy McPherson had his feet under Razenbrook's desk as Blue walked in, with Wally Aitken sitting cross-legged to one side. The Anglo-African boss was a bit of a blusher, and it was him, rather than Mork or Mindy, who gave the game away. They were plotting, that was for certain, and it was just as certain that what they were up to boded no good for Blue Harding.

'You should have knocked,' Razenbrook protested.

Blue grinned. 'Mike said you were with my guys, so I didn't think it would be necessary.'

'We were just having a wee chat, Blue,' said Sandy, without the least trace of embarrassment. You had to hand it to the bastard. He had skin like a rhino.

'That's right,' added Wally unnecessarily.

'Anything to do with recovering barges filled with rutile?'

That deepened the redness in Razenbrook's cheeks. But Sandy acted like the man in charge, nodding sagely before he replied. 'I was just telling Mr Razenbrook here that in my opinion we should just go in and get it. All this farting about is getting nobody anywhere. If anything, it's threatening our contract.'

'And what did you say, Tony?'

'I agreed. I'm getting hell from London. And you can witter on as much as you like about the High Commission putting the block on it. I might remind you that you don't work for him, and neither do I.'

'Anybody ask Dave Heffer about this?'

'What's it got to do with him?' demanded Sandy.

'Do you know how much work Charter Security does for the British government? He might not take too well to us upsetting someone like Quentin-Davies. This job is worth fuck all compared to the government contracts.' Blue's voice rose as he broke a personal doctrine, which was never to bollock an inferior in front of a superior. He jabbed his finger towards Razenbrook, because he too was in the bollocking frame. 'This man does not pay our wages. He pays Charter Security and they pay our wages. But that hasn't occurred to you, has it, Sandy? Your brain is so full of fucking sea water that you've gone doolally.'

Sandy moved his leg, unwinding it from the other, and made to get up.

'Stay in that chair and listen, Sandy. You too, Wally, or I'll mullah the pair of you. I'm in charge of this job. I work for Dave Heffer, and I want to do that again, so you will fuck off out of here now and stop kissing arse. And you, Mr Razenbrook, either accept that I know more about what I'm doing than you or get on the blower to London and ask for me to be replaced.'

'You can't talk to me like that.'

Blue jerked his thumb. 'Sandy, Wally. Out!'

The ex-RSM grinned then, sure that Blue had gone too far. Razenbrook would have him off the case so quick his feet wouldn't touch the ground. And as the man on the spot, and flavour of the month with the client, there was little doubt who'd be taking over the AAR team.

'Come on, Wally,' he said, slipping out of the chair and moving to the door. His gopher followed him, a worried look on his face. Aitken didn't have the brains to suss what was happening, even when Sandy McPherson started to whistle 'Everything's Coming up Roses'.

231

Blue waited until the door shut before turning to face the clenched jaw and furious gaze of Tony Razenbrook. 'I've just been on a little trip.'

'Have you indeed?'

'You haven't asked me how it went.'

'No. I have not.'

'You should do. It might just help you keep your job.'

'How I do or do not maintain my job is none of your concern.'

That had been said as confidently as he could, but there was just a trace of nervousness at the back of the voice.

'You'll be wanting to replace me.'

'I most certainly shall.'

'Pity that,' Blue said, with a grin. 'I was just about to tell you that you can have your rutile out, your maintenance crews in, and the mine sites reopened.'

'What!'

Blue tapped his head. 'The plan is right here in my head. Now I might be able to do that, but those two arseholes who've just walked out of here can't. So I want you to pick up the phone and ask Dave Heffer to send them a fax telling them that their contracts are terminated forthwith. He didn't act on it when I asked him, but I'm sure you have more juice.'

Razenbrook looked at him hard, trying to reassure himself that Blue was telling the truth. What followed was par for the course for a bastard like him. There was no protest, no attempt to protect the men who had been sucking up to him ten minutes before, but it was always like that with selfish bastards. They could slip through a 180-degree turn and not even notice they'd done it.

'How do I know I can trust you?'

'Because I know what I'm doing, and you don't. I didn't walk into this job, I spent twenty years learning it. Now either do as I ask or I will pack in now and leave you with Mork and Mindy there. Who, I might add, will probably fuck things up so comprehensively that you'll never get your mine sites reopened.'

That threat struck home, enough to produce almost physical panic. Razenbrook grabbed the phone, but then he nodded towards the door. For a second Blue wondered whether he was going to dump him after all, but then he decided he didn't really care. He found Sandy and Wally waiting outside, the marine looking at him keenly.

Blue pulled a serious face and said, 'I need a fucking drink!'

McPherson beamed at him and threw out a hand to slap him on the back. 'I think I must buy that, John. It's the least I can do. After all, I have been a wee bit naughty.'

'You certainly have, Sandy.'

'It was well-intentioned, mind. I only ever do these things for the best.'

Razenbrook got Dave Heffer on the phone. 'Harding is a first-class chap, David, and I'm very grateful to you for sending him out, but I'm afraid that fellow McPherson has done nothing but try to undermine him. Then there's Aitken, who is a bit like a Siamese twin.'

Dave Heffer knew what Sandy and Wally were like, and he knew Blue Harding. He would never have put them together if it hadn't been a rush job.

'In what way?' he asked, stalling.

'Well, David, there's any number of things, but the final straw was not ten minutes ago. I was forced to listen to some wild plan they had to take over the mine sites regardless of the hostage situation. I might have only done my bit in the CCF, but even I could see the idea was deeply flawed. And this when Harding, who is of a different opinion, is running the show. I do not, repeat not, like the notion of inferiors going behind their superior's back.'

'Blue knew nothing about it?'

'No!'

'What would you like me to do?'

'Well, my feelings are this. It is a boil that is better quickly lanced. I must retain Harding, since he's such a super chap, but I think that AAR can dispense with the services of McPherson and Aitken. If you agree, I should fax that through straightaway. Let's get them out of Sierra Leone as soon as possible.'

'As you wish, Tony. Could you ask Blue to call regarding replacements?'

'Of course.' Razenbrook put down the phone then pressed the intercom button. 'If either that McPherson chap or his friend Aitken want to see me, I'm not available. And ask Mike to come in.'

Blue saw Mike Layman striding towards the table, his hand going into his breast pocket and half a smile on his face. That told him all he needed to know. His glass was empty anyway. Sandy might buy him one drink, but there would never be a time when the RSM would buy two on the trot. It had been interesting to observe the way he reacted, suddenly fonder of John Harding and more concerned for his welfare than he'd been since they'd met at Heathrow.

'I must be going, Sandy.'

'Aye,' the man replied, before suddenly realising it could be miscon-strued. 'Are you bound back to Bonthe?'

'No. It's deepest Freetown and a hunt for Willy Rakiba.'

Sandy misunderstood that as well, it being a good place for a man to go if he was looking for a job. 'You want to watch that Fijian, John. He's more of a danger to his own than to anyone he chooses to fight against.'

'I've got no choice, have I, Sandy?'

'Not a lot,' McPherson replied, sticking out a hand. 'No hard feelings, eh?'

Blue returned a perfunctory handshake, nodded to Mike Layman who was now behind Sandy, and headed for the exit. As he got to the door he turned to see McPherson reading the fax. He handed it to Wally, then looked up at Blue, which earned him a small wave, fingers only, the kind you give to a child.

Willy wasn't hard to find. For all his reputation as a boozer, he had a strong responsible streak. He might get pissed at night, but whoever was paying him could rely on his undivided attention during the day. He had his own office at the headquarters of Sieromin, where he'd been employed as security chief. They had more than one mining site in the country, and it was his job to make sure that what happened at the Mokanje facility didn't happen anywhere else, so he'd recruited his own mercenary force. They were now engaged in a very noisy series of training exercises designed to persuade the RUF to stay away. His company also owned one of the twin jetties at Port Nitti, the secondary one, up-river from AAR's. There was no way to take one without the other and it was their kit on site, so any notion of taking it back had always included the need, at the very last possible moment, to involve Willy.

Being ex-SAS Blue felt he could trust him, but the hostage rescue wasn't his call so he had to be very circumspect. That led to a round-the-houses approach in which Willy was invited to draw conclusions, without ever being treated to any hard facts. The Fijian knew the rules of the game.

234

Whatever he sussed out for himself he kept hidden behind that dark, heavily lined forehead, sticking to the bones of what Blue was after.

'You want to take back our site at Port Nitti?'

'Yep. Just as soon as you help us take back ours.'

The pockmarked cheeks split into a grin. 'I'd rather it was the other way round, man.'

'It would be if ours wasn't on the way.'

'And I can forget the hostage thing?'

'I'm inviting you to a party, that's all. Blue's big night in Bonthe. We might go out and do a little hunting, or we might just end up getting shit-faced.'

'What the hookers like down there?'

'Cheap and cheerful.'

That made the deep brown eyes light up. 'Sounds like my kind of place.'

'But if we have a go situation on the Port Nitti jetties, and I think we'll get one, I have the water transport to get us from Bonthe to the target, as well as the men to secure and get out Anglo-African barges. Those we could take on our own, but if we want to clear the area around the whole facility, including the Sieromin jetty, I want someone from your mob on hand to take possession and assess the damage.'

'Why stop at the storage sheds, Blue? Let's kick those fucking rebels all the way back to the Guinea border.'

That was typical of the Fijian. Start men like Willy going forward and they were like the cavalry at Waterloo, impossible to stop. To call it stupid was a real understatement. The AAR team would be out on a limb at Port Nitti, never mind pushing on. And a couple of dozen guys, out in the bush, unsupported and well away from any kind of base, facing the kind of numbers that the RUF could muster, would just end up like Fizzin' Frank, with their heads on poles.

'I can just see you in the middle of fucking Africa, Willy, trying to take them on in their thousands.'

'I'm a black bastard. They'd worship me as a god.'

'Not as much as you worship yourself, old son.'

Willy winced at that. 'I heard the Gurkhas have a little plan around Moyamba. You basing things on that?'

'This place leaks like a sieve,' Blue replied, not pleased.

'I needed to know that. I have responsibilities up that way too. And man, don't give me that shitty face. You knew and weren't going to say fuck all.'

'It's not relevant.'

Willy sat for a bit, thinking, and Blue left him to it. In his own mind he was clear. If the stand-by squadron went in, the hostage situation was resolved, and that applied even if they failed. The RUF would slot their captives or let them go, because the whole thing, threat or bluff, would have been called. He needed to take advantage of the mayhem to get his own task sorted out. And it was just possible, with the SAS hitting them up-country and the Gurkhas clobbering them in the middle, that the AAR team might just add the sauce that cooked them, freeing the whole country from the threat.

'I'll come to the party, man, and I'll bring my hardware.' Then the great square face creased in a look of deep suspicion. 'But I ain't setting foot in no boat until I know what is going down.'

Blue nodded and then agreed the pickup time to Bonthe. 'I've already worked out the plan. You and I talk first. If you've any objections I'll take them on board, but there's no way I want a Chinese parliament. There's no time for that.'

'Okay, man.'

'I'll expect you first thing in the morning,' Blue said finally, holding out a hand that was gripped in a numbing embrace. 'Don't forget to bring a bottle.'

'Would I, man?'

'And Willy, spread it around. Let every ear in Freetown know that Blue Harding is throwing a monumental piss-up in his private Bonthe holiday camp.'

Willy grinned and gave him a thumbs up. 'I'll tell my girls. When it comes to spreading stuff they be better than fibre optics.'

Sergei was Blue's next port of call, and with the Russian he had to show some care. He had to use him to get Paul Hill and the sponsoring team to Bonthe, then they had to be lifted out to an RV point on Edmonton Island, carrying with them a strobe light powerful enough to be seen from the air. Once they'd been dropped Sergei would have to return to Bonthe, where he would become his special guest.

Even if he liked the guy, there were others he worked with whom he'd never met, and trust was a luxury he couldn't afford. None of the helicopter crew, fliers or ground staff, socialised with mercenary types. They were all husbanding the dough, trying to build up the kind of dollar pile that would see them safe and sound when they got back to Russia. When they drank, which they did to excess, it was together, the kind of occasions that usually ended up with mournful songs or furious punch-ups.

Fortunately, thanks to Tony Razenbrook, Blue had a big wad for private use. He shelled out several high denomination notes, told the pilot what he wanted and when he wanted it, and hinted that if he so much as picked up a whisper that the info had been leaked their livelihood would be finished. The man was used to the Russian mafia, so the threat didn't have to be very subtle.

'So, Sergei, I'm just going back into town to buy a whole load of booze and food for a party. Then, when I bring it back here, if you don't mind, you can wing me down to Bonthe.'

'That fine, Blue. But I must wait for Sandy and Wally. They ask me to.'

'Don't bother waiting for them,' Blue snapped. Then he smiled, because doing that had driven home the message he just given the Russian. 'They are history.'

The SAS headshed were not the only people involved in planning. Toby Flowers was with his own officers, studying a map of the Tinanhun district, which was already marked with the proposed lines of advance. The Gurkhas intended to use their superior mobility to cut through and trap the RUF rebels using that town as a base. Careful intelligence gathering had identified some of the routes by which they might seek to escape, and these were selected ambush points for specified patrols. And the order was so simple that it hadn't even been issued. There was to be no taking of prisoners.

Blue continued to leave his AAR team in the dark. They'd already planned and rehearsed the Port Nitti assault, and that they could do blindfolded. Blue spent an hour aboard the *Adelaide* with Willy Rakiba giving him the briefing on the assault plan. Onshore there was some range work going on, the final zeroing of weapons. That would be followed by an overall equipment check and a good meal. Blue was waiting for Paul Hill and his team to come in, Sergei tasked to drop them close to the boat.

They had with them the radios for the Cougar net, comms that would put Blue in touch with the incoming SAS. He had a satcom link to Hereford, the High Commission and the director of Special Forces in London.

As soon as the Fijian saw the four troopers jump out of the Hip, in combat gear and carrying their kit, he nodded. That confirmed what he'd already sussed. 'So we got the heavy shit going down here, man?'

'Just you and me, Willy. Let's not make it a general discussion.'

'We're not the only ones who can figure this, man. The guys on this boat ain't no mugs.'

'Yeah, but they're SBS and will stay stum. The others will wonder but won't ask. And it doesn't make any difference, Willy, they're not going out on the town tonight.'

Paul and his team came straight aboard the *Adelaide*, staying out of sight while Blue took over the billiard room for their final briefing. Maps were issued for the country beyond Port Nitti, targets identified and the last intelligence reports circulated.

'This is a bit different from what we planned for, guys,' Blue said, addressing his AAR team. 'We should be going into an empty site, but our latest sitrep shows the RUF have wandered back in. Why, God only knows 'cause there's fuck all left to loot.'

'They'll find something,' said a voice from the back.

'So we're going to have to fight them if they're still about. We would have had to do it some time. We're just going after the bastards a bit quicker than originally intended. Remember the job is to get them to run. If they show signs of putting up a good fight, break off contact and get back inside our defensive perimeter.' He paused, and deliberately hardened his voice and manner. 'Nobody is to lose contact with the main group. We're not here to do the army's job for them. No frontal assaults. No John Wayne stuff, okay?'

'Preaching to the converted, Blue,' said Jamie Padden.

The engines on the C-130s were already turning as the stand-by squadron loaded their gear. The main kit was the quartet of Avon medium inflatable boats, each with twin Mariner 30hp engines and compressed air bottle for self-inflation. The snipers carried 7.62mm PMs with nightsights and a suppresser silencer. Light order meant each sniper also carried an MP5 strapped to his back for personal protection in the event of a close-action firefight. Every trooper had a combat weapon, either a Minimi LMG, an M203 with its underslung grenade launchers, or a 66mm shoulder-fired rocket launcher. The assault team, the guys who would get the hostages out, carried MP5 machine guns fitted with a laser sight and torch.

There wasn't much talk on the planes as the tailgates lifted, though there was a lot of thinking going on, the troopers running through everything they'd learned in the last few days. The tension they felt came from the responsibility. Each man had a job to do. Get it right and it was no contest; fuck it up and you could put the whole op in jeopardy.

Blue was standing on the jetty when the call came through to the satcom. Paul answered it, then turned to him.

'We have a go. They're airborne.'

CHAPTER EIGHTEEN

The first task was to get Paul and his team into place on the agreed drop zone, Edmonton Island. Chosen by Blue, it was perfect for the job, a low-lying uninhabited salt marsh island right in the middle of the Bagru estuary. They would take all the necessary precautions to check the security of the DZ regardless. The SAS would drop into the sea; getting wet in a warm environment was not a problem. Square parachutes and constant training meant that they would land at the water's edge. The MIBs, on their own 'chutes, would drop close by to await recovery.

The distance from the mouth of the Bagru river to its tributary, the Gbangbia, with every twist and turn and other river mouths, had been programmed into the GPS already, and since it was marshland all round the rescue team could cover the first five kilometres at full speed. From drop through to recovery was an unknown, but from the time a trooper put a hand on the donut ring holding the Avon boat to the craft being fully operational in the water would be a maximum of seconds rather than minutes.

Blue would be long gone by then, the aim being for contact with the SAS to be kept to a minimum. He would go back to Bonthe to pick up his people. Their job was to proceed up-river, the *Adelaide* in company with a push boat big enough to take the barges out and his own inflatables, long after the SAS had left the area. The need to be in position well before time would require them to lie-to, in pitch darkness, in the small offshoot of Gbangbia creek, the connection between the two rivers. They would remain invisible. Only Blue knew they'd time their attack to coincide, as closely as was feasible, with the SAS going in on the hostage rescue. The communications were transmitted over a secure network; all the radios had been programmed prior to the op by a cipher gun carrying an unbreakable code. Anyone inadvertently listening in would hear nothing but scrambled garbage.

Blue would have liked to go earlier, in daylight, but he had no absolute knowledge of the state of the RUF's comms. He'd seen that they had a radio in that old displaced persons' camp. The rebels, in a settled and high-risk locality like Port Nitti, might have set up an emergency signal throughout the areas they controlled, so the sound of gunfire might just see the hostages shot out of hand. Besides, Blue's primary task – to retrieve the processed rutile and to secure the access road to Port Nitti – could be carried out in darkness. It was all about firepower married to ability, he and was sure he had his enemy beaten on both counts. By the time first light came he'd know what was happening, and then he could initiate phase two in which he and the AAR team would push slightly inland, clearing the RUF away far enough to secure a defendable perimeter for Port Nitti. At the same time the Gurkha Guard Force would commence its own operation. The rebels, hit on three fronts, and used to facing the SL army would begin to wonder what had hit them.

At Bonthe there was, generally, an air of silence and suppressed expectation, though that was punctuated occasionally by the usual gallows humour. Most of the guys in the room were ex-Paras, and there was no group of soldiers anywhere on God's earth who enjoyed a scrap more than they did. Their discipline was what any Rupert alive would call first-rate and they would go in and do whatever they were told in a way that standard Green Army regiments could only envy. It was easy to see that despite their attempts at humour, they were champing at the bit. They made jokes to each other about places like Mount Longden and Goose Green, where they'd taken on and beaten many times their own number, sometimes in assaults that bordered on the suicidal. One of them, Tom McAdams, had been at Warren Point when the Parachute Regiment lost eighteen of their men to an IRA bomb. He had clawed himself away from the carnage leaving his own personal signature drawn in flesh and blood, as well as a serious amount of body fluids, only to find himself invalided out of the army. This was nothing to do with his physical wounds, but because the trick-cyclists in the psychiatric department deemed him emotionally unstable. He'd never had his chance for revenge, so any action he was on after that usually resulted in the guys he was up against paying the price.

Tom was just an example. They'd all seen action at some time in their service lives, which made them even better material for the up-coming job. And for the few who hadn't, they'd trained for it so hard that any natural fear was tempered by faith in their ability. The scale model they'd made of the facilities at Port Nitti now sat unobserved on the snooker table, just like the sketch maps on the wall of the bar that showed routes of attack, distances, estimates of the forces they would engage and the route from those to their secondary objectives. The weapons checks were over, the pre-prepared explosive charges examined for the last time. Every man had a day sack on carrying the kit he needed to do his part of the job. Willy was like a caged bear, but Blue reckoned that was because he needed a drink or a woman, since fear was alien to him.

Sergei, who'd been obliged to stay after he'd dropped the BG team in, at last understood what was going on. Perhaps it was the atmosphere, or maybe there was still enough of the fighting man left in him. Whatever the reasons, he offered his services in a medevac capacity. Blue thanked him but could not tell him that his task was already allocated. He was in Bonthe for a purpose, to take the hostages from here to the helipad in the High Commission compound in Freetown.

Eventually the watches clicked round to 1800 hours and Blue, with the last light fast approaching, could at last break the tension. 'OK, guys. Let's get loaded.'

They heard the drone of the C-130 engines when they were still to the south of Kendall Island, following the sound as they swung round from the main Sherbro river channel to begin their run into the DZ. Blue could imagine the atmosphere aboard the plane, a place where the SAS had no control, the whole drop operation being controlled by the pilot and the RAF despatchers. The latter would have already given a warning at fifteen minutes to drop, when the guys would have put on their parachutes. At the five-minute warning they would clip on their reserve 'chutes to the front of their harnesses. That would be immediately followed by the command to 'stand up and hook on'. The first thing on standing was to ensure that the reserve 'chute was properly attached, before taking their stations, static lines hooked on to the overhead strop either side of the MIBs. After a last check on their 'chutes and equipment, the man behind working with the man in front, the despatcher would call off the numbers, working from the back until each man had responded with an okay. When jumper number one said okay, that was his signal to inform the pilot that the drop was ready.

The Hercules would come in low, the ground-to-air radio contact backed up by Paul Hill's strobe light. Aimed through a narrow funnel, it threw an immensely bright beam of light into the air. From a low drone the noise would suddenly increase as the C-130 put on power to climb to the drop height where the aircraft would slow to facilitate the drop. There would be a deafening roar as the tailgate opened; the sound of the slipstream would blot out everything as the jumpers moved forward to take station on the ramp. All eyes would be on the lights, while in the cockpit the co-pilot listened to the ground signals set out by the BG team. At the appropriate point he would flick the switch that turned on the green light, and the handlers in the rear would hit the front jumpers. The despatchers, aided by the troopers, would slide out the MIBs, the men keeping up the momentum for the jump, each adopting a good, stable parachute exit position before dropping out into the night sky. Falling into silence, the last sound the breaking of the static line that released the 'chute, each man would take hold of the toggles that controlled the guide lines, and begin to steer himself on to the drop zone.

Paul Hill kept the strobe light going. There was moonlight enough to see the men he was guiding, forty highly trained parachutists weaving as they brought themselves into a copybook water landing. The twenty-two-foot steerable squares were accurate to within a few metres, depending on the individual skill of each trooper. Just before they entered the warm water, a welcome change from the cold North Sea, they hit the quick-release harness. It was the job of the man nearest to inflate the boats, breaking the donut ring and cracking open the inflation bottle.

Then the chatter started as the secure Cougar net was used to get some order into a situation that was mildly untidy. The salt-water lights, set off as the batteries contacted the water, guided those who had the boats to pick up the rest. Goring was in contact with Paul Hill, and once they'd established that the situation was secure the Squadron commander went over the orders while his men loaded one MIB with the spare fuel bags that had dropped in on the second pass.

Paul was in the lead boat with the primary Garmin, and within ten minutes the rescue team was ready to move off at speed. The Garmin ground positioning system, using the US Department of Defense precise positioning service, told them exactly where they were, receiving from the satellites overhead a fundamental geometric equation, which it then solved to present continuous navigation updates in an easy-to-understand visual display. The boat held four other troopers, each of whom had his weapon out covering the arc for which he was responsible. There was nothing haphazard about their positions; they had been worked out in Gibraltar. Every man was in the right boat and knew exactly where in that boat he should be. One member of each crew had on passive night goggles, and his arc was forward, right in the lead boat, left in the second, the positions replicated all the way down to the tail-end Charlie.

At speeds approaching thirty-seven kilometres per hour they ate up the distance along the Bagru to the Gbangbia in fifteen minutes. The 30hp Mariner engines, especially designed for Special Forces, didn't roar at twenty knots. There was sound, yes, but it was muted, hemmed in by the thick vegetation that lined the riverbanks. The Garmin told them they were approaching a point within hearing distance of Port Nitti, which led to a diminution of speed and a dearth of sound, until they were in the main creek leading to Gbangbia. They slowed significantly for the bridge at Sigimi, but only to idling speed, which with the Mariners was near silent. There was no disembarkation. It was a trade-off, speed as against secrecy. The SAS were less concerned about concealment and cared little if they raised a bit of attention. By the time anybody from the SL army responded they'd be long gone.

By comparison the *Adelaide* chugged up the Bagru channel, making seven knots. Blue was in no hurry. He had an age to get into position and had already plotted the Garmin information they were using. The SAS had an estimated time on target of 2100 hours, an attack window of twenty minutes and an exfil timing of another twenty. He would be on dry land himself just as they were going in.

The MIBs couldn't go flat out all the way: there were sandbars and points of precaution that slowed the speed, but Goring had been adamant at the planning stage that the trick was to stay ahead of the opposition's information system. The only thing to avoid was a firefight until they were on target. So at the ferry crossing at Sigimi, which had a known piquet, the MIBs passed at minimum speed, and it was not until they'd cleared the sandbanks round the double bend that they could open up again. Then it was as fast as possible all the way to one kilometre short of the target. There they halted while Paul sent a brief message by satcom phone.

Donald Quentin-Davies put down the phone, then immediately picked it up again, asking to be put through to Government House, personal to Valentine Strasser if possible. He was not surprised when that was stated as being impossible. He knew that the leader was in his own home, but an enquiry produced the information that the Defence Minister was available, so he asked to speak to him.

'Ah! Minister Lumulo.'

'Ambassador.'

That offended Quentin-Davies. He and Lumulo didn't like each other. In his book a High Commissioner was a good cut above a mere ambassador, a fact of which he made little secret, but being a diplomat he said nothing regarding what he suspected was a calculated insult. 'I just thought you'd like to know that our man Welford thinks there might be a breakthrough on the hostage crisis.'

'What kind of breakthrough?' Lumulo asked suspiciously.

'A negotiated release. All of the remaining hostages set free and brought to Freetown.'

'At what price?'

'Their standing internationally. Welford and his man Deen have done a wonderful job. Thanks to their constant refrain, the RUF, especially after the accidental death of Doctor Mondeh, are worried that they will be seen as nothing more than terrorists.'

'Which, Ambassador, is exactly what they are. Do not believe what that practised liar Alimany Bakaar tells you. That was no accidental death. He must have known about it.'

'Of course, but the constraints of negotiation preclude our man from telling them that. Let's just concentrate on the positives, shall we, since that gets us somewhere. It is my view that we will see the hostages in Freetown very soon.'

'When?'

'It would not surprise me in the slightest if it was all over within the next twenty-four hours.'

'Where will they be released?'

'They have not yet said, on the very good grounds that such information would indicate to us where they are, up to this point, being held captive.'

'I will inform Captain Strasser.'

'Please do. He may contact me at the High Commission if he wishes to. And perhaps someone should stay on call overnight to take any further information.'

'It would be best if I came to the—'

'High Commission? I think not, sir.'

'The release should be overseen by a government official.'

'These affairs are very delicate, Minister. Not even I am allowed to interfere. I'm sure if you ask Captain Strasser, he will confirm to you that such an approach is best.'

The phone was down before Lumulo could argue.

Blue had left his lying up point and set the prow of the *Adelaide* towards Port Nitti, the engine barely turning over as he made for the junction of the Gbangbia creek and the Jong river. He'd lost the luxury of listening to the SAS team go in, they were out of range, but in his head he could hear the commands and responses and could see in his mind the whole operation unfold, the whole attack preparation carried out in whispers.

He doubted Goring would actually race up-river, ignoring all precautions, but he would definitely move faster than he had, powering his way to each obstacle, the troopers piling out to drag their MIBs across the sandbars that had already been identified and plotted on the Garmin. The one thing the SAS would seek to avoid was premature contact. That could involve gunfire and alert the very people he intended to surprise. Those guys would be keyed up, doing what they had trained for, the best the British Army had to offer when it came to brains, balls and skills. The concentration would be immense. Every man in the squadron would be on total alert, every sense and nerve end tuned to the task. And that was nothing to do with bravado or showing off. It was the way it was done, the only way it worked.

Train hard and fight easy. The six P's – proper preparation prevents piss-poor performance. Get in without being seen; bring down too much shit for the enemy to cope with; isolate the hostages and kill anyone outside the secure corridor. Then get out as fast as you came in. Only an idiot stays around to trade bullets with a superior enemy, or one that has support when you don't. To do that you need cool heads and intelligent thinkers. Everyone knew the plan, but that was not a set of orders if things went wrong. When that happened every man had to be able to react to

246

the individual threat in a way that secured his own safety, that of the hostages, and the needs of the whole group. There would be a lot of talking going on though. It wasn't that the guys were chatterboxes, they just used the kit they had, the best comms equipment in the world, to ensure that everyone had a clear overview who needed to know what they were doing. Their position, what target they had, how they were sighted; could they do exactly what they planned and rehearsed in Gibraltar? War was a messy business. Even if you trained for a year, there were always slight adjustments to make before actually engaging.

They would idle up to the drop-off point and secure the area before moving on to their objectives. Paul would be there, as frustrated as anybody else that he wasn't front-line, but he and his guys couldn't take a wound because it would be hard to explain away. Not that they would just sit still and do nothing. Once the boats were refuelled they'd patrol out two at a time, going to each side of the designated exfil route, turning the forest around it into a death trap.

Blue was right. Paul was waiting to do that very thing once the rescue teams moved off. The assault teams took point, moving up through the undergrowth, the guys with night goggles up ahead to lay out the route. The distraction team had the furthest to go and the most to do, their aim to get to the point in the camp furthest from the boats so that they could set up positions from which to lay down enough covering and suppressive fire to dominate the whole camp area. They didn't rush. There are drills for moving through heavy bush at night, and they were applied with rigid self-discipline. The four men mutually supported each other, weapons up and trained, their eyes glued to the nightsights that gave them a clear if negative vision of the ground that lay ahead. Each man checked his pacings, relating that to the distances they'd studied back at Gibraltar. They needed to know exactly where they were in relation to their primary target, and not one of them would rely on PNGs or Garmins to get it right. Any clear ground was searched silently before they moved on, the patrol commander using hand signals or taps on the shoulder to relay his orders.

Once in position they stopped, searching the ghostly green camp for any sign of activity. The snipers moved into place to either side of them, opposite the two stone buildings, ranging over the area around and in front, to the side and above, looking for targets. The eight men of the assault team got into their final jump-off positions, while just outside the

247

central group the main fire support team set up their Minimi light machine guns. At the edge of the occupied zone were the rest of the fire support teams, without specified targets, tasked to take on whatever opportunity presented.

All of this was accomplished in silence. Anyone five feet away would not have heard a thing.

At Port Nitti Blue checked his watch, then led his primary assault team into the first inflatable, while Jamie Padden led the second team. With two jetties a kilometre apart, they had to get into position to attack both simultaneously. If what was going on up-river was high tech, the assault the AAR team planned to put in was old-fashioned SAS stuff. The comms were basic, relayed back through Ray Kavanagh at Bonthe. There were no nightsights. Instead every man in the boats carried in his mind's eye a picture of the battle and his part in it, all provided by the close target reconnaissance carried out by the observation teams that had occupied cross-river hides in the last two days.

Blue knew the SAS attack time, which was close to a rigid thing, not an approximation. There was always a chance of error, but he had done so many timed operations that he wasn't worried. When they went active, so would he, his primary target the men guarding the rutile barges. Jamie would get his people into position and await a radio signal from Bonthe. On the initiation, he would take out the rebels' sentries around the buildings on the Sieromin jetty. As far as possible this first phase of the action was to be without a firefight, but once that was no longer sustainable then the teams had to open up with everything they had, which would bring in the rest of the guys still on the *Adelaide* as support.

Blue's inflatable was paddled in to a pre-selected point, an area of deep sand one hundred metres below the first loaded barge. The team was out and ashore within seconds, the boat secured and each man moving to his appointed position. They made the line of the primary growth bush and began to move in on target. The words Jamie had imparted to him were buzzing in Blue's ears. 'Never trust a Kaffir to be where he's supposed to be. They're wanderers, man.'

'Bravo One. Number one sniper. I have the shot.' A different voice followed in Goring's ear. 'Number two sniper, no target.' Three and four reported in positive, which meant that three RUF sentries would, if they remained in the sniper's sights, be dead in a few minutes. Goring listened while all his teams reported in, telling him that they were ready to go.

Most of Blue's concentration was on the strand of sand to his left. He'd seen them himself on his OP stags, the rebels who wandered about all over the place, sometimes even fishing instead of protecting the site, but mostly searching for any loot left lying about. It wasn't him that found one but Jamie. The guy, with his AK47 beside him, was laid out just off the beach, snoring gently. Jamie called forward one of his men, and while the second guy secured the body and lower trunk Jamie went for the head, his knife slicing hard down and through the throat, cutting the windpipe and vocal chords. The guy jerked, but he was held still, the only sound a slight gurgling of escaping blood. As soon as he was still and they had each individually checked his pulse, they moved on.

Goring was ready, only waiting for the hands on his watch to give the order to go. The distraction team was on target and ready. The support groups had their weapons trained and the assault team opposite the stone building that should house the hostages. And all the time the snipers kept their commander informed of the state of their targets. Sentries move about, putting vegetation between them and sniper, or moving out of view. Having the shot is not continuous, nor does the same sniper always have the same target. The commander needs constant updates.

Blue came up behind a sentry. He could smell him. The guy was bored stiff, looking at the stars, occasionally lifting his rifle and pretending to shoot one out of the sky. He had his AK47 up when Blue took him, jamming his knife down through the left shoulder blade at the same time as he dragged the head back. Vaguely he was aware of the scuffling sounds as the other sentries died.

Goring's voice came on the net. 'Bravo One. I have control. Stand by, stand by. Go!'

The ripple of the explosions from the far end of the camp had the trio of sentries outside the hostage building spinning round in alarm. All three died with the first flicker of those bright orange flashes in their eyes, as each one took a bullet to the head that blew their brains out. They wouldn't have heard the 7.62mm sniper rifles fire even without the barrage of sudden noise and even if they had not been suppressed. A bullet travels faster than the speed of sound. You only hear the ones that miss. The assault team was halfway to target when the distraction team's explosives went off. They were at the entrance before sentries' bodies hit the ground. There was no fiddling with handles. Two men with MP5s went forward, blowing off the hinges with a small charge, while behind them, as soon as they opened, stood the guys who would go in. Rushing into a pitch-dark room in PNG goggles, with a clear notion of who might a be target and who was a hostage, gave them the edge. They didn't expect any of the RUF to be inside anyway. Behind them the fire support teams had engaged, those without specified targets using suppressive fire to cause mayhem. A pair of Minimis were laying down a curtain of fire on either side of the stone building. Anything that walked through that in an attempt to interfere with the rescue, taking on a Minimi light machine gun firing at 850 rounds a minute, would be cut to pieces.

They'd practised it in the CT house at Hereford, and in the mocked-up structure in the gym at Gibraltar. They knew that in this case, just as in every other rescue, the hostages would be just as shocked as the rest of the encampment, a sea of pale green faces, eyes and mouths wide open. The men who'd come to get them had no time to be gentle or polite.

'Out! Out! Out! Move!'

They couldn't afford to be gentle, these SAS guys. Even with the firepower they had available, they were outnumbered. The aim was to get everyone out unscathed, rescuers and rescued alike. That could only be done if they moved at speed.

All around the building the world had gone mad, as the M203s laid down a barrage of 40mm grenades on all the other buildings. The 66mm rockets did even more damage, ripping through the command huts and blowing apart everything inside: flesh, equipment and furniture. They had to take out the leadership and the comms. It was nothing personal, just good tactics; a headless fighting force reacts poorly and will struggle to regroup. The snipers had shifted their aim, taking on opportunity targets, individuals as they tried to evacuate the wooden huts either through door or window. Flash-bang grenades were going off everywhere outside the cordon of fire, and the rescuers were still shouting, grabbing at the people they'd come to get out, hustling their terrified quarry out into what looked like their worst nightmare. They couldn't know it in such mayhem, but they were the only people in the camp at practically no risk of taking a bullet.

The return fire, when it came, was sporadic, poorly aimed and uncoordinated, and the men who fired revealed themselves to troopers who were marksmen, and paid the price. All the time the troopers talked on the net. Goring knew that they had two hostages on stretchers, that four could barely walk and would have to be half carried, that the rest were either stunned and vague or terrified and panicky. But the SAS trained for that too and if the handling was a little rough it had to be for safety's sake.

The distraction team had pulled out to make for the boats. They knew that the corridor back was secure, as was the exfil RV. The hostages were out and at the edge of the compound, still with the assault team, moving to link up with the hostage reception team so that both groups could escort them to the boats. Behind them the fire support teams continued to lay down fire with their Minimis and M203s. It sounded like mayhem, but it was cold, professional killing at its most proficient.

It was time for Blue to go in. He informed Ray Kavanagh, waited precisely sixty seconds, then tapped the shoulder of the man with him, an ex-Para called Jimmy. He lifted the twelve-inch tube that contained the para-illum flare, a fire-once-and-throw-away piece of kit, which made a satisfying whoosh as it shot up into the sky, leaving behind a thin trail of grey smoke. At the top of its arc the small parachute opened with a dull plop. The whole area was suddenly illuminated in a ghostly white light. The *Adelaide* had come in to tie up alongside the now unguarded barges, and Blue's team poured over the side, breaking off to take on their individual assignments. Jamie Padden's para-illum went off a split second later.

The targets were human, not buildings. The men had orders to take out what was necessary but not to engage in wanton destruction. Kill the software, respect the hardware. High explosive grenades they had, but they stuck to stun where possible, throwing them into confined spaces in the AAR buildings and following that up with a burst of rapid rifle fire aimed through window or door. They had a good idea of the enemy they were dealing with and Blue reckoned they would run, so he had set as priority the need to get the 12.75 mm machine guns deployed.

Under a constant canopy of para-illums they wreaked havoc. Sited to cover the only road out with an established zone of cross-fire, they could, with short bursts, take out anyone trying to escape. In the rest of the compound Blue's team had fanned out to cover the bush on either side, seeking individual targets, those who had escaped the assault on the buildings. Jamie was doing almost as well with one machine gun, but they knew from the information provided by the CTRs that he faced fewer men than Blue. In a firefight time stands still; a minute is a lifetime, ten minutes an age. But that was all it took to clear the main danger at Port Nitti, a red flare shooting skywards to tell his men to cease pursuit, the point at which they would automatically carry out an ammunition and casualty check. They began work on ensuring the security of the area, with a special word from Blue to Jamie to find Willy and restrain him before he set off for Kenya. The heavy machine gun teams, with support, raced up to the junction of the two roads that connected the twin port facilities to set up a defence position that would deal with any counter-attack that might develop.

Up-river the hostage rescue team was busy on the net. 'Bravo Two One complete towards pickup.'

Goring knew, as there was no mention of any problems, that all the hostages were now being moved down the exfil corridor towards the pickup point. The distraction team were next. 'Bravo One One, Roger, moving to assist.'

Goring acknowledged, then informed the fire support teams to remain in position. He needed confirmation that the hostages were clear, that the remaining callsigns had acknowledged completion of their exfil to the pickup point.

The call came in from Paul Hill. 'Bravo Three One. Position secure, ready to move.'

That told Goring that all the hostages were loaded into their respective boats. He could now give the code for the final exfil. 'All callsigns this is Bravo One. Red Dragon, I say again, Red Dragon, out.'

The fire support teams bugged out immediately on that signal, making their way back to the pickup point. On arrival all callsigns were accounted for, and after a quick ammunition and casualty check the squadron moved off.

Looking at his wristwatch, Blue guessed they would be pulling away, the man in the front on his Minimi wearing his goggles, the hostages, still bemused, crowded into the middle, with the troopers around them covering the arcs. The engines would race as they bugged out, each GPS reading programmed in on the way up giving them an exact distance to the first sandbank. Behind them the rebels, no longer under fire, would rush through the bush to exact revenge, setting off the Claymore mines Paul Hill and his patrol had laid to catch them out. He was right. Paul had an arc to cover like everybody else, and he concentrated on that, but he saw the flashes as his mines went off, and if he couldn't hear the screams he could imagine them.

Blue was back aboard the *Adelaide*. Jamie Padden was now in control, working to get the push boat in to hook up on the rutile barges. That was the primary requirement. They would cover them until they were clear: then and only then would a judgement be made to stay or bug out. Blue was at full throttle in the AAR boat, heading for his rendezvous, listening hard on the Cougar net for the point at which they would come into range. He heard the first whisper, and it was finally time for him to make his one contribution. He knew they'd had a one hundred per cent success.

'Bravo One, this is Blue Harding. Nitti secure. Heli standing by.'

Goring answered. 'Bravo One, roger. Phase one complete. RV junction of Gbangbia Creek zero three hundred hours.'

'Blue Harding. Acknowledge zero three hundred hours. Congratulations.' Blue switched to his own comms. 'Ray?'

'Boss?'

'Jamie has taken over command of the AAR team.'

'Roger.'

'Sergei to stand by to fly out at first light, acknowledge.'

'Roger that.'

Blue got the *Adelaide* to the RV well ahead of Goring. That didn't matter. If the SAS had turned up first they would have waited for him. He took the satcom on to the deck and set it up. But he waited, listening to the Cougar net, until he was sure that the SAS had cleared the Sigimi bridge without being compromised. Only then did he dial, his first call to the High Commission to give the estimated time of arrival of the hostages in Freetown. Then he phoned Mike Layman, who was sound asleep in bed. 'You can give our boy wonder the good news, Mike. We have the Port Nitti site under control, and the push boat is in the process of extracting his barges.'

'You went in?'

'We did.'

'The hostages?'

'Don't worry about them. There's been a negotiated release.'

'You're kidding.'

'Read your morning paper. Or maybe the evening one.'

'Anybody hurt?'

'No reported casualties.'

Razenbrook wouldn't have asked that, he thought to himself as he put the phone down.

Eddie Welford and Ian Cannon had no idea why the High Commissioner had asked them, and their mouthpiece, Chendor Deen, to be on stand-by throughout the night. But they sussed it when he came to see them at two in the morning.

'I want you to initiate contact with Alimany Bakaar immediately. Wake the bugger up if necessary. He has two choices. He can announce to the world that the RUF have agreed to a hostage release, or he can acknowledge that they have been taken from under his nose. If he does the first, we will do the same and confirm his report.'

'And if he says no?'

Quentin-Davies grinned. 'He won't.'

In the MIBs the hostages were just beginning to come to terms with the notion that they were safe. Surrounded by silent SAS men they were a bit bemused. Somehow Geoff and Mary had ended up in the same boat, and she was lying down with her head cradled on his shoulder. Both of them ached from the wounds of both capture and rescue, bruises where their less-than-gentle fellow countrymen had dragged them to safety.

'When I get back to Freetown, Mary Kline, I'm going to take you out for the best meal money can buy.'

'Okay.'

'And then, woman,' he said, dropping his voice to a whisper. 'I am going to take you up to my room and give you the night of your life.'

She didn't speak, but the squeeze she gave him was encouraging.

EPILOGUE

MIBs, cramped and uncomfortable, prone to bounce on the least swell, were no place for weak and injured hostages, especially when the boats got to sea. Blue got them aboard, with the four SAS in the Freetown bodyguard team acting as medics to treat them. Then he took the inflatables under tow and headed back for the Bagru channel. There was a brief stop at Edmonton Island to pick up a cache of fuel the stand-by squadron had left behind, and then they headed out to sea, the prow of the *Adelaide* set for the north point of Sherbro Island.

Orders had been issued from Fleet HQ at Northwood the day before and the frigate HMS *Canterbury* had changed course to close with the West African shore, heaving-to just outside the twelve-mile limit. With full tanks and a precise rendezvous, the SAS Avons powered out to sea. Within two hours they had made radio contact, rendezvoused and got aboard. They were now below deck, having a good scoff, with the frigate steaming back to Gibraltar. To the world, press and public alike, the 22nd Special Air Services Regiment had never been in Sierra Leone.

Blue set course for Bonthe, while on the satcom Paul ran through the condition of the hostages. Some would require quite serious medical treatment, but all were stable and some actually cheerful. Mary Kline hadn't left Geoff Hinchcliffe's side, hanging on to him for dear life. Once they docked in Bonthe they helped the other passengers off the boat. They were loaded straight on to the Hip for transfer to the High Commission or a hospital. Once a nurse always a nurse: Mary Kline took over their care during the half-hour flight, with Geoff fetching and carrying as if nothing in their recent life had changed.

Sergei flew straight into the British High Commission compound, where the required ambulances and medical personnel were waiting. There were also diplomats on hand to talk to those who were fit enough, and minders to keep the press away from those who were not. Apart from the matter of their health, the hostages had to be persuaded to maintain the line that would go out on all the wire services; the release had been negotiated and the RUF had voluntarily surrendered them. To people suffering from shock and malnutrition, with only the vaguest sense of the events that had got them out, only a small amount of pressure was required to gain initial compliance. What would surface when they were well again mattered less, because the attention of the world would have moved on. Besides, many would never divulge the truth about the rescue for the sake of others who might, anywhere in the world, suffer a similar fate.

'I think I owe you a drink,' said Paul, just before he clambered into Sergei's helicopter. The Russian, having dropped his first cargo, had come straight back to get them. They had to be got out too, cleaned up to look like they had a hangover from boozing not fighting, and back to Freetown so that their absence could be minimised. 'A big drink.'

'It'll take gallons, mate,' Blue replied. 'If I'm lying on my back with my mouth open, just keep pouring.'

'See you in Paddy's Bar tonight then.'

'You will. Suited and booted.'

That's the way it was with Special Forces and mercenaries alike. You could be up to your neck in shit and bullets at dawn, and into your Armani, strutting your stuff with some floozie on the dance floor in some sprauncy bar the very same night.

Toby Flowers and his Gurkhas hit the RUF around Moyamba like a typhoon. He'd never known troops so fired up to exact revenge. Their rule was simple: in a situation in which you didn't know who was on whose side, if you had a gun you dropped it or died. Everyone who did just that was asked one question.

'Where is the American's head?'

It took a sweep covering over fifteen square miles, during which they killed over a hundred rebels, before they found it, stuck on a post outside a big hut. Captain Dennis was in there, and he died a death as painful as any he'd inflicted. The head was put in a box and shipped back to Freetown. Added to the rest of Buckhart's remains, it was, after a brief ceremony, taken back, by his wife to the United States.

Donald Quentin-Davies sealed the letter, sellotaped it for double security and marked it 'confidential'. It would go home in the diplomatic bag, to be handed to Jimmy Heriot to read at his leisure. Then he had to move quicker than normal. Captain Joshua Lumulo had lost his job as Minister of Defence in a reshuffle that had seen him and several others on the NPRC escorted from their houses to the Battery Street police barracks. It was full dress stuff, the feathers in the hat as well, for a ceremony at Government House. Strasser was in full military rig as well, unusual for a man who always wore combat gear. But the person who outshone them all in the gleam of his insignia and medals was the new Minister, Colonel Eustace Tumbu. His face shone and his teeth gleamed as he accepted the tokens of his office and embarked on a short speech.

'Gentlemaan,' he intoned, droning on about it being a privilege to serve. Then he came to the interesting bit. 'The RUF have seen the folly of holding on to innocent people. I hope that my personal intervention had something to do with the negotiated release. The country, under its great leader Captain Strasser, needs peace to rebuild itself. Our friends from abroad need stability to increase both their profits and our revenues. I hope I have gone some small way to helping this to come about. I shall work for my nation from this moment as hard as I have in the past, so that we can become the envy of Africa.'

Quentin-Davies was watching Strasser throughout this. His expression was like that of a man eyeing a very venomous snake that was about to bite him. Which only went to prove he was, as had been proved by recent events, no fool.

'We have a written question, Minister, from Jock Mayhew, regarding the situation in Sierra Leone.'

The Secretary of State for Foreign Affairs didn't look up from the mass of papers on his desk. There were too many to sign or initial. 'That man's a bloody pest, Jimmy.'

Heriot agreed. Mayhew was a veteran Scottish MP who had a knack of posing awkward questions. 'It's about British involvement.'

'As usual.'

A hand went out to take the sheet of paper and the minister scanned it quickly. 'He thinks we engineered the whole thing. And the SAS as well. Where does he get it from?'

The minister looked at his permanent under-secretary. Both men knew very well, if not the finer details, the facts of the recent operation. The need was now to avoid saying so. A written question, answered in

257

Parliament, was a tricky affair; the House of Commons was no place to be telling lies. Mayhew would be allowed a follow-up enquiry and that could lead the unwary into a personal and political minefield.

'I think in this case,' said Jimmy Heriot, 'we could get him to settle for a written reply, that is if you have a quiet word with him.'

'And?'

'Tell him that SO10 were involved.' That made the minister look up, to face the bland expression Jimmy Heriot wore. The civil servant nodded to the red box on the desk. 'You did have it, sir, read and initialled. I passed it to you myself. Deny the SAS or any involvement by our High Commission other than in a purely technical sense.' The pen stayed poised, awaiting further explanation. Heriot smiled and continued. 'Mayhew has just picked up some loose gossip from the underbelly of the press.'

'He seems to spend an inordinate amount of time there.'

'The more to discomfit us, sir. But he is not the man to make a meal out of a successful negotiated release. I think if you tell him on the quiet that our Scotland Yard chaps were there and played a major role he will see the sense in not pursuing the matter. Even Jock Mayhew is a fan of SO10.'

'The question getting into the press is the problem, Jimmy, you know that. These things have a nasty habit of spinning out of control.'

'I think we're safe on this one, sir. Any journalists who tried to file the story from Freetown were spiked by their editors here in London.'

'And what did we have to feed the sharks in return?'

'Precious little, sir. Anything to do with the SAS seems to bring out the best in them, and Africa has a limited hold on what is already a short attention span.'

'A famine a year, a coup a month,' said the minister, repeating a well-known mantra.

'That's it, sir. The world moves on.'

The Secretary of State for Foreign Affairs looked out of the huge sash windows of what was the biggest office in the British government on to the Mall, teeming as usual with tourists. 'So the betting is we can kill it stone dead?'

'I'd say so, sir. After all, the result was very positive.'

'Right,' the minister said, his head dropping back to the mass of papers before him, 'Arrange for me to buy Jock Mayhew a drink at the terrace bar.'

'A good idea, sir. Now can I move you on to Russia?'

'You are ignoring me again, John,' said Leila, her face creased in anger.

'Sorry. It's just with what Paul's told me about Tumbu not only surviving but getting a new job, the old brain box is racing.'

'Let it go mate,' said Paul. 'Just take the money and run.'

'Even if it's blood money?'

'There's no other kind. And that applies if you're in the regiment or out of it.'

'Whenever there's a stitch up, look for who gains the most.'

'You'll drive yourself nuts trying to figure this one out.'

'It could only be Strasser,' said Blue, thumping the table. 'He must have set the whole thing up.'

'He hasn't got the fuckin' brains,' scoffed Paul.

'You don't need brains. You need to be a foxy bastard, and I bet you he'd own up to that.'

'Tumbu got the most out of it.'

'He's done well, but he's not the main spider. He led Fizzin' Frank Buckhart into an ambush and he lost his head. The only thing Tumbu lost, according to the word going round, was his hat. Why?'

'To wind everybody up!' said Paul, enjoying the baiting he was giving Blue. He knew the whole thing stank, but he'd been in too many shit ops for dodgy reasons to care. Blue had always been a man to dot the Is and cross the Ts.

'He had to be playing both ends against the middle, working for Strasser and pretending to side with the RUF. It was probably him that started the hostage taking by telling the rebels they were getting nowhere. How did he know where those nuns were, get there, and come out alive? Then when they need to stage a big rescue, one of the poor buggers gets wasted. What happens next? In come the fuckin' cavalry and wipe out half the RUF leadership. You lot got Tarawali and Jalloh, the rest are taken care of by the Gurkhas. Then half the government goes to the cells. Suddenly Strasser, who you wouldn't have put ten pence on a week ago, is sitting pretty.'

'Blue likes crosswords too,' Paul said to Leila, who was looking less than pleased at the lack of attention she was getting.

'The bastard cooked this whole thing up with our High Commissioner.

Strasser gets his enemies slaughtered. He has an excuse for a clear-out of his fellow crooks, a way to bang up most of his ministers.'

'What does Quentin-Davies get?'

'The businessmen off his back. They get their mines opened again and can start making money, and for that prize poor buggers like us risk getting slotted.' Blue picked up his drink and looked at Paul hard. 'We've been had over, mate.'

'So what? It's nothing new. The Ruperts have been doing it to us for years.'

'Now that's a fact.'

'So fuck Strasser,' said Paul, 'fuck Sierra Leone and all those diplomatic bastards who get us in the shit to help their careers. And fuck your question-and-answer session. The real and only question, Blue, is what are we going to do now?'

'Get shit-faced,' Paul smiled and Leila groaned. 'How about you?'

Jimmy Heriot liked the Connaught Hotel. Five star, it had a lot of old-world charm and the Mayfair location was an added bonus. Sir Patrick Molloy was late, but that didn't matter since he was already drinking off the old man's tab. He'd adopted the French habit of drinking port as an *aperitif*, and the one he had in his hand now, a second helping, was a fifty-year-old vintage.

He stood up as Molloy came bustling in, a big man in a suit of heavy stripes, greeted obsequiously by all and sundry. The man was imposing with that presence few people have. Some actors have it, one or two politicians, a few businessmen. It was sad to reflect that it was entirely absent in the civil service to which he belonged.

'Sorry I'm late!'

'Sir Patrick.'

Molloy held out his hand and gave him a firm shake. 'Call me Paddy. And if you don't mind I shall call you Jimmy.'

'Delighted!'

'Let's eat. I'm famished.' He turned to the waiter standing by his side. 'Do you still have any of the Montée de Tonerre Chablis?'

'We have, sir.'

'Then let's have a bottle of that. And fetch up a bottle of the '47 Haut Brion.'

'I say,' said Jimmy Heriot. He nearly blurted out that it cost a fortune, but he bit his tongue in time.

'Jimmy, you deserve better. The reason I'm late is that I've just disposed of my stake in some stuff in West Africa. Rutile extraction. Forgeham-Lowry said I had to get out. The whole place is too febrile.'

Heriot was hardly surprised, since it was his appreciation, based on a letter from Quentin-Davies, that had been used to make the suggestion. 'Oh I agree, as I said to Sir George, the situation won't last. The last little upheaval was only temporary. Our man out there, Quentin-Davies, was quite adamant about that.'

'He's due to move on I gather.'

'Saudi ambassador when the present incumbent steps down. He's come home on leave if you'd like to meet him.'

'What a good idea. Could you set it up?'

'Happily.'

'You know, old George started working for me this very week. Didn't even take a break after retirement. Said work was better than fishing, walking the dog and arguing with your wife.'

'I wish him well. He's been very kind to me.'

'Speaks highly of you.' Molloy paused to taste the Chablis, pronounced it fine and continued while the waiter filled both glasses. 'Says that I'm to keep an eye on which way you go.'

'Let's hope it's up,' said Heriot, slightly too loudly and emphatically, the effect of that double aperitif.

'My dear Jimmy, for people of talent there's no other route.' Molloy raised his glass. 'I think we ought to raise a toast to Sierra Leone.' Jimmy Heriot hoisted his glass up as the financier continued. 'May God rot the bloody place.'

We're going home, mate,' said Paul Hill. 'The training job has been terminated, by guess who?'

'Tumbu,' Blue replied.

Paul nodded, but refused to ask how Blue had guessed. 'They've got a South African team in for personal protection. Executive Outcomes, they're called.'

'That makes sense.'

'How come?'

'Because of why you were here in the first place.'

'Which was, smart arse?'

'You were here to make sure that while Strasser was stitching up the RUF and his own mates no one could get near him. If you want total protection you get the SAS, regardless of the cost. If you don't need it that badly they're too expensive.'

'And Tumbu?'

'He's got the men you trained back. And who do you think they are going to be looking after now? None other than the new Minister of Defence, old buddy. I hope these Executive Outcomes blokes are good. Cause if they ain't Tumbu is going to have them over. If I was Strasser, I'd be shitting myself.'

'You're staying, I take it?' asked Paul.

'Still got a job to do, mate. And now Razenbrook thinks the sun shines out of my arse, I even get bonuses.'

'What a life. Ordering people about, strutting your stuff, then coming back to get pissed and laid in Freetown.'

'Beats working, mate.'